Praise for
Meredith Efken

@HOME FOR THE HOLIDAYS

"[Efken] offers a balanced and loving take on gender roles, faith and child-rearing. Both stay-at-home and working Christian moms will recognize their struggles here, and feel the novel's lighthearted humor lessening their load."
—*Publishers Weekly*

SAHM I AM

"Can a novel consisting entirely of e-mails be enjoyable faith fiction? Efken's charming, light debut offers a resounding and surprising yes. Efken keeps the mood light, although she's not afraid to tackle serious topics such as infertility, marital difficulties and chronic illness. Christian readers will savor this fresh entrée."
—*Publishers Weekly*

"Written in the tradition of Erma Bombeck, this fine first novel is recommended."
—*Library Journal*

"*SAHM I AM* is hysterically funny and I lost count of how many times I laughed out loud. I loved the cast of quirky characters and I could hardly turn the pages fast enough. Erma Bombeck was a funny lady, but Meredith Efken is even funnier."
—Christy Award-winning author Randall Ingermanson

Also by
Meredith Efken

SAHM I Am
@Home for the Holidays

Meredith Efken
Play It Again, SAHM

Steeple
Hill
Café™

Published by Steeple Hill Books™

Recycling programs
for this product may
not exist in your area.

STEEPLE HILL BOOKS

ISBN-13: 978-0-373-78646-6
ISBN-10:   0-373-78646-8

PLAY IT AGAIN, SAHM

www.SteepleHill.com

Printed in U.S.A.

To my mom and dad, Judi and Mike, for filling my childhood with love, my soul with laughter, and my shelves with good books.

And for all the readers who asked me so sweetly for another SAHM story—this one I wrote for you.

ACKNOWLEDGMENTS

Collecting inspiration for my SAHM stories has always been something of an accidental treasure hunt. I never know when I'll stumble across the next gem. I'm very thankful to the following people whose crazy behavior, odd mistakes and other personal quirks have proven so useful to my story. (Because yes, it really is all about me!)

For Tosca Lee, the queen of text messaging. Thanks to you, my cell phone company has increased their profits because I had to get a new service to accommodate all our messages to each other. You've trained me well, and now I'm working on getting my husband hooked, too.

Thanks to Scott Ross for his brilliant discovery that glass stove tops can be broken with a pan. His wife may not have appreciated it, but I found it was most instructive and inspiring.

Thanks to my friend Richard Vasey, the original Tiara Man, for showing me how cute a dad can look when his daughter dresses him like a fairy princess.

Thanks to my agent, Steve Laube, not just for being a fabulous agent, but also for telling me about the people in Phoenix who trucked in snow for their kids' birthday party. He told me about giant roof rats as well. Too bad I don't write horror.

A big thanks to Morgan Busse for having the creative foresight to bring a child into this world who would nearly nuke a kitten, thereby providing me with yet another entertaining disaster for my book.

And thanks to my own daughter whose talk-the-babysitter-into-letting-us-play-with-lit-candles scheme nearly drove me over the edge... And the crawling out on the porch roof... And the Queen of the World remark... And...well, I'd better not share any more of her secrets, I guess. Since I was able to use it all in my book, everything is forgiven.

Much appreciation and love to Camy, Randy, Steve, Gina, Chip, Tosca, Jim, Brandilyn and all the many others of my late-night writers conference buddies. The retreat in this book was written with you guys in mind—for your friendship, laughter, support, and for all the sleep hours we've given up in order to hang out together.

Finally, a special thank-you to my editor, Melissa Endlich, for being such a great supporter of my writing and letting me do a third SAHM book. I appreciate your insight, enthusiasm and how much fun we've had working together. The campfire scene at the end of the book—that's for you. Thanks, Melissa!

Beloved Moms,

I am SO pleased to have the honor of welcoming back our dear Rosalyn Ebberly to our SAHM I Am loop. As many of you know, Rosalyn made the wise decision about a year ago to take some time away from our loop family so that she could focus on some intensive therapy and counseling with her own family. Praise God, He blessed them with much healing. Today, they are stronger and healthier than ever. And Rosalyn feels at peace with returning to the loop.

She will return to her moderator duties immediately, and none too soon. The other half of my news isn't nearly as wonderful. My mom, who is in her seventies and lives all by herself in Santa Fe, is going in for double hip replacement surgery next week. We've been discussing it for several months, and it only made sense that she come live with us for the surgery and through the rehabilitation period. This is going to be a HUGE upheaval in my family's routine, since James (who's thirteen now!) is going to have to either move in with little brothers John and Josiah or let them move in with him. Rachel and Rebecca were already sharing, and we didn't have a guest room.

And Mom is going to need so much help with everything for a long time. So just as Rosalyn is returning, I'm afraid I'm going to have to say goodbye for a while. I'll miss you all terribly, but I know I'm leaving the loop in the best hands possible. Rosalyn will take care of everything. Please give her the same cooperation and respect you've always given me. If you want to e-mail me privately, you can. May Jesus bless all of you.

With all the mother-love in my heart,

Your loop mom,

Connie Lawson

SAHM I Am Loop Mom

From:	Rosalyn Ebberly <prov31woman@home.com>
To:	SAHM I Am <sahmiam@loophole.com>
Subject:	[SAHM I AM]
	TOTW June 1: Total Honesty

Sweetest Sisters,

It is SUCH a joy to be back among you! I feel like I've been sojourning in a strange land and have finally returned home. It's been a bit more than a year since I took my sabbatical, and yet you girls have made me feel like I never left.

This past seventeen months has been a time of growth and healing for me and my family. I'm looking forward to sharing what I've learned with all of you. I think the best way to do that will be through my resumed duty of moderating the

Topic of the Week. My sister, Veronica, has, from what I've heard, been doing a great job in my absence, but when she heard how eager I was to take my old place again as TOTW facilitator, she graciously agreed to step aside.

Most of you know I've been involved in intensive therapy and counseling along with my family. One of the most important things I've learned is that I must be COMPLETELY HONEST with those around me. So this is our TOTW— Total Honesty.

It's difficult to be honest and vulnerable with other people, even the ones we love. But I've learned that this is the ONLY way to truly break the cycle of dysfunction and strife.

So let's practice this week, shall we? I'd like each of you to share with us one deeply personal thing that you've never shared before. As we bare our hearts to each other, grace and friendship will be released, and we'll be closer than ever. With that in mind, here is my confession. I give it to you with trembling fingers and a full heart:

I HATE to cook. In fact, sometimes when it's been a really bad day, I call my husband and ask him to stop at McDonald's on the way home from work. I can down a Big Mac in under two minutes, and we have a bin of Happy Meal toys that we stash in the basement when company comes over.

Whew! It's great to have that out in the open at last! See, honesty isn't so hard. What about you? Get that secret off your chest. And remember, this is for posterity, so…be honest. Peace to you all,
Rosalyn Ebberly
SAHM I Am Loop Moderator

"The wise woman builds her house, but the foolish tears it down with her own hands." Proverbs 14:1 (NASB)

From:	Zelia Muzuwa \<zeemuzu@vivacious.com\>
To:	"Green Eggs and Ham"
Subject:	**She hates to cook????**

THAT'S her big confession? After all the pomposity, after all the "I'm so much better than you, you poor things, why can't you be more like me…ah, but you can't and never will, you LOSERS"…after waging a war on Christmas because retailers weren't saying the greeting SHE thought was most correct…after being so paranoid about her husband that she hired a detective to spy on him…after her kids were freaking out and drawing pictures of themselves in COFFINS…

She expects us to be impressed that she's confessed to a lack of interest in the culinary arts???

Air. I need air. I'm hyperventilating. Her first day back, and I'm already developing a nervous tic. At this rate, we'll ALL need intensive therapy.
Z

From:	Dulcie Huckleberry
	\<dulcie@homemakerinteriors.com\>
To:	"Green Eggs and Ham"
Subject:	**Re: She hates to cook????**

How do you really feel, Ham? *Honestly.* Share it on the loop, dear one. You know it's for posterity. The emotional health of your children hangs in the balance.
Dulcie

From:	Zelia Muzuwa <zeemuzu@vivacious.com>
To:	"Green Eggs and Ham"
Subject:	**Re: She hates to cook????**

Don't tempt me.
Z

From:	P. Lorimer <phyllis.lorimer@geemail.com>
To:	"Green Eggs and Ham"
Subject:	**Re: She hates to cook????**

Poor Zelia, it sounds as if you may have some unforgiveness toward her. Are you certain you don't need to confess it on the loop? It will do you much good.
Teasing,
Phyllis

From:	Zelia Muzuwa <zeemuzu@vivacious.com>
To:	"Green Eggs and Ham"
Subject:	**Re: She hates to cook????**

Phyllis, darling, don't you have a graduate class to study for? Something along the lines of "Dripping Faucets: A Survey of the Most Irritating Women of Western Civilization"? You could write a paper on our loop moderator.

Besides, the TOTW was about honesty, not forgiveness.
I've never struggled with being honest.
Z

From:	Dulcie Huckleberry
	<dulcie@homemakerinteriors.com>
To:	"Green Eggs and Ham"
Subject:	**Re: She hates to cook????**

Betcha five bucks that forgiveness is next week's topic.
Dulcie

From:	P. Lorimer <phyllis.lorimer@geemail.com>
To:	"Green Eggs and Ham"
Subject:	**Re: She hates to cook????**

Dulcie,
I'll see your five and raise you one. ☺
Phyllis

From:	Zelia Muzuwa <zeemuzu@vivacious.com>
To:	"Green Eggs and Ham"
Subject:	**Re: She hates to cook????**

Aaaarrrgghhh!!! You're a PASTOR'S WIFE! You don't
make bets! And besides, you did it wrong. If you think

Dulcie's bet is right, why would you raise it? Oh, never mind…I have to go pick up my children from school. Why they have to schedule school all the way into June boggles the mind.

Z

From:	P. Lorimer <phyllis.lorimer@geemail.com>
To:	Dulcie Huckleberry
	<dulcie@homemakerinteriors.com>
Subject:	**Zelia?**

Oops. Do you think I made her angry? I was only trying to joke around with her. All of you know I think betting is stupid. I was truly just kidding.

Phyllis

From:	Dulcie Huckleberry
	<dulcie@homemakerinteriors.com>
To:	P. Lorimer <phyllis.lorimer@geemail.com>
Subject:	**Re: Zelia?**

LOL! I think you're okay, Phyllis. You know she's been really touchy about Rosalyn ever since The-Incident-That-Must-Not-Be-Mentioned last year. But Z's been a bit stressed out lately. No wonder—things haven't been going too well with Lishan and Duri. I think she's really worried about them. It's been eighteen months since they brought those two home

from Ethiopia, and they're still having a lot of language problems. She told me Duri has been wetting the bed almost every night, and Lishan has terrible nightmares. I feel bad for her—wish there was something I could do to help.
Dulcie

From:	Hannah Farrell
	<boazsmom@farrellfamilylovesjesus.net>
To:	SAHM ! Am <sahmiam@loophole.com>
Subject:	**[SAHM I AM]**
	Re: TOTW June 1: Total Honesty

Hi! I'm new—so I guess anything I share will fit the topic of the week because I've never told it to any of you! LOL!

I'm Hannah, and I'm nineteen years old. I have a two-month-old baby named Boaz, and in two weeks I will celebrate my FIRST year of being married to my totally awesome husband, Bradley. We live in South Carolina, and I always wanted to be a stay-at-home mom with lots of kids. My best friend, Krissy, went off to college in Florida to be a marine biologist. I guess I'm majoring in the Domestic Arts here at home. I joined up with this group because our moms' group at church doesn't meet during the summer, and Krissy decided to spend the whole summer in Hawaii. I'm hoping to make lots of good friends here!

And Rosalyn, I'm like *totally* impressed that u can talk so easily about being in family counseling! I read through the archives and found out what happened to u—thinking your husband was having an affair and then the woman turned out to be a Lesbian! And all the problems with your kids! That's so humiliating! You're really brave to come back to a big loop like this where everyone knows all that bad stuff about you.

I'm just trying to say don't feel bad about not liking to cook. Compared to all that other stuff, it's no big deal. But if you want, I'll be glad to share some recipes with you that I like. I've been getting more into organic cooking, so anytime you want some help, just let me know. Okay?

Oh, I'm so happy to be here. You're all going to be my best friends forever (BFF). I can just FEEL it!

In the love of Jesus,

Hannah Farrell

From:	Brenna L. <saywhat@writeme.com>
To:	"Green Eggs and Ham"
Subject:	**Hmm…**

Is it my imagination, or did that new chick just like *totally* dog Rosalyn?

Brenna

From:	Dulcie Huckleberry
	<dulcie@homemakerinteriors.com>
To:	"Green Eggs and Ham"
Subject:	**Re: Hmm…**

Like, she so *totally* did, Brenna! I like, LIKE her, you know? Like, how cool is that? She's so like going to be my new BFF!

Like totally Dulcie

From:	The Millards
	\<jstcea4jesus@familymail.net\>
To:	"Green Eggs and Ham"
Subject:	**Re: Hmm...**

Come on, guys! She's only nineteen. Yikes! That's only seven years older than Tyler! Anyway, I think she was rude. Rosalyn's been through a lot. We shouldn't mock her.

Jocelyn

From:	Zelia Muzuwa \<zeemuzu@vivacious.com\>
To:	"Green Eggs and Ham"
Subject:	**Re: Hmm...**

Jocelyn wrote:

\< Rosalyn's been through a lot. We shouldn't mock her.\>

WHAT? Are my eyes seeing correctly? Jocelyn, babe, come back from the Dark Side. Did she slip you some Kool-Aid while we weren't looking? Did you DRINK IT?

Z

From:	The Millards
	\<jstcea4jesus@familymail.net\>
To:	"Green Eggs and Ham"
Subject:	Re: Hmm...

Of course not, I'm not stupid!

But I do feel a bit sorry for Ros. She's had a hard time of it the last couple of years. We should be kind. However, that new...*child* does look like she might provide some entertainment. Nineteen! My goodness. And since when is "lesbian" a proper noun? And is there a problem with her fingers that she is unable to type out the word "you"?
Jocelyn

From:	P. Lorimer \<phyllis.lorimer@geemail.com\>
To:	"Green Eggs and Ham"
Subject:	Re: Hmm...

Jocelyn wrote:
< And since when is "lesbian" a proper noun? And is there a problem with her fingers that she is unable to type out the word "you"?>

Ahhh, Jocelyn, now u r speaking my language! ☺
Phyllis

From:	Brenna L. <saywhat@writeme.com>
To:	"Green Eggs and Ham"
Subject:	**Re: Hmm...**

Phyllis wrote:

< Ahhh, Jocelyn, now u r speaking my language! ☺>

Hey, great joke, Phyllis! Your sense of humor is really improving!

Brenna

From:	P. Lorimer <phyllis.lorimer@geemail.com>
To:	"Green Eggs and Ham"
Subject:	**Re: Hmm...**

Thank you! It was the elective graduate course in Joking 101 that did the trick.

Phyllis

From:	Brenna L. <saywhat@writeme.com>
To:	"Green Eggs and Ham"
Subject:	**Re: Hmm...**

Oh, man. I'm in awe.

Like *totally*.

Brenna

From:	VIM <vivalaveronica@marcelloportraits.com>
To:	Rosalyn Ebberly <prov31woman@home.com>
Subject:	Ouch!

Hey Rossie-girl,

Saw that post on the loop from that new *chica*. She made you look about as sharp as a…oops, never mind. Was going to lapse into a Texasism, and I promised you not to. But sheesh, sis—Houston is really growing on me for real! I've perfected the "y'all" and "wajeet" (what did you eat). Not such an act for me anymore.

Anyhow, I'm sorry about what Hannah said. She was rude. You going to talk to her about it? I've half a mind to let her know what we Texans do to little chits who diss on our family members.

You hang tough now, you hear?

Veronica

From:	Rosalyn Ebberly <prov31woman@home.com>
To:	VIM <vivalaveronica@marcelloportraits.com>
Subject:	Re: Ouch!

Dearest sister,

You can relax—I'm perfectly fine. Hannah obviously has a lot of repressed anxiety and an emotional hunger for acceptance and a sense of superiority. These things are inflicted on the juvenile psyche and manifest themselves in a variety of ways, include an inability to gauge appropriate social behavior. I wonder how her relationship with her father is? Regardless, I'm not planning to speak to her about it at all. It's not my problem.

Anyway, rest assured I am not allowing her emotional unrest and woundedness to disturb my personal sense of peace and well-being. I just picture Jesus as my bubble of light, surrounding me as I float down the sewers of life. No matter how murky the waters, they don't need to contaminate my inner wholeness. Oh, Ronnie, I can't tell you how freeing it is! This sort of thing would have made me so angry a year and a half ago, but now…it just rolls right off.

Though I would like to know what you were going to say… Sharp as a what? You have my permission, dear girl, to "speak Texan." I don't even care if it's put on or genuine. Those sort of petty issues no longer have the power to upset my spiritual centeredness.

With love,

Rosalyn

"The wise woman builds her house, but the foolish tears it down with her own hands." Proverbs 14:1 (NASB)

From:	VIM <vivalaveronica@marcelloportraits.com>
To:	Rosalyn Ebberly <prov31woman@home.com>
Subject:	Re: Ouch!

Was going to say, "She made you look about as sharp as a mashed potato."

Therapy or not, you are still one bizarre chick, sis. Shrink turned you into a Buddhaesque freak. Either that, or you're on some pretty strong drugs.

Veronica

From:	Rosalyn Ebberly <prov31woman@home.com>
To:	VIM <vivalaveronica@marcelloportraits.com>
Subject:	Re: Ouch!

LOL! Neither. ☺ I'm high on the peace of Jesus and emotional wholeness.

Rosalyn

"The wise woman builds her house, but the foolish tears it down with her own hands." Proverbs 14:1 (NASB)

From:	VIM <vivalaveronica@marcelloportraits.com>
To:	Rosalyn Ebberly <prov31woman@home.com>
Subject:	Re: Ouch!

I think Buddha-enhanced drugs would be less scary than your evangelical-induced Nirvana. But you know I love ya anyway.

Veronica

From:	Thomas Huckleberry
	<t.huckleberry@showme.com>
To:	Dulcie Huckleberry
	<dulcie@homemakerinteriors.com>
Subject:	**Whatcha doin'?**

Hey, hotstuff, what are you doing?

From:	Dulcie Huckleberry
	<dulcie@homemakerinteriors.com>
To:	Thomas Huckleberry
	<t.huckleberry@showme.com>
Subject:	**Re: Whatcha doin'?**

Working, of course. Nobody warned me that interior design would entail marital counseling. I've got a meeting tomorrow with the Kerricks, who are fighting over the design of their master suite. She said she wanted "red walls and gold satin curtains" and his response was "Great, we'll be sleeping in a bordello."

She said, "And how would you know about that?"

"Well, how else is a guy going to get some action, huh?"

And then they were off. I know FAR too much about the Kerricks now. Blech!

So my job tomorrow is to calm them both down before

they decide to get a divorce and leave me with an outstand-
ing bill. This is NOT what they trained us for in school!

What are you doing? Where are the kids?

Love ya!

Dulcie

From:	Thomas Huckleberry
	<t.huckleberry@showme.com>
To:	Dulcie Huckleberry
	<dulcie@homemakerinteriors.com>
Subject:	**Re: Whatcha doin'?**

I'm e-mailing *you*. The kids are…let's see…MacKenzie is
doing a hair-singeing experiment with the lighter, and I
gave the twins permission to take their dolls to the roof and
play up there for a while.

From:	Dulcie Huckleberry
	<dulcie@homemakerinteriors.com>
To:	Thomas Huckleberry
	<t.huckleberry@showme.com>
Subject:	**Very. Funny.**

Your humor is sad, as in S-A-H-D, stay-at-home DAD SAD.
You obviously are bored and don't have enough to keep you
busy. You could bring me a snack or something. ☺

From:	Thomas Huckleberry
	<t.huckleberry@showme.com>
To:	Dulcie Huckleberry
	<dulcie@homemakerinteriors.com>
Subject:	Re: Very. Funny.

A snack? Do I look like a live-in maid? Sheesh. I cook for
you, I clean for you, I care for the kids—and this is the
thanks I get? Bring me a *snack?* I'm insulted.

From:	Dulcie Huckleberry
	<dulcie@homemakerinteriors.com>
To:	Thomas Huckleberry
	<t.huckleberry@showme.com>
Subject:	Re: Very. Funny.

You might as well—you've still got a dish towel over your
shoulder. You look like housekeeper material to me. Just
missing the apron.

From:	Thomas Huckleberry
	<t.huckleberry@showme.com>
To:	Dulcie Huckleberry
	<dulcie@homemakerinteriors.com>
Subject:	Re: Very. Funny.

Shoot! I forgot again. I hate that—I put it there when I load the dishwasher, and then it's there the rest of the day. But an apron? Not even on my dead body, got it? A SAHD has to have SOME boundaries.

And why are you e-mailing me when I'm sitting not four feet away from you?

From:	Dulcie Huckleberry
	<dulcie@homemakerinteriors.com>
To:	Thomas Huckleberry
	<t.huckleberry@showme.com>
Subject:	Re: Very. Funny.

Me? You started it!

☺**Instant Message**

Huck: True. This better?

Dulcet: No! I can't IM. I have to work!

Huck: Chill, sweetheart. It'll be okay.

Dulcet: No, it won't. How would you like this little entre-preneurial endeavor of Homemaker Interiors to fail before it's even two months old? Right now, the Kerricks are my ONLY clients.

Huck: You're not going to fail.

Dulcet: If they bail on me because their marriage breaks up, we're not going to make the house payment next month.

Huck: They won't bail.

Dulcet: From your lips to God's ears.

Huck: And don't worry about the house payment. That's what our year's worth of savings is for.

Dulcet: Yeah, but I don't want to use it! It takes at least three years to get a business going. And about half that money is from our parents. Even though

Huck: Yes, it's called an "investment."

Dulcet: it's a gift…yeah, or "investment," I still don't want to use it until absolutely necessary.

Huck: I know. But it will be okay.

Dulcet: Thanks for the vote of confidence. I just know how much is riding on me succeeding with this. It's really scary sometimes.

Huck: Don't put so much pressure on yourself—it's not just you. We're in this together, remember? And WHY are we having this conversation via IM when we are sitting in the same room?

Dulcet: YOU STARTED IT!!! And anyway, I have to get back to work. Somebody has to earn money in this family, mister.

Huck: Hey, you can't be so high and mighty with me, Ms. Self-Employed Business Woman.

Dulcet: Why not?

Huck: Because I've seen you wake up, and it's impossible to be a snob to someone who snuggled you first thing this morning.

Dulcet: Snuggled? Is that what you're calling it now?

Huck: Is that inaccurate?

Dulcet: I am WORKING! I am professional and very busy!!!

Huck: You're blushing…it's so cute.

Dulcet: I cannot IM you about stuff like that right now or else the Kerricks' master suite WILL end up looking like a bordello! Don't you have some preschool disaster to clean up or something?

Huck: I love you, Dulcie. ☺

Dulcet: I love you, too. Now go away.

Dulcet: And stop laughing at me!

Huck signed off at 3:48:23 p.m.

Dulcet signed off at 3:48:35 p.m.

From:	Brenna L. <saywhat@writeme.com>
To:	SAHM I Am <sahmiam@loophole.com>
Subject:	Re: [SAHM I AM]
	TOTW June 1: Total Honesty

Okay, I'll play. I just got home from my twins' ten month checkup. Tess is doing great. But we're worried about Patrick. He is just now sitting up without support, but he can't get himself there on his own yet. And the doctor says he should be able to pull into a standing position!

Tess is such a go-getter, but Patrick doesn't do anything. He doesn't try to reach for toys, and he hardly ever makes a sound. He's a lot smaller than Tess, too. At first, I thought he's just a really laid-back kid, but now I'm afraid he's actually behind. Lots of studies talk about how in vitro fertilization babies are at higher risk for developmental delays, and my two were from a frozen embryo adoption, too! What if all the antiembryo adoption people are right, and it's our fault that Patrick is delayed? They all say that frozen embryos are weaker and more prone to developing birth defects.

The pediatrician said we need to look for hidden ear infections. But I'm worried it might be worse than that. We love Patrick, but if there's something wrong with him, Darren will be devastated. He's under a lot of pressure to do the whole "have a son to take over the farm" thing with his family. What if Patrick can't do that?

And yeah, I got the guilt thing going on, too. It shouldn't matter if there's anything wrong with Patrick or not. We will still love him anyway. We shouldn't be disappointed or put expectations on our kids. I know. And I feel bad because I'm doing it anyway.

How's that for total honesty?
Brenna

From:	Marianne Hausten <confidentmom@nebweb.net>
To:	Brenna L. <saywhat@writeme.com>
Subject:	Re: [SAHM I AM] TOTW June 1: Total Honesty

Brenna, thanks for being so honest. I don't want to make light of your worries, but I used to also worry a lot about Helene. She's always been so obstinate and headstrong—I thought maybe she had some psychopathic disorder. But she's just strong willed. And now that she's three and a half, she's getting better. My slowly stiffening backbone about being firm with her is helping a lot, too.

I guess I'm trying to say that ten months old is a little early to be too worried about developmental stuff. Kids grow at different rates. Your pediatrician wasn't too worried, right?

I've got "boy troubles", too—of a different sort—with little Neil, who is now just over two years old. Actually, it's not him so much as it is me. Me and my lifelong inability to stand up to anybody or deal with disapproval or conflict. I've gotten so much more confident about being firm with Helene that I thought it wouldn't be a problem with Neil, either. And it's not…well, not directly.

I know I'm not making much sense, but I don't have the energy to explain it right now. I definitely don't want to get into it on the loop quite yet. That's *my* honest confession. I still have a lot of clashes with Helene. Sometimes I just can't deal with any more conflicts, and this thing with Neil will definitely create a controversy there.

Anyway, try not to stress about Patrick. He's probably just fine.

Love,
Marianne

From:	The Millards
	<jstcea4jesus@familymail.net>
To:	SAHM I Am <sahmiam@loophole.com>
Subject:	Re: [SAHM I AM]
	TOTW June 1: Total Honesty

Okay, everyone, here's my deep, dark confession. I haven't told ANYBODY on the loop this yet…

About a month ago, my husband, Shane, got a huge pro-

motion—to VP of the web design firm he works for. Came
with a big raise, and we're all really happy about it. But here's
the kicker—Shane and I had a long discussion. Seems he's
STILL not satisfied about my ability to say "no" to doing
stuff. I mean, it's a lot better than it was a couple of years
ago. We're still homeschooling, and with four kids—one of
whom is now a teenager—there's bound to be a lot of activities. We only let the kids pick three extra things per week
to be involved in. So it's only twelve total! But I'm not di-
recting the church Christmas production, or teaching the
marriage classes, or coordinating the home school co-op
classes. I still lead a women's Bible study group, but that's
ministry so it doesn't count!

I tried to explain all this to Shane. He says that since I
am pathologically unable to maintain anything resembling
a sane schedule that his only alternative is to…

HIRE EXTRA HELP!

That's right—he forced me to hire a housekeeping
service! And he's making me allow a teen home school
student come over to be a "mommy's helper." As if I need
help or something! Can you believe it?

So now, I have to go away once a week and when I come
home, the Happy Housekeepers have been all over my
home—straightening, vacuuming, dusting, cleaning the
bathrooms. Yes, they CLEAN my bathrooms! It's so embarrassing.

And Tasha, the homeschooler, comes twice a week to
tutor and watch Evelyn and Audra so I can take Cassia to
dance lessons and Tyler to home school band. (He's playing
the saxophone—isn't that terrific?)

My life is ruined. A mom ought to be able to manage

running her own household. I didn't need help. What do these Happy Housekeepers know about my home anyway? Well, other than that Tyler sometimes misses the toilet bowl…

Oh my goodness! They KNOW my son has bad aim!

I can never show my face again in public.

Jocelyn

From:	Dulcie Huckleberry
	<dulcie@homemakerinteriors.com>
To:	SAHM I Am <sahmiam@loophole.com>
Subject:	Re: [SAHM I AM]
	TOTW June 1: Total Honesty

She's mad that her husband insisted on hiring a housekeeping service? Somebody shoot her.

☺**Instant Message**

JocelynM: Hey! Be nice! ☺

Dulcet: I am. I could have said you sounded like Rosalyn. But I didn't.

JocelynM: Yeah, okay. You were nice.

Dulcet: Seriously, what is your problem? I would LOVE to have a housekeeping service. We can't afford it.

JocelynM: I just feel like if I'd been doing the job I should be doing, Shane wouldn't have gone and hired someone else to do it. How would you feel if you had to hire someone else to do your design work for you?

Dulcet: If I had to hire another designer, I'd be thrilled because it would mean my business is really growing. Most people view hiring as a step up.

JocelynM: It just feels like a big failure to me. Maybe I *should* be shot.

Dulcet: I'm sorry.

JocelynM: I gotta run. Tonight is piano lessons and we have to leave in a half hour.

Dulcet: Have fun.

JocelynM signed off at 6:18:04 p.m.

From:	VIM <vivalaveronica@marcelloportraits.com>
	SAHM I Am <sahmiam@loophole.com>
To:	**Re: [SAHM I AM]**
Subject:	**TOTW June 1: Total Honesty**

Hey Jocelyn,

Frank and I got ourselves a cleaning lady right after we got married a few years ago. It's been a lifesaver. Or at least a sanity saver for me, anyway. Don't know what I would have done without the extra help.

Don't worry—once you get used to it, you'll wonder how you ever survived without it. I can't remember the last time I actually had to clean the bathroom myself!

Veronica

From:	Dulcie Huckleberry
	<dulcie@homemakerinteriors.com>
To:	SAHM I Am <sahmiam@loophole.com>
Subject:	**Re: [SAHM I AM]**
	TOTW June 1: Total Honesty

Can't remember the last time she had to clean the bathroom? Somebody shoot her, too.

From:	Rosalyn Ebberly <prov31woman@home.com>
To:	Dulcie Huckleberry <dulcie@homemakerinteriors.com>
Subject:	Re: [SAHM I AM] TOTW June 1: Total Honesty

Dulcie dear,

You seem a little tense or unhappy about the good fortunes of Jocelyn and Veronica. Do we have a bit of an envy problem?

I used to feel the same way. But you know what I've learned? The key to inner peace is learning to be content. That's what the Apostle Paul learned—contentment no matter what. Everything is a blessing—even a dirty bathroom! It really is.

Here's a challenge for you—the next time you are elbow deep in the toilet bowl, giving it a good scrub, just start praising God for the blessing of having to clean a toilet. And what, you may ask, is there to be thankful for about a dirty toilet?

It means, dear one, that you have a family to make it dirty. Blessings and peace,

Rosalyn

"The wise woman builds her house, but the foolish tears it down with her own hands." Proverbs 14:1 (NASB)

From:	Dulcie Huckleberry
	<dulcie@homemakerinteriors.com>
To:	"Green Eggs and Ham"
Subject:	**FW note from HMS Pollyanna**
	(see attached)

Never mind someone else. I'll shoot her myself.
Dulcie

From:	P. Lorimer <phyllis.lorimer@geemail.com>
To:	SAHM I Am <sahmiam@loophole.com>
Subject:	**Re: [SAHM I AM]**
	TOTW June 1: Total Honesty

Fellow loopers,
I think this is a wonderful topic. Thanks, Rosalyn!

Here is my honest confession: I am a pastor's wife. Rightly or not, we're held to unreasonably higher standard of behavior than everyone else. But I am also a graduate student with an advisor that, frankly, I can't stand.

She was my professor this past semester for a class called Women's Voices: Misogyny, Religion and Community in Early Modern Europe. It was actually a fascinating study about the cultural and political treatment of women during this time period. I absolutely loved the class. We studied primary sources, private journals of women, letters, stories, sermons, books—some were humorous and others were heartbreaking.

My advisor is actually a brilliant woman and an amazing teacher. At first, I was so impressed with her and the research she's done, that I chose her as my advisor. But I didn't know until I had her for class this summer what she was really like.

She's quite the feminist, and when she found out that I am married to a pastor, she made barbed comments about it during class. It was embarrassing and demeaning. And stupid. She's very intelligent, but her sarcastic remarks made her sound immature and not very bright.

I feel guilty for not liking her. After all, I know that God loves her, and if Jesus were in my shoes, He'd forgive this woman and be able to see past the petty smallness and into her heart.

But for once in my life, I'd like to not do the "spiritually correct" thing. My husband, Jonathan, told me that he thinks God led me to my advisor for a reason. I'm sure He did, but I'm not happy about it at all. A normal person would request an advisement change. A normal person would not put up with this crap.

I, however, don't feel I have the freedom to be a "normal person." (No quips about that, you guys!) It would affect my funding for my dissertation, and it would not be good for my reputation. Right now, I'm not too happy about that at all.

So that's the confession—Ms. Holy Pastor's Wife doesn't want to be the "light and love of Christ" to this bitter woman. Ms. Holy Pastor's Wife is tired of doing the right thing and would like to do the usual human thing of writing her off permanently.

Ms. Holy Pastor's Wife is grumpy.

Phyllis

☺**Instant Message**

ZeeMuzzy: hey phyllis—you trying to bait rosalyn or what?

PhyllisLorimer: No. I just needed to vent.

ZeeMuzzy: well, i don't blame you. but you know ros is going to have something to say about it.

PhyllisLorimer: Something along the lines of "Thanks for your honesty, dear, but I'm a little concerned about the example you're setting for the other women. We who are in a position of leadership need to be conscious of what our actions are saying to others," perhaps?

ZeeMuzzy: precisely

PhyllisLorimer: Too late. I've already preached that sermon to myself and the effect lasted about as long as people's memories of Jonathan's sermons do on Sunday morning.

ZeeMuzzy: the amount of time it takes for the congregation to walk from their seat to the back of the sanctuary?

PhyllisLorimer: The average for that is 21.6 seconds. So a little less than that, yes.

ZeeMuzzy: poor girl. wish i had something spiritually profound to say.

PhyllisLorimer: I do, too. You know I'd listen.

ZeeMuzzy: ☺ my best advice is avoid checking your email for the next few minutes. any minute here, and you'll have a rosalyn-bomb in your inbox.

PhyllisLorimer: Happy thought, indeed.

ZeeMuzzy: shouldn't be long now. wait for it…

PhyllisLorimer: Waiting. Nothing yet.

ZeeMuzzy: wait for it...
PhyllisLorimer: Waiting with anticipation and mortal dread.
ZeeMuzzy: 3...2...1...

From:	P. Lorimer <phyllis.lorimer@geemail.com>
To:	Zelia Muzuwa <zeemuzu@vivacious.com>
Subject:	**Nothing!**

How very odd—six hours later and no response! I wonder what happened to her?
Phyllis

From:	Zelia Muzuwa <zeemuzu@vivacious.com>
To:	P. Lorimer <phyllis.lorimer@geemail.com>
Subject:	**Re: Nothing!**

Huh. Therapy session run long, maybe?
Z

From:	VIM <vivalaveronica@marcelloportraits.com>
To:	SAHM I Am <sahmiam@loophole.com>
Subject:	**Re: [SAHM I AM]**
	TOTW June 1: Total Honesty

Okay, y'all…I mean, all of you (sorry Ros),

All y'all (argh, I can't help it! I may not be native Texan, but I tell you…I have the soul of one!)—anyway, you all have inspired me with your honesty, so here's what's going on in lil' old Ronnie's corner of the earth…

Ashley's now thirteen years old, and as determined to make her momma miserable as ever a teenager was. Keeps talking nonsense about how she wants to go live with her "real mom" instead of her dad and me—despite the fact that "Real Mom" sent BACK the Christmas presents the kiddos made for her last year! I know Ashley's just trying to annoy us, but it's super irritating to have to admit it works.

Courtney's nine and Stanley's seven. And other than the sibling war that the two girls have been waging since… birth, I guess, they're not doing too badly.

And my baby, Stephenie is eighteen months old now! I shouldn't phrase it like that, I suppose. I feel like the other three are mine, too, after being the only real mama they've ever had for three years now. But y'all know what I mean, I hope.

Lest you start thinking this is sounding an awful lot like a Christmas newsletter, I'm saying all this because of the thing I want to talk about for this Honesty topic of the week thingy.

Frank, my sweet Francesco, has been telling me that since the kids are getting older and especially with Ashley being a pain in the behind lately, and also since he wants to avoid the mistakes he made with his ex…

He thinks we should try attending church! His family back in Italy is 100% Catholic, and he's wanting to check out our local parish.

I know most of you all on this loop are churchgoing

folks, so this is where that hard-core honesty is coming in for me. I'm not real sold on the idea of going to church. I don't think it's very responsible of us to expect religion to solve our problems or fix our kids. You all are generally sincere and genuine people, and I respect that. I'm just not sure I'm the religious type.

But Frank really is pushing for it. I told him if he wanted to take the kids and go, I wouldn't put up a fuss. But he doesn't want to go without me. Not sure if there's a senti-mental reason for that or if he just doesn't want to handle all four kids by himself. But we're kinda at a standoff with it.

And that there's my confession. Hey…confession! I don't need to go to church. I've got all of you.
Veronica

From:	Iona James
	<poetsmystique@brokenwrenchandcopperbucket.com>
To:	SAHM I Am <sahmiam@loophole.com>
Subject:	[SAHM I AM]
	An Honest Greeting From Iona

Dia daoibh! ("Hi there" in Gaelic),

I will not reveal my given name, but I am called Iona—ever since I discovered that my great-great-grandmother was born there. I had a dream about her three years ago and she called me "her Iona." When I woke up, I knew I had been renamed. I'm studying Gaelic, but it's slow going because I don't have anyone to practice it with.

I am a poet and songwriter for my husband's band, Broken Wrench and Copper Bucket. I've recently joined your lovely little brigade because the Angel Child (my ten-month-old, Gabriel) and I are trying to learn our Life Dance with each other a bit better—and we've been stepping on each other's toes too much.

My moment of utter honesty is thus:

I never intended to become a mother. What started as a moment of passion has become a never-ending progression of confusion. I love the Angel Child, but I don't understand him. And the more I become his mother, the less I understand myself, as well.

I can't share further with you right now, but I will in time. At the moment, I'm waiting for Francine to return. I was soaking up the beauty of God's Word this morning and felt a strong urge to open the Bible to a random page. Every time that happens, it's always a life-changing moment for me. So I did, and my finger landed on Psalm 141:2 "May my prayers be counted as incense before Thee; the lifting up of my hands as the evening offering."

And I knew. It was clear to me that God was calling me to burn incense in our apartment so that we would no longer view prayer as something we do, but something we live. So I took the Angel Child and was on my way to a Tats 'N Wicks shop three blocks away to buy incense. But the Angel Child's diaper sprung a leak about a block from our apartment. Just as I turned around to go home, a woman appeared and asked if she could help me. She said her name was Francine, and that she has eight children of her own and spent twenty years as a stay-at-home mother.

I gave her twenty dollars and asked her to pick out something that smelled like Jesus and bring it to my apartment.

I believe God gave me that scripture verse so I would meet Francine today. She's a treasure and blessing. She looks like a homeless prostitute—probably a meth addict. But Jesus visits us in the most unlikely disguises.

We're going to invite her to live with us for a while.

May you live in the divine mystery of God, my friends,
Iona James

From:	Brenna L. <saywhat@writeme.com>
To:	"Green Eggs and Ham"
Subject:	Re: [SAHM I AM]
	An Honest Greeting From Iona

What was THAT???
Brenna

From:	The Millards
	<jstcea4jesus@familymail.net>
To:	"Green Eggs and Ham"
Subject:	Re: [SAHM I AM]
	An Honest Greeting From Iona

I have no idea, but I think it's gone now. Do you suppose it will come back?
Jocelyn

From:	P. Lorimer <phyllis.lorimer@geemail.com>
To:	"Green Eggs and Ham"
Subject:	Re: [SAHM I AM]
	An Honest Greeting From Iona

It? *She* was beautiful, and I hope she does come back. Don't scare her off, understand? I think I'm in love…
Phyllis

From:	Hannah Farrell
	<boazsmom@farrellfamilylovesjesus.net>
To:	Kristina Shaw <krissyshaw@loopy.com>
Subject:	What have I gotten into?

Hi Krissy,

U R so NOT going to believe this. I joined this loop for stay-at-home moms this week, and they're like really bizarre. The loop moderator just got out of some sort of mental hospital, I think. I guess she crawled into a coffin because she thought her husband was having an affair with a Lesbian! Can u imagine?

And then her sister is even worse! She's not even a Christian. And she married a divorced guy! The scariest part is…he was raised CATHOLIC! In Italy, where the pope lives! He's trying to talk her into going to church again. But she says she's not "the religious type." And they actually let her post on the loop!

There's another new girl this week, too. She's psycho. She has a ten-month-old baby, and she's inviting a prostitute to live with her and her husband! I would NEVER be so totally stupid! If a prostitute even looked at my Bradley, she'd be sorry! Is sharing your home with a homeless hooker even Biblical? Nobody in our church would ever do that, I'm sure. What if she tempts the husband to, you know, SIN or something? And she thinks God told her to burn incense, too! I'm pretty certain incense is new age. You can't be new age and still believe in Jesus, can you?

So I'm hugely bummed. I thought this was going to be a loop full of Christian SAHMs like me—well, sure, I figured they'd be a little older than me. But these people are really weird. I don't think they're what I'd exactly call "Christian" even.

I thought about just unsubscribing from the loop. But I really am very lonely without you here. Bradley is nice and all, but it's SO not the same as having a best girlfriend. I decided not to leave the loop just yet, because maybe it'll be better and I'll meet some normal moms. I don't want to be all like judgmental or anything, you know?

Well, write me and tell me all about Hawaii. YouTube it and send me some pics, okay?

BFF,
Hannah

From:	Kristina Shaw <krissyshaw@loopy.com>
To:	Hannah Farrell
	<boazsmom@farrellfamilylovesjesus.net>
Subject:	Re: What have I gotten into?

Hey you! Hawaii is awesome. Check out the attached pics. Tried 2 txt them 2 u, but they were 2 big. Weird about that mom loop. U going 2 stay on loop? Lots of my new friends are kinda whacked like that 2. But they r fun. Lots better than our stuffy old high school! I told them all about South Carolina Crusading Lambs of God High School. They think it's the best joke. LOL! I gotta run. Some of the guys in our group are taking me surfing this afternoon. We did all our research/school stuff this morning. Can you imagine—I'm going surfing with hot guys! My parents would totally freak out, but there's nothing they can do about it. It's great to be FREE!

LUV U!!!!

Kris

From:	Thomas Huckleberry
	<t.huckleberry@showme.com>
To:	SAHM I Am <sahmiam@loophole.com>
Subject:	Re: [SAHM I AM]
	TOTW June 1: Total Honesty

Hi ladies,

It looks like I'm about the last one to check in this week on the TOTW. Here's something I bet no guy up until now has confessed to in your hearing:

I'm sitting at my computer wearing a plastic jeweled princess crown on my head and strap-on fairy wings on my back. My sparkle wand is on the desk. And I'm having a great time!

MacKenzie is playing Cinderella, and I'm her Fairy Godmother. Two years ago, if you'd suggested that I'd ever make a statement like that (or be dressed like this), I probably would never have talked to you again. But since then, I've discovered that only a real man has the courage to play make-believe with his daughter. She tried to put dress-up heels on me, but my feet were too big…thankfully.

Whoa, gotta go. Sounds like Mac has given the twins the choice between being the ugly stepsisters or the mice. They're not happy.

Tom

From:	Zelia Muzuwa <zeemuzu@vivacious.com>
To:	SAHM I Am <sahmiam@loophole.com>
Subject:	**Re: [SAHM I AM]**
	TOTW June 1: Total Honesty

Awww, Tom!!! Fairy wings and a tiara? This is the only (and I do mean ONLY) context I'd ever say this in, but…THAT IS SO DARN CUTE! Aw, you're a good dad. A really, really good dad!

Rock on, Tiara-man!

Z

From:	Hannah Farrell
	<boazsmom@farrellfamilylovesjesus.net>
To:	SAHM I Am <sahmiam@loophole.com>
Subject:	**Re: [SAHM I AM]**
	TOTW June 1: Total Honesty

There's a MAN on the loop???

This is supposed to be a loop for MOMS! How am I supposed to be all share-y and open if there's a guy lurking around? I can't talk about…you know…STUFF—in front of a man!

What kind of a weird place is this? What wife would ever be idiotic enough to let her husband on a loop full of other women?

What is WRONG with you people?

Hannah

From:	Dulcie Huckleberry
	<dulcie@homemakerinteriors.com>
To:	SAHM I Am <sahmiam@loophole.com>
Subject:	Re: [SAHM I AM]
	TOTW June 1: Total Honesty

Hannah,

I'm the "idiot" who "lets" her husband on a loop with other women. Charmed to meet you.

If you have a problem with our loop, you're welcome to find yourself a different loop that is more to your liking. We voted to let Tom join our loop, and he's been a great addition.

If you don't feel comfortable discussing things in front of him, that's your problem, not his. He is the most trust-worthy, sympathetic, sweetest person in the whole world, and anyone who decides not to take the time to get to know him is a big-time loser.

Stay-at-home dads need encouragement and friendship, too. There's no reason why only moms should get that privilege.

I knew you were young, but good grief! Apparently, you haven't gotten past the "Ew, boys have cooties" stage yet. Sincerely,
Dulcie Huckleberry

From:	Dulcie Huckleberry
	<dulcie@homemakerinteriors.com>
To:	Rosalyn Ebberly <prov31woman@home.com>
Subject:	My loop post

Go ahead and slap my wrist now, Rosalyn. I'm so angry, I don't care at the moment.
Dulcie

From:	Rosalyn Ebberly <prov31woman@home.com>
To:	Dulcie Huckleberry
	<dulcie@homemakerinteriors.com>
Subject:	Re: My loop post

I should. I really should. But…I'll let it go this time. The line about boy cooties was worth it. However, Dulcie dear, would you like to borrow one of my books on anger management? I'm sure you would find it so helpful!

Go soak in a nice bubble bath with candles—relieving

stress and anxiety will go a long way to helping you control
your temper.
Much love,
Rosalyn

"The wise woman builds her house, but the foolish tears it
down with her own hands." Proverbs 14:1 (NASB)

From:	Dulcie Huckleberry
	<dulcie@homemakerinteriors.com>
To:	"Green Eggs and Ham"
Subject:	**Whaaaaat?**

Rosalyn was just nice to me.

Rosalyn. Yes, THAT Rosalyn.

She was nice.

To me.

I've been wandering around the last ten minutes repeat-
ing this to myself and still can't grasp it. My brain has
exploded. I feel as if I've entered a *Twilight Zone* episode.

There's something very weird afoot. Very weird, indeed.
Dulcie

☺**Instant Message**
Huck: How's my damsel in shining armor doing?
Dulcet: Still steamed.
Huck: You didn't have to do that, you know.
Dulcet: Do what?
Huck: Defend me. I'm a big boy. I can handle it.

Dulcet: Of course you can. But you really think I was going to let that little brat publicly slam you without saying a word in protest?

Huck: Well, it would have shocked me if you had. ☺

Dulcet: We stick together. Attack one, and you tangle with us both. You'd have done the same for me.

Huck: Sure. But only if you weren't able to do it yourself. I was going to post a reply of my own, you know.

Dulcet: Oh. Really?

Huck: Yeah. Was working on it when yours posted. It was going to be a good post, I think.

Dulcet: Not a rant like mine, huh?

Huck: A gentler rant. Remember, I'm on the loop strictly because of everyone's good will. I have to be a little more diplomatic.

Dulcet: You're not going to be able to send yours now, huh?

Huck: Probably not. Wouldn't want to keep things stirred up.

Dulcet: I'm sorry.

Huck: Forgiven. You sure you're okay? Her post wasn't that bad, you know. Lots of those women had stronger objections when you first brought up the idea of me joining the loop.

Dulcet: I lost the Kerrick account.

Huck: Whoa.

Dulcet: They called today and cancelled—said they're definitely getting a divorce. They still have to pay me for the design work to this point, but nothing more.

Huck: Okay, so we

Dulcet: I think it'll be enough to make the bills for this month and part of next, but I don't have any more clients! I can't even talk to any of the clients from my previous job. And the ads I placed aren't bringing in enough inquiries.

Huck: Dulcie, let's

Dulcet: I'm going to fail! I was stupid for even trying this.

Huck: No, you weren't.

Dulcet: What are we going to do? I should have done something. Stopped it from happening. I could have fixed it. I didn't try hard enough.

Huck: DULCIE!

Dulcet: What?

Huck: Don't you think we should take this conversation out to the living room couch? I can't hold you when I'm typing.

Dulcet: Yeah…that sounds good.

Dulcet signed off at 5:01:56 p.m.

Huck signed off at 5:01:58 p.m.

⌨Text Message From Jeff Ebberly: For Rosalyn Ebberly

———June 15 10:13 a.m.———

Mom, jst got n fyt. Im k. Nt my falt. Principel wl cll u. Sry. Jeff.

From:	Rosalyn Ebberly <prov31woman@home.com>
To:	SAHM I Am <sahmiam@loophole.com>
Subject:	[SAHM I AM] TOTW June 15: Meeting the needs of our children

Marvelous Mommies,

After last week's scintillating discussion on forgiveness, I thought we should turn our attention to a topic sure to warm and encourage every mother's heart:

Meeting the needs of our children.

I've had to learn the hard way that EVERYTHING we do as mothers—every word, every glance, every touch—deeply affects our children for the *rest of their lives!*

So when you shrieked, "Can't you be quiet for just ONE SECOND?" after breakfast this morning? Sliced their tender little souls like a piece of deli ham. They'll forever struggle with voicing their own wants and needs. Assertiveness will never come easy for them and they'll probably get taken advantage of by every emotional manipulator who crosses their path.

When you said you were too tired to read your son a book? Five years from now, that moment will fester into resentment that will cause him to punch another child in summer school. Ten years from now, it will blossom into a full-scale rebellion that will get him kicked out of school and placed into a juvenile detention center.

Every time you pushed their eager little hands away and impatiently told them, "here, let me do it"…it was one more blow to their fragile sense of worth. It will probably result in a total inability to sustain meaningful relationships as adults.

Not to mention a permanent spelling handicap.

How many wounds we inflict on our children every hour of every day! It's no wonder they end up so screwed up. And it's our fault as mothers for not meeting their emotional needs.

So let's encourage each other on how we can do better at not ruining our children. Obviously, it's not an easy task, considering that our own parents did a thorough job of wounding us to the point where we wouldn't recognize a healthy psyche if it tackled us to the sidewalk. But as adults and mothers, it's our responsibility to try to do better with the next generation, even if it kills us.

Blessings,

Rosalyn Ebberly

SAHM I Am Loop Moderator

"The wise woman builds her house, but the foolish tears it down with her own hands." Proverbs 14:1 (NASB)

From:	Zelia Muzuwa <zeemuzu@vivacious.com>
To:	SAHM I Am <sahmiam@loophole.com>
Subject:	**[SAHM I AM] sahmiam totw**

Ooookay. Looks like somebody needs to dial back on her happy pills…WAY too cheerful this morning!

Z

From:	Dulcie Huckleberry
	<dulcie@homemakerinteriors.com>
To:	Zelia Muzuwa <zeemuzu@vivacious.com>
Subject:	Your note!!!

Z,

Did you realize that note went to the SAHM loop instead of our Green Eggs and Ham group? ROSALYN saw it! You'd better apologize quick. She's going to be SO mad! Dulcie

From:	Zelia Muzuwa <zeemuzu@vivacious.com>
To:	SAHM I Am <sahmiam@loophole.com>
Subject:	[SAHM I AM] Re: sahmiam totw

Hey gorgeous mom-babes, (and Tom, of course)
Hope nobody took my previous message too seriously. Just trying to lighten the mood on this Monday. It's rainy and foggy here in Baltimore—needed to cheer myself up a bit. No offense intended.
Z

☺**Instant Message**
Pr31Mom: Zelia, dear.
ZeeMuzzy: ros, honey.
Pr31Mom: Thank you for your apology on the loop.
ZeeMuzzy: no prob. you know i could never bear the thought of offending anyone.
Pr31Mom: Of course not. You're sweetness itself.
ZeeMuzzy: takes one to know one, babe.
Pr31Mom: That's kind of you to say so. I hope you are feeling sufficiently cheered now?
ZeeMuzzy: vastly.
Pr31Mom: Great. Well, then, I'll let you get back to your

day. Since I'm sure you're far too busy for more loop humor today, we'll have to just get along without the giggles. Okay?

ZeeMuzzy: you never know. i might have a few spare moments later on.

Pr31Mom: That's a relief. Wouldn't want you to be too stressed out.

ZeeMuzzy: yes, because you're just that kind of compassionate person, aren't you.

Pr31Mom: Zelia, I'm serious—

ZeeMuzzy signed off at 2:38:02 p.m.

From:	Brenna L. <saywhat@writeme.com>
To:	SAHM I Am <sahmiam@loophole.com>
Subject:	Re: [SAHM I AM] TOTW June 15: Meeting the needs of our children

This is the biggest pile of male cow manure I have ever read in my life! First off, Rosalyn, your parents did not screw you up. You want to compare dysfunctions? You all know I had Maddy at age sixteen. Yep, teen mom. I was the poster child for dysfunction. It would be easy for me to whine and say it was the fault of my parents—they were no Clair and Cliff Huxtable for sure. But my family was no worse than many of my friends' and not all of them became teen moms. I made my own choices. We all do. So if your life has a lot of problems, then it's up to you to make the choices you need to make in order to fix those problems.

As far as our kids go—I doubt any of us on this loop are doing anything less than our best for our kids. We're not going to get it right all the time. Our kids will survive. At least they have so far. Guilt trips and self-loathing for our shortcomings are only going to make it harder to see what our kids really need. And when it comes down to it, our kids are the only ones who can actually make their lives successful and fulfilling. They have to choose to be that way. We can't guarantee it for them.

You want to meet your kids' needs? Stop being so hard on yourself. They need a mom who isn't drowning in self-inflicted condemnation. Or whining. A mom who is happy and still realistic about who she is and her own weaknesses. And who isn't afraid to make changes to improve but who doesn't beat herself up for her imagined failures.

By the way—who won the fight?
Brenna

From:	Zelia Muzuwa <zeemuzu@vivacious.com>
To:	Brenna L. <saywhat@writeme.com>
Subject:	Re: [SAHM I AM] TOTW June 15: Meeting the needs of our children

Girrrrrl!!!!!

From:	Brenna L. <saywhat@writeme.com>
To:	Zelia Muzuwa <zeemuzu@vivacious.com>
Subject:	Re: [SAHM I AM] TOTW June 15: Meeting the needs of our children

Um, am I a good "girrrrl" or a bad "girrrrrl"?

From:	Zelia Muzuwa <zeemuzu@vivacious.com>
To:	Brenna L. <saywhat@writeme.com>
Subject:	Re: [SAHM I AM] TOTW June 15: Meeting the needs of our children

You are an amazing, gutsy, tough-as-nails, I'm-in-awe, totally correct, couldn't-have-said-it-better-myself, wish-I'd-have-said-it-first, love you to pieces…girrrrrrl!!!
Z

From:	Hannah Farrell <boazsmom@farrellfamilylovesjesus.net>
To:	SAHM I Am <sahmiam@loophole.com>
Subject:	Re: [SAHM I AM] TOTW June 15: Meeting the needs of our children

I sort of like don't really agree—with either Rosamund or Brenda. I think it's better to just not do all those mean things to our kids in the first place. Then we don't have to worry about messing them up. And there's lots and lots of books about child development that will explain everything you need to know about what kids need.

Most moms have trouble with that because they aren't focusing on their kids like they should. I'm totally into hanging out with friends and stuff, but my little Boaz always comes first. 'Cause I'm his mommy and that's what mommies do—I'm the center of his world, and as long as he feels secure about that, he won't ever have any problems.

I'm always into keeping it simple, you know? And it doesn't get more simple than that—just being there for them. All the time, any time.

Hannah

From:	Rosalyn Ebberly <prov31woman@home.com>
To:	SAHM I Am <sahmiam@loophole.com>
Subject:	Re: [SAHM I AM] TOTW June 15: Meeting the needs of our children

Hannah,

Thank you so much for sharing that incredible nugget of wisdom. I'm very impressed with the depth of the insight you've gained from just two months of motherhood and a handful of parenting books. We must never underestimate the power of the written word combined with our own deep maternal instincts. I don't know why I didn't see it before—all I have to do to make my children happy is be

everything to them! It really is that simple. Thanks, honey.
You've changed the entire course of my life.
ROSALYN

**"The wise woman builds her house, but the foolish tears
it down with her own hands." Proverbs 14:1 (NASB)**

From:	Hannah Farrell
	<boazsmom@farrellfamilylovesjesus.net>
To:	SAHM I Am <sahmiam@loophole.com>
Subject:	Re: [SAHM I AM] TOTW June 15: Meeting the needs of our children

Really? Wow! I'm SOOOO relieved. I was afraid you'd all
be like ticked off at me for disagreeing with you. I really
DO love my books—everything I know about kids comes
straight off those pages. Since you were so interested in
them, I posted a list of them in the loop files.

The newest book I have is about how to educate infants.
I'm going to teach Boaz sign language so he won't ever feel
frustrated about not being able to communicate his needs.
Then we can avoid all those nasty temper tantrums later
on.

And the book also talks about how important it is to
make good faces at our babies. Did you know that if you
frown and talk to a baby in an angry tone of voice before
they're two years old, it will cause brain damage? I'm totally
serious! So this book says you should always approach your

baby with a big smile on your face, even if he's crying. Otherwise, you could scar a kid for life!!!

Gotta go—Boaz needs me to grin at him some more. Sometimes I just sit and smile at him for a half hour at a time. I'm hoping it will make up for any frowns he might have accidentally seen on other people.
Hannah

From:	Marianne Hausten
	<confidentmom@nebweb.net>
To:	"Green Eggs and Ham"
Subject:	**Grinning at babies**

Did anyone else find this idea a bit creepy? Reminds me of a clown. I was terrified of clowns when I was little.
Marianne

From:	Brenna L. <saywhat@writeme.com>
To:	"Green Eggs and Ham"
Subject:	**Re: Grinning at babies**

Hate to break it to you, Marianne, but there are clowns on SAHM I Am—and they've been posting all morning!

My goodness, has Rosalyn learned NOTHING from the disaster that is her life the past two years? And that Hannah… I'm sorry, but nineteen-year-olds have NO business being parents. I can say that because I had a three-year-old by that time, and I was totally clueless. The difference is that I made a mistake by being a teen mom. But Hannah?

She did it on purpose!

It makes me furious. And the weird thing is I really don't know why. It's her life. Her business. But everything in me just screams that it was a stupid decision. Maybe getting married at eighteen was fine for women hundreds of years ago, but it's foolish now.

I know…I must sound like a grumpy middle-aged woman. She just gets on my nerves.

Brenna

📧Text Message From Jeannine Hash: For Dulcie Huckleberry

——June 16/7:45 a.m.——

Hi i just got a cell phone with text messaging sorry for no punctuation but i cant find it do you want me to ask some of my friends if they need a decorator text messages take a lot of time to write this one took me 20 minutes

📧Text Message From Dulcie Huckleberry: For Jeannine Hash

——June 16/10:01 a.m.——

Thx 4 offer, mom. But no need. No big deal. Get more clients soon. Write shorter mssg, takes less time.

From:	Jeanine Hash <ilovebranson@branson.com>
To:	Jeanine's Friends
CC:	Dulcie Huckleberry
	<dulcie@homemakerinteriors.com>
Subject:	Re: My daughter-in-law needs help!!!

Dear Friends,

As many of you know, my daughter-in-law, Dulcie, has been working ever so hard the past few months to start her own interior design business. Well, things just aren't going so well! She could only get one client, and they've dumped her because they decided to get a divorce after meeting with Dulcie!

It would just break my heart to see her fail! She's trying to support the whole family—three children and a "house husband." Poor thing—it's just not right for a woman to have such a burden on her. But I know how that feels—I was a single mom for years before marrying my beloved Morris.

So I'm starting a "let's help Dulcie" campaign! We all could use some home decorating help, right? And I know many of you are…shall we say…"gifted" with plenty of financial resources (Hi, Mr. Tabuchi!!!) so there's no reason not to hire my daughter-in-law. You'll get a prettier house or theater or office building, and she'll be able to put food on the table.

She really is the sweetest little thing. And very talented,

too! You all should see how she decorated the bedroom for her twins—a woodland fairy theme with hand-painted trees and twelve fairies hidden in different corners and crannies all over the room! Who wouldn't want such a good mom working on their project?

You should look at her Web site: www.homemakerin-teriors.com and give her a call! Besides, I'm fixing to make a whole new batch of my famous peach butter later this summer. I'd be more likely to give jars of it to people who are supportive of my kids. :)

Blessings,

Jeanine Hash

P.S. Please feel free to forward this to lots and lots of people!!!

From:	Dulcie Huckleberry <dulcie@homemakerinteriors.com>
To:	Jeanine Hash <ilovebranson@branson.com>
Subject:	**Re: My daughter-in-law needs help!!!**

Mom, tell me you did NOT just send that message to Shoji Tabuchi! The "hi Mr. Tabuchi" referred to some other guy and NOT the Branson megastar with the most-photographed theater bathrooms in America...RIGHT???

By the way, who ELSE was on your friends list???
Dulcie

From:	Jeanine Hash <ilovebranson@branson.com>
To:	Dulcie Huckleberry
	<dulcie@homemakerinteriors.com>
Subject:	Re: My daughter-in-law needs help!!!

Well, of course I sent it to Shoji, darling! He's been my employer and Morris's employer for years, and a good friend, too. Not to mention how sweet he was in letting us have our wedding ceremony at his theater! Wasn't it beautiful—with Morris on the white horse and us girls floating down on stage from sparkly stars? It seems like it was just yesterday…

Anyway, Mr. Tabuchi knows a LOT of people, dear. Plus, if you were able to do a project for him or his family, just think of all the business you'd get!

As for who I sent the e-mail to? Well, everyone I know—which is nearly all of Branson and half of Springfield! Just consider me your marketing and PR machine, sweetie.

Love,

Jeanine

🖂Text Message From Dulcie Huckleberry: For Tom Huckleberry

——June 16/10:08 a.m.——

I'm going to kill your mother. Just wanted to warn you. How is the park?

⌨Text Message From Tom Huckleberry: For Dulcie
Huckleberry
——June 16/10:12 a.m.——
Park is fine. Girls having fun. Will it be Dulcie, with the candlestick, in the library?

⌨Text Message From Dulcie Huckleberry: For Tom
Huckleberry
——June 16/10:14 a.m.——
Hah! Candlestick 2 gentle 4 her. Will be me, in kitchen, drowning her in own peach butter.

⌨Text Message From Tom Huckleberry: For Dulcie
Huckleberry
——June 16/10:15 a.m.——
Yikes! Why? Or do I have 2 wait 4 testimony at trial?

⌨Text Message From Dulcie Huckleberry: For Tom
Huckleberry
——June 16/10:15 a.m.——
Plea will be temporary insanity. Hers. Xplain at home.

From:	Zelia Muzuwa <zeemuzu@vivacious.com>
To:	SAHM I Am <sahmiam@loophole.com>
Subject:	[SAHM I AM] This stinks

"This" being my house. I can't figure it out. Something smells awful! Like garbage—only I've emptied every single trash can in the entire house. I even rinsed them all out with bleach and water! I scrubbed the fridge, replaced the baking soda in there, and put baking soda down all the drains. I cleaned the toilets, the microwave, and even did all the laundry.

And it still reeks!

I'm so mad! All that work, and for nothing!
Zelia

From:	The Millards
	<jstcea4jesus@familymail.net>
To:	SAHM I Am <sahmiam@loophole.com>
Subject:	Re: [SAHM I AM] This stinks

How can you say it was all for nothing? You got your house cleaned, didn't you? And at least you didn't have a stranger scrubbing your toilets.
Jocelyn

From:	Zelia Muzuwa <zeemuzu@vivacious.com>
To:	SAHM I Am <sahmiam@loophole.com>
Subject:	Re: [SAHM I AM] This stinks

Joc, babe, are you still whining and moaning about the pain of having someone clean your house FOR you? I love you, girl, but… Get. A. Grip.

As for my own housecleaning efforts (done by the sweat of my brow and the grease of my elbow, I might add)… it was for nothing because I was trying to get rid of the garbage smell in my house. I was not trying to *clean* my house. If I'd known that all that cleaning was still not going to help, I would have saved myself the trouble.

And we did have near-strangers victimized by our olfactory pollution. My DH Tristan had a coworker and her husband over for dinner last night. It wasn't until after we were done eating that we first noticed the problem. I thought Tristan had forgotten to take out the garbage like I asked him to.

I kept jerking my head toward the kitchen, trying to signal to him that we needed to talk privately. The blockhead. (Whom I love with all my heart, but still…) Totally oblivious.

Carla, his work colleague (who happens to have just been made a partner in his firm—somebody he needs to impress), started sniffing the air. I pretended I wasn't watching. Then she checked the bottoms of her shoes.

DUH—it wasn't that kind of smell. Anybody ought to have known that!

Then she leaned over, like she was getting something out of her purse, but I could tell she was smelling under her arms.

Tacky. But it was making me nervous. Something reeked. In my house! And one of the partners of Tristan's company was definitely noticing it!

I excused myself to the kitchen and checked the garbage can. It had a few scraps in it from fixing dinner, but nothing that smelled. In fact, the kitchen didn't smell as bad as the family room.

By the time the couple left, both of them looked like they were going to pass out soon from trying not to take any deep breaths. They gave us these tiny frozen smiles and scuttled out of the house. I'm almost certain I heard them both gasping for air before we had barely shut the door.

I am utterly mortified! I spent all day trying to track this down and no such luck!

Tristan apparently has a nearly nonexistent sense of smell. He thinks I'm imagining the whole thing—including Carla's little sniff-check.

Next on my list—bathing all the kids.

Z

From:	P. Lorimer <phyllis.lorimer@geemail.com>
To:	SAHM I Am <sahmiam@loophole.com>
Subject:	Re: [SAHM I AM] This stinks

A quote, in your honor, Zelia:

"Something is rotten in the state of Maryland." —slight paraphrase from *Hamlet,* Act 1, Scene 4

Seriously, I wouldn't be overly concerned. I doubt it's as bad as you think it is. And it might be something outside—like a sewer pipe or your neighbors' trash cans or something.

Phyllis

From:	Zelia Muzuwa <zeemuzu@vivacious.com>
To:	P. Lorimer <phyllis.lorimer@geemail.com>
Subject:	Re: [SAHM I AM] This stinks

Ack! My own Shakespeare predilection thrown back at me. A perfect example of this:

"Hoist with his own petard." (*Hamlet,* Act 3, Scene 4) You want to have a Shakespeare war, girlfriend? I'll win.

And I'm not overreacting. I know a bad stink when I smell it! And last night after dinner, definitely "there was the rankest compound of villainous smell that ever offended nostril." (*The Merry Wives of Windsor,* Act 3, Scene 5)

TOP THAT!

Z

From:	Brenna L. <saywhat@writeme.com>
To:	SAHM I Am <sahmiam@loophole.com>
Subject:	Re: [SAHM I AM] This stinks

Oh no! Everyone take cover! The Great Shakespeare Quote War has broken out again! Run for your lives!!! Or as the Bard would say: "Cry havoc and let slip the dogs of war!"

Brenna

From:	Zelia Muzuwa <zeemuzu@vivacious.com>
To:	SAHM I Am <sahmiam@loophole.com>
Subject:	**Re: [SAHM I AM] This stinks**

Ah, Brenna… I salute you, Mistress Lindburg. You are truly magnificent. Here's one for you:

"Methinks a woman of this valiant spirit
Should, if a coward heard her speak these words,
Infuse his breast with magnanimity
And make him, naked, foil a man at arms."
    (*King Henry VI Part iii,* Act 5, Scene 4)

Z

From:	Hannah Farrell
	<boazsmom@farrellfamilylovesjesus.net>
To:	SAHM I Am <sahmiam@loophole.com>
Subject:	**Re: [SAHM I AM] This stinks**

That's NOT a real Shakespeare quote! Shakespeare would never have written about naked…*people* in his plays! That's not appropriate to joke about! I studied *Romeo and Juliet* last year in Senior English, and there wasn't ONE mention of anything remotely risqué!!!
Hannah

From:	P. Lorimer <phyllis.lorimer@geemail.com>
To:	SAHM I Am <sahmiam@loophole.com>
Subject:	**Re: [SAHM I AM] This stinks**

Hannah, out of curiosity…what school did you attend?

From:	Hannah Farrell
	<boazsmom@farrellfamilylovesjesus.net>
To:	SAHM I Am <sahmiam@loophole.com>
Subject:	**Re: [SAHM I AM] This stinks**

South Carolina Crusading Lambs of God Christian High School. Affectionately knows as SCCLOG. Their academic quality is unsurpassable. I tied for valedictorian with my best friend, Krissy.
Hannah

From:	P. Lorimer <phyllis.lorimer@geemail.com>
To:	SAHM I Am <sahmiam@loophole.com>
Subject:	**Re: [SAHM I AM] This stinks**

Ah. Congratulations. And you studied the entire play of *Romeo and Juliet?* The original, unabridged version?

From:	Hannah Farrell
	<boazsmom@farrellfamilylovesjesus.net>
To:	SAHM I Am <sahmiam@loophole.com>
Subject:	Re: [SAHM I AM] This stinks

Yes, the WHOLE thing! Like I said, SCCLOG is a very advanced school academically. Three of my graduating class even went to college! I was going to go to college, but I met Bradley instead.
Hannah

From:	P. Lorimer <phyllis.lorimer@geemail.com>
To:	SAHM I Am <sahmiam@loophole.com>
Subject:	Re: [SAHM I AM] This stinks

Thanks for the clarification. I'm just a little confused. How did you manage to study the entire play *Romeo and Juliet* and come away with the impression that Shakespeare was NOT in any way risqué?

Did no one ever explain to you the Queen Mab speech, honey?
Phyllis

From:	Zelia Muzuwa <zeemuzu@vivacious.com>
To:	P. Lorimer <phyllis.lorimer@geemail.com>
Subject:	Be nice!

Down girl! Behave yourself. Lest you bring the wrath of Rosalyn down on all our heads.

Z

From:	Hannah Farrell
	<boazsmom@farrellfamilylovesjesus.net>
To:	SAHM I Am <sahmiam@loophole.com>
Subject:	**[SAHM I AM] Shakespeare**

Hi Phyllis,

I'm SOOO like not confrontational or anything, but Shakespeare happens to be something I know about. I got an A+ in that class!!!

I know all about the Queen Mab speech. Mercutio was talking about a dream fairy, like Tinker Bell or the Sugar Plum Fairy. What's so risqué about that?

It's impossible for Shakespeare to have written anything naughty. After all, he wrote hundreds of years ago, when people were a lot more pure-minded and innocent. We all should try to be more like that instead of making inappropriate remarks about things that are immodest.

I'm not trying to be a prude or anything. I mean, after all I AM a married woman! But I love Shakespeare, and I don't like to see his reputation ruined—especially not on an e-mail list of (mostly) Christian stay-at-home moms! I'm sure William Shakespeare loved Jesus—everyone did back then. He most certainly did NOT write about naked people fencing. I'm very offended by the suggestion and by the images that brings to mind.

I'd like to ask the loop moderator to bring this topic to a close. It doesn't even have anything to do with stay-at-home mom stuff!

Hannah

P.S. Zelia, your smelly-house problem reminded me of what happened at my school my junior year. Some boys stuffed some tuna fish sandwiches down the air vents and the whole school smelled like rotten fish for weeks.

From:	P. Lorimer <phyllis.lorimer@geemail.com>
To:	SAHM I Am <sahmiam@loophole.com>
Subject:	Re: [SAHM I AM] Shakespeare

Well, Hannah, it does sound like your English teacher did an interesting job with your education. Here's a quote in her honor, from *As You Like It*, Act 2, Scene 7:

"And in his brain,
Which is as dry as the remainder biscuit
After a voyage, he hath strange places cramm'd
With observation, the which he vents
In mangled forms."

Love,

Phyllis

From:	Hannah Farrell
	<boazsmom@farrellfamilylovesjesus.net>
To:	SAHM I Am <sahmiam@loophole.com>
Subject:	**Re: [SAHM I AM] Shakespeare**

I don't get it. But I heard that you weren't very good with humor, so that's probably why.
Hannah

From:	Zelia Muzuwa <zeemuzu@vivacious.com>
To:	SAHM I Am <sahmiam@loophole.com>
Subject:	**Re: [SAHM I AM] This Stinks**

Before our Beloved Moderator puts an end to this conversation, I just wanted to let everyone know I found the source of our stink problem. Hannah's comment about the tuna fish sandwiches at her school gave me an idea.

We live in an older house with old-fashioned air ducts. Big enough for food to be shoved through. I had Tristan check the ductwork when he got home this evening, and sure enough, there's so much old food rotting in one of the ducts that we could start our own compost pile.

At first, I figured Seamus did it. Almost any trouble in our family is a direct result of that boy. But the duct connects to Duri's room. Duri is one of the children we adopted from Ethiopia about fifteen months ago. We asked him if he knew anything about the food in the duct, and at first he said no.

We showed him the food. He stared at it like he'd never seen it before. Then he said something about "That's not my food. I'm saving my food."

To make a very long story about an even longer, depressing evening short, it comes down to this:

Duri has started hoarding food. He sneaks it to his room and shoves it down the air vent.

I don't get it! We feed him plenty! And there's always snacks available. I know he and his sister didn't have much to eat in the orphanage, but they've been with us over a year. Why would he suddenly start doing this?

I don't think he even knows why. He doesn't even connect his actions with the pile of food in the duct. He says he's not hungry, and he has plenty to eat. I don't think he's really even aware of what he's doing.

And to make matters worse, Seamus is mad at me now for accusing him of doing it. And he's mad because we didn't punish Duri. But I don't think Duri was trying to be naughty. It's not the same, but Seamus doesn't understand.

I'm going to have to call our doctor in the morning and maybe see about taking Duri to a psychologist. I'm more than a little freaked out. And we're going to have to get our ducts cleaned out.

But after that—what am I going to do? I don't want to become the Food Police, but we can't let him hoard food like that. What if he'd eaten it later? He'd make himself sick.

All right, Ros—you got me. I'm answering your TOTW.

Apparently, I DON'T KNOW HOW TO MEET MY KIDS' NEEDS! Otherwise, Duri wouldn't be stuffing food down the air vents, and Seamus wouldn't be glaring at me as if I'd betrayed him.

Z

From:	Iona James
	<poetsmystique@brokenwrenchandcopperbucket.com>
To:	SAHM I Am <sahmiam@loophole.com>
Subject:	Re: [SAHM I AM] TOTW June 15: Meeting the needs of our children

How can I meet the needs of the Angel Child when I can't even meet my own needs? The poetry that used to flow from me has been replaced by a steady stream of milk that never seems to satisfy a growing boy. He's growing—but am I? I feel like the host of a parasite—I'm providing nourishment by having the life sucked from me.

I want to write! I want to create. I know the Angel Child should be my greatest poetry, but it's a poem that drains me. I need something that will refresh my soul so I can keep giving.

In other news, Francine—the homeless woman we tried to help—has gone back to selling her body to buy meth. She was a stay-at-home mom for over twenty years. And I can't help but wonder if someday that will be me—used up, empty, hopeless.

Whoa! That's a thought. In fact, I think it might be a poem! I think I'll call it "Weaning." Thank God for dark, depressing thoughts! Life has been way too cheerful recently, and I've had absolutely no inspiration.

I must be off to my writing corner. Angel Child is sleeping. Maybe I'll be extra blessed by him waking up crying. The inner turmoil that creates in me is fantastic for truly tortured emotions!

Iona James

From:	Rosalyn Ebberly <prov31woman@home.com>
To:	SAHM I Am <sahmiam@loophole.com>
Subject:	Re: [SAHM I AM] TOTW June 15: Meeting the needs of our children

Are you INSANE? If you want turmoil and pain, I'll be glad to send you some from our household. I understand your creative drive, but, dear one—you should be glad your baby is healthy, and that there's only one "angel child" to drain your energy. You're not going to end up on the street unless you choose to be there. Can't you find inspiration in a less masochistic way?

Rosalyn Ebberly

"The wise woman builds her house, but the foolish tears it down with her own hands." Proverbs 14:1 (NASB)

From:	Iona James
	<poetsmystique@brokenwrenchandcopperbucket.com>
To:	SAHM I Am <sahmiam@loophole.com>
Subject:	Re: [SAHM I AM] TOTW June 15: Meeting the needs of our children

You killed it. You killed my poem. It was there, ready to be poured out on the page in all its raw glory. But now it's gone, slaughtered by your optimistic good sense. First truly promising burst of inspiration I've had in weeks. Dead. My poetry, killed by your happy prose. That's tragic.

In fact…this might work out even better. How about a song called "When the Poetry Dies"? Ooohhh…thanks, Rosalyn, for the inspiration.

But do not e-mail me again, for at least…a few hours! You're not depressed and twisted enough. You'll jeopardize the entire work!
Iona James

From:	Rosalyn Ebberly <prov31woman@home.com>
To:	VIM <vivalaveronica@marcelloportraits.com>
Subject:	Iona

How dare she say I'm not depressed enough! When she's been through what I've been through, THEN let her accuse me of having "optimistic good sense"! And "happy prose"?

I'm insulted! I am in a very delicate mental condition. What does she know about it anyway?

Poets and their need for tortured angst. So annoying.
Ros

"The wise woman builds her house, but the foolish tears it down with her own hands." Proverbs 14:1 (NASB)

From:	VIM <vivalaveronica@marcelloportraits.com>
To:	Rosalyn Ebberly <prov31woman@home.com>
Subject:	Re: Iona

Well, sis, you're certainly twisted enough.
Veronica

From:	Zelia Muzuwa <zeemuzu@vivacious.com>
To:	Iona James
	<poetsmystique@brokenwrenchandcopperbucket.com>
Subject:	Did you get your song written?

Hey Iona,
I just wanted to see if you got that thing written. If not, don't read any more of this e-mail because it's supposed to be encouraging! :)

Listen, I know it's hard to do creative stuff when the kids are little. I'm an artist, too, not that you'd know it recently.

But it sounds like you're doing the right thing—grabbing the time and the inspiration as it comes. It won't be like this forever. Almost, but not quite forever.

E-mail when you get a chance, okay? I'd love to get to know you better. And you already have a big fan in my friend Phyllis. You should share your poems on the loop sometime.

Hugs,

Z

From:	Iona James
	<poetsmystique@brokenwrenchandcopperbucket.com>
To:	Zelia Muzuwa <zeemuzu@vivacious.com>
Subject:	Re: Did you get your song written?

Dear Zelia,

The song is written. I'm attaching it if you'd like to read it, but please don't feel obligated. Thank you for the sweet words. It's been a trying afternoon. I'm sorry to hear about the troubles with your children. Makes my "angst" seem petty—as Rosalyn implied. She was probably right.

I hope nobody thinks I don't love the Angel Child. I adore him. I just always thought that if we ever did have children, my husband and I would share the load more equally—since neither of us have what anyone would consider a "real" career. But he gets so caught up in his music and in the band that the parenting falls mostly to me. He's a dreamer, and I don't know how to wake him up. I love him, too, but I feel alone most of the time. That's why I

joined SAHM I Am. I'm tired of being alone—even if it is good for tragic inspiration. :)
Iona James

From:	Zelia Muzuwa <zeemuzu@vivacious.com>
To:	Iona James
	<poetsmystique@brokenwrenchandcopperbucket.com>
Subject:	Re: Did you get your song written?

I hear you, girlfriend! Listen, Phyllis and I and several other gals have a sort of small loop we post on. The main loop is so big, and we needed a way to connect better (and to gripe about one crazy loop moderator). We also chat every Monday night on the loop Web site. You're welcome to join us. I'll include you on the next e-mail we send to each other. We call ourselves "Green Eggs and Ham." They're the eggs. I'm the ham. :)

You don't have to be alone, okay? Not sure how this will affect your creativity, but maybe you can learn to be inspired by happiness, too.
Z

From:	Iona James
	<poetsmystique@brokenwrenchandcopperbucket.com>
To:	Zelia Muzuwa <zeemuzu@vivacious.com>
Subject:	Re: Did you get your song written?

You are so kind, Zelia! I only get on the Internet when I go downstairs to the tea shop and use their wireless network, so I probably wouldn't be around for your chat. But I'll keep it in mind.

I wouldn't mind meeting the others on your subloop, though. That might be fun. I can probably learn to be inspired by light, as well as dark, I suppose.

Iona James

From:	Rosalyn Ebberly <prov31woman@home.com>
To:	SAHM I Am <sahmiam@loophole.com>
Subject:	[SAHM I AM] TOTW July 13: Housecleaning as Worship?

Dear Domestic Divas,

I just returned from another AMAZING session with my counselor. I seriously do not know how I ever managed without this woman. It's like she sees into my soul, and no matter how ugly it gets, she never even cringes. In fact, I think she likes me. There's always that client-therapist reserve, but I get the feeling that I'm probably one of her favorite clients. If I ever stop needing her as my therapist, I bet we could be really good friends.

Anyway, one of the things we talked about today was how much I've always resented housecleaning. Can you believe it? I know…I've always made such a big deal about how good a housekeeper I am. And I AM good! But I really dislike it.

In fact, I loathe it. Detest it.

If my entire housekeeping experience could be concentrated into a single human being, I would pull that person's hair out one hair at a time, even her eyelashes. And then I'd put clothespins on her nose!

Oh! And I could make her wear food-encrusted rubber gloves...

AND spray her with disinfectant cleaner instead of perfume.

I'm liking this picture!!!

Then I'd SHOVE HER HEADFIRST INTO THE TRASH CAN, where hopefully she'd die a slow and smelly death. THAT'S what I'd do to housecleaning if I could!

Whew! Felt good to express all that inner rage. Very cleansing. See what I'm learning in counseling?

My therapist suggested that perhaps if I thought about cleaning the house as another way of worshipping God, then I wouldn't feel so resentful about it.

I don't know. I've always cleaned house because it was my job, my duty. I was expected to do it, so I did. And I expected the very best from myself, and I got it. I know everything is supposed to be done for God's glory.

But I don't know if I want to think of it as worship. Worship is supposed to be enjoyable. I don't know if I want to ruin that picture by connecting it to doing the dishes.

What do you think?

Chat away, dear ones,

Rosalyn Ebberly

"The wise woman builds her house, but the foolish tears it down with her own hands." Proverbs 14:1 (NASB)

From:	Hannah Farrell
	<boazsmom@farrellfamilylovesjesus.net>
To:	SAHM I Am <sahmiam@loophole.com>
Subject:	Re: [SAHM I AM] TOTW
	July 13: Housecleaning as Worship?

Wow, Rosalyn. I hope when I've been married twenty years or whatever that I won't be as violent-minded as you are! You're a little scary. Good thing you're seeing a shrink, huh?

I think that housecleaning SHOULD be totally like worship, especially for women that are Christians. I mean, that's like the highest calling for a woman—to be a good housekeeper. I know it says so in the Bible. So it should be worship.

I think it's bad to feel resentment about that. I mean, sure, it would be nice to have a little help now and then. My Bradley would be glad to help out around our house, except he works a lot, and like he says—I have to earn my keep somehow since I don't have a job. And he's really grateful for what I do, because if he didn't have me, he says he'd have to hire a cleaning lady. So I'm saving him a lot of money. That makes me feel glad—it's nice to be needed.

I do have a question, though. What is the correct way to clean a stovetop? We just got one of those glass-top ranges, and I totally don't want to ruin it.

Thanks,
Hannah

From:	Thomas Huckleberry
	<t.huckleberry@showme.com>
To:	SAHM I Am <sahmiam@loophole.com>
Subject:	**Re: [SAHM I AM] TOTW**
	July 13: Housecleaning as Worship?

Hey Hannah,

Just the guy on the loop, here. Don't want to freak you out. Might want to check your Bible concordance, though. I don't think it says anywhere that a woman's highest calling is to keep house.

I don't think there's such a thing as the "correct" way to clean a stovetop. There might be a "best" way, but pretty much whatever gets it cleaned should work.

And it's not true that a stay-at-home spouse has to "earn their keep." I didn't think that way about Dulcie when she was at home and I worked. And she doesn't think that way about me now that she is working from home. We share housecleaning duties.

I don't know if cleaning can be worship or not. I just try to get it done as fast as I can so I can do stuff I like to do. Tom H.

From:	Dulcie Huckleberry
	<dulcie@homemakerinteriors.com>
To:	SAHM I Am <sahmiam@loophole.com>
Subject:	**Re: [SAHM I AM] TOTW**
	July 13: Housecleaning as Worship?

Hannah,

Don't listen to a thing Tom says! (Well, at least not about how to clean a stove. The rest was good.)

There IS a right way to clean a glass-top range! Don't use anything abrasive on it, and get the special cleaner for it.

Most importantly, DON'T let your husband anywhere near the stove—he might, oh…I don't know…USE CAST IRON ON IT AND BREAK THE WHOLE TOP! Hypothetically, of course.

Love,

Dulcie

From:	Thomas Huckleberry
	\<t.huckleberry@showme.com\>
To:	SAHM I Am \<sahmiam@loophole.com\>
Subject:	Re: [SAHM I AM] TOTW
	July 13: Housecleaning as Worship?

Hannah,

In that hypothetical situation, you'd probably be quite happy to get a new stove, considering you didn't even like the glass-top stove and were constantly harping on your husband "Don't scratch it! You're scratching it!"

Tom

From:	Dulcie Huckleberry
	<dulcie@homemakerinteriors.com>
To:	SAHM I Am <sahmiam@loophole.com>
Subject:	Re: [SAHM I AM] TOTW
	July 13: Housecleaning as Worship?

Except that in that hypothetical case, what she probably liked best about the glass-top stove was that it was already paid for. So she didn't have to scrape together money with no warning to get a new stove!

From:	Zelia Muzuwa <zeemuzu@vivacious.com>
To:	SAHM I Am <sahmiam@loophole.com>
Subject:	Re: [SAHM I AM] TOTW
	July 13: Housecleaning as Worship?

Ah, yes, the Argument By Hypothesis technique. Pay attention, Hannah—you're watching true masters of this high and noble art.

Check the loop archives for their "Hypothetical Shrunken Sweater" discussion—BRILLIANT!

Z

From:	Hannah Farrell
	<boazsmom@farrellfamilylovesjesus.net>
To:	SAHM I Am <sahmiam@loophole.com>
Subject:	Re: [SAHM I AM] TOTW
	July 13: Housecleaning as Worship?

This is why I am so like "Having a guy on the loop is a bad idea." No offense, guys, but don't put me in the middle of this. I'm not the one that broke the hypothetical stove. I just want to know how to clean my real one.

Hannah

From:	The Millards
	<jstcea4jesus@familymail.net>
To:	SAHM I Am <sahmiam@loophole.com>
Subject:	Re: [SAHM I AM] TOTW
	July 13: Housecleaning as Worship?

There most certainly is a right way to clean a glass-top stove, but the ninny cleaning my house isn't doing it.

See, a glass-top range is kind of like a work of art. You have to treat it carefully. My kids let oatmeal boil over last week, while I was out running some errands. It got baked on, and when our cleaning lady went to work on it, she must have scraped it off using a razor blade or something, because now the surface is pitted and gouged.

I called to complain, hoping that maybe I could just cancel the service. But the supervisor was SO nice and friendly—she even gave us two extra months for free to make up for it! I couldn't just dump them after that expression of goodwill.

The good thing is, having her come out every week is good incentive for me to get things picked up and ready for her. I need something to do…it's getting boring around here.

As far as worship—yes, I think cleaning can be worship. I like making everything shiny and bright—reminds me of what God has done for me.

Jocelyn

From:	Dulcie Huckleberry
	<dulcie@homemakerinteriors.com>
To:	SAHM I Am <sahmiam@loophole.com>
Subject:	Re: [SAHM I AM] TOTW
	July 13: Housecleaning as Worship?

Jocelyn, honey, you really are sick. Have Rosalyn's shrink suggest one in your area—you need major help. :)

But speaking of cleaning ladies, you guys will NOT believe what happened to me today.

I was supposed to meet with a potential client—has a big home overlooking Table Rock Lake, and wants it professionally decorated. The WHOLE house! If I could land this, it would pay all our family expenses for the next three months—just by itself.

I was ready. I spent three hours just putting together some ideas. And I got up extra early to make sure my hair and makeup and clothes all looked great.

I brought my portfolio, including a DVD of previous work, and my briefcase.

I looked professional!

The house is palatial. There's a winding path to the front door, flanked by tree roses. And giant fir trees line the lawn. Look one direction, and the Ozarks are spread before you. Look the other way and Table Rock Lake sparkles on the horizon below.

By the time I got to the front door, I was almost shaking, and my heart was pounding. I rang the doorbell, and a man opened the door. My client's husband. I offered him my hand and started to introduce myself, but he interrupted me.

"Staff use the side entrance that way."

I was so shocked, I just stared at him. I've never been forced to use a separate entrance at any client's house. Normally, everyone is very friendly and tries to feed me, which is the last thing I need.

He scowled at my silence. "Can't we ever get a girl that speaks English? Country's being overrun with Mexicans—don't even bother learning the language when they sneak across!" Then he looked over his shoulder, stepped out the door and shut it behind him. "Where are your papers?"

A hot steam started roiling inside me. This was unbelievable. "What…papers?"

He rolled his eyes and leaned closer. "Pa-pers." He drew out each syllable, nearly shouting at me. "Are…you… legal?"

Just as I was trying to decide whether slapping him would be worth it or not, the door swung open again. My client leaned out. "Dulcie, is that you?"

"Yes, I just arrived." This time my offered handshake was accepted.

She frowned at her husband. "Is there a problem, sweetie?"

"Who is this?" He nodded at me.

"That's Dulcie Huckleberry, dear! You know, she's Shoji Tabuchi's *personal* decorator." (WHAT? Must have serious talk with Jeanine about exaggeration and false advertising!) She turned to me. "I'm so glad you were able to come. Let's get you in out of this oppressive heat."

I risked one brief glare at the husband as I followed her through the door. His face was red and he looked embarrassed.

He should be! I have never been so insulted. And believe me, I've met some pretty insulting idiots. I'm used to people thinking I'm Mexican instead of Guatemalan. All us Hispanic people "look alike," you know. And I've even been spoken to in Spanish, though I can't do more than count to ten.

But I have never been treated like so much trash or with such suspicion! And what really hurts about it is that I can't afford to tell them to take their fancy house and shove it. So in a way, I really am "staff"—I need them far worse than they need me. And that burns.

So I apologize to Tom and the rest of you for being a bit grumpy. Work really stunk today.

Dulcie

From:	Iona James
	\<poetsmystique@brokenwrenchandcopperbucket.com\>
To:	SAHM I Am \<sahmiam@loophole.com\>
Subject:	Re: [SAHM I AM] TOTW
	July 13: Housecleaning as Worship?

Dulcie,

What happened to you was inexcusable. I work on a part-time basis at the tea shop downstairs, and I know how rude customers can be. I'm sorry you had a rough day.

For everyone,

I've been lying on the grass in the park, watching the Angel Child play on a blanket. And thinking about worshipping God through cleaning my home. And I wondered, maybe it's not so much a matter of us choosing to worship God through housecleaning. Maybe it's a matter that we've gotten to the point of worshipping housecleaning itself.

Worship is supposed to be something that brings glory to God. Is He glorified when we spend all our time polishing our material possessions? Or is it our possessions that are glorified?

But I'm just a dreamer and poet—so maybe I'm lost when it comes to the path of a good homemaker. It's certainly never a life I envisioned in any of my dreams.

In three days' time, I will attend my ten-year high school reunion. And in my heart of hearts, I dread it.

I fear they will all find me unchanged—the same dreamy, head-in-the-clouds Iona that I was back then. Not many of my dreams have come true that I had then. I am happy with my life, except for the times when those old dreams tug at my spirit.

Before I accepted the invitation to go, I didn't care a bit that I have stretch marks and circles under my eyes. Now, I look in the mirror, and that's all I see. That, and a girl-woman whose poetry has had to take a backseat to baby food and diapers, and whose husband will look almost un-employed compared to everyone else.

And it angers me that I even care!

I can't judge any of you for polishing your possessions. I am guilty of wanting to polish myself—so I can be glori-fied by a bunch of people who never liked me in the first place. I don't even know why I am going. Curiosity, I suppose. Or that small sense of self-hate?

I'm getting into a bit of a black mood with all this. Too much self-analysis. I will now set that all aside, take the Angel Child down to the tea shop, and have chamomile tea with people who know and love me. I may even write a poem about it. I'm trying to learn to be inspired by things other than pain.

Dwell in mystery, my friends,
Iona James

From:	P. Lorimer <phyllis.lorimer@geemail.com>
To:	SAHM I Am <sahmiam@loophole.com>
Subject:	Re: [SAHM I AM] TOTW July 13: Housecleaning as Worship?

Great post, Iona! I have often wondered if a stay-at-home parent's job is actually to clean the house. I am not so certain it is. As much as I enjoy vacuuming in my heels and pearls and pencil skirt, I'm just not so sure that's what our highest calling really is.

As I understand it, the highest calling of any human being is to love God with all our heart and soul and mind, and love our neighbors as ourselves. We can do that regardless of whether or not we're married, have a career, stay at home, or…

Ugh. I hate it when God takes my little homilies and pokes me with them. My highest calling, according to my own post here, is to love my advisor as I love myself. Even though she refuses to return my calls and is not helping me develop the proposal for my dissertation. I am still supposed to love her. That is, I'm afraid, the worship to which I am called right now.

Drat. Cleaning the house would be a LOT easier!
Phyllis

From:	Hannah Farrell
	<boazsmom@farrellfamilylovesjesus.net>
To:	SAHM I Am <sahmiam@loophole.com>
Subject:	Re: [SAHM I AM] TOTW
	July 13: Housecleaning as Worship?

Dear Phyllis,
As much as I respect your perspective as a pastor's wife, I really don't agree with the idea that we're not called to keep

house! If that is true, then what ARE we SAHMs supposed to be doing? We can't all be in graduate school, you know!

And Bradley works so hard all day long. How would he feel if he came home to find a messy house? He'd feel like I wasn't doing my share.

Plus, I think women are just naturally more skilled at keeping house. Look at Tom—he's no good at stove cleaning or laundry! My Bradley is the same way. Men just aren't built for household chores, any more than women are really built to go out and support a family. (Sorry, Dulcie, but you wouldn't have had that problem at your client's house if you were a guy.) We all have our roles in life, and I think we should be content with that. THAT'S how we glorify God.

Hannah

☺**Instant Message**

Dulcet: Okay, I know you're a big boy. But can I just please tell her off?

Huck: Tell who off? I've been busy all morning with the kids.

Dulcet: Check your sahmiam posts.

Huck: ok. brb

(Huck is idle.)

Huck: Ah. I see. No. Don't tell her off.

Dulcet: Please? Just one little barb? Something so subtle and straight-faced, an idiot like her wouldn't even understand?

Huck: Dulce, honey. It's not worth it.

Dulcet: You ALWAYS say that! What IS worth it? Why do

you have to be so passive about everything? Didn't her post make you mad?

Huck: She's some kid on an email loop. Why would I let her make me mad?

Dulcet: I hate it when you're reasonable.

Huck: You hate it when I'm not. I can't win. :)

Dulcet: Don't you have laundry to do or something?

Huck: You know, I don't really think I'm built for laundry. I think that's something God has called YOU to do. :)

Dulcet: Interesting. I think God is calling YOU to sleep on the couch tonight, buster.

Huck: Funny. I'm not hearing that call.

Dulcet: Selective hearing. Apparently the kids inherited it from you, darling.

Huck: Hmm. Listening…nope, definitely sounds more like "Tom…Tom…go kiss your wife until she forgets the Hannah chick…and then see if she'll help you fold the load of clothes that just beeped in the dryer."

Dulcet: That might be…we could always try it and see if you heard correctly. :)

Huck signed off at 8:27:13 p.m.
Dulcet signed off at 8:28:35 p.m.

From:	Marianne Hausten
	<confidentmom@nebweb.net>
To:	SAHM I Am <sahmiam@loophole.com>
Subject:	[SAHM I AM] Gender expectations

Hannah's comments brought up a sore spot for me. It's something that has been bugging me recently, but I was reluctant to bring it up on the loop because it's a little controversial.

Those of you who have both boys and girls—do you find that people expect totally different behavior from each one? Here I've spent the past three years or so trying to get a handle on how to expect good behavior from Helene. And now with Neil, who is two, when I expect him to sit still or be quiet, I get chewed out from people. "He's a BOY" they protest. "He can't be expected to behave nicely!"

Then what on earth was all my work for? Do you know how awful life was when Helene was so out of control? How can they even suggest that I throw it all out the window now that I have a boy?

I'm sure some of you will say the same thing—that boys can't be expected to behave. But I can't accept that. I'm determined to prove otherwise. MY kids are going to be nice children—not little beasts that no one wants to have around.
Marianne

From:	P. Lorimer <phyllis.lorimer@geemail.com>
To:	Marianne Hausten <confidentmom@nebweb.net>
Subject:	Re: [SAHM I AM] Gender expectations

Tell it like it is, Marianne! Good for you. I never had different standards for Bennet than I do for Julia. I think there are some developmental differences, but with the basics like respect and obedience, keep up your expectations.

Don't listen to the Hannahs of the world. It used to be that people thought women were incapable of learning, that they couldn't be expected to achieve what a man could. So now it's the other way around? It was wrong then, and it's wrong now.

You're doing a great job. I'm proud of you.

Hugs,
Phyllis

From:	Marianne Hausten
	<confidentmom@nebweb.net>
To:	P. Lorimer <phyllis.lorimer@geemail.com>
Subject:	Re: [SAHM I AM] Gender expectations

Thanks, Phyllis. That means a lot to me. I'm getting a lot of pressure from my mom and Brandon's sister especially. And my playgroup. And some days, I wonder if I know anything at all.

Marianne

⌨Text Message From Veronica Marcello: For Rosalyn Ebberly
——July 18/5:30 p.m.——
Posts like Hannah's are why I don't want to be part of a church. Could she B more medieval?

⌨Text Message From Rosalyn Ebberly: For Veronica Marcello
——July 18/5:32 p.m.——

I wouldn't expect you to agree with her. But a lot of people do.

✉Text Message From Veronica Marcello: For Rosalyn Ebberly
——July 18/5:38 p.m.——
Do u?

✉Text Message From Rosalyn Ebberly: For Veronica Marcello
——July 18/5:45 p.m.——
I don't know. I used to. But if this is what it feels like to be created for something, I think I'd rather pass.

✉Text Message From Veronica Marcello: For Rosalyn Ebberly
——July 18/5:46 p.m.——
Wow. Was not xpectN that from u.

✉Text Message From Rosalyn Ebberly: For Veronica Marcello
——July 18/5:49 p.m.——
:) Me neither. Did you go to church on Sunday?

✉Text Message From Veronica Marcello: For Rosalyn Ebberly
——July 18/5:54 p.m.——
Yeah. Not as bad as I thot might b. Peaceful. Frank very happy.

✉Text Message From Rosalyn Ebberly: For Veronica Marcello

——July 18/6:02 p.m.——
I'd never dreamed you'd go to any church. I'm not happy with the choice of church, but I'm glad you weren't miserable. Will you go back?

📧Text Message From Veronica Marcello: For Rosalyn Ebberly
——July 18/6:04 p.m.——
I think so. Only bc Frank wants to.

📧Text Message From Rosalyn Ebberly: For Veronica Marcello
——July 18/6:07 p.m.——
That's great—for Frank.

From:	Iona James
	<poetsmystique@brokenwrenchandcopperbucket.com>
To:	SAHM I Am <sahmiam@loophole.com>
Subject:	[SAHM I AM] High School Reunion

I will be brief because I only have a few moments before the Angel Child wakes from his nap. The reunion last night was horrible. Here's what happened:

   * All my old crowd—the nonconformists and artists—have turned into suburban sellouts. None of them are pursuing their art. None are standing for their principles of justice or concern for the environment. They're all

driving SUVs and drinking expensive, non-fair-trade coffee!

★ Our homecoming queen asked me if it was some sort of jungle illness that made my hair twist into dreadlocks. She never was the brightest star in our sky. Everyone laughed, though. It shouldn't hurt, but it does. I tried to explain my spiritual connection to my dreadlocks, but nobody wanted to listen. Just laugh.

★ My ex-boyfriend from tenth grade told our whole table about how he'd recently discovered the world's worst alternative/folk band—Broken Wrench and Copper Bucket. He did a very loud, beer-enhanced parody of their signature song. Not two minutes later, he turned to Jeremy to ask him what he did for a living. Jeremy looked him straight in the eye and said, "I am the lead musician for Broken Wrench and Copper Bucket." They thought it was a great joke until they saw we weren't laughing.

★ The worst moment, though, was toward the end. I still nurse the Angel Child, even at ten months old, and I have a lot of milk. I could feel the pressure building through the evening, because I rarely go that long without nursing him. At the end of the evening, one of my classmates' husbands showed up with their twin babies. They started to cry…and my milk let down. My top was soaked, and no way to hide it because I didn't have a jacket.

I cried all the way home. Why did I go? My pride? Some twisted sense of dependence on these insignificant people? Or maybe it was a way for my spirit to remind me of my own insignificance.

On a positive note, I'm sure to get at least seven or eight truly raw, pain-filled poems from this experience.
Iona James

From:	Zelia Muzuwa <zeemuzu@vivacious.com>
To:	"Green Eggs and Ham"
Subject:	**For Iona**

Hey Iona,
The rest of us Green Eggs and Ham gals decided to all buy the latest Broken Wrench and Copper Bucket CD. If jerks like the ones at your reunion don't like it, it's got to be good! I just started listening to mine, and I love it!

Sorry—hope we didn't ruin any good, angsty poetry. :)
Z

From:	Iona James
	<poetsmystique@brokenwrenchandcopperbucket.com>
To:	"Green Eggs and Ham"
Subject:	**Re: For Iona**

Thank you, everyone! Don't worry, Z—this will knock my poem output down to maybe three poems. But I suspect I can survive. Maybe I'll even write a small happy poem about you Green Eggs—and the Ham, of course.
Iona James

From:	The Millards
	<jstcea4jesus@familymail.net>
To:	SAHM I Am <sahmiam@loophole.com>
Subject:	[SAHM I AM] A suggestion

Seems to me that the only people that actually understand us and can put up with us are...US! Iona's awful reunion experience got me thinking.

Why don't we have our own "reunion"? We could arrange to meet up somewhere over a weekend, and just have a small get-together.

I remember when Phyllis and Jonathan needed a place to stay and they went to visit Brenna for several weeks. The rest of us were so envious they got to meet up. But why couldn't we plan a meet-up for everyone?

I'd be willing to coordinate it if Rosalyn or someone would help me. Give me something to do since I'm not allowed to so much as polish ANY of my own belongings. :)
Jocelyn

From:	Rosalyn Ebberly <prov31woman@home.com>
To:	SAHM I Am <sahmiam@loophole.com>
Subject:	Re: [SAHM I AM] A suggestion

That's a brilliant idea, Jocelyn! If the rest of you are as excited about it as I am, I think we should go for it. I'd be glad to cocoordinate with Jocelyn. Perhaps Connie could even join us. I know we all miss her terribly.

What do the rest of you think? It would be so amazing to see some of you in person after so many years of knowing you online. Wouldn't it be fun?
Rosalyn

"The wise woman builds her house, but the foolish tears it down with her own hands." Proverbs 14:1 (NASB)

From:	Dulcie Huckleberry
	\<dulcie@homemakerinteriors.com\>
To:	SAHM I Am \<sahmiam@loophole.com\>
Subject:	Re: [SAHM I AM] A suggestion

Yes PLEASE! Let's do this! I wish I could volunteer to help, but I won't have time. But I do want to come. I would LOVE to see you all.
Dulcie

💬Loophole Groups: SAHM I Am Chat Room
Dulcie: Green Eggs and Ham, we all have to try our best to get to the meet-up!
Brenna: Agreed.
Marianne: I'm there. Brandon already said he'd take extra time off if needed to take care of the kids. Isn't that nice?
Zelia: this is all great, but jocelyn, how could you agree to work with HER?
Jocelyn: Her? You mean Rosalyn? Easy. Because I'm not holding a year-long grudge against her.
Zelia: not a grudge. i just can't ever respect or trust her

again. can't believe you'd work directly with her on something like this. you're gonna get hurt. she's like a spider.
she'll catch you in her web.

Phyllis: Z, I love you dear. But don't you think it's time to
let go?

Zelia: et tu, Brute?

Dulcie: Let's not get into that right now. Just think how
fun it will be when we all get together—no matter who
arranges it! You will come, won't you, Z?

Zelia: yeah, sure. wouldn't miss it.

From:	Rosalyn Ebberly <prov31woman@home.com>
To:	SAHM I Am <sahmiam@loophole.com>
Subject:	[SAHM I AM] TOTW July 27: What do you do for relaxation?

Dear Stressed SAHMs,

At my counseling session today, my dear therapist said something I don't think I've ever heard before. "Rosalyn," she
said, "you need to relax."

"Relax?" I had to laugh. "I have three children. When
am I supposed to relax?"

But she was serious. She wanted to know what I do for
fun. FUN! So I told her about how I make scrapbooks of
all my kids' photos.

"And you spend six hours stitching the photos to the
page using special llama hair fibers imported from Peru.
Then you spend another hour trying to decide between six
different kinds of brads to put at the center of a collage

flower in the corner. It takes you another two days to rest up from the ordeal. You call that relaxation?"

"You're exaggerating" I told her. "I only spend a half hour choosing brads."

For some reason, she almost glared at me.

Since I clearly wasn't going to convince her that scrapbooking is relaxing, I tried again. I told her that I enjoy gourmet cooking.

"Really?" she asked. "Even after eight hours and three tries to get some French concoction exactly right, and then end up bleary-eyed at 1:00 a.m. trying to put the finishing touches on a chocolate-ginger tort with handmade marzipan fruit? That makes you feel relaxed?"

"I always sleep well when I DO get to bed."

"Sleep deprivation contributes heavily to depression, you know."

Then she asked me, "Do you actually ENJOY these activities?"

I had to admit I didn't know. I always did them because they were things I could do that no one else was as good at.

She asked me, "Do you ever read a book just for fun?" No, never.

"Take a walk that's not for exercise?" Not that I recall.

"Do you have ANY hobbies that you aren't very good at, but you do them just because you enjoy them?" Why would I do that?

"Watch any movies? Hang out with friends? Visit a coffee shop and read the newspaper?" Isn't that what people do when they're retired?

I think I frustrated her. So obviously, this is something I

need to work on. I think with enough help, I could become an expert on relaxation. It's just a matter of working hard at it and practicing. I've never been one to shy away from a challenge!

Which leads me to the Topic of the Week:

How do YOU relax? I'm sure I can figure it out if I just have a little guidance. So give me your ideas.

Rosalyn Ebberly,
SAHM I Am Loop Moderator

"The wise woman builds her house, but the foolish tears it down with her own hands." Proverbs 14:1 (NASB)

From:	Hannah Farrell
	<boazsmom@farrellfamilylovesjesus.net>
To:	SAHM I Am <sahmiam@loophole.com>
Subject:	Re: [SAHM I AM] TOTW July 27: What do you do for relaxation?

Hi Rosalyn!

I'm totally surprised that it takes you six whole hours to do a simple stitch embellishment on your scrapbook page. I can show you how to do it in less than an hour! I do that in between chatting with friends on MySpace.

As for the gourmet food—I think you should lay off the cake, personally. When you get to be, well…your age, your metabolism slows down and that frosting is going to go straight to your thighs. I would think it would be awful to actually LOOK middle-aged, even if you are.

What I do to relax is stuff like MySpace or Second Life—which is this virtual world where you can have a job and take trips and shop—all with a made-up character who has their own house and everything! It's super cool, and I'd probably make a lot of friends if I had more time.

Lately, I've also been absolutely gone over learning how to write little plug-in programs for my blog so it does more stuff. It's just a matter of learning the code for it. I'm hoping that Bradley will let me fix up his Web site for his job—it's pretty lame right now.

But you're probably not into all that technology stuff. It's more a thing for the younger generation. If you want me to show you anything, though, just let me know.
Hannah

From:	Rosalyn Ebberly <prov31woman@home.com>
To:	SAHM I Am <sahmiam@loophole.com>
Subject:	Re: [SAHM I AM] TOTW July 27: What do you do for relaxation?

Hannah, dear,
How old, exactly, do you think I am?

And please…I would never eat the cake myself. I usually give it to the local homeless shelter. It's such a treat for them after all the cafeteria-style food they usually get!

As for the stitch embellishment—it's far from simple. I can do a simple stitch in about ten minutes, so no need to help me out with that. No…this one was a special stitch known only to a remote tribe in Tibet, used only for wedding garments and ceremonial robes for their religious rites. There are thirteen steps involved in each stitch, and an entire story that goes with each step. It's a dying art, and an old woman in the tribe was kind enough to teach it to me the last mission trip I took there. We had to travel by mule and had nothing to eat but grubs and this very dodgy-smelling gruel. But anyone who has known me long will tell you I'd do anything to bring the love of Jesus to even the remotest parts of the world. I'll tell you about it sometime, if you like.

I wouldn't expect someone your age to understand what a profound experience that was. Most of you guys think a mission trip is spending a week painting a church building in a border town in Mexico. A whole week without MySpace. Sacrifice indeed. :)

But I never like to compare—that's not the point of the Gospel, is it?

Enjoy your blog, dear. That's so cute.

Rosalyn Ebberly

SAHM I Am Loop Moderator

"The wise woman builds her house, but the foolish tears it down with her own hands." Proverbs 14:1 (NASB)

☺**Instant Message**

JocelynM: Well, THAT was like a blast from the past! I thought you'd moved beyond those sort of one-upping posts.

Pr31Mom: I was weak! I couldn't help it!

JocelynM: I think I'm going to have to tell your therapist.

Pr31Mom: No, please! I couldn't bear her disappointment.

JocelynM: I was teasing. :)

Pr31Mom: Oh.

JocelynM: Hey look, she replied.

Pr31Mom: I'm scared to read it.

From:	Hannah Farrell
	<boazsmom@farrellfamilylovesjesus.net>
To:	SAHM I Am <sahmiam@loophole.com>
Subject:	Re: [SAHM I AM] TOTW July 27: What do you do for relaxation?

Wow, you've done lots of cool stuff. I've been to Asia, too. I spent the summer after my junior year of high school helping prostitutes in Thailand learn jobs so they didn't have to sell themselves anymore. I found out about that program through MySpace.

However, I am pretty impressed with all that you've done, Rosalyn. Most women my mother's age don't do anything more than shop and get pedicures. You sound pretty cool. I like meeting older women that I can respect for their wisdom and experience. You've gone through some rough times, but I'm learning a lot from that, too, so hopefully I'll be able to avoid ruining my family like that.

Hugs,

Hannah

☺**Instant Message**

Pr31Mom: I was NEVER that bad!

JocelynM: True. You were worse.

Pr31Mom: Really?

JocelynM: Fraid so.

Pr31Mom: Oh my goodness. Can I just die now? Can I?

JocelynM: What? And deprive us of your "wisdom and experience"?

Pr31Mom: Gack! God is punishing me.

JocelynM: If so, it would show some remarkable good sense on His part. :)

Pr31Mom: You don't really think that...

JocelynM: No, I don't. I think Hannah is probably every bit as miserable as you were. Just for different reasons.

Pr31Mom: Like what?

JocelynM: Don't know yet. I'm sure we'll get to find out. It's part of the joys of an email loop.

☺**Instant Message**

ZeeMuzzy: hey joc, did you see ros and hannah's little spat? just like old times!

JocelynM: Yeah, just read it.

☺**Instant Message**

Pr31Mom: We need to talk by phone about planning for the retreat/meet-up. Will you be available this evening?

JocelynM: How about tomorrow—during the day or evening is fine.

Pr31Mom: Okay. Oh, that's right—you always chat with Zelia on Monday nights.

JocelynM: I didn't know you knew about that.

Pr31Mom: I try to keep tabs on what's going on with the loop. Does Zelia ever…you know, mention me or anything?

☺**Instant Message**
ZeeMuzzy: still determined to work with her? it sounds like she's regressing.
JocelynM: Wouldn't you if a 19 year old basically called you elderly in front of everyone? Give Ros a break.
ZeeMuzzy: not a chance. and i think you're insane to co-ordinate this retreat with her. it will end in disaster—trust me. anything with rosalyn at the helm is bound to end in disaster.

☺**Instant Message**
JocelynM: Sometimes, Ros. She mentions you occasion-ally.
Pr31Mom: Probably not in a positive way.
JocelynM: Z is going through a tough time right now. I think she'll come around eventually.
Pr31Mom: I think you're more optimistic than I am.

From:	VIM <vivalaveronica@marcelloportraits.com>
To:	SAHM I Am <sahmiam@loophole.com>
Subject:	[SAHM I AM] Need Birthday Party Ideas

Howdy girls,
I don't know about y'all, but around here, the hobby du jour seems to be planning elaborate birthday parties for fun and relaxation.

My stepdaughter, Ashley, is turning thirteen in a couple of months, and she's already campaigning for a big blowout bash. It started last week when her friend Libby threw a thirteenth birthday party that had a "magazine shoot" theme to it.

They dolled these little girls up like models, hired some fancy-schmancy photographer (who was NOT my husband!) to do a photo shoot, complete with hair-blowing fans, designer clothing and makeup and hair artists.

Then, as if that wasn't enough, they compiled it all into a "magazine" with the birthday girl as the front cover and sent each guest a copy. Ours arrived today. Ashley has been clutching it all day as if it were her dearest possession and begging us to "do something just as cool."

And when I suggested maybe her dad could do something similar, since he is one of Houston's top photographers, she was appalled. "But Veronica!" she wailed, "That would be copying! Nobody would want to come and they'd all make fun of me!"

Poor child was almost in tears. Okay, fine. No photo shoot. But what are we going to do to equal that? I'm not sure we can afford to top it! That party cost thousands of dollars, I'm sure. For a BIRTHDAY PARTY! And it's not like we're all filthy rich, either.

So if you have any good ideas, send them my way. My suggestion was to get all her friends together, throw them downstairs in the rec room with some balloons and streamers, pizza and music, and let them play "spin the bottle."

Frank said something in Italian that I think was the equivalent of "Over my dead shotgun!" But I wasn't sure.

So I don't get any relaxing until I have secured my daughter's social future with a kicking birthday party. Help!
Veronica

💬 Loophole Groups: SAHM I Am Chat Room

(Dulcie has entered the room)

Dulcie: Hey guys, sorry I'm late. But I just signed that big account! You know—the one where the husband thought I was the illegal cleaning lady?

Zelia high-fives Dulcie

Zelia: way 2 go, girlie! but are you sure you WANT to work with them?

Dulcie: Oh, it actually worked out perfect. The wife could tell I was really angry, and she figured out pretty quick that her husband had offended me. She was so mortified that she gave me a bonus if I'd still work with them!

Jocelyn: That's awesome. Before we know it, you'll be the hottest designer around—and we'll be like "Oh, yes, we're Ms. Huckleberry's particular friends. Known her for years." And everyone will be so impressed.

Dulcie: You have obviously been inhaling too much cleaning solution today, Joc.

Brenna: That rocks, Dulcie. When do you start?

Dulcie: Next week. Hey, how is little Pat doing? I know you were worried about his development.

Brenna: About the same. Darren doesn't say much about it, but he watches Pat a lot. Gets impatient with him when he can't do something that Tess can do. Makes me want to shake him! Darren, of course, not Pat.

Dulcie: I'm sorry. ☹

Dulcie hugs Brenna

Brenna: Thanks. But Phyllis here was just telling us about how her class is going—with that professor who hates her.

Phyllis: Not good. She went on a huge rant today about how misogynistic Martin Luther was. She glared at ME the whole time! As if I had anything to do with it! I know Luther was a chauvinist. Pretty much all men were at that time. Why does she have to assume I think that's terrific?

Marianne: Because you're the evil evangelical pastor's wife, so it must be your fault.

Phyllis: I'm so sick of her judging me according to my husband's job.

Zelia: pretty hypocritical attitude for a feminist.

Phyllis: Exactly!

Jocelyn: I've got news—Ros and I decided the retreat is going to be in Colorado Springs.

Zelia: oh sure. make it easiest for yourself to get there! what about those of us on the east coast?

Jocelyn: Hey, it would be hard to plan if we didn't have it in one of our towns. Would you rather have gone all the way to Washington?

Zelia: i just don't know if this whole retreat thing is a good idea. what does shane think about it?

Jocelyn: He thought it sounded cool. Why wouldn't he?

(Hannah has entered the room)

Hannah: Hi everybody!

Dulcie: Hi…Hannah. This is a big surprise.

Dulcie Whispers to Zelia: Did you invite her? What is she doing here?

Marianne: How are you, Hannah? How's Boaz?

Hannah: Boaz is terrific. He rolled over today! That's almost a whole month early. He's SOOO advanced!

Marianne: Well, that's special.

★Zelia Whispers to Dulcie★: i didn't invite the chick! i have no idea why she's here.

Brenna: Do you often check the chat room, Hannah?

Hannah: Actually, I made this nifty little plug-in that tells me when anyone is in the chat room. I just got the alert, and would have been here sooner, but had to finish nursing Boaz.

Brenna: I had NO idea that was possible.

★Brenna Whispers to Dulcie★: She's spying on us? How do we get rid of her?

★Dulcie Whispers to Brenna★: I don't know. I don't want to be rude to her.

Hannah: So what's everyone chatting about?

Jocelyn: Oh you know, just stuff. Nothing important.

Hannah: That's great! I didn't expect any of you to be so up on technology.

Jocelyn: Yeah, we noticed today. You know, we're not THAT much older than you. We do know how to do stuff online.

Hannah: I SO keep forgetting that! You all seem a lot older.

★Phyllis Whispers to Dulcie★: I cannot deal with this tonight. Please do me a huge favor and get rid of her somehow.

★Dulcie Whispers to Phyllis★: Why do you all think I can do it?

Hannah: Hey, I was just reading this super-cool article in The Journal of Child Development—which I started subscribing to this month. It's about how you can actually help your baby's language development by showing them genuine emotion when you talk to them.

Brenna Whispers to Dulcie: Shoot. Me. Now.

Phyllis: I feel almost sorry for her. I mean, she's walked into the middle of a private chat and has no idea none of us want her here. One of us has to do something.

Marianne: PHYLLIS!!!

Hannah: I think you already did do something, Phyllis.

Zelia: well, this is awkward.

Hannah: Were you all "whispering" behind my back?

Jocelyn: We're sorry, Hannah. We've been having Monday-night chats for years. Nobody ever joined us before.

Hannah: And that gives you the right to totally humiliate me?

Phyllis: I am so sorry, Hannah. It wasn't right for us to do that.

Hannah: I think you are a very poor example of a pastor's wife, Phyllis. You don't do ANY of the stuff a good PW is supposed to do, and you make your husband look HORRIBLE because of it!

Phyllis: Do you have any idea what it's like to be in my position? You want to know why you don't get invited to chats, and why we weren't all jumping up and down to see you? Comments like that, little girl. Do us all a favor and grow up. Adults know the world isn't black and white. Stop acting like the teen you are.

Hannah: You are all horrible, mean people! You think you're so mature. But you're just like the popular clique in high school—only you have wrinkles and stretch marks and wear baby spit up on your clothes!

Dulcie: Whoa! Everyone calm down. Hannah, Phyllis has had a really rough day. She didn't mean to hurt your feelings. We all totally screwed up this evening. I think the best thing to do would be

(Hannah has left the chat room)

to give each other lots of grace and start over.

Brenna: Guess this means our chat is over for the night, huh?

Phyllis: I am SO horrified. I totally lost it. My hands are shaking and I think I'm going to go cry. I've never been that mean to anyone in my life! I'll email her and try to smooth things over.

Marianne: We were all guilty, Phyllis. You're just the one that got caught. I'll try to email her, too. I get along pretty well with her overall.

Dulcie: I think we probably all owe her apology emails. Maybe even chocolate. :(

★Dulcie hugs Phyllis★

Jocelyn: You guys, Hannah's right.

Zelia: speak for yourself—i don't have any stretch marks!

Jocelyn: I'm serious, Z. We've been behaving just like those girls we couldn't stand in high school.

Dulcie: No we have not.

Jocelyn: I think so. For years, what have we done about Rosalyn? Nothing except talk about her among ourselves.

Brenna: We've always tried to be fairly nice. And you know she CAN be difficult. We needed a support group!

Jocelyn: I've been talking to Rosalyn more lately because of the retreat stuff. I think she—and Hannah—need friends. Friends who won't backstab them.

Marianne: Maybe we should just all call it a night, apologize to Hannah, and start over tomorrow.

Zelia: well, if jocelyn is going to be all sensitive about everything from now on, i'm not sure if it's even worth keeping our monday chat tradition going. and besides, we'll have to find a new chat room anyway, because this one is under surveillance.

Phyllis: Marianne's suggestion is a good one. I need to go—I feel ill. Good night all.

(Phyllis has left the chat room)

(Marianne has left the chat room)

(Jocelyn has left the chat room)

(Zelia has left the chat room)

(Brenna has left the chat room)

Dulcie: I was going to ask for some advice—about Tom. But it's just me, posting to myself. Pathetic. What a wretched evening.

(Dulcie has left the chat room)

From:	Hannah Farrell
	<boazsmom@farrellfamilylovesjesus.net>
To:	Kristina Shaw <krissyshaw@loopy.com>
Subject:	I'm miserable

Do you know how jealous I am of you right now, Krissy? I would give absolutely ANYTHING to trade positions with you. Nobody takes me seriously, not even Bradley. He's always so busy with work, and he thinks he's such a big shot because he has a bachelor's in business administration. He treats me like I'm slightly retarded.

The moms at church are nice, but my mind feels like it's being smothered when I'm around them.

And this mom loop I'm on! I think they hate me because some of them have kids close to my age. Some of them are really smart, but I just don't fit in. I've tried and tried and tried. But they treat me like I'm some sort of mosquito they can't get rid of. They did their best to squish me tonight, though.

Bradley came in a minute ago. He didn't even notice I'm crying. He just wanted to know if I'd loaded the dishwasher yet or not, because he had a mug that needed washing. I notice he left it on the table for me to load.

Is this what I have to look forward to? An endless round of dishes, laundry, diapers and feedings? A husband who couldn't care less, and always feeling like I don't belong?

Krissy, I'm dying here. I'm trapped, and there's nothing I can do about it. What did I do wrong? I tried to do everything the right way, and it's all falling to pieces.

I think I made a huge mistake.

Wish you were here,

Hannah

From:	Kristina Shaw <krissyshaw@loopy.com>
To:	Hannah Farrell
	<boazsmom@farrellfamilylovesjesus.net>
Subject:	Re: I'm miserable

Hey girl,

I'm sorry u r having such a tough time right now. Wish I could be there for you. I can't write long—a bunch of us are going scuba diving in about a half hour. I'm miserable, too, actually—just thinking about how I've only got two weeks left before leaving Hawaii. The summer has gone by sooooooo fast! Waaahhh!!!

I thought I was going to have a week at home before going back to school, but one of the girls on my team here invited me to stay with her a week. She's from Maine. I'm so excited about visiting there! So I won't get to see you. But maybe over Christmas we can get together, okay?

Hang in there—I'm sure Bradley loves you. You just need to tell him how you're feeling. It's probably how all new moms feel. It'll get better. And don't worry about all those other moms—they're just jealous because you're young and have your whole life ahead of you. Probably a midlife crisis thing, you think?

Anyway, gotta run. Maybe I can call you later this week, okay?

Love,

Krissy

From:	P. Lorimer <phyllis.lorimer@geemail.com>
To:	Hannah Farrell
	<boazsmom@farrellfamilylovesjesus.net>
Subject:	I am sorry.

Dear Hannah,

I don't know what else to say. I am truly, truly sorry for what happened yesterday evening. You are completely justified in your hurt and anger. What I did and what I said to you was inexcusable. Not because I'm married to a pastor, but because I am a follower of Jesus. And as we both know, Jesus would NOT have done that to you. I'm sorry I was such a poor example of Him to you.

I don't expect you to move past this quickly. But I really sense that there's a lot of hurt and stress in your life, even without the pain we've added. I would like to make restitution in some small way by being your friend and by supporting you however I can.

Would you be willing to let me do that? I'd like to prove to you that I'm not the monster I acted like last night. I feel absolutely ill about the whole thing. Please let me know what I can do to make it right.

Sincerely,

Phyllis Lorimer

From:	Hannah Farrell
	<boazsmom@farrellfamilylovesjesus.net>
To:	P. Lorimer <phyllis.lorimer@geemail.com>
Subject:	Re: I am sorry.

Phyllis,

I forgive you. Not because I'm over it, but because I'm supposed to forgive people. I don't really feel like being friends with you. But I was griping to my friend Krissy on

Monday night that I don't have any real mom friends. And maybe this is God's weird way of solving that problem.

But I don't think I want to start being friends until next week, okay? I need a few more days.

You want to know what hurt me the most? I thought you were the coolest person on the SAHM loop! Not only are you a pastor's wife (I think it's pretty special), but you must be really smart, too, to be going to school for a Ph.D. I know I get snarky about it, but I think I'm jealous. I gave up college to marry Bradley. But I could have done great in college. I'm like totally a brainiac.

So anyway, you were the one mom I really admired beyond everyone else on the loop. And so what you said hurt me even worse. That's not really your fault because I totally should know better than to put people on pedestals. But no worries of that happening now.

If you want to start being friends next week, you can e-mail me on Sunday. But I don't think we should take it very fast. You understand, don't you?

Thank you for e-mailing me and apologizing. It was a very nice thing to do. I'm not that brave.

Okay then…until next week,

Hannah

From:	Rosalyn Ebberly <prov31woman@home.com>
To:	SAHM I Am <sahmiam@loophole.com>
Subject:	**[SAHM I AM] TOTW**
	August 10: Household budgets

Savvy SAHMmies,

I have been learning that one of the prime reasons we SAHMs are prone to depression is that we often feel a lack of empowerment. After all, we are completely dependent on our hubbies to provide financially for us. I used to think that was the way it was meant to be—that I'd be happier to have all that taken care of for me.

But my therapist (who really is brilliant) has been helping me to see that I need to be involved in financial decision making in our family.

So Chad and I have started doing our budget together. And you know what? I DO feel empowered! I came up with a simple budgeting system that I'm thinking of patenting and selling because it's just so intuitive and effective. But since I love you all so much, I'm going to let you have it for free.

First, you have to

Step One: Pull out all your bills, receipts, check stubs, and check carbons. Then get ledger paper or a spreadsheet and start entering in all the stuff you bought or bills you paid.

Step Two: Color code all your purchases according to what category they fit in. Then group your categories into "S"—for "set expenses," or "V"—for "variable expenses."

Step Three: Rate each item a 1, 2, or 3 according to how typical it is to spend that amount of money on that item. Then put an ⑦ if the amount is usually more, and a ⑨ if the amount is usually lower.

Step Four: Add up all the purchase amounts for each category. Then add up all the ratings for the items in that category. Divide by the number of total items in the category to find your overall rating. Now you'll have a Code for each category: S or V, Average rating, up or down, and dollar amount. So for the Transportation Category, it might look like this: V 1.976⑨ $682.96.

Step Five: For the next two steps, you'll have to do some math. Since most of you aren't math experts, I found this nifty program online that translates any set of math steps into a nice, simple formula.

Just go to the Web site and put in the following formulas with your particular numbers instead of the variable letters.

IF VC_N < estimate then new month VC = (^{TM}TAC— (.1)VC_N^2). IF VC_N > estimate then new month VC_N = ^{TM}TAC (1+ 1/VC_N).

Step Six: VC_N = VC_N / ((^{TM}EIC- ^{TM}TAC) $\star$ ((^{TM}SC+^{TM}VC)/(^{TM}TAC)))

SC = SC $\star$ (((^{TM}SC/^{TM}TAC)/ (^{TM}EIC- ^{TM}TAC)))

Isn't that simple? Just between us, when I unveiled this plan to Chad, he was speechless! My new interest in our finances obviously meant a lot to him, because he sounded a bit choked up after I explained everything. But he also seemed pretty stressed out. I didn't say anything about his tension. I'm sure he'll work through it and come to appreciate my input.

So tell me, what methods do the rest of you use for budgeting? How do you work with your husband (or wife, Tom) to make financial plans for your family? And if you're not currently participating in that aspect of running your household, what do you intend to do to become more involved?

You know, the Proverbs 31 woman was a wise financial manager. Let's become more like her!

Blessings,

Rosalyn

SAHM I Am Loop Moderator

"The wise woman builds her house, but the foolish tears it down with her own hands." Proverbs 14:1 (NASB)

From:	Thomas Huckleberry
	<t.huckleberry@showme.com>
To:	Dulcie Huckleberry
	<dulcie@homemakerinteriors.com>
Subject:	Re: [SAHM I AM] TOTW
	August 10: Household budgets

Dave Ramsey's head would explode.

From:	Dulcie Huckleberry
	<dulcie@homemakerinteriors.com>
To:	Thomas Huckleberry
	<t.huckleberry@showme.com>
Subject:	Re: [SAHM I AM] TOTW
	August 10: Household budgets

It's kind of like the budgeting equivalent to Calvin Ball, don't you think? :)

From:	The Millards
	<jstcea4jesus@familymail.net>
To:	"Green Eggs and Ham"
Subject:	Re: [SAHM I AM] TOTW
	August 10: Household budgets

Chad was speechless and tense because that is the worst, most confusing "budget" system that has ever been designed! What is she thinking? Should I e-mail the loop and suggest they do NOT "try this at home"?

Why does she have to make everything so utterly complicated? Did you know she created an entire rubric to determine the best possible date for the retreat?
Jocelyn

☺**Instant Message**

ZeeMuzzy: thought you weren't going to "gossip" about rossie anymore.

JocelynM: Gee, you're cranky today. Come on, Z. This bitterness is not attractive.

ZeeMuzzy: not bitterness. just think you should walk the talk. that's all.

JocelynM: Well, don't you think her budget is a horrible idea?

ZeeMuzzy: sure. but i'm not the one who has pledged to be her new bff either.

JocelynM: I didn't make any such pledge. Deciding to be friends with someone doesn't mean that I can't disagree STRONGLY with them.

ZeeMuzzy: behind their back? or maybe you do that to ALL your friends, huh?

JocelynM: I'm not even going to respond to that.

JocelynM signed off at 10:40:23 a.m.

From:	Hannah Farrell
	<boazsmom@farrellfamilylovesjesus.net>
To:	SAHM I Am <sahmiam@loophole.com>
Subject:	Re: [SAHM I AM] TOTW
	August 10: Household budgets

Hey Rosalyn, your little budget system is fabulicious! I am utterly in awe of it.

Hope it's okay to give you a couple of itty-bitty nitpicks. I think you left something out in Step 4. Isn't it true that your Set Categories are cohomologous with your Variable Categories? (I SO totally could be mistaken, but I'm pretty sure that when you compute eigenvalues for the covariance matrix, you find a degeneracy. Yes, really!!! If I'm right, then cobordism implies that your budget won't satisify the Lipschitz condition, and we ALL know what that means! *shudder*

But really—it was a great attempt. Totally elegant approach. Won't help you reserve enough money to buy groceries, but the mental exercise did you good, I'm sure. XOXO,

Hannah

From:	P. Lorimer <phyllis.lorimer@geemail.com>
To:	SAHM I Am <sahmiam@loophole.com>
Subject:	Re: [SAHM I AM] TOTW
	August 10: Household budgets

Wow, Hannah, I didn't realize you were so proficient in math! I don't have any idea what you said, but I'm convinced.

Maybe we should have YOU teaching us about keeping track of our finances.

Phyllis (who is cramming madly for an exam from the Professor of Doom. What prof gives Ph.D. students summer exams anyway?)

From:	Hannah Farrell
	<boazsmom@farrellfamilylovesjesus.net>
To:	SAHM I Am <sahmiam@loophole.com>
Subject:	Re: [SAHM I AM] TOTW
	August 10: Household budgets

Hi Phyllis,
Like I told you a couple weeks ago, I'm like a total brainiac. If I'd have gone to college, I would have majored in physics and computer engineering so I could design a quantum computer and become rich and famous. I bet a quantum computer would destroy Microsoft, and then open-source

would like totally rule the world. And that would be awesomely cool.
Hannah

📧Text Message From Rosalyn Ebberly: For Veronica Marcello
——August 10/2:15 p.m.——
"Such a brainiac I would have designed a quantum computer"—well isn't that special. Little twerp.

📧Text Message From Rosalyn Ebberly: For Veronica Marcello
——August 10/2:16 p.m.——
I'd like to give HER a Lipschitz condition! Sounds delightfully painful.

📧Text Message From Veronica Marcello: For Rosalyn Ebberly
——August 10/2:18 p.m.——
Poor Ros. Pwned by the Lipstick Kid. Wht happened to Jesus as ur bubble of light n the sewer of life?

📧Text Message From Rosalyn Ebberly: For Veronica Marcello
——August 10/2:19 p.m.——
I worked hard on my system and she made me look stupid.

📧Text Message From Veronica Marcello: For Rosalyn Ebberly
——August 10/2:21 p.m.——
SHE did?

⌨Text Message From Rosalyn Ebberly: For Veronica Marcello
——August 10/2:22 p.m.——
You irritate me.

⌨Text Message From Veronica Marcello: For Rosalyn Ebberly
——August 10/2:23 p.m.——
Sounds like time for another visit to ur shrink, sister-dear. Uv fallen off the nice-wagon again.

⌨Text Message From Rosalyn Ebberly: For Veronica Marcello
——August 10/2:23 p.m.——
Shut up.

⌨Text Message From Veronica Marcello: For Rosalyn Ebberly
——August 10/2:24 p.m.——
LOL. Luv u 2! :)

From:	The Millards
	<jstcea4jesus@familymail.net>
To:	SAHM I Am <sahmiam@loophole.com>
Subject:	Re: [SAHM I AM] TOTW
	August 10: Household budgets

Corbordism aside, I think Rosalyn's main point was important. Being totally dependent on a working husband does tend to make a lot of SAHMs depressed. Maybe that's why I'm having such a hard time with this whole cleaning-service thing. I mean, if I'm NOT cleaning house, and I'm NOT doing all the mom-taxi stuff, and if I'm NOT spending all my time cooking or homeschooling or whatever…

Then what purpose do I have? I mean, nobody in their right mind would say that my job is to do all the parenting. In fact, everyone is constantly harping on how terribly important dads are. And somehow our husbands are managing to do their full-time jobs and be good fathers.

Or maybe I'm just grumpy today because Tyler told me he wishes Anna could come every day and make his bed for him. I said, "You can't make it yourself?"

"She does it better. She makes it all tight and folds the sheets down and lines my baseballs up on the edge. Why don't you do that, Mom?"

What are we teaching our kids? I'm going to end up with a son who doesn't remember how to make his bed. I told Shane my concerns, and he said there's plenty of time for him to learn that when he goes to college.

He'll probably con some poor, sweet girl into doing it for him. I'll have to send him off to school with a disclaimer: "Looks cute, but extremely devious. Befriend at own risk."

Jocelyn

From:	Rosalyn Ebberly <prov31woman@home.com>
To:	The Millards
	<jstcea4jesus@familymail.net>
Subject:	**Thanks...**

…for getting the subject back on track on the loop. I appreciated it.
Rosalyn

"The wise woman builds her house, but the foolish tears it down with her own hands." Proverbs 14:1 (NASB)

From:	The Millards
	<jstcea4jesus@familymail.net>
To:	Rosalyn Ebberly <prov31woman@home.com>
Subject:	**Re: Thanks...**

Yeah, no big deal. But you really need to focus here, Ros. We HAVE to get the contract signed for the retreat hotel. Otherwise, we're going to lose our weekend. And I do NOT intend to go through your torturous rubric again to pick a new date!

So put down the convoluted budget system. Just concentrate on deciding which one of the hotels I visited sound the best to you. This MUST be done by tomorrow, okay?
Jocelyn

From:	Rosalyn Ebberly <prov31woman@home.com>
To:	The Millards
	<jstcea4jesus@familymail.net>
Subject:	**Re: Thanks...**

You don't have to get testy about it. I'm not trying to delay on purpose, you know. I just want everything to be RIGHT. I know a lot of you probably doubt this—but I really do love the ladies in our loop. They deserve a beautiful weekend getaway, and I'm determined to give it to them.

Rosalyn

"The wise woman builds her house, but the foolish tears it down with her own hands." Proverbs 14:1 (NASB)

From:	The Millards
	<jstcea4jesus@familymail.net>
To:	Rosalyn Ebberly <prov31woman@home.com>
Subject:	**Re: Thanks...**

IF YOU LOVE US THEN PICK A BLASTED HOTEL ALREADY!

Jocelyn

P.S. Are you certain that we're going to be able to recoup our costs on this? You know that I'll be signing the contract and making the deposit with my own money, right? I can't afford for this to flop.

From:	Rosalyn Ebberly <prov31woman@home.com>
To:	The Millards
	<jstcea4jesus@familymail.net>
Subject:	Re: Thanks...

Trust me...they'll come. It'll be a huge success. When have I EVER planned something that turned out to be a disaster?
Rosalyn

"The wise woman builds her house, but the foolish tears it down with her own hands." Proverbs 14:1 (NASB)

From:	The Millards
	<jstcea4jesus@familymail.net>
To:	Dulcie Huckleberry
	<dulcie@homemakerinteriors.com>
Subject:	(no subject)

I am so screwed. I just want to let you know, now, before the coming Apocalypse, that you've always been a dear friend to me. And after this whole retreat thing blows up in my face and Shane kills me for bankrupting the family,

I want you to have Cuddie my teddy bear from when I was three. If you can grab him before the IRS does.
Jocelyn

From:	P. Lorimer <phyllis.lorimer@geemail.com>
To:	SAHM I Am <sahmiam@loophole.com>
Subject:	[SAHM I AM] Economic Dependence

This is becoming more and more of a sore spot for me. Jonathan does NOT like spending money, and I absolutely despise the feeling that I'm begging him every time I want to go shopping. It's not like I don't have equal access to the money. But if I spent it without his blessing then I'd get the wrinkled-nose, pursed-lip, terse little nod of his. Plus, if it's clothing, then every time I'm getting ready to go somewhere, he says something like "You're going to wear that new shirt-thing aren't you?"

And if I say no, then he raises his eyebrows and says, "Well, I would just think you'd want to get your money's worth out of it after…you know…what you paid for it."

Do you know how that ruins any pleasure I used to have in that purchase?

I hate feeling like every stitch on my back and everything in the house down to the very last butter knife has ultimately been provided by him. Not that a pastor's income provides much of any of that stuff. But it is rather humiliating after a while to realize that if my nose is running, I don't even have enough money of my own to buy a tissue.

I've held off getting a job because a lot of our congregation would probably be horrified at the idea. They'd feel like it was either because I'm a bad wife, or because they're a bad congregation and not providing enough for us. I truly love them and don't want them feeling either way.

And right now, I don't have time for a job even if I could take one. I did get a grad assistant position starting in just a couple weeks, so that will help. But the pay is minuscule. I might be able to buy TWO tissues if I saved up for them!
Stalling on studying,
Phyllis

From:	Rosalyn Ebberly <prov31woman@home.com>
To:	SAHM I Am <sahmiam@loophole.com>
Subject:	Re: [SAHM I AM] Economic Dependence

Dearest Phyllis,
I think a lot of your dissatisfaction probably has to do with your attitude and mindset. My therapist is constantly helping me learn to reframe situations in my mind to make them more positive. The result is that I can change my emotions and feelings merely by changing how I think about something. Isn't that amazing?

So with this, I think your biggest problem is that you are viewing your finances as "belonging" to Jonathan. Shouldn't you be thinking of the money as "our" money instead of "his" and "hers"? I think you'll find that you feel much more "one" with your husband if you learn to cleave together financially, as well as in other areas.
Rosalyn
SAHM I AM Loop Moderator

"The wise woman builds her house, but the foolish tears it down with her own hands." Proverbs 14:1 (NASB)

From:	P. Lorimer <phyllis.lorimer@geemail.com>
To:	"Green Eggs and Ham"
Subject:	**Re: [SAHM I AM] Economic Dependence**

Yes, thank you SO much, Dr. Laura. And to think I sacrificed ten minutes of study time for that.

Phyllis

P.S. Jocelyn, I do not care if you think this is gossip. She is driving me loony, all right?

From:	Dulcie Huckleberry <dulcie@homemakerinteriors.com>
To:	SAHM I Am <sahmiam@loophole.com>
Subject:	**Re: [SAHM I AM] Economic Dependence**

I think Phyllis knows that it's "their" money and not "his." But I could see where it would feel burdensome after a while to always feel so dependent.

I never felt that way so much, even when Tom was working and I was home full-time. Since he traveled almost all the time, I did the bills. So I felt like I had a lot of control over our money. I don't know who does the bills in Phyllis's family, but maybe if she did them or they did them together, it might help. (Sorry, Rosalyn, but I can't recommend that budget thing…too confusing.)

I think it also helps if a parent stays home because it was truly their first choice. I know Tom doesn't feel overly dependent on me because he wanted to be a stay-at-home dad. Plus, he's developing his own hobby that will eventually bring him some pin money, too, and that will help.

Hang in there, Phyllis. You're taking steps to be able to bring in money as a professor. And I know that Jonathan supports that and is excited about it. :)
Dulcie

☺**Instant Message**
Huck: PIN MONEY?
Dulcet: What was wrong with that?
Huck: Why didn't you just say how you give the "little man" a pocket allowance? Sheesh.
Dulcet: I didn't mean it that way. I'm sorry.
Huck: I know you didn't. But that was embarrassing.
Dulcet: I didn't know you were so sensitive about it. Do you feel like Phyllis then?
Huck: Sometimes, maybe a little.
Dulcet: Well, it's not like I'm acting like Jonathan.
Huck: No.
Dulcet: And you never have to have "permission" to buy anything. You're always good at making sure we can afford it. I trust you.
Huck: I know. It's not that.
Dulcet: Then what? We've been doing this for two years. I thought you were fine with it.
Huck: I did too. But the comments on the loop—it made

me realize I feel the same way. It's not always easy, especially being a man.

Dulcet: Oh, and you think it's easy for a woman?

Huck: I did NOT say that.

Dulcet: Look, I don't want to argue about this, especially over the computer. What can I do to help you feel better about this?

Huck: I really want to learn more woodworking so I can do it professionally. You know Morris can get me connected with the vendors in Branson. People are wild there for homemade furniture. And I love doing it. I just need to pick up more techniques and practice.

Dulcet: I have no problems with that.

Huck: There's a woodworking show in Kansas City next spring. I'd like to go.

Dulcet: Sure. That would be great. Find out the details and we'll make it happen.

From:	Rosalyn Ebberly <prov31woman@home.com>
To:	SAHM I Am <sahmiam@loophole.com>
Subject:	[SAHM I AM] TOTW
	August 24: Did I Hear You Correctly?

Ladies, (well…and Tom)

This week, we're all going to practice our Active Listening skills! Now, in case some of you were sleeping during that session of your premarital counseling, here's a quick review:

1) Focus on what the other person is saying—even if you

disagree. Even if they want to talk about something totally stupid, like quitting counseling or something…try to keep an open mind!

2) Show empathy by reflecting back their emotions. "Gee, Chad, it IS frustrating how much time and money our sessions are taking. Also, weekly sessions are exhausting, especially after two years without a break."

3) Show you have understood by rephrasing their thoughts. "So what I hear you saying is that you want to stop going to counseling."

4) Ask open-ended questions: "So if we stop going to counseling, what effect will this have on our marriage and family? How do you propose we move forward in our quest for emotional wholeness if you aren't willing to go the distance and stay in the game? What sort of effect do you think this will have on MY outlook on life?—You know, any question that does NOT have a "yes" or "no" answer.

Don't you think in that scenario, Chad felt like I was really listening to him and engaged in the discussion? THIS is why counseling is so important! We're learning so many more positive ways of communicating with each other!

So let's practice on each other this week. We can "active listen" in our e-mails and with our families. Report back and tell us how you're doing with it.

Ready… Set… LISTEN!

Rosalyn Ebberly

SAHM I Am Loop Moderator

"The wise woman builds her house, but the foolish tears it down with her own hands." Proverbs 14:1 (NASB)

From:	Zelia Muzuwa <zeemuzu@vivacious.com>
To:	"Green Eggs and Ham"
Subject:	Re: [SAHM I AM] TOTW
	August 24: Did I Hear You Correctly?

Ah, Rosalyn! Yet another exercise in MISSING THE POINT.

Zelia

From:	Brenna L. <saywhat@writeme.com>
To:	"Green Eggs and Ham"
Subject:	Re: [SAHM I AM] TOTW
	August 24: Did I Hear You Correctly?

So what I hear you saying is…you think Rosalyn is missing the point of active listening. That must be very frustrating to you. What things would you have liked to see her do instead?

Brenna

From:	Zelia Muzuwa <zeemuzu@vivacious.com>
To:	"Green Eggs and Ham"
Subject:	Re: [SAHM I AM] TOTW
	August 24: Did I Hear You Correctly?

Brenna, babe, you are like the teacher's pet who sits in the front row of class and knows all the answers.

Z

From:	Brenna L. <saywhat@writeme.com>
To:	"Green Eggs and Ham"
Subject:	Re: [SAHM I AM] TOTW
	August 24: Did I Hear You Correctly?

No, that's Phyllis!

From:	P. Lorimer <phyllis.lorimer@geemail.com>
To:	"Green Eggs and Ham"
Subject:	Re: [SAHM I AM] TOTW
	August 24: Did I Hear You Correctly?

HEY!

Don't I wish I was the teacher's pet! Right now, I am the teacher's whipping boy…er, girl. I did manage to get a B on my exam. So now if I can just get this final paper done and turned in, I will be supremely relieved.

But right now I have to run—I am taking Julia to kindergarten. Her first day. She has the pretty dress, the little backpack, a lunch box, and her own parental paparazzi to mark the occasion.

Phyllis

From:	VIM <vivalaveronica@marcelloportraits.com>
To:	SAHM I Am <sahmiam@loophole.com>
Subject:	**[SAHM I AM] Birthday Party update**

This is going from bad to worse, y'all. We thought we had the whole birthday party issue resolved. Ashley was going to have a limo party—she and five of her friends were going to get picked up in a limo, driven around and eventually dropped off at the mall, where Ashley could go buy herself a present, and then the limo would take them to a restaurant for dinner, and then back home where we were going to let them end the evening by watching a movie.

She was happy. We were happy (though soon-to-be significantly poorer).

But the child made the mistake of telling her friend about it. And so guess what we got in the mail today from that child?

Yep, an invitation to her birthday party…a LIMO PARTY.

Ashley is crushed. She says she won't go to the party because this other girl "stole her idea" and if she has a limo party of her own now, everyone will call her a copycat even though it was her idea first.

ARGH! Is this what I get to deal with for the next seven years? She begged me to talk to this girl's parents and ask them to reconsider. She's acting for all the world like her life is going to end if she can't have her limo party.

I'm off to call the parents. Nothing like a good catfight with another mother.

Wish me well!

Veronica

From:	Iona James
	<poetsmystique@brokenwrenchandcopperbucket.com>
To:	SAHM I Am <sahmiam@loophole.com>
Subject:	Re: [SAHM I AM] Birthday Party update

Hello from my world, Veronica,

When I was eleven, I wanted more than anything to have a horse-riding birthday party. I longed to gallop through a forest glade with the wind in my hair and the warmth and glow of a horse's back under me—with no one but my best friend Allison beside me.

I dreamed about that party for months. When it finally arrived, and my parents took Allison and me to the stables, there was no forest glade. There was a riding ring and a grumpy instructor. There was no wind, which was unfortunate because none of my dreams included the smell of horse manure and feed. Allison was so frightened of the horses that she spent the entire party sitting on an overturned feed bucket crying and griping about the smell. And the next day, my muscles were so sore, I could hardly walk.

The next year, I didn't dream about a party. My parents planned it a week in advance, and Allison and I camped out in my backyard. We got bit by mosquitoes, and I was still sore the next day. But we ate M&M's and made s'mores over the stove and shared our secrets late at night. It was the best birthday I ever had.

I hope Ashley has a wonderful birthday, too.

Iona

From:	Rosalyn Ebberly <prov31woman@home.com>
To:	SAHM I Am <sahmiam@loophole.com>
Subject:	Re: [SAHM I AM] Birthday Party update

Uh, Iona, dear, don't forget that this week we're working on our active LISTENING. It's easy sometimes to forget that when we're listening, we should be focused on what the other person's problems are, not sharing our own stories.

I just think it's an important distinction to remember.

So for example, what you could have said to Veronica is "So you're saying that this other family has really hurt your daughter by stealing her idea for a birthday party." (Reflecting) And then you could say, "Wow, Veronica, I can see how that would be really agonizing for a parent to watch their daughter feel so betrayed by one of their friends." (Empathy)

Then Veronica would know that you've really heard her.

Let's all remember, it's ACTIVE LISTENING WEEK, okay?

Rosalyn Ebberly

SAHM I Am Loop Moderator

"The wise woman builds her house, but the foolish tears it down with her own hands." Proverbs 14:1 (NASB)

From:	VIM <vivalaveronica@marcelloportraits.com>
To:	SAHM I Am <sahmiam@loophole.com>
Subject:	Re: [SAHM I AM] Birthday Party update

Thanks, Ros, but I thought Iona's post was just peachy. In fact, here's a little ol' active listening just for Iona, 'cause I appreciate her so much:

So y'all dreamed forever about your horse party, and then when it came, all y'all got was a grumpy old galoot of an instructor, a blinky friend, and a smelly, plug-ugly nag. That must've got you all choked up, sweetheart!

Veronica

☺**Instant Message**

Pr31Mom: You aren't supposed to do your Texas shtick anymore, remember?

Ronnie_M: And you aren't supposed to do your "I'm the nightmare you'd get if you crossed Donna Reed with Napoleon Bonaparte" shtick anymore, either! I figure you asked for it.

Pr31Mom: I wasn't that bad!

Ronnie_M: A string of pearls around your neck and a bicorn hat are all that you were missing, darlin'.

Pr31Mom: I just really wanted them to take the whole active listening thing seriously.

Ronnie_M: You know, dear sis, sometimes the loudest way to speak is through actions. Maybe if you just model it, they'll get the message. We do listen to you, even if not always actively.

Pr31Mom: Really?

Ronnie_M: Yeah. So you can stop yelling already.

Pr31Mom: Sometimes you are weirdly sensible.

Ronnie_M: Well, we all have our faults.

From:	Iona James
	<poetsmystique@brokenwrenchandcopperbucket.com>
To:	"Green Eggs and Ham"
Subject:	Wounded

My fellow Eggs, and Her Eminence, the Ham,

Are posts like Rosalyn's the reason you have your own little subgroup? That hurt! And as much as I take pleasure from the inspirations my own emotional pain brings me, I honestly wasn't in the mood for these sort of jabs today. The Angel Child has an ear infection, and there's been nothing but his screaming here today. He was so loud that the tea shop manager called up here to see if we were all right. And she casually mentioned that the noise was disturbing her customers.

It was probably mean of me, but I told her that this should give her a good opportunity, then, to promote her chamomile-lavender tea to calm their nerves.

She hung up on me. ☹
Iona James

From:	Zelia Muzuwa <zeemuzu@vivacious.com>
To:	"Green Eggs and Ham"
Subject:	**Re: Wounded**

Hey you eggie Tea-Babe,

Love your snark to the tea shop manager! Sorry to hear your Angel Child has an ear infection. Those are the worst.

And absolutely—Rosalyn is the main reason we ended up with this loop. We're like refugees, banding together for support and comfort while trying to survive in her world of cruelty. ☺

Although…Ms. Depressed-Cuz-She-Has-A-Housekeeper has recently decided we shouldn't say bad things about our dearest loop mod, so I'd better cut it short here. But I am sorry she hurt your feelings. Her sister made up for it, though, don't you think? Veronica is all right. I'd say she'd be a great addition to our merry little band, except that some of our Ros-inspired angst might be a bit awkward for her.

Channel your pique into a poem, okeydokey, chica? And be thankful it wasn't worse!

Hugs,

Z (though the title "Her Eminence" was brilliant)

From:	Iona James
	<poetsmystique@brokenwrenchandcopperbucket.com>
To:	P. Lorimer <phyllis.lorimer@geemail.com>
Subject:	**Zelia and Rosalyn?**

Greetings Phyllis,

I hope you don't mind my e-mailing you with a personal concern. But I thought since you're a pastor's wife, you are probably used to dealing with sensitive personal matters, and could be counted on for wisdom and discretion.

I just read Zelia's response to the post I sent you and the other Green Eggs and Ham group. She's always so amusing and fun to read, but I think I detect an edge of bitterness in her words. This has me quite concerned. Honestly, I don't mind venting with you all, but I'm not a mean-spirited sort of person. And if your group spends all its time talking badly about someone—even Rosalyn—I don't think I want to be part of it.

Can you illuminate this situation for me? I'm not asking you to betray any confidences, but I need to know whether or not this is something I want to be part of. Zelia's e-mail made me uncomfortable. I certainly don't hate Rosalyn. I just feel that her way of dealing with people can sometimes be hurtful.

Advice or insight, please?

Thank you, and many blessings,

Iona James

From:	P. Lorimer <phyllis.lorimer@geemail.com>
To:	Iona James
	<poetsmystique@brokenwrenchandcopperbucket.com>
Subject:	Re: Zelia and Rosalyn?

Hi Iona,

It was perfectly fine for you to e-mail me about this. I think that any of our group would have been equally discreet and understanding. There's nothing about full-time ministry (by profession or by marriage) that gives a person an edge in the wisdom department! Trust me—I have personal proof this is true. ☺

But I would love to help you understand about Zelia. Our little group is definitely NOT about bashing anyone. In fact, until last year, Zelia herself would have been the first to say that we actually care a lot about Rosalyn. Certainly, she's frustrating, but there was no "mean-spiritedness" or "bitterness" as you noted. And most of our chatter wasn't even about her—still is not.

Zelia was one of the first SAHM I Am loop members. She's known Rosalyn a very long time and has stuck with her and the loop through a lot of Rosalyn's shenanigans. They've had an odd sort of friendship—equal mix of frustration and admiration, I think.

But all that changed last year. You may have heard about the Christmas adventures she and her husband had that year. She thought Chad was having an affair, but in reality, he was working against her "Boycott Christmas" campaign in their town. She let Veronica send a private investigator to shadow Chad. Then Veronica showed up, too, and went into labor at a restaurant, right in the middle of the big fight between Rosalyn, Chad and the P.I.

They got things patched up after that, but Rosalyn's family and marriage were so broken that the whole family has been in counseling since. I don't know if you're familiar with how emotional and psychological problems work, but it's usually the case that things have to get worse before they get better.

The counseling brought up many painful issues in Rosalyn's life, and that spring, some of her personal problems spilled over to the loop. She said some very spiteful, hurtful things to Zelia about Z's adopted kids and her ability to parent them. It caused such an uproar that Connie—our loop owner and Rosalyn's best friend—had to remove Rosalyn from the loop for a year. She was only allowed to come back this June.

Zelia has let herself get bitter about the whole thing. She won't forgive Rosalyn, and I have a feeling that the problems with her adopted children just keep that wound open.

It doesn't excuse her, but I hope that it will help you have some patience with Zelia. She was never like this before. The attachment troubles with her kids have been killing her, and Rosalyn was more than she could handle.

Does this help you feel better about our group? Please let me know if you have any other questions. None of this is private, so it's okay to share it with you.

Thank you for asking me. I'm honored by your trust.

Phyllis

From:	Iona James
	<poetsmystique@brokenwrenchandcopperbucket.com>
To:	P. Lorimer <phyllis.lorimer@geemail.com>
Subject:	Re: Zelia and Rosalyn?

Dear Phyllis,

Your e-mail has made me so very thankful to know you and the other Eggs. And the Ham, too. She is extremely blessed to have a friend like you who loves her so much. I don't think I've ever had a friend that faithful.

And yes, your e-mail helps me understand Zelia and have compassion and patience for her. I feel compassion for Rosalyn, too. I wish there was something we could do to help them both.

Thank you again.

Iona James

From:	P. Lorimer <phyllis.lorimer@geemail.com>
To:	SAHM I Am <sahmiam@loophole.com>
Subject:	[SAHM I AM] Just sent my baby off to kindergarten!

Dear friends,

I've come home from dropping Julia off for her first day of kindergarten. Bennet is still here, but the house feels so empty! I think I am going to cry—which surprises me greatly because I would not have thought I'd be the sort to get weepy about the first day of school.

But it's all I can do to not grab the phone and call the school and see if she's okay. What if she is scared? What if the other kids are mean to her?

Or…even worse…WHAT IF I'VE DONE A BAD JOB OF PREPARING HER FOR SCHOOL? Academic failure would likely be harder on me than it would be for her.

I've spent five years wishing for this day, and now I'm miserable! What's wrong with me?
Phyllis

From:	Dulcie Huckleberry <dulcie@homemakerinteriors.com>
To:	SAHM I Am <sahmiam@loophole.com>
Subject:	Re: [SAHM I AM] Just sent my baby off to kindergarten!

Hi Phyllis!
Don't worry—you're totally normal! When MacKenzie went off to school last year, it took me two hours before I could pull out of the parking lot.

I finally crept inside and asked the secretary if there was anyone who could just peek in on Mac and tell me if she was doing okay. I was certain I'd discover that Mac was hiding in the corner of the room sobbing and nearly wetting her pants.

The secretary sort of smirked at me—like I wasn't the

first nervous kindergarten mommy she'd ever met. She went personally to check on Mac for me.

And here's what she said—Mac was doing centers…some alphabet thing. She was with another little girl, giggling and having the time of her life.

So then I went home and had a good, long cry…because obviously my baby didn't need me as much as I still needed her. :)

So see, Phyllis—both Julia AND you will be just fine. I promise.

Love,
Dulcie

From:	P. Lorimer <phyllis.lorimer@geemail.com>
To:	Dulcie Huckleberry
	<dulcie@homemakerinteriors.com>
Subject:	Thanks

I gave up and called the school and did pretty much what you did with the secretary—asked her if someone could check on Julia. Our secretary was just as good a sport as yours. She told me Julia was in front of the room reading *If You Give A Moose A Muffin* to the rest of the class, just like we do it at home, complete with the "And what do you suppose will happen next?" shtick that I started with her.

First day at school and already leading the class! That's MY GIRL! :)

Phyllis

From:	Dulcie Huckleberry
	<dulcie@homemakerinteriors.com>
To:	P. Lorimer <phyllis.lorimer@geemail.com>
Subject:	Re: Thanks

LOL! That's terrific. Kindergarten today, grad school tomorrow. Go get a latte or something—you deserve it! Dulcie

From:	Kristina Shaw <krissyshaw@loopy.com>
To:	Hannah Farrell
	<boazsmom@farrellfamilylovesjesus.net>
Subject:	My class schedule

Hi from Maine! This is the week I'm staying with Lissa, my friend from the Hawaii trip. We're having a great time. Just about ready to zip off to a real, live clambake so can't write too much.

But I had to tell you—I'm so excited! I get to take zoology this fall. Usually you can't get into the class until your junior year, but Dr. Talbot recommended they let me in. She's the professor who coordinated our Hawaii project this summer and she's fabulous! She's even going to help me get an internship this next summer—maybe working with whales!

It's so weird—I e-mail you about zoology and whales, and you e-mail me about how your boobs hurt from nursing Boaz. I just love him, you know that. But I can't imagine being a mom already! The whole world feels like it's mine to explore. I wouldn't want to be stuck changing diapers just yet. But I know it's what you've always wanted, so I'm glad for you.

Off to bake clams, or whatever it is they do here…

Luv ya!

Krissy

From:	Hannah Farrell
	<boazsmom@farrellfamilylovesjesus.net>
To:	P. Lorimer <phyllis.lorimer@geemail.com>
Subject:	Advice please

Hey Phyllis,

Since you've been like all nice to me and everything the last couple of weeks, I thought maybe you could give me some suggestions about what to do with Boaz. I keep trying to get him to stop sucking his thumb, but he tears off the little socks on his hands. He won't take his binkie, either. I just know he's going to end up with buck teeth and braces if I don't get him to quit!

Hope u r having a good day.

Hannah

From:	Hannah Farrell
	<boazsmom@farrellfamilylovesjesus.net>
To:	P. Lorimer <phyllis.lorimer@geemail.com>
Subject:	Forgot

Sorry to bother you again, but I also meant to ask you if you had any good ideas for how to talk to Bradley about maybe letting me take some classes at our community college. Since you had to go through all that with your husband, I figure you know all the tricks to getting him to give you what you want.

Thanks,

Hannah

From:	Marianne Hausten
	\<confidentmom@nebweb.net\>
To:	SAHM I Am \<sahmiam@loophole.com\>
Subject:	**[SAHM I AM] Supersonic Hearing**

I was at playgroup this morning, upstairs with the other moms. The kids were playing in the basement. I made a simple remark to the mom sitting next to me.

"Looks like it's almost time to get going."

I promise you—the mom sitting at the other end of the room didn't hear me. But soon there was a rumbling on the steps, and Neil stormed into the room.

"Don't want get going! No get going!"

How on EARTH did that child hear that from all the way in the basement? And yet when I tell him time for bed, he acts stone-deaf! This is a truly amazing feat, I tell you. My child has supersonic hearing. He's like Larry-Boy with suction-cup ears—latching on to the faintest whisper if he thinks it's something that might have to do with him.

Anyway, he was going into tantrum mode, so I took him into the kitchen and scolded him for being rude and for whining. Then I told him he had five more minutes to play and get toys put away. Not that he understands time or anything, but it usually helps him get ready to leave so we don't have as many problems.

The minute he scampered downstairs, one of the moms said to me, "You know, I don't think he was really being rude. He's just a boy, and they're rough-and-tumble. You don't want to try to teach him to be too polite—you'll emasculate him."

Another one chimed in with "And you can't expect boys to be as compliant as girls, either. They're made to challenge authority and be aggressive. This is your first boy, but you'll find out really fast that they're just not like girls."

I should have told them I think they're full of it. But I just hate confronting! So I just nodded and gathered my stuff and my children to leave.

They're not right, are they? I haven't ever raised a boy before. Do I have to let my son be a jerk in order for him to be a "real" guy?

And speaking of supersonic hearing! They somehow managed to continue their own conversations and listen to my discussion with my child in the kitchen. Then they butted in even though they don't really know anything about how Brandon and I have decided to raise our kids. I think that took a lot of nerve!

I just wish I'd had the nerve to say so to them.

Marianne

From:	Zelia Muzuwa <zeemuzu@vivacious.com>
To:	SAHM I Am <sahmiam@loophole.com>
Subject:	Re: [SAHM I AM] Supersonic Hearing

Hey Marianne,

About that supersonic hearing—amazing gift, isn't it? Comes and goes. Wish Tristan had it sometimes.

Speaking of, I think your playgroup moms are full of it, too. Tristan is EXTREMELY well-mannered. If he ever tried something like that, I bet his mother would have said something like, "And you, young man…you think someone made you a prince? You think you can snap a finger and stomp your feet and we all come running? I have some news for you—you are nobody's prince, and if you keep acting in such a way, never will you be, either." And even though a two-year-old wouldn't understand all the words, there'd be NO mistaking her meaning. She's even better at being intimidating than Tristan is!

There's nothing remotely effeminate about Tristan, either. (Good heavens, no! *blush*) So I think he's pretty good proof that you can raise a polite, well-mannered son who is ALL hunky, yummy man. In fact, the manners make him just that much hotter. Oh my, yes, some woman is going to REALLY thank you for that someday.

Z (who is now wishing it was closer to 6:00 p.m. when Polite Hottie gets home instead of only 11:42 a.m. and time to fix lunch for my own two-year-old son)

From:	Marianne Hausten
	<confidentmom@nebweb.net>
To:	SAHM I Am <sahmiam@loophole.com>
Subject:	Re: [SAHM I AM] Supersonic Hearing

Thanks, Z, but I do NOT want to even think about Neil in terms of being anyone's hottie. EWWWWW!!! He's my baby!
Marianne

From:	Zelia Muzuwa <zeemuzu@vivacious.com>
To:	SAHM I Am <sahmiam@loophole.com>
Subject:	Re: [SAHM I AM] Supersonic Hearing

LOL, Marianne! I understand, babe, but you're going to wake up someday and find it happened without you even knowing when. Might as well get used to the idea now.
Z

☺**Instant Message**
HannieBananie: Hey Phyllis! Did you have a chance to look at my emails yet? I saw you were online, and I thought we could chat.
PhyllisLorimer is working on the Graduate Paper From Hades.
HannieBananie: R U trying 2 avoid me? I thought we were going 2 B friends.

☺Instant Message

PhyllisLorimer: Dulcie, could you please IM or email Hannah and explain to her that I HAVE to finish my paper by 5:00 p.m. tomorrow and can't chat or email right now? I've been sort of avoiding her because if I start talking to her I know I won't get her to leave me alone.

Dulcet: Tired of your new little buddy already? :)

PhyllisLorimer: That's not what I mean. Please help me! I don't want to hurt her feelings, but she's asking me for advice and information I don't have time to give right now. Maybe you can help her with it. I'll forward the emails to you.

Dulcet: Why me? She doesn't even like me!

PhyllisLorimer: Because she likes all my other friends even less, I'm sure. Besides, you'll be patient with her. Come on...please? I'll love you forever.

Dulcet: That would be a better incentive if it weren't already the case. :) All right, fine. Send me the emails and I'll see what I can do.

PhyllisLorimer: THANK YOU!!!

From:	bellasmom16425870@loopy.com
To:	VIM <vivalaveronica@marcelloportraits.com>
Subject:	**Bella's Birthday Party**

Dear Veronica,

This is Bella's mom. You left us a voice message a few days ago about Bella's party. I'm sorry if your daughter felt like

Bella "stole" her idea for a birthday party. I'm sure Bella would never do that. Maybe Ashley simply felt envious that Bella had come up with the idea for a limo party and told a little fib about it. You know how girls can be at that age.

It just so happens that Bella had the idea for a limo party months ago. We had this planned since the beginning of summer. I'm sorry Ashley was disappointed, but that's how it goes. I suppose she could always have her own limo party for her birthday, but it seems as if that's not "cool" right now to copy birthday party ideas. Crazy, huh?

I hope this all won't keep Ashley from coming to the party. I know Bella has been looking forward to having her come.

See you soon!

Jennifer Sanderson

From:	VIM <vivalaveronica@marcelloportraits.com>
To:	SAHM I Am <sahmiam@loophole.com>
Subject:	[SAHM I AM] Birthday Party Update 2— Declaration of War!

See the attached message from Bella's mom. That lying, conniving, manipulative little viper! She accused MY daughter of "fibbing"! When Ashley told Bella about her limo party idea, Bella had to ask Ashley what a limo was! Not the sharpest crayon in the box, that child. Absolute nonsense that she "had the idea months ago."

Okay, fine. No limo party for Ashley. Who wants to ride around in a boring old limo anyway?

I'm telling you, this means WAR. Ashley is going to have the mother of all creative, fun birthday parties if I have to take out a second mortgage on our house to do it! Jennifer Sanderson will be wishing she never even thought of pinching our idea by the time we get done with this celebration! Sorry, Iona—I agree with you in principle, but this goes beyond merely the lessons of childhood.

Off to strategize with Ashley…I'll let you know what we come up with!

Veronica

From:	Dulcie Huckleberry
	<dulcie@homemakerinteriors.com>
To:	"Green Eggs and Ham"; Thomas Huckleberry
	<t.huckleberry@showme.com>
Subject:	**Why do we do that?**

This thing with Veronica and the birthday parties—is it a psychological response to being shut in the house too long, breathing dirty diaper and baby food fumes? We've become the SAHM equivalent to *Lord of the Flies*. It's starting to scare me—we're all a bit mentally imbalanced, ready to attack and eat each other over the most unimportant things.

So if I start running around wielding a spear, please forgive me. It just means I've been stuck on my island a bit too long.

Dulcie

From:	Dulcie Huckleberry
	<dulcie@homemakerinteriors.com>
To:	Hannah Farrell
	<boazsmom@farrellfamilylovesjesus.net>
Subject:	Phyllis sent me

Hi Hannah,

Phyllis said you'd had several questions for her. She's working REALLY hard on a paper for her class—the one with the awful professor—and so she asked me to help you out. I thought maybe you'd like to chat in the chat room this evening? Or whenever you're available. Just let me know.

Dulcie

From:	Hannah Farrell
	<boazsmom@farrellfamilylovesjesus.net>
To:	Dulcie Huckleberry
	<dulcie@homemakerinteriors.com>
Subject:	Re: Phyllis sent me

Thanks, Dulcie, but I don't think I feel all that welcome in the chat room. I think I'll just wait for Phyllis to get done with her big important paper. My questions about taking care of my child obviously aren't as high a priority as her education.

Hannah

From:	Dulcie Huckleberry
	<dulcie@homemakerinteriors.com>
To:	P. Lorimer <phyllis.lorimer@geemail.com>
Subject:	**Hannah**

Your little "let's be friends with Hannah" project? Yeah. Good luck with that. She's being a big baby. I say let her figure out how to stop sucking her own thumb before she worries about Boaz's.

Hope your paper is going well.

Dulcie

From:	Rosalyn Ebberly <prov31woman@home.com>
To:	
Subject:	**DRAFT email to Chad**

Dear Chad,

This is my homework assignment for counseling today. Shelley was talking to me about being assertive, instead of aggressive or passive-aggressive. ~~She seems to think~~ I ~~should think about~~ ~~probably need to~~ am going to work on that.

~~Of course, it would help~~ ~~I'd rather~~ ~~if you weren't so~~ I feel that you are ~~dead-set on~~ ~~stubbornly determined to being mulish about~~ firmly decided on quitting counseling.

~~It's always about you and your needs. What about what I need?~~

I ~~sense that~~ ~~figure~~ ~~suppose~~ understand that you feel ~~this~~

~~completely unreasonable aversion to actually improving our marriage, and instead are intent on sabotaging every step forward that we've made in the last two years just because you despise sitting in Shelley's office week after week having to admit where you've been wrong in our relationship instead of being able to just gripe about all my shortcomings which admittedly I have a lot of~~ tired.

~~You always act like I'm~~ I don't ~~think~~ ~~feel~~ agree that I'm too dependent on Shelley. ~~The thing you don't seem to get is~~ ~~I'm sorry but~~ ~~Why can't you understand~~ I have realized that ~~I need her~~ ~~I need help~~ I benefit from our sessions. ~~She's showing me~~ I'm ~~finally coming to understand things about myself that I never knew for all those years. I'm learning and growing, and hopefully~~ changing ~~if you hadn't noticed~~ ~~not that you seem to care~~

Hang it all.

From:	Rosalyn Ebberly <prov31woman@home.com>
To:	SAHM I Am <sahmiam@loophole.com>
Subject:	[SAHM I AM] TOTW
	September 7: Being Assertive

Look up "assertiveness" on Google and figure it out for yourselves. I'm done.

Rosalyn Ebberly

SAHM I Am Loop Moderator

"The wise woman builds her house, but the foolish tears it down with her own hands." Proverbs 14:1 (NASB)

From:	P. Lorimer <phyllis.lorimer@geemail.com>
To:	"Green Eggs and Ham"
Subject:	**Frustrated!**

All I wanted was to help pay for my education. That is the only reason I ever applied for a Graduate Teaching Assistant position.

So now I get told by my beloved advisor that as a GTA, I need to make sure to schedule office hours on either Monday or Wednesday evening, since I have a class on Tuesday and Thursday, and I'm required to offer a certain number of evening hours and Friday is pretty much pointless since no one would come on a Friday night anyway.

The problem is that Mondays are our "Sabbath" day. Since Sundays really are a workday for any pastoring family, most of us take Mondays as our day off. Jonathan and I decided from the start that Mondays were strictly NOT available for anything but family. We've had to bend that a little bit when I have a Monday class. But I'm trying to avoid putting too much on Mondays.

That leaves Wednesday, which has traditionally been a "family night" at church. I've led a women's Bible study that evening for several years. I tried to explain this to my advisor. I should have saved my breath.

"You are being employed by the university. I think that your obligations to us far outweigh some 'women's Bible study.'"

She spit that last part out with the same contempt that Bennet spits out lettuce and green beans. I should have known better than to mention exactly what the time conflict involved!

The worst part is that she's right. As much as I don't like it, I do have a contractual obligation to the university. So I chose Wednesday nights.

When I called our women's ministry director to tell her, you would have thought I'd announced to her that I was leaving the study in order to pursue employment as a stripper or something.

"It seems to me that your first obligation is to the church, Phyllis. What do you think Jesus would say about you choosing secular instruction over spiritual instruction?"

I didn't tell her what I thought Jesus would say, because I had a feeling my response would have been mostly Phyllis and not so much Jesus.

Is it too much to ask the warring forces NOT to put me in the middle of their mutual hatefest?

Phyllis

From:	Zelia Muzuwa <zeemuzu@vivacious.com>
To:	"Green Eggs and Ham"
Subject:	Re: Frustrated!

Sorry, babe! That stinks. Can Jonathan call off your women's ministry director for you?

Z

From:	P. Lorimer <phyllis.lorimer@geemail.com>
To:	"Green Eggs and Ham"
Subject:	**Re: Frustrated!**

He probably could if I asked him to. But I don't want to do that. I know it's silly of me, but with my advisor digging at me every chance she gets about how we married women (pastors' wives especially) have no life outside our husband, and are so dependent, etc., etc....well, I just can't quite bring myself to prove her even a tiny bit right by asking Jonathan to solve this problem for me.

It's a pride issue, I know. And I shouldn't let her get to me. But sometimes I wonder if maybe she's right—in some small way. Maybe I do rely too much on him. So I just want to see if I can manage this one myself.
Phyllis

From:	The Millards
	<jstcea4jesus@familymail.net>
To:	SAHM I Am <sahmiam@loophole.com>
Subject:	**[SAHM I AM] Retreat**

Hi Loopers!
Hope you've marked your calendars for March 18–21 when we all meet in Colorado Springs to hang out for the weekend! We'll be getting total costs to you as soon as we can.

We were thinking… Wouldn't it be fun if we had just a couple of presentations at the retreat, like little workshops on being a stay-at-home mom? Would you guys be interested in something like that? Nothing complicated or overly structured—we're still going mainly to spend time together. But since we're there, and I'm sure we all have a lot of the same questions, we thought why not do a little teaching time if people are interested?

Let's talk about that, okay?

Jocelyn

From:	Brenna L. <saywhat@writeme.com>
To:	SAHM I Am <sahmiam@loophole.com>
Subject:	**Re: [SAHM I AM] Retreat**

I think a couple of workshops would be great. Here's my list:

1) Better housecleaning—so I don't feel like I have to do it every day.

2) Dealing with in-laws—especially ones that live on the opposite end of the driveway and co-own the farm you work for a living.

3) Talking to spouses about difficult topics—like his critical attitude toward his son.

4) Recognizing potential health or development problems in our kids and how to get help—like when that son is falling further behind every single day.

Any of those spark some ideas?

Brenna

From:	Dulcie Huckleberry
	<dulcie@homemakerinteriors.com>
To:	SAHM I Am <sahmiam@loophole.com>
Subject:	Re: [SAHM I AM] Retreat

Hey Brenna, sorry to hear little Pat is still having some problems!

I think maybe we should have workshops for those of us who are trying to work from home. Stuff on business topics like taxes and managing a home office when you have clients and you don't want them seeing your kids' toys and dirty dishes all over.

Dulcie

From:	VIM <vivalaveronica@marcelloportraits.com>
To:	SAHM I Am <sahmiam@loophole.com>
Subject:	Re: [SAHM I AM] Retreat

Those are terrific ideas, y'all! Maybe we could have some workshops on how to deal with kids at certain ages—like terrible twos, terrible tweens and terrible teens?

Sure could use the advice!

Veronica

From:	Iona James
	<poetsmystique@brokenwrenchandcopperbucket.com>
To:	SAHM I Am <sahmiam@loophole.com>
Subject:	Re: [SAHM I AM] Retreat

Hello everyone,

This is starting to sound like so much fun, but couldn't we keep this retreat simple and uncluttered? That is how my soul recharges, anyway. We can always learn from books and teachers, but the chance to connect with our friends is rare indeed.

Your friend in spirit,

Iona James

From:	Zelia Muzuwa <zeemuzu@vivacious.com>
To:	Dorian Keller <d.keller@Paeninnashealth.com>
Subject:	Mental Health Services
	Pre-Approval #51862439665B

Dear Mr. Keller:

I'm writing in regards to Paeninnas Health Insurance of Maryland's denial of our request for mental health services for our two children. We would like for them to be approved to visit Dr. Jamison at the Attachment and Post Trauma Adoption Clinic in Baltimore. Our request for approval has been denied, and we would like further explanation on this as quickly as possible.

Thank you,

Zelia Muzuwa

From:	Dorian Keller <d.keller@Paeninnashealth.com>
To:	Zelia Muzuwa <zeemuzu@vivacious.com>
Subject:	**Mental Health Services**
	Pre-Approval #51862439665B

Dear Mr. Muzuwa:

Thank you for contacting Paeninnas Health Insurance of Maryland. You are a valued member of our health family. In order to answer your question, I need the Mental Health Services Pre-Approval number from your Pre-Approval Form. Once I have that number, I can look up the account info and respond to your question.

Thank you,

Dorian Keller,

Pre-Approval Claims Representative

Paeninnas Health Insurance of Maryland

From:	Zelia Muzuwa <zeemuzu@vivacious.com>
To:	Dorian Keller <d.keller@Paeninnashealth.com>
Subject:	**Re: Mental Health Services**
	Pre-Approval #51862439665B

Dear Mr. Keller,

I am a female. It's "Ms. Muzuwa." And would the Mental Health Services Pre-Approval Number be that long one I put in the subject heading of the e-mail? The one labeled "Mental Health Services Pre-Approval Number" #51862439665B?

The sooner we can settle this, the better. My children's appointment is next week and it took nearly six months to get an appointment, so we need to have this settled before Tuesday, September 15.

Thank you,

Zelia Muzuwa

From:	Dorian Keller <d.keller@Paeninnashealth.com>
To:	Zelia Muzuwa <zeemuzu@vivacious.com>
Subject:	**Mental Health Services** **Pre-Approval #51862439665B**

Dear Mr. Muzuwa:

Thank you for contacting Paeninnas Health Insurance of Maryland. You are a valued member of our health family. In order to assist you with Pre-Approval #51862439665B, I need to know what your question is about the Pre-Approval request. Please e-mail me with that information at your convenience.

Sincerely,

Dorian Keller,

Pre-Approval Claims Representative

Paeninnas Health Insurance of Maryland

From:	Zelia Muzuwa \<zeemuzu@vivacious.com>
To:	Dorian Keller \<d.keller@Paeninnashealth.com>
Subject:	**Re: Mental Health Services**
	Pre-Approval #51862439665B

Dear Ms. Keller:

Apparently, you did not keep my original e-mail. I'm cutting and pasting it below:

< I'm writing in regards to Paeninnas Health Insurance of Maryland's denial of our request for mental health services for our two children. We would like for them to be approved to visit Dr. Jamison at the Attachment and Post Trauma Adoption Clinic in Baltimore. Our request for approval has been denied, and we would like further explanation on this as quickly as possible.>

Thank you,

Zelia Muzuwa

From:	Dorian Keller \<d.keller@Paeninnashealth.com>
To:	Zelia Muzuwa \<zeemuzu@vivacious.com>
Subject:	**Mental Health Services**
	Pre-Approval #51862439665B

Dear Mr. Muzuwa:

Our records indicate that you are not the primary insurance-holder on the account. We will need to have a signed affidavit from Tristan Muzuwa giving you permission to make decisions for the account. I will be happy to fax this form to you or mail it if you will send me either a fax number or your mailing address.

Thank you for contacting Paeninnas Health Insurance of Maryland. You are a valued member of our health family.
Sincerely,
Dorian Keller

From:	Zelia Muzuwa <zeemuzu@vivacious.com>
To:	Dorian Keller <d.keller@Paeninnashealth.com>
Subject:	Re: Mental Health Services Pre-Approval #51862439665B

Dear Miss Keller:
Considering we have been with your insurance company for EIGHT years now, and I have called before on other matters, I find it very strange that you now need a signed affidavit in order to reply to a simple request for information. I am NOT feeling like a "valued member of your health family" at all.

My husband, Tristan Muzuwa, is on his way to your office at this moment to sign the affidavit, and then we are expecting to receive our information immediately following that.
Sincerely,
Zelia Muzuwa

⌨Text Message From Tristan Muzuwa: For Zelia Muzuwa

——September 9/11:48 a.m.——
Still at ins. co. Am #846, currently serving #825. Taking rest of day off. Will be here long time.

📧Text Message From Zelia Muzuwa: For Tristan Muzuwa
——September 9/11:49 a.m.——
Ths is ridiculous! Wnt company?

📧Text Message From Tristan Muzuwa: For Zelia Muzuwa
——September 9/11:50 a.m.——
No. Stay home. I know your bad temper.

📧Text Message From Zelia Muzuwa: For Tristan Muzuwa
——September 9/11:51 a.m.——
I can b good when I try!

📧Text Message From Tristan Muzuwa: For Zelia Muzuwa
——September 9/2:15 p.m.——
Just got done. They will email you with explanation.

📧Text Message From Zelia Muzuwa: For Tristan Muzuwa
——September 9/2:19 p.m.——
they kept u 4 nearly 3 hours! we should lodge a complaint! worst customer service EVER! Outrageous!

📧Text Message From Tristan Muzuwa: For Zelia Muzuwa
——September 9/2:22 p.m.——

This is why I said stay home, love. Good part is that I have rest of p.m. off now. No children. Can vent our angst together. Yes?

▭Text Message From Zelia Muzuwa: For Tristan Muzuwa
——September 9/2:22 p.m.——
OH YES.

From:	Dorian Keller <d.keller@Paeninnashealth.com>
To:	Zelia Muzuwa <zeemuzu@vivacious.com>
Subject:	**Mental Health Services** **Pre-Approval #51862439665B**

Dear Mr. Muzuwa:

Your approval request was denied because Attachment Disorder is not on Paeninnas Health's list of approved services that we cover. We suggest that you work with your family physician for a referral to one of our approved providers and to receive a diagnosis from among the ones on our approved list.

Thank you for contacting us. You are a valued member of our health family.

Sincerely,

Dorian Keller,

Pre-Approval Claims Representative

Paeninnas Health Insurance of Maryland

From:	Zelia Muzuwa <zeemuzu@vivacious.com>
To:	Dorian Keller <d.keller@Paeninnashealth.com>
Subject:	Re: Mental Health Services
	Pre-Approval #51862439665B

Mr. Keller:

First of all, I AM A WOMAN! "Zelia" is a female name, not a man's name! I am "Ms." Or "Mrs." Hey, I'll even take a "Miss" at this point!

Second, what do you mean you don't cover attachment disorder!!! After the runaround you have given us? The "can't find your number" "can't find your e-mail" "need to sign an affidavit" nonsense—THEN you tell me it's not an approved diagnosis? As if I'm shopping for a pair of shoes or something!

Reactive Attachment Disorder is a legitimate mental disorder! My children are hoarding food, freaking out in grocery stores, destroying their sibling's toys, lying and can't even give us hugs without going nearly catatonic. We need help before they tear apart our family. You can't deny us that help just because you don't approve of the diagnosis!

Please, I'm begging you. We need this coverage. We need to make this appointment.

And if this is how you treat "members" of your "health family" I'd hate to see how you treat nonrelatives.

Zelia Muzuwa

From:	Dorian Keller <d.keller@Paeninnashealth.com>
To:	Zelia Muzuwa <zeemuzu@vivacious.com>
Subject:	**Mental Health Services**
	Pre-Approval #51862439665B

Dear Mr. Muzuwa:

I understand your concern. Please know you are a valued member of our health family. I have spoken with my department supervisor, and he said that if you change the diagnosis to "Developmental Trauma Disorder" it will meet our approval requirements.

However, I also am noting that you have used up your available Mental Health Service Visits for the year. This will mean you are not eligible for Mental Health Service Coverage until the start of the next calendar year. Please plan accordingly when you choose your mental health services for next year.

You are always welcome to visit the health provider of your choice, regardless of coverage. We cannot prevent you from receiving care for any health issue you desire. But in order to provide the highest quality service to all our health family, we have to enforce the limitations of your particular plan. We regret the inconvenience this may have caused you.

Sincerely,

Dorian Keller,

Pre-Approval Claims Representative

Paeninnas Health Insurance of Maryland

From:	Zelia Muzuwa <zeemuzu@vivacious.com>
To:	SAHM I Am <sahmiam@loophole.com>
Subject:	Slow typing for a while

Hey everyone,

Fractured my right wrist yesterday while throwing a temper tantrum about our insurance company. Long story—wrist too sore to tell you right now. Had to go to emergency room, and have a soft cast for next six weeks.

Just got e-mail today from insurance company. Cut and pasted here:

<Dear Mr. Muzuwa:

Regarding Emergency Care Claim #5987123406346478C: This claim is denied because Paeninnas Health Insurance of Maryland does not cover out-of-network emergency room visits. We regret the inconvenience this may have caused you, and we encourage you to choose in-network facilities for your next emergency care visit.

Thank you for doing business with us. You are a valued member of our health family.>

I'd cry, but it makes my wrist hurt too bad. There had better be a special place reserved in the Land of Fire and Brimstone especially for insurance companies. And in the meantime, I really hope and pray that somehow we can afford to get our kids to the Attachment Specialist next week.

Z

From:	Rosalyn Ebberly <prov31woman@home.com>
To:	SAHM I Am <sahmiam@loophole.com>
Subject:	**[SAHM I AM] TOTW**
	September 21: Killing Comparisons

Dear SAHMurais,

Thanks to the enlightening insights of my counselor—despite the fact that Chad has indeed decided to quit going to our sessions—I have come to see the danger of the Comparison Enemy.

This silent killer ruins our own lives and happiness by polluting them with thoughts about how much better other people are. We MUST attack and destroy this enemy of comparison!

I never before realized how much I do this. I have learned it's a harmful game to play, even when you feel like you are coming out on top. So I've come up with a way to destroy once and for all the comparisons that make me feel inadequate or inferior to others—or at least I hope this will work.

What I have done is use pictures or written descriptions of the people in my life who I compare myself to. Then I wrote down how I compare myself to them and why they make me feel inadequate. I put it all into a little booklet—using the finest handmade paper and environmentally responsible soy ink, complete with the photos and/or illustrations and thoughts from me. I have even hand-bound the pages together. It's now a handsome little folio. I call it my Comparison Hall of Shame.

Now, I am about to take the sharpest knife I own and

PLUNGE it into this book! I'm going to hack away at all the pages until every last photo is mutilated beyond recognition. I'm going to slash away at each and every word until there are none left to accuse me!!! I WILL MAIM AND DESTROY WITHOUT MERCY EVERY LAST COMPARISON!

brb.

Ahhhh, that felt good! But I'm not yet done.

Now, I'm going to throw all the shreds and scraps of my once-beautiful book INTO MY FIREPLACE! The pieces ignite and fire laps them up, making them glow and curl and blacken! I am visualizing myself free from the chains of comparison! My spirit SOARS on the wings of newfound confidence!!!

Slight mishap just now…the flue didn't open properly and we now have smoke all over our living room. Chad is going to be furious!

I will let you know how it goes the rest of the week. In the meantime, feel free to share your inadequacies and what you're doing about them.

Confidently yours,

Rosalyn Ebberly

SAHM I Am Loop Moderator

"The wise woman builds her house, but the foolish tears it down with her own hands." Proverbs 14:1 (NASB)

From:	Brenna L. <saywhat@writeme.com>
To:	SAHM I Am <sahmiam@loophole.com>
Subject:	**Re: [SAHM I AM] TOTW**
	September 21: Killing Comparisons

So, Ros, who was in your book? We want to know who you symbolically murdered. Anybody we know?

Brenna

From:	Rosalyn Ebberly <prov31woman@home.com>
To:	SAHM I Am <sahmiam@loophole.com>
Subject:	**Re: [SAHM I AM] TOTW**
	September 21: Killing Comparisons

I am not telling who was in my book. And it was NOT symbolic murder! What an awful idea! It was a spiritual and psychological exercise is all. And it was private, so as far as you are all concerned, NO—nobody you know.

Rosalyn

SAHM I Am Loop Moderator

"The wise woman builds her house, but the foolish tears it down with her own hands." Proverbs 14:1 (NASB)

From:	Brenna L. \<saywhat@writeme.com\>
To:	"Green Eggs and Ham"
Subject:	**Re: [SAHM I AM] TOTW**
	September 21: Killing Comparisons

Definitely somebody we know, or she wouldn't be so reluctant to tell us who. The whole loop is buzzing about it—I've gotten a bunch of e-mails. They're all speculating about which one of us was in her book.

Who do you think? Who in the world could possibly make Rosalyn Ebberly feel inadequate? I think we need to find out! Imagine how much confidence that person would get from that knowledge. Being able to intimidate The Great and Mighty Roz. Who would have thought that was even possible?

Brenna

☺**Instant Message**

ZeeMuzzy: you're joking, right?

Farmgirl04: About?

ZeeMuzzy: being interested in rosalyn's stupid little book.

Farmgirl04: I don't know. I think it's interesting. Half-joking, maybe.

ZeeMuzzy: i think rosalyn gets far too much of our attention.

Farmgirl04: I know you do. But you're bitter and jaded. :) Besides, it's a nice distraction from the doctor's appointment hanging over my head.

ZeeMuzzy: what appointment is that?

Farmgirl04: For Little Pat. To figure out why he's so far behind. I'd rather drag Darren in to a shrink and have his head checked—his attitude toward Pat is getting worse all the time. Makes me SO mad!

ZeeMuzzy: kids with problems can really stress out a family. i should know.

Farmgirl04: That reminds me—were you able to work out the appointment with the attachment specialist for your kids?

ZeeMuzzy: not exactly. the insurance company refused to find a way to grant us more visits. so we're stuck until the end of the year.

Farmgirl04: That's rotten.

ZeeMuzzy: yeah, but it turned out okay after all. somebody anonymously paid for the doctor's visit.

Farmgirl04: WOW! Any idea who it was?

ZeeMuzzy: no, but whoever it was is my hero. i betcha it was someone from our church. we were on their prayer list about it.

Farmgirl04: That's great.

ZeeMuzzy: the specialist was hugely helpful. and thanks to our anonymous donor, we'll be getting weekly appointments for both lishan and duri through the end of the year. after that, if they still need therapy, i guess we'll have to work out a payment plan with the doctor after we use up our allotted visits. i'm just relieved we were able to get them in and onto his patient roster.

Farmgirl04: So you think the doctor can help with their problems?

ZeeMuzzy: yeah. we found out that they've made a LOT of progress in understanding attachment problems in the last 20 years. most kids that have been in orphanages have had some amount of trauma that can make them have a hard time adjusting after they're adopted. i just wish we hadn't waited so long to get help. i kept thinking all i had to do was give them more love and attention. but that wasn't enough. and now our other kids are going to need some help, too.

Farmgirl04: I'm sorry. I wish there was more I could do to help.

ZeeMuzzy: hey, where would i be without my brenna-buddy? :) i'm just SO relieved to know there's something that can be done—i'm practically giddy!

Farmgirl04: I hope things go as well for Little Pat.

ZeeMuzzy: me, too. hey, i need to scoot. you've got enough to think about—don't add rosalyn's neuroses to the mix, okay?

Farmgirl04: Yes ma'am.

ZeeMuzzy signed off at 4:18:12 p.m.

Farmgirl04 signed off at 4:18:35 p.m.

From:	The Millards
	\<jstcea4jesus@familymail.net\>
To:	SAHM I Am \<sahmiam@loophole.com\>
Subject:	[SAHM I AM] Wanna do a workshop at the retreat?

Gals,

We've decided to definitely do workshops at our retreat in March. So we're opening it up for applications. If you have something you want to teach, then e-mail your ideas to me, and Rosalyn and I will put together the schedule.

You'd all better be glad I'm working with Ros because otherwise you'd be filling out a TEN-page workshop application! :)

We are going to have a BLAST! I'm getting so excited about this.

Jocelyn Millard

From:	Zelia Muzuwa <zeemuzu@vivacious.com>
To:	The Millards
	<jstcea4jesus@familymail.net>
Subject:	**Workshop ideas**

Jocelyn,

I'm taking a stab at the whole workshop idea thing. I was skeptical at first, but this might end up being really great for everyone. Sorry I've been such a brat about everything lately. The stress of dealing with Lishan and Duri was really getting to me. It wasn't supposed to be like this. We were supposed to come home with two adorable children who were happy to have a real family. And they are adorable, and at times they are happy, too. But we weren't prepared for the intensity of their problems.

I'm just relieved that we're finally getting some help. And

I know I should let the whole Rosalyn incident go. But...I'm just not there yet. I'm glad you've stuck by me, even though I've been a big grouch. Sounds like you're doing a rock-awesome job on the retreat so far. I'm looking forward to coming.

Suggestions for workshops:

1) Fun ways to get your kids involved in art.

2) Tax information for work-at-home parents. Since Tristan is a CPA, he would help me put this one together, and be available by phone to answer any questions afterward.

3) Unschooling—remember we used to do that before Tristan insisted on putting the kids into private school? Anyway, I thought it would be fun to do a workshop on it, to explain what it is and the benefits, etc.

Hope one of those will work for you.

Z

From:	The Millards
	\<jstcea4jesus@familymail.net\>
To:	Zelia Muzuwa \<zeemuzu@vivacious.com\>
Subject:	Re: Workshop ideas

Hey girl,

No apology necessary. Your family is going through some rough times, and you can always count on me to be your friend. Love you!!!

Thanks for the workshop ideas. We'll let everyone know what we come up with.

I'm praying that God helps you find a way to work through the issue with Rosalyn. It happened over a year ago—and she really is trying to make changes in her life. I'm sorry it was so painful for you. Don't you think it's time to let God do a little healing for it, though?

Much love,

Jocelyn

From:	VIM <vivalaveronica@marcelloportraits.com>
To:	SAHM I Am <sahmiam@loophole.com>
Subject:	[SAHM I AM] Ashley's birthday party

Yep, it's time for another chapter in the Ashley's Birthday Party Saga. In our previous episodes, twelve-year-old Ashley was angsting over what to do for her birthday party. One "friend" stole her limo party idea, with her parents as accomplices! So now, it's up to us to defend our daughter's party reputation and come up with something truly memorable.

I think we finally done it! We kept it top secret. We didn't even tell y'all, in case there's a birthday party mole among us, waiting to snatch innocent children's unique party ideas. But the invitations went out today, so we decided to lift the ban of secrecy.

We decided who wants to do a dumb old limo ride

anyway? What will REALLY impress those conniving, idea-thieving parents is…A MEDITERRANEAN CRUISE!

Now, we don't quite have that much money to cart a bunch of squealing teen girls to the real Mediterranean. But since we live in Houston, right near the Gulf, it was a fairly simple (albeit pricey) job to rent a yacht for a couple of days. The girls are going to go on a "cruise"—complete with cruise-type food and on-board entertainment in the form of a local boy band (the girls will be drooling over the lead singer), who will be locked in their cabin at all times if they're not performing.

Then, they'll end up on a little island owned by one of Frank's photography clients. We'll send hot boy band home via causeway, and then pretend that we've arrived at our port of call in Italy. This guy's got a big house that we're com-mandeering that happens to look remarkably like an Italian villa. Perfect, since Ashley is half-Italian. They'll have dinner there, and Frank will take their photos. And then they're going to get a "spa" experience, thanks to the hot tub and some of my friends who are coming to help. After that, they'll get back on the yacht and get to have a slumber party on the boat, including movies on the big-screen TV. (I'm campaigning for *Roman Holiday* with Audrey Hepburn, but Ashley's not quite old enough to appreciate classic romantic movies like that, I guess.)

Now, I'd like to see anyone top that! And it's an unsteal-able idea, too, because none of the other parents are friends with our island villa guy. HAH!

Veronica

From:	Rosalyn Ebberly <prov31woman@home.com>
To:	SAHM I Am <sahmiam@loophole.com>
Subject:	Re: [SAHM I AM] Ashley's birthday party

Funny…I thought the point of a birthday party was to celebrate the birth of a child, not to show up all the other parents.

Rosalyn

"The wise woman builds her house, but the foolish tears it down with her own hands." Proverbs 14:1 (NASB)

From:	VIM <vivalaveronica@marcelloportraits.com>
To:	SAHM I Am <sahmiam@loophole.com>
Subject:	Re: [SAHM I AM] Ashley's birthday party

Normally, sis, I'd agree with you. However, if all we wanted to do was celebrate Ashley's birth, we'd take her out to Dave and Buster's for dinner and buy her some more iTunes gift cards. And maybe a new pair of boots. She's all about boots.

But this goes way beyond a simple celebration of her birth. This is about family honor! It's about making sure our children can hold their heads high among their peers. It's about not having to listen to all the other parents brag about their birthday party triumphs and make cutting little remarks about how sad it is that our children are being so deprived.

This is war! And even though our budget may end up as the primary casualty, we are determined to do whatever it takes. Ridiculous? You betcha. But it's twenty-first century America, and we do petty, pointless things like this to make ourselves feel more courageous and important than we really are.

So onward with the parties!

Okay, okay, it's pathetic. I can't help it! I want to be the best! (If y'all notice, that's a family trait...)

Veronica

From:	Hannah Farrell
	<boazsmom@farrellfamilylovesjesus.net>
To:	P. Lorimer <phyllis.lorimer@geemail.com>
Subject:	Baby food

Hi Phyllis,

I think I did something wrong. I decided to try giving Boaz baby food for the first time. I did all this research and found out that homemade baby food is the best. And that u shouldn't start with rice 'cause it's like all hard to digest and stuff.

I've done SOOOO much research the past couple of days. I decided to start with a sweet potato puree. I followed the recipe exactly, and used organic sweet potatoes and everything. It took over an hour to steam the potato, but it's better than boiling it because it keeps all the nutrients in the potato that way.

Then I pureed it in the blender and added some breast milk until it was pretty thin. Then I put a little bit in a bowl.

I bought this special bamboo baby spoon that is ergonomic and coated with rubber. I put Boaz in his little bouncy seat…

And from there, nothing went the way it was supposed to. The books said to put just a little on the edge of the spoon and let him smell it, or rub the spoon on his gums.

So I did that, just like it said. And Boaz blew a big raspberry and sprayed the food in my face! I was just wiping it off when he got all excited and kicked his feet, hitting the bowl. It went flying—and then we BOTH were covered with sweet potato puree!

About that time, my mother showed up at the door. And after she about died laughing at the two of us wearing the puree, she cleaned Boaz up, cleaned my carpet and the bouncy seat, and then even got Boaz to eat a couple bites of the food—all while I was cleaning myself up!

I was totally embarrassed. It's MY baby—why does he cooperate for my mom better than for me? It made me feel like the babysitter when the parents come home.

And then I got an e-mail from Krissy. She won some undergrad research competition and gets a big scholarship for school next year. And meanwhile, I'm wearing sweet potato puree while my mom feeds and takes care of my baby.

Could you like maybe tell me that this is all going to get better sometime? PLEASE!

Hannah

From:	P. Lorimer <phyllis.lorimer@geemail.com>
To:	Hannah Farrell
	<boazsmom@farrellfamilylovesjesus.net>
Subject:	Re: Baby food

Dear Hannah,

I'm sorry you had such a bad day. I would imagine it was more than a little funny, though. Hopefully, you'll be able to laugh about it later…maybe MUCH later! As far as getting better…I've been told it does, though I would not be able to comment from personal experience.

Today, I arrived at first day of classes for this semester, only to discover that the professor for one class had been changed, and it is now being taught by my advisor who despises me because I'm a pastor's wife. Required class, and no way to get out of it. She seemed carnivorously happy to see me. I'm dreading the next several months!

To make it all even more fun, my phone vibrated about halfway through class. It was my daughter Julia's kinder-garten teacher. Julia was too intent on whatever activity she was doing, waited too long to go potty, and wet her pants. My husband was in back-to-back counseling appointments this morning, so I had to leave class (which didn't earn me any points with Cruella de Vil) and pick Julia up from school—where she was hiding in the nurse's office because she was so embarrassed about her "accident." I had to take her home, clean her up and give her a new outfit. She begged me not to send her back today because she's scared all the kids will laugh at her. So I skipped my other class and kept her home. I'm thinking that may have been a poor idea because now she's asking me if she can stay home tomorrow, too. And she was loving school until this happened!

So, you see, Hannah, the reason I can't say for sure if it gets better is because, while your child will learn to eat solid food, there will be just another challenge waiting for you after that. However, your mother survived you and mine survived me. So I think chances are pretty good that it DOES get better at some point. Either that, or we just get tougher.

Blessings,
Phyllis

From:	The Millards
	<jstcea4jesus@familymail.net>
To:	"Green Eggs and Ham"
Subject:	Retreat workshops!

Hey ladies,
You would not BELIEVE the number of workshop suggestions I've received this week! Of varying merits, too. I believe the weirdest suggestion award goes to one I got today called *Health Benefits to Bathing Your Child In Dark Chocolate*.

Anyway, if you guys want to get in on the fun, let me know. Z already gave me some good suggestions. Anyone else game?
Jocelyn

☺Instant Message

Dulcet: Hey Tom. How are the kids?

Huck: Hey yourself, gorgeous. Aren't you supposed to be at the library studying how Nero's wife decorated her kitchen or something?

Dulcet: "Or something." But I had to check my email—you know I'm addicted. Anyway, Jocelyn sent an email out to the loop earlier this week about doing workshops at the retreat. I was thinking I'd like to do one on starting your own business. What do you think?

Huck: I didn't think you were going to the retreat.

Dulcet: WHAT? Why wouldn't I be going to the retreat?

Huck: Well, isn't it the same weekend as my woodworking convention? I thought we both agreed on me going to that.

Dulcet: It's not the same weekend, is it?

Huck: Pretty sure it is.

Dulcet: NOOO! I didn't realize that!

Huck: Maybe they'll have it again next year.

Dulcet: I don't want to miss it THIS YEAR.

Huck: I know, but we can't both be gone. Someone has to watch the kids.

Dulcet: Why are you assuming it has to be me?

Huck: Because we already made plans for me to go to my convention.

Dulcet: But you don't understand! I've never met most of these people before, and they're my closest friends! And you've gotten to travel a lot. I hardly get to go anywhere!

Huck: So…you're asking me to cancel our pre-arranged plan of attending a convention that could help me reach some business goals of my own, just so you can hang out with your girlfriends for the weekend?

Dulcet: There's gotta be other woodworking shows around here. You could take a class or join a club or something, couldn't you?

Huck: Did you "take a class or join a club or something" in order to start your business?

Dulcet: It's not the same! That's actually providing our income and supporting the family—or it will. With you, it's just pretty much monetizing a hobby.

Huck: Gee thanks. Well, that's even more reason for you to stay home.

Dulcet: What do you mean?

Huck: First, you shouldn't be taking time off your all important JOB to go socialize with friends. After all, you have to PROVIDE for your family! We're all depending on you, oh great entrepreneur. Or are you going to let us starve in the streets so you can gab with the girls?

Dulcet: That's unfair!

Huck: It's a retreat for stay-at-home moms. You're a working mom that happens to have a home office. I don't think you qualify anymore.

Dulcet: You are being childish.

Huck: Maybe. But you know, I spend all day with children, so it's probably natural.

Dulcet: Then maybe you'd better go get your blankie and take a nap. You're cranky.

Huck: I am going to that woodworking convention. We had an agreement. We paid the registration fee. I even have a hotel reservation. I can't believe you'd be so selfish as to ask me to give that up when I have spent the last two years doing everything I could to support and encourage you with your work. I'm not giving this up.

Dulcet: You think TWO years of staying home, a year of that with me also in the house, is comparable to the YEARS I spent basically as a single parent while you traveled all the time? Whenever you want, you go over to your mom and Morris's house or hang out with Flynn or your other friends and I take over with the kids. Who spotted for me like that while you were working all the time? Don't talk to ME about being selfish, Tom. I put in my time.

Huck: Ok, fine. Nobody has suffered or endured as much as you, Dulce. Look I don't care if you go to your retreat. But you'll have to find someone to take care of the girls, because I'm holding you to your agreement—that weekend is mine, to myself. And that's something I haven't had in a LONG time. So if you want to do something, too, then you'll have to arrange childcare.

Dulcet: Fine. Now, I'd better get back to WORK. Because I'm just selfish that way—you know, wanting to provide for the family and all.

Huck: Now who's being childish? See you at home.

Dulcet signed off at 4:52:17 p.m.
Huck signed off at 4:52:55 p.m.

From:	Rosalyn Ebberly <prov31woman@home.com>
To:	SAHM I Am <sahmiam@loophole.com>
Subject:	[SAHM I AM] TOTW
	October 5: Family Meetings

Communicative Caregivers,

Our family is returning to a tradition that we used to do when the children were younger, but that we forgot as our lives grew busier—FAMILY MEETINGS. My therapist recommended that we go back to having meetings, so that we can find positive ways of dealing with life's everyday ups and downs, such as:

An eight-year-old son who has got into four fights since June and is in danger of being expelled;

A nine-year-old daughter who has started stressing about whether or not she's gaining weight and if her jeans make her look fat;

A six-year-old daughter who is very intelligent, but so worried about failure that she threw a two-hour temper tantrum because she didn't know how to spell the word *coelenterate;*

A dad who is discouraged about counseling and quit going and is threatening to stop paying for the rest of the family to go because he didn't get the results he was hoping for;

A mom who just wants to be happy and wants her family to be happy, and who is starting to care less and less about what other people think about them or about being the "best" family in the world. She just wants them to STAY a family.

These are just typical examples, you know, of the sort of thing your average family faces every single day.

We're going to be using the "4-Round" method. Family Meetings are supposed to be democratic, so everyone gets to take turns facilitating the different meetings. The first round, we go around and everyone gets to say something that made them feel good that week. Then the second round, each person gets to share something that bothered them this week.

Third round, we share something we want to work on or improve this week, with Action Plans. And fourth round is discussing our schedule for the week.

The goal is to make each member of the family feel empowered and a full-fledged partner in the family-creation continuum.

How many of you do regular family meetings? What method do you use? If you don't do family meetings, why not try it out and report back to us on how it goes?

Your Mother of Meetings,

Rosalyn Ebberly

SAHM I Am Loop Moderator

"The wise woman builds her house, but the foolish tears it down with her own hands." Proverbs 14:1 (NASB)

From:	Brenna L. <saywhat@writeme.com>
To:	SAHM I Am <sahmiam@loophole.com>
Subject:	Re: [SAHM I AM] TOTW
	October 5: Family Meetings

Maybe I should throw a two-hour tantrum for not knowing the meaning of the word *coelenterate*.

Seriously, I think a family meeting might be a good idea. Except what do you do with toddlers? Little Tess is starting to talk, but of course, Little Pat isn't saying a word. *sigh* I think most of our meeting would be taken up with Darren's angst about that. Maybe I DON'T want a family meeting. Sometimes conflict avoidance is okay, don't you think?

Brenna

From:	Hannah Farrell
	<boazsmom@farrellfamilylovesjesus.net>
To:	SAHM I Am <sahmiam@loophole.com>
Subject:	Re: [SAHM I AM] TOTW
	October 5: Family Meetings

Coelenterate is like a jellyfish or coral or sea anemone.

Boaz is too little to have meetings with, but I would be glad to start the tradition with Bradley. Unfortunately, he is too busy with work right now. I tried to get him to do date nights with me, but he didn't seem interested. He said as long as there was a hot dinner waiting for him at home, he was happy.

Do you think it was, like, wrong of me to be upset about that?
Hannah

From:	Brenna L. <saywhat@writeme.com>
To:	SAHM I Am <sahmiam@loophole.com>
Subject:	Re: [SAHM I AM] TOTW
	October 5: Family Meetings

Hannah,
Figures you'd be a wordsmith,, as well as a mathematician. But honey, seriously…YES you should be upset at Bradley! What does he take you for—the live-in maid? Get a spine, girlfriend, and let him know that makes you feel neglected.
Brenna

From:	Hannah Farrell
	\<boazsmom@farrellfamilylovesjesus.net\>
To:	SAHM I Am \<sahmiam@loophole.com\>
Subject:	Re: [SAHM I AM] TOTW
	October 5: Family Meetings

Brenna,

When your BFF is in college to be a marine biologist, you pick it up after a while.

As far as letting Bradley know how I feel, well, it's not like I'm all mad at him or anything! He's my Bradley-sweet-ykins, and I just felt a little upset that he wasn't as excited about date night as I was. But I think that, you know, talking about my needing to get a "spine" is a bit much coming from you, Miss "Sometimes conflict-avoidance is okay, don't you think?" :) I don't think it's nice to be all like "You should do this" when you won't do it yourself.

Hannah

From:	Brenna L. \<saywhat@writeme.com\>
To:	"Green Eggs and Ham"
Subject:	Re: [SAHM I AM] TOTW
	October 5: Family Meetings

Grrrr. The child is right. You guys aren't going to make me actually admit it on-loop, though, are you?

Brenna

☺**Instant Message**

Pr31Mom: Hi Jocelyn, I'm glad you're online.

JocelynM: Yeah, what's up?

Pr31Mom: I've been looking through all these proposals for workshops for the retreat. There are a LOT of them!

JocelynM: We had a great response, didn't we?

Pr31Mom: Yes. And so I was thinking

JocelynM: Uh-oh…

Pr31Mom: What?

JocelynM: Every time you start thinking, it invariably makes my life more complicated.

Pr31Mom: Sorry. I didn't realize my ideas were so offensive to you.

JocelynM: Whoa there! I was teasing you. Hasn't your therapist worked with you on how to laugh at yourself?

Pr31Mom: We haven't gotten to that point yet, no.

JocelynM: After TWO years?

Pr31Mom: Yeah, I decided working through suicidal depression and a marriage on the brink of divorce would be easier. Slacker that I am.

JocelynM: Wow. I'm sorry.

Pr31Mom: Anyway, I was thinking since we have so many workshop ideas, why not just see if the hotel will let us have an extra meeting room? Then we can have two workshops running at the same time, sort of like a mini conference.

Pr31Mom: Also, I just found out through one of our loop members that we can book a certain nationally-known women's speaker to be our keynote address, if we want.

JocelynM: Keynote? I don't know, Ros. That's getting pretty complicated. Who is it?

Pr31Mom: Kathy Keller.

JocelynM: Oh. My. Goodness. Ros, that's amazing—but we CANNOT afford her! That woman fills stadiums that would make a rock star jealous! We couldn't afford her pinky finger, much less her entire self!

Pr31Mom: She happens to be the cousin of one of our loop members, and she's got young kids herself. She offered us a fantastic discount. We'd be fools to say no.

JocelynM: We'll have a lot of women come just to see her. That's going to mean re-negotiating our contract with the hotel, you know. We'll need more room.

Pr31Mom: Yeah, but you said there weren't any other large groups using the conference facilities that weekend. It should be okay.

JocelynM: It's going to cost more, too.

Pr31Mom: With Kathy Keller, I think we'll get enough attendees to cover it.

JocelynM: You THINK? You do realize that I've paid the entire deposit out of my own pocket, right? And that makes me responsible for the ENTIRE amount, regardless of whether or not we get enough women to show? And if we make it too expensive, not enough people will come, and then I will be left holding the bag, and Shane is going to be furious at me for bankrupting our family!!!

Pr31Mom: Gee, now who needs therapy? Stop worrying. No wonder Shane keeps trying to get you to slow down—you stress too much about everything.

JocelynM: I just think it's incredibly risky.

Pr31Mom: Anything worth doing is worth doing well. Our group will love the extra choices. And besides, anyone who is doing a workshop has to come, so we'll have at least that many guaranteed to be there. Plus, with Kathy coming—we'll be turning people away, not begging them to come!

JocelynM: You have your heart set on this, don't you.

Pr31Mom: Trust me. It will work out just fine.

JocelynM: You'd better hope it does.

From:	Iona James
	<poetsmystique@brokenwrenchandcopperbucket.com>
To:	SAHM I Am <sahmiam@loophole.com>
Subject:	**[SAHM I AM] Cast aside**

Jeremy told me today that he thinks I should spend more time taking care of the Angel Child instead of writing song lyrics for the band. And he wants me to get a full-time job, too!

I said if I had to give up my art and get a job then he should, too. And it hurt me when he seemed confused by that. "But my art IS a paying job."

He's right. Before the Angel Child, we could live quite comfortably on the $200 a week or so that his playing gigs and my part-time work at the coffee shop brought in. And there was always a little extra cash from the random sale of one of the band's CDs.

But Angel Child has yet to appreciate the joy of living simply. He needs so much! And we want to give him good quality organic food and hemp diapers and natural baby lotion and all the other assorted accessories that go along with a baby. It's NOT simple! It seems we can't go for even a week without realizing there is something we need for the baby.

So we are slowly being crushed into the suburban mold, and Jeremy is on the verge of giving in to it completely. He thinks we need more space, more money, more…everything.

It used to be that if we had a few extra dollars, we'd give it away to a charity or someone in need. Now we put it all toward the Angel Child.

I didn't want to live like this. I don't like all the trappings of materialism. I don't WANT to drive an SUV and contribute to global climate change! All I ever wanted was to live in bliss with the sunlight of my life and write poetry and lyrics for his band. I never wanted possessions or a fancy place to live.

And now, I am angry—at Jeremy for pressuring me, and at the Angel Child for making it a necessity. That makes me feel like a horrible person. How can I be angry at my own family? I love them! How can I resent the needs of a helpless little being? Do I love my art more? If I did not, then I don't think I would be so angry.

Why is it that I must be the one to give up my art to raise a child? Shouldn't we both be making these sacrifices?

Somehow, I have to find a way to speak through the smoke of our argument and extinguish the fire causing it. This never happened before the Angel Child. And that makes me angry, too. And frightened because surely it's an unforgivable thing to be angry at a child.

Iona James

From:	Zelia Muzuwa <zeemuzu@vivacious.com>
To:	SAHM I Am <sahmiam@loophole.com>
Subject:	Re: [SAHM I AM] Cast aside

Iona,

It's never, ever unforgivable to be mad at your kids. Believe me, babe—if it were, we'd all be in big trouble!

And I get why you're upset—no woman should ever be pressured to give up her art for her child. If it's really necessary, any good mom (including YOU) would sacrifice everything, including art, for their child. But you're mad because you know deep down it's not necessary. There are other ways to do what you need to do without giving up part of who you are to do it. And you're right—sacrifices should be made by both parents, not just one.

I sort of had to help Tristan understand this. I am a very artistic person, too, and Tristan is so not. He didn't always see why it was so important to me. But you are in a much better position because your husband is also artistic, so he can understand why it's important to you.

Tristan came around because he loves me and because I told him honestly how it made me feel to be asked to give up something so important to me. I imagine if you talked with Jeremy and told him how you feel, you two could work out a compromise.

And don't forget—even though a child IS more expensive than just you guys on your own, there's lots of ways to save money and still have good quality baby supplies. You're a creative person—you'll find ways of doing it.

I'm really glad you shared what you're going through with us. It's nice to get to know you a little better.

Z

From:	Thomas Huckleberry
	<t.huckleberry@showme.com>
To:	SAHM I Am <sahmiam@loophole.com>
Subject:	Re: [SAHM I AM] Cast aside

Hi Iona,

Dulcie and I know how tough this can be. We had to get pretty creative to figure out a way for her to do her interior design business and still make sure the kids were taken care of.

We ended up with me staying home with the kids and her working from home. And now, I want to develop my "creative" side, too, by making furniture and stuff. So we're working on a way for me to get the training and network I need in order to do that. I think that's what being married and being a family is all about—working together so everyone gets to do what they've been created to do.

Maybe you could figure out how to make money from your poetry and then you could work from home, too? Just an idea.

Tom

From:	Iona James
	<poetsmystique@brokenwrenchandcopperbucket.com>
To:	Zelia Muzuwa <zeemuzu@vivacious.com>;
	Thomas Huckleberry
	<t.huckleberry@showme.com>
Subject:	You are a blessing!

Both of you gave me such hope today. I WILL talk to Jeremy. And I do so love the Angel Child—even when I am angry and frustrated. And I love Jeremy, too. We both are still learning how to be parents and spouses and friends. It helps greatly to hear how other people like you manage it.

Thank you. You've been part of God's Divine Grace to me today.

Iona James

From:	Jeanine Hash <ilovebranson@branson.com>
To:	Dulcie Huckleberry
	<dulcie@homemakerinteriors.com>
Subject:	Re: Can you take our kids in March?

Hi Dulcie, sweetie,

I got your e-mail! It was so nice of you to think of Morris and me taking the girls. We would LOVE to have them so you can go to your retreat. We'll play dress-up and have a tea party and watch movies! Do you think they'd like *Beach*

Blanket Bingo or *How To Stuff a Wild Bikini?* Can't beat Frankie and Annette!

This will be SO FUN!!!
Love,
Mom Hash

From:	Dulcie Huckleberry
	<dulcie@homemakerinteriors.com>
To:	Jeanine Hash <ilovebranson@branson.com>
Subject:	**Re: Can you take our kids in March?**

THANKYOUTHANKYOUTHANKYOU!!!!!! You are terrific! You are the absolute best mother-in-law in the world!!!

However, regarding movies…since MacKenzie is only six, and the twins are just four, I don't really think beach movies are appropriate for them.
Thanks SO much!!!
Dulcie

From:	Jeanine Hash <ilovebranson@branson.com>
To:	Dulcie Huckleberry
	<dulcie@homemakerinteriors.com>
Subject:	**Re: Can you take our kids in March?**

Of course! Silly me. What about *Gidget?* I know—we could have a SURFING-THEMED TEA PARTY!!!
Mom

From:	Dulcie Huckleberry
	<dulcie@homemakerinteriors.com>
To:	"Green Eggs and Ham"
Subject:	Surf's Up

I just want to say that this retreat had better be AMAZING because I'm going to come home to three little girls running around in bikinis pretending that they're surfing with Moondoggie and the Big Kahuna.

Stuff of nightmares.

Dulcie

From:	Thomas Huckleberry
	<t.huckleberry@showme.com>
To:	SAHM I Am <sahmiam@loophole.com>
Subject:	[SAHM I AM] Question for the moms

Hi ladies,

It's me, the SAHD. I have a question. Anyone know how to get grease stains out of a fancy dress? Haley and Aidan were playing dress-up in their brand-new Sunday dresses (yes, I know I should have caught that sooner) and they came down to the kitchen and grabbed the can of hamburger grease on the cabinet (yes, I realize it should have been kept out of their reach—I'd been fixing supper earlier and left it). They fought over it and ended up dumping the entire can on each other. Wasn't hot enough to burn them, thankfully, but the dresses are soaked.

Any suggestions?

Tom

From:	Zelia Muzuwa <zeemuzu@vivacious.com>
To:	SAHM I Am <sahmiam@loophole.com>
Subject:	Re: [SAHM I AM] Question for the moms

Hey Tom!

Liquid dish soap should do it. Just soak the dresses in it for about a half hour and then wash them with some dish soap and regular detergent. Dish soap is a great degreaser.

Zelia

From:	P. Lorimer <phyllis.lorimer@geemail.com>
To:	SAHM I Am <sahmiam@loophole.com>
Subject:	Re: [SAHM I AM] Question for the moms

Hi Tom,

In addition to Zelia's suggestion, I would advise that you try some baby powder. Sprinkle it over the dresses while you soak them. That should help.

Phyllis

From:	The Millards
	<jstcea4jesus@familymail.net>
To:	SAHM I Am <sahmiam@loophole.com>
Subject:	Re: [SAHM I AM] Question for the moms

Poor guy! Cooking grease is a pain to deal with. Especially that much of it. I think the other suggestions you've gotten are good. You also might try a can of cola. Put it in the wash and it should degrease everything.

Let us know how it turns out!

Jocelyn

From:	Thomas Huckleberry
	<t.huckleberry@showme.com>
To:	SAHM I Am <sahmiam@loophole.com>
Subject:	Re: [SAHM I AM] Question for the moms

Hello again,

You gals wanted an update. Here you go.

First, I coated the dresses with dish soap—actually drenched them both in straight dish soap. Then I dumped nearly an entire large container of baby powder over the top of that. It made sort of a paste over the dresses, but I wasn't worried.

Then I put most of the rest of the bottle of dish soap into the washing machine, along with extra detergent, and an entire six-pack of cola, and set everything to warm. (Was going to do hot but then remembered that it might shrink the dresses.) Put the dresses in. Washed them.

Not too many minutes later, I smelled a weird sweet soapy burned smell from the basement. Went to check. Sticky soap suds had FILLED the wash room and were oozing out into the rest of the basement.

Apparently, I overdid it on the dish soap and the cola.

Now we have to pay to have the basement carpet cleaned. And when the cola-dish-soap-powder brew overflowed, it got into the electronics of the machine and shorted out the timer, which caused the burned smell. We're lucky I didn't burn the house down! However, now we need a new machine.

And the dresses are still toast.

But thank you all for the excellent suggestions. I'm sure that in your more capable hands, it would have turned out great.

Tom

From:	Zelia Muzuwa <zeemuzu@vivacious.com>
To:	SAHM I Am <sahmiam@loophole.com>
Subject:	Re: [SAHM I AM] Question for the moms

Tom, honey, you're going to hate me for this, but it can't be helped. This absolutely MUST be said:

Double, double, toil and trouble;
Fire burn and cauldron bubble.

(*Macbeth,* Act IV, Scene 1)

Shakespeare is always relevant.

Z

From:	Dulcie Huckleberry
	<dulcie@homemakerinteriors.com>
To:	"Green Eggs and Ham"
Subject:	I've had a BAD day!

First, I was on the phone with a potential client—that rare species of creature that actually offers me money in exchange for doing something I enjoy—when what should my wondering ears hear? But of course…the screeching howl of a four-year-old reverting back to a terrible-two-style tantrum—RIGHT OUTSIDE THE OPEN DOOR OF MY OFFICE!

Potential client gets all worried. "What's that? Is somebody screaming? Is everything okay?"

I have to explain that it is my four-year-old. Client says, "Oh, is it Take Your Child To Work Day?"

I should have lied and said yes. But the piercing noise was addling my brain. And Tom was nowhere to be found. So I said, "No. I have a home office, and my child is upset about something."

Client says, "Oh, dear, well I'd better let you go do your mom-thing. I'll contact you again at a more convenient time." And before I know it, she's off the phone and out of my life.

Probably FOREVER!

And why was Tom absent instead of keeping my children "not seen and not heard"?

Because he was in the basement trying to fix the mess YOU GUYS TALKED HIM INTO!!!

Sheesh! I asked him why he didn't just ask me what to do with the dresses. He said he "didn't want to bother" me. Yes. And chasing off my clients because of a screaming child certainly was less bother.

Please, my sweet friends…the next time my beloved husband needs advice, SEND HIM BACK TO HIS WIFE! You don't know how to communicate with him to avoid tragedy. He may appear normal enough. But he has just enough of his mother in him that you have to handle him carefully! Got it???

I can't even be happy that we're getting a new washing machine out of the deal. Nothing like being responsible to earn every penny for the family to take the joy out of shopping. :(

Dulcie

From:	Rosalyn Ebberly <prov31woman@home.com>
To:	SAHM I Am <sahmiam@loophole.com>
Subject:	[SAHM I AM] TOTW October 19: Giving Children What They Want

Magnanimous Mommies,

We used to do this—giving our blessed children everything in our power to give them. We sacrificed our own material pleasure for their sakes! And where did it get us?

Suzannah just announced to us that she would NEVER wear any more clothing that wasn't from her select list of expensive, trendy shops. She said she was "sick and tired of looking like some Midwestern hick" and that it was time she developed her own "fashion style" so she wouldn't end up looking like ME! She's nine. I'd like to see what would have happened to me or my dear sister if we had pulled such an attitude with our parents at that age!

And what is wrong with my sense of fashion? I've always prided myself on keeping up my appearance and not letting myself go just because I don't have an office to go to every day.

We told her that she'd better be thankful she has clothing to wear, and that we're certainly not going to spend half our family budget on overpriced, trendy clothing for her, at the expense of everyone else.

She had the nerve to say that if I would just go get a job instead of moping at home trying to manage everyone else's lives, that then I'd be able to afford the important stuff— like clothes, of course.

Where did we go wrong? I did everything anybody told me was good to do for kids. We've given them as many opportunities and activities as we could! We've volunteered as a family for ministry events and to serve the poor! We've made crafts and sold them to raise money for charity!

We've done everything we can to model service and humility and contentment. And what do we get in return?

All she cares about is designer clothing.

So I guess the TOTW is this: What do you do with a child like that?

Rosalyn Ebberly

SAHM I Am Loop Moderator

"The wise woman builds her house, but the foolish tears it down with her own hands." Proverbs 14:1 (NASB)

▭Text Message From Brenna Lindberg: For Dulcie Huckleberry
——October 19/9:21 a.m.——
Gt 2 ur computer NOW! Ros jst postd real live rant!

▭Text Message From Dulcie Huckleberry: For Brenna Lindberg
——October 19/9:36 a.m.——
What? Ok will chk out. A rant as in "I'm actually a real person w/ real problems" rant? N how did u get my # 2 text me?

▭Text Message From Brenna Lindberg: For Dulcie Huckleberry
——October 19/9:36 a.m.——
Yes that sort of rant. Marianne gave me #, hope its ok.

▭Text Message From Dulcie Huckleberry: For Brenna Lindberg
——October 19/9:40 a.m.——
Jst fine. Text r cll anytime. Wow! Never in my lifetime would I have dreamed…

☺**Instant Message**
Dulcet: Tom! Check your email! Rosalyn RANTED!

Dulcet: Tom?

Dulcet: Hey Tom! Am I going to have to talk to you the old fashioned way? You're staring at your computer screen in a daze. You okay?

Huck: Yeah...I'm here. Just in shock. Speechless. She really ranted?

Dulcet: Totally. Gotta read it!

⌨Text Message From Jocelyn Millard: For Zelia Muzuwa
——October 19/10:03 a.m.——
Did u c the rant?

⌨Text Message From Zelia Muzuwa: For Jocelyn Millard
——October 19/10:04 a.m.——
Yes. Saw it. Nearly feel sorry 4 her.

⌨Text Message From Jocelyn Millard: For Zelia Muzuwa
——October 19/10:05 a.m.——
Come on. She's almost acting like a normal person!

⌨Text Message From Zelia Muzuwa: For Jocelyn Millard
——October 19/10:06 a.m.——
And margarine almost tastes like real butter. The trans-fat will still kill u.

⌨Text Message From Jocelyn Millard: For Zelia

Muzuwa
——October 19/10:06 a.m.——
U r hopeless.

From:	Hannah Farrell
	<boazsmom@farrellfamilylovesjesus.net>
To:	Kristina Shaw <krissyshaw@loopy.com>
Subject:	**U Won't Believe This!!!**

Hi Krissy,
You know Rosalyn, the crazy lady that's the moderator of the SAHM loop I'm on? Well, she totally lost it today and went on this huge rant about how we should all do charity work instead of buying designer clothes. I'm attaching the e-mail so u cn read it. Just don't say anything bc it's supposed to be a confidential loop.
Love ya!
Hannah

From:	Thomas Huckleberry
	<t.huckleberry@showme.com>
To:	Becky Schwartzendruber
	<schwartz@ozarkmail.net>
Subject:	**Rosalyn RANTED!**

Hey sis!

I'm not really supposed to do this, but since you've been following our stories about Rosalyn Ebberly for years, you have to read her rant. Yes, a real rant! So I attached it.

It's historic, and I knew you'd want to see it.

I'll write more later. Gotta go find out what Aidan is getting into.

Love,

Tom

From:	Rosalyn Ebberly <prov31woman@home.com>
To:	VIM <vivalaveronica@marcelloportraits.com>
Subject:	Did you pass around...

...my loop post from this morning? The TOTW one where I was talking about Suzannah? A local news reporter called me wanting to do a story about the girl who refuses to wear anything but designer clothing, even though her family is locally known for their charity work.

And MOM called! Said if it were her, she'd make Suzannah wear nothing but garage sale clothing for the next six months!

What did you DO, Ronnie?

Rosalyn

"The wise woman builds her house, but the foolish tears it down with her own hands." Proverbs 14:1 (NASB)

From:	VIM <vivalaveronica@marcelloportraits.com>
To:	Rosalyn Ebberly <prov31woman@home.com>
Subject:	Re: Did you pass around...

Hey now! I haven't even checked my e-mail until just now. I have no idea what you're even talking about. Don't blame me. Besides, I know the loop rules—posts are strictly confidential. No forwarding.

So Suzannah's developed a taste for style? Must be her auntie Ronnie coming out in her. I'll have to go read your post.

Veronica

From:	Rosalyn Ebberly <prov31woman@home.com>
To:	VIM <vivalaveronica@marcelloportraits.com>
Subject:	Re: Did you pass around...

THEN HOW IN THE WORLD DID ALL THESE PEOPLE OFF LOOP FIND OUT IN LESS THAN THREE HOURS???

I bare my heart, and the whole world seems to know. This is NOT fair!

Rosalyn

"The wise woman builds her house, but the foolish tears it down with her own hands." Proverbs 14:1 (NASB)

From:	VIM <vivalaveronica@marcelloportraits.com>
To:	Rosalyn Ebberly <prov31woman@home.com>
Subject:	**Re: Did you pass around...**

Well, it WAS a good rant. And coming from YOU, it was practically like if Paris Hilton became a Buddhist monk and gave all her money to Mother Teresa's orphanage. I checked with mom, and she said Aunt Doris forwarded it to her. And Aunt Doris said she got it from her friend's daughter who got it from another friend in Michigan. We tracked it back and lost the trail somewhere south of Nashville about 12:30 this afternoon.

It's on its way to becoming the latest e-mail forward. You'll probably see it on Snopes.com in a few days—likely under the subject heading "The Rant—You GOTTA See This!"

You enjoy your 15 minutes of fame, sis. I'm headed into the depths of despair over this birthday-party thing. Ashley's party was a smashing success. Everyone is still talking about it! But now, we're getting more party invitations. And they're all getting more elaborate.

So now my question is…what are we going to do for Courtney's party? If we don't blow away the competition again, everyone will think Ashley's party was just a fluke!

Veronica

From:	Rosalyn Ebberly <prov31woman@home.com>
To:	VIM <vivalaveronica@marcelloportraits.com>
Subject:	Re: Did you pass around...

It's good to know that when push comes to shove, you have a solid sense of what is really important in life, sister-dear.
Rosalyn

"The wise woman builds her house, but the foolish tears it down with her own hands." Proverbs 14:1 (NASB)

From:	Rosalyn Ebberly <prov31woman@home.com>
To:	SAHM I Am <sahmiam@loophole.com>
Subject:	[SAHM I AM] LOOP RULES

LOOP POSTS ARE TO BE KEPT STRICTLY CONFIDENTIAL!!!! NO SHARING THEM WITH ANYONE!

How many times do I have to remind you? NO passing around, NO sharing. NO FORWARDING!!!

It's not that hard, my friends. Take the finger off the forward button. If any of you so much as THINK about sending one of our posts to your off-loop friends or family, I will ban you from this loop—and your children, and grandchildren and great-grandchildren, too!

I MEAN IT!
Rosalyn

"The wise woman builds her house, but the foolish tears it down with her own hands." Proverbs 14:1 (NASB)

☺**Instant Message**
PhyllisLorimer: My goodness, what's her problem today?
Farmgirl04: I know! Sheesh—lets loose one little rant and then she can't stop!

From:	Brenna L. <saywhat@writeme.com>
To:	SAHM I Am <sahmiam@loophole.com>
Subject:	[SAHM I AM] Where did my daughter go?

It must be Cranky Tween Day or something. I doubt I can top The Rant, but…

All I did was tell Madeline, my ten-year-old, to go clean her room. Didn't yell. Didn't order or strong-arm or anything. Just said, "Hey, Maddy, time to clean your room."

You would have thought I told her to bring the cattle in from the north pasture by herself before bedtime! Usually she just fusses or stomps to her room and pouts if she doesn't want to clean it.

This time, she put her hands on her hips and glared at me, her eyes glittering with resentment. "Why should I do it? You're not the queen of the world."

I could hardly breathe! She's never been that blatantly mouthy and defiant before. How dare she talk to me like that! I couldn't believe it, but here I was—scowling at my own daughter like I was about to get in a catfight with her. "As your mother, I AM queen of your world, and don't you forget it!"

The look in her eyes—it was like she hated me in that instant. I could feel my heart cracking just a little. "Tess and Pat got in there and made most of the mess."

"I'm sorry, but that's what little brothers and sisters do sometimes. Get it cleaned up, and we'll do a better job of keeping them out next time."

"I didn't want any brothers and sisters ANYWAY!"

I didn't know what to do. I didn't recognize this angry, spiteful little person standing in front of me. All I could think of to say was "That is enough. Get going now!"

I can't believe this. What happened? Have I done something wrong? Did we do a bad job at handling the twins being born? I didn't even know she was so upset. How could she act like that?

My biggest fear is that if she's already getting that bad teenager attitude, what will she be like when she IS a teen? I do not want her to make the same mistakes I did!

What do I do? What did I do?

Somebody please help me—I think I'm panicking.
Brenna

From:	VIM <vivalaveronica@marcelloportraits.com>
To:	SAHM I Am <sahmiam@loophole.com>
Subject:	Re: [SAHM I AM]
	Where did my daughter go?

Hey Brenna,

Your guess is as good as mine, sweetheart. Ashley has been like that since she was about ten. Freaked me out at first. I didn't think girls started that nonsense until they were teens. I doubt you've done anything wrong, though. And I don't think it means that she'll turn out bad.

You hang in there, okay?

Veronica

From:	Hannah Farrell
	<boazsmom@farrellfamilylovesjesus.net>
To:	SAHM I Am <sahmiam@loophole.com>
Subject:	Re: [SAHM I AM]
	Where did my daughter go?

Hi Brenna,

Don't you remember being ten? I do! Maybe that's like an advantage to being so young and all. I remember wanting so bad to be like all grown-up and have people take me seriously. (I still totally feel that way some days.) And yet, you're still just a kid and everyone seems to want to remind you of it. (Still feel like that, too, sometimes.)

I think I also started my period when I was eleven. My mom said that for about a year before that, I got really cranky and moody for a couple days each month. Maybe you should keep track of Madeline's moods and see if there's a pattern.

I do remember that I didn't actually hate my parents. And

I wasn't like seriously, deep down, MAD mad. I was just...
cranky mad.

I bet Madeline is the same way. Give her some credit.
After all, just because you went off the deep end and got
pregnant doesn't mean she's going to be that stupid, too.
Hannah

From:	Brenna L. <saywhat@writeme.com>
To:	SAHM I Am <sahmiam@loophole.com>
Subject:	Re: [SAHM I AM] **Where did my daughter go?**

You were doing great until that last sentence, dear. You
really gotta learn when to quit.
Brenna

From:	P. Lorimer <phyllis.lorimer@geemail.com>
To:	SAHM I Am <sahmiam@loophole.com>
Subject:	**[SAHM I AM] Cranky kids become cranky young adults**

...And that makes for cranky teachers! My children aren't
at all close to that stage, but if I can survive teaching, I think
I'll be ready for whatever an adolescent Julia or Bennet can
fire at me.

Frankly, the worst of the entire lot are the Christian
students. Many of them have tremendous chips on their
shoulders. I am teaching an undergraduate Western Civi-

lization course—a gen. ed. class full of students who aren't interested and wish they were somewhere else…usually at a location that includes a keg.

We were studying the Enlightenment, and one of my students went off on a huge rant about how "the Enlightenment was the most devastating phenomenon in the past thousand years" because it produced "rampant humanism" (as if it were a disease epidemic) and led to the collapse of "all Christian morals and traditions" and most importantly, it gave rise to EVOLUTION. (Cue dark, scary music, I suppose.)

I should have just thanked the young sir for his unenlightened position, and let it go. But I was in my "earnest teacher" mode and decided to have a discussion on his points—most of which I disagreed with. I was polite! I gave him the same sort of respect that I would have given a fellow Ph.D. candidate! His response?

"You're just saying that because you've been brainwashed by liberal academia. I don't expect to hear anything different from a secular teacher. But I believe that all truth is based on the Bible, and I have the right as a person of faith to express my opinion!"

Oh, so now college is all about expressing our various opinions? What is this? Oprah's book club?

I told him that now was not an appropriate time to interrupt the lecture to express opinions. He got very angry about that and said he was going to complain to the dean about the "antireligion bias" in my classroom.

I couldn't help it—I laughed! Then I said, "Go right ahead. The interesting thing about all this is that I'm married to a pastor" and I told him which church. It's NOT a "liberal" church by any definition. He looked like he was choking. Didn't say anything else, just slumped in his seat.

Afterward, I intended to try to speak to him. But he zoomed out without even looking at me.

And now, the whole campus probably knows I'm a pastor's wife. I meant to keep that information as private as possible. But I definitely blew that goal today. Now they've started calling me "PW"—Pastor's Wife. I hate that!

What I do not understand is this bitterness and anger that I see, particularly from our Christian students. I do not see how this is a Christlike attitude. Why do they think that the college classroom is suddenly a debate forum where they are supposed to point out the error of their professor's way? Where is the respect for teachers? Where is the thoughtful consideration of new ideas? Why are they even here if all they want to do is argue?

I'm sorry. I'm sure this steps on some people's toes on this loop. But I just had to vent. It's no wonder the faculty lets out a collective groan when they hear that they've got another Christian student enrolled. It doesn't need to be that way. And it makes my life just that much harder because people assume I'm the same.

Phyllis

From:	Hannah Farrell
	<boazsmom@farrellfamilylovesjesus.net>
To:	SAHM I Am <sahmiam@loophole.com>
Subject:	Re: [SAHM I AM] Cranky kids become cranky young adults

Hi Phyllis,

I totally don't think there was anything wrong with what that student did. We learned at SCCLOG that as Christian students we have to be SO CAREFUL because secular colleges all want to indoctrinate us with pagan ideas that will make us become ATHEISTS! And that would be like so totally bad I can't describe it!

He had no way of knowing you were on his side. Probably, he couldn't really even tell. So he just was standing up for his beliefs. I think that was brave of him.

Hannah

From:	Dulcie Huckleberry
	<dulcie@homemakerinteriors.com>
To:	SAHM I Am <sahmiam@loophole.com>
Subject:	Re: [SAHM I AM] Cranky kids become cranky young adults

I don't know, Hannah. When I was in college, I didn't really think it was my job to argue with my professors every time I didn't agree with them. I thought it was my job to learn the material they were teaching me—at least long enough to regurgitate it on the test.

If I'm strong enough in my own beliefs, then I should be able to listen to the perspectives and thoughts of other people without feeling the need to argue about it, don't you think?

Dulcie

From:	Hannah Farrell
	<boazsmom@farrellfamilylovesjesus.net>
To:	Dulcie Huckleberry
	<dulcie@homemakerinteriors.com>
Subject:	**Re: [SAHM I AM] Cranky kids become cranky young adults**

You like totally went to PUBLIC school, didn't you!
Hannah

From:	Rosalyn Ebberly <prov31woman@home.com>
To:	SAHM I Am <sahmiam@loophole.com>
Subject:	**Re: [SAHM I AM] Cranky kids become cranky young adults**

Hi everyone,
I'm just going to bring this discussion to a close now before
it starts an argument here on the loop. We all have different ideas and opinions of how our faith should be expressed
in public situations. We could argue all day long about what
is and isn't the best expressions of that faith, but that would
really defeat the idea of our faith UNITING us. Don't you
think?
Thanks,
Rosalyn Ebberly
SAHM I Am Loop Moderator

"The wise woman builds her house, but the foolish tears it down with her own hands." Proverbs 14:1 (NASB)

From:	Dulcie Huckleberry
	<dulcie@homemakerinteriors.com>
To:	"Green Eggs and Ham"
Subject:	**A real loop moderator**

Whoa! She actually made a good call! She actually acted like a normal loop moderator on a normal loop! I'm shocked. This is a week that will go down in history—first, Rosalyn RANTS, and then it's the first time that SAHM I Am has ever had a discussion moderated that probably really needed it. And she did it NICELY! I'm impressed.

Of course, she has good reason for not wanting any more ugly fights on the loop. I'm kind of glad she stepped in. Dulcie

From:	The Millards
	<jstcea4jesus@familymail.net>
To:	"Green Eggs and Ham"
Subject:	**Re: [SAHM I AM] Cranky kids become cranky young adults**

Dulcie, you should e-mail her and tell her that. Maybe without the snark. :) But I think she could probably use the

positive reinforcement—if you want the behavior to continue. It's just like potty training!
Jocelyn

From:	VIM <vivalaveronica@marcelloportraits.com>
To:	P. Lorimer <phyllis.lorimer@geemail.com>
Subject:	[SAHM I AM] Cranky kids become cranky young adults

Hey girl,
I feel your pain, my friend. Stuff like that is why I've resisted going to church for so long. We've been visiting a Catholic church lately, and I just wanted to let you know that part of the reason I finally gave in and decided to go with Frank is because of knowing you and other gals on the loop who aren't like that.

So I just betcha that the way you responded to that kid in your class probably gave all those other kids a more balanced view of Christians and showed them that you all aren't idiotic, angry jerks. You might just have done a lot of good there—even if it was frustrating. So hang in there, okay? Don't be embarrassed about what your husband does. I know it creates lots of expectations for you, but I just bet that anyone who meets you comes away with a LOT to think about because you've challenged all those expectations. That's a good thing. We "heathens" need our expectations challenged sometimes. :)
Veronica

From:	P. Lorimer <phyllis.lorimer@geemail.com>
To:	VIM <vivalaveronica@marcelloportraits.com>
Subject:	[SAHM I AM] Cranky kids become cranky young adults

Thanks, Veronica. You have no idea how much I needed that encouragement—especially from you.
Phyllis

⌨Text Message From Tom Huckleberry: For Dulcie Huckleberry
——October 21/3:32 p.m.——
At animal shelter looking at kittens. I like small white one. Grls wnt lrge shaggy orange one w/ missing tail. Grls will likely win.

From:	Hannah Farrell <boazsmom@farrellfamilylovesjesus.net>
To:	SAHM I Am <sahmiam@loophole.com>
Subject:	[SAHM I AM] Car Seats?

Are any of you like all into which car seats are the best? Boaz is getting too big for his carrier seat, and I am utterly overwhelmed by all the choices. Only the very best for my wittle Boey-Booboo!
Hannah

From:	Marianne Hausten
	\<confidentmom@nebweb.net\>
To:	SAHM I Am \<sahmiam@loophole.com\>
Subject:	**Re: [SAHM I AM] Car Seats?**

I think you should go with the JoyRider 6000.
Marianne

From:	Brenna L. \<saywhat@writeme.com\>
To:	SAHM I Am \<sahmiam@loophole.com\>
Subject:	**Re: [SAHM I AM] Car Seats?**

Ooohh, do you have one of those, Marianne? They've got that nifty little computer that automatically adjusts the height to improve side-impact protection. And the cover comes in washable suede that acts like a temperature control so the baby doesn't get too warm or cold.

I WISH I had one. It can go all the way from 5–25 lbs. rear-facing, and up to 70 lbs front facing!
Brenna

From:	Iona James
	\<poetsmystique@brokenwrenchandcopperbucket.com\>
To:	SAHM I Am \<sahmiam@loophole.com\>
Subject:	**Re: [SAHM I AM] Car Seats?**

We were given a JoyRider 6000 from my in-laws. It's wonderful. Sometimes, the only way we can get the Angel Child to fall asleep is to put him in the JoyRider and drive for an hour. I don't believe possessions should define us or own us, but the JoyRider 6000 might be the one exception I'd make to that rule.

Iona James

From:	VIM <vivalaveronica@marcelloportraits.com>
To:	SAHM I Am <sahmiam@loophole.com>
Subject:	Re: [SAHM I AM] Car Seats?

I've got one! It makes me feel happier just looking at it. And what I really like is that you can take it to any of their Joy-Centers at malls or baby stores, and they have car seat experts who will install the seat for you, inspect all the components, and even clean it for you! It's a spa for your car seat!

Veronica

From:	Dulcie Huckleberry <dulcie@homemakerinteriors.com>
To:	SAHM I Am <sahmiam@loophole.com>
Subject:	Re: [SAHM I AM] Car Seats?

It's a car seat cult! When we had to get car seats, I just went to the local department store and got the simplest one we could find. Works fine. The only thing I don't like is that

the fabric faded quickly, and the padding didn't hold up too well. We just stick a foam pad under the cover and it works.
Dulcie

From:	VIM <vivalaveronica@marcelloportraits.com>
To:	SAHM I Am <sahmiam@loophole.com>
Subject:	Re: [SAHM I AM] Car Seats?

Listen to yourself, Dulcie! "It works just fine" "the only thing I didn't like"…you are not happy with your car seat. You tolerate it, but you have no love for it because deep down, you know it's a worthless piece of plastic! :)

You don't hear that sort of thing from a JoyRider family. We can't help but rave about our car seats because they're great quality, and they've got pizzazz and all the features you could want. Award-winning design, excellent customer service…I mean, you walk into a JoyCenter, and you're treated like a queen!

Did I mention they have play spaces for your kids while your car seat is being serviced?

Come over to the Light, Dulcie. Trade up—they've got great booster seats for older kids, too.
Veronica

From:	Marianne Hausten <confidentmom@nebweb.net>
To:	SAHM I Am <sahmiam@loophole.com>
Subject:	Re: [SAHM I AM] Car Seats?

Non-JoyRider people just don't get it. I would absolutely adore a JoyRider 6000. We're going to save up for one. Those of you with them, e-mail me off-loop and tell me what you think about the built-in lockoffs and top tether. Are they really as easy to install as all the reviews say? You are SOOOO lucky to have one—I hope you know that!
Marianne

From:	Dulcie Huckleberry
	<dulcie@homemakerinteriors.com>
To:	SAHM I Am <sahmiam@loophole.com>
Subject:	Re: [SAHM I AM] Car Seats?

All you JoyRider people ought to get your own e-mail loop! You're cluttering up ours with all your floaty hearts. Do the car seats come equipped with smelling salts to revive swooning adorers?
Dulcie

▧Text Message From Tom Huckleberry: For Dulcie Huckleberry
——October 21/4:46 p.m.——
Orange kitten adopted. Mac named him Rosie. I said not good name 4 boy cat. She said don't care. So Rosie he is. On way 2 pet store 2 get food n stuff.

▧Text Message From Dulcie Huckleberry: For Tom Huckleberry

——October 21/4:48 p.m.——
Gr8t. Can't wait 2 meet little Rosie.

✉Text Message From Tom Huckleberry: For Dulcie
Huckleberry
——October 21/5:07 p.m.——
Do u think its ok if boy cat has pink rhinestone collar and
purple glitter cat bed? Grls r going nuts here.

✉Text Message From Dulcie Huckleberry: For Tom
Huckleberry
——October 21/5:08 p.m.——
LOL! I think Mr. Rosie will b jst fine. Not like kitten has
sense of gender identity. & will b neutered soon anyway.
No worries.

From:	Hannah Farrell
	<boazsmom@farrellfamilylovesjesus.net>
To:	SAHM I Am <sahmiam@loophole.com>
Subject:	**Re: [SAHM I AM] Car Seats?**

Hey everybody! Thanks so much for the awesome advice
on the car seats. I'm happy to announce that… WE'RE
GETTING A JOYRIDER 6000!!!!

We're going to a JoyCenter tonight—I'll send pictures!
Hannah

From:	Dulcie Huckleberry
	<dulcie@homemakerinteriors.com>
To:	SAHM I Am <sahmiam@loophole.com>
Subject:	Re: [SAHM I AM] Car Seats?

Ack! Another initiate into the JoyRider cult. NO pictures!
You all are nuts!
Dulcie

From:	Rosalyn Ebberly <prov31woman@home.com>
To:	SAHM I Am <sahmiam@loophole.com>
Subject:	[SAHM I AM] TOTW November 16: Will
	My Children Hate Me?

Much-loved Ladies:

Don't worry, this TOTW is not as dismal as it might sound
from the subject. I want to encourage you! If you've ever ex-
perienced one of your children—who you've labored over,
nursed through stomach flus, comforted after a 2:00 a.m.
nightmare, bandaged, held, rocked, fed, and clothed—if one
of these children ever loses it and starts screaming "I hate you!"
simply because you told them to turn off the television...

Please be encouraged—they can't possibly hang on to
that resentment through adulthood. In another decade or
so, it should (probably) vanish.

Or you might have the misfortune of losing your own

temper and screaming at your child—yes, the very same one you dreamed about holding in your arms—"Do you enjoy making my life miserable? Why can't you JUST FOR ONCE do what you are told to do?" And then you feel a load of guilt the size of the city dump because you made them cry, and what kind of parent yells at their kids and makes them cry!?!

And even when you tell them "no" fifty thousand times in one afternoon, and they are shooting daggers at you with their eyes, and when they ask you for the 136th time "Is Dad going to be home soon?" and when you feel bad because you just can't bring yourself to endure ONE more game of Candy Land, and when all you want to do is lock yourself in the bathroom, and when you've grounded them to their rooms for an entire week and they skulk down to dinner as if they are part of a chain gang sentenced for life…

Odds are fairly good that it's all going to turn out fine. They're notorious for having poor long-term memory. They'll probably forget. Or the trauma you've inflicted on them will fade. To some extent. They'll get perspective as they get older, and they will hopefully come to understand that you were just doing the best you could, and that it's not really that they are impossible little brats or that you're the world's most incompetent and unfeeling mother. As they mature, they'll understand that parents spend most of their parenting careers exhausted, overworked, and in the grip of a King-Kong-size inferiority complex.

And they'll forgive you everything you ever did to them, and you'll all be best friends for the rest of your life.

Don't you think?

Rosalyn Ebberly

SAHM I Am Loop Moderator

"The wise woman builds her house, but the foolish tears it down with her own hands." Proverbs 14:1 (NASB)

From:	P. Lorimer <phyllis.lorimer@geemail.com>
To:	"Green Eggs and Ham"
Subject:	Re: [SAHM I AM] TOTW November 16: Will My Children Hate Me?

I can't believe I'm actually typing this, but I'm having a complete "Rabbit and Tigger" moment. I want the old Tigger back! The one that pompously pontificated about parenting, and patted herself on the back all the time. The impossibly perfect one with her impossibly perfect children. The Tigger I could dislike without feeling very guilty about it!

I don't like this new Tigger. This Tigger makes the book of Lamentations read like chick-lit! What am I supposed to do with this Tigger? How am I supposed to respond? St. John's Wort, anyone? You'll need it after her posts.

I never thought I'd feel this way, but I'm definitely Rabbit today.

Phyllis

From:	Dulcie Huckleberry <dulcie@homemakerinteriors.com>
To:	"Green Eggs and Ham"
Subject:	Re: [SAHM I AM] TOTW November 16: Will My Children Hate Me?

You know what the most wonderful thing about Tigger is, don't you?

SHEEEEE'S the only one! :)

Dulcie

From:	Brenna L. <saywhat@writeme.com>
To:	"Green Eggs and Ham"
Subject:	Re: [SAHM I AM] TOTW November 16: Will My Children Hate Me?

WRONG! You forgot the other Tigger...

Cheer up, Phyllis. You've still got Hannah. And she LUVVVVS you! :)

Brenna

From:	P. Lorimer <phyllis.lorimer@geemail.com>
To:	"Green Eggs and Ham"
Subject:	Re: [SAHM I AM] TOTW November 16: Will My Children Hate Me?

Thank you, Brenna. Now I really need an antidepressant.

Phyllis

From:	Rosalyn Ebberly <prov31woman@home.com>
To:	Shelley Dalton <shelley@hibiscusmentalhealth.org>
Subject:	Idea for dealing with my kids

Hi Shelley!

Thank you very much for suggesting I e-mail you instead of calling you. I LOVE e-mailing! Did I ever mention to you that I am the moderator/co-owner of an e-mail discussion loop with over 1,500 moms on it?

I just wanted to run an idea past you, since you are always so good at helping me figure out what to do and how to handle my children! I know we're supposed to be working on teaching them social skills so that we have a plan for how to deal with conflicts when they arise. I LOVE your idea of teaching a new social skill each week and breaking it down into its component parts.

So I'm attaching a list of the top fifty social skills I think we need to teach the kids, and I broke each one down into about thirty steps so we can systematically teach them. I used the list you gave me, and added a few, plus created a few more steps just to get in some stuff I felt was left out.

Could you do me a huge favor and look this over for me and let me know what you think? Was I thorough enough? I just think if teaching social skills will eliminate this conflict we've been having with them, then I want to go all the way with it…NOW! We can't afford to wait another day.

Thanks so much. You are really the BEST therapist there ever was.

With love,

Rosalyn Ebberly

"The wise woman builds her house, but the foolish tears it down with her own hands." Proverbs 14:1 (NASB)

From:	VIM <vivalaveronica@marcelloportraits.com>
To:	SAHM I Am <sahmiam@loophole.com>
Subject:	Re: [SAHM I AM] TOTW November 16: Will My Children Hate Me?

MY children had better adore me by the time this week is over! It's Courtney's birthday party on Saturday. She's turning ten, and we decided to have a fairy party for her. She just about ruined the whole thing a couple weeks back by blabbing to her friend. This friend went and told her parents—so we were inches away from a repeat of the Ashley Limo Party disaster. We bribed the parents to not steal our idea by Frank offering to do a FREE family photo session for them. And let me tell you—that was a sacrifice on his part. I dare you to try to find a more unphotogenic family!

Okay, so we're doing this fairy party, right? Y'all should SEE the boxes of stuff arriving in our basement. Tulle netting, giant silk flowers, yards of ivy garland, chicken wire, brown and green fabric, landscaping stones, and bunches of other stuff. We're creating a woodland fairy-land in our basement—complete with child-size fairy hide-aways and houses, and special lighting and even a waterfall!!!

The girls will have a sleepover down there, and there will be a scavenger hunt for fairy treasure, including a ton of party favors, and hidden treats to eat. We're inviting ten girls (since Courtney is turning ten) and I hired a local seamstress to create a unique fairy costume for each one. We're also having a makeup artist come in to do fairy makeup on each girl. And then Frank is going to photograph the entire thing so each girl has their own "fairy foto" in a special frame.

Doesn't that all sound like fun? Courtney is SO excited. I think she was a tad bit envious after Ashley's party—got her panties in a twist over how elaborate Sis's party was, and convinced she was going to get shortchanged for her party. We had to do a TON of convincing and planning to reassure her. It's all costing a pretty penny, though. I had no idea all that floral fabric stuff could be so expensive!

But I DO believe in fairies! Especially ones that help me keep the title "Queen of Birthday Parties" around here.
Veronica

From:	Hannah Farrell
	<boazsmom@farrellfamilylovesjesus.net>
To:	SAHM I Am <sahmiam@loophole.com>
Subject:	Re: [SAHM I AM] TOTW November 16:
	Will My Children Hate Me?

Oooooh!!! I LOVE fairy stuff!!! I wish I could go to that party, Veronica. It sounds fab-u-licious! Only, except, I would be so much older than everyone else. Well, except you, of course.

I have a fairy collection. In fact, before we found out Boaz was a boy, I was going to do my nursery in fairies. Maybe I still will if I get to have a girl next. Bradley thinks I should get over liking fairies. But I don't think anyone is ever too old to enjoy fairy tales. I often like to dream that

I'm the fairy princess in the story. I'm sure you all like doing stuff like that, too, right?
Hannah

From:	Brenna L. <saywhat@writeme.com>
To:	"Green Eggs and Ham"
Subject:	Re: [SAHM I AM] TOTW November 16: Will My Children Hate Me?

Hannah Farrell wrote:
    < I often like to dream that I'm the fairy princess in the story. I'm sure you all like doing stuff like that, too, right?>
    Yes, my fairy tale would include the fairy princess locked in a tower, babysitting my children until her hair grows long enough for her precious Bradley to climb up it and release her. By which date, I will have saved up enough money to buy my own tropical island where a resort full of staff will cater to my every desire and where my husband will have nothing to do but give me massages and take me shopping.
    Hey, it's MY fairy tale, after all!
Brenna

From:	Rosalyn Ebberly <prov31woman@home.com>
To:	Shelley Dalton <shelley@hibiscusmentalhealth.org>
Subject:	Christmas presents?

Dear Shelley,

Sorry to bother you again, but I had a question…do you think part of the reason my children are so resentful is because we haven't always gotten them the same number of Christmas presents? We always try to spend about the same money on each child, but we sometimes get one child several less-expensive presents while another one gets one big one. And I was just thinking that maybe they are subconsciously assuming that if they didn't get as many presents as their siblings, that means that we don't love them as much.

Not that I'm trying to psychoanalyze them or anything! (That's YOUR job, LOL!) But I was just going through the gifts we have put away for this year (I finished my shopping in August) and wondering if we ought to return any of them or add some to make it more even.

For example, last year we got Suzannah her very own prayer journal and a donation to a children's relief fund in her name. She seemed unhappy about those things, and I thought maybe she was jealous because we got Jefferson a whole set of math flash cards and workbooks, as well as new socks and a contribution to his college savings fund. And I thought maybe he was envious of Abigail's presents of new bedsheets, photos of her grandparents, and the picture dictionary and spelling cards we got her. Abigail was only five, so she couldn't have been jealous of anyone. After all, kids that young just like opening the packages!

So what do you think? Should we do the same number of gifts for everyone? That should make them happier, right?
Rosalyn

"The wise woman builds her house, but the foolish tears it down with her own hands." Proverbs 14:1 (NASB)

✉Text Message From Dulcie Huckleberry: For Tom
Huckleberry
——November 17/6:32 p.m.——
Cn u also pick up some antibiotic ointment at the store?
Rosie just bit MacKenzie again. Thxs.

✉Text Message From Tom Huckleberry: For Dulcie
Huckleberry
——November 17/6:33 p.m.——
Sure. Why Rosie bite her? Resents his pink rhinestone
collar?

✉Text Message From Dulcie Huckleberry: For Tom
Huckleberry
——November 17/6:34 p.m.——
Mac dressed him in doll clothes again. Poor thing had on
a pink sparkle princess doll dress. Final straw—caught
Mac trying to tie tiara to cat's head with yarn. Rosie had
enough n bit her.

✉Text Message From Tom Huckleberry: For Dulcie
Huckleberry
——November 17/6:34 p.m.——
Smart kitten.

✉Text Message From Dulcie Huckleberry: For Tom
Huckleberry
——November 17/6:35 p.m.——
Don't encourage him! He has 2 learn 2 deal w/ the girls.
Can't nip at them jst bc they treat him like a doll. Needs
to accept his lot in life.

✉Text Message From Tom Huckleberry: For Dulcie
Huckleberry
——November 17/6:36 p.m.——
I feel sorry for the poor thing. I identify w/ him.

☺**Instant Message**
JocelynM: Hey Z, I'm glad I caught you online. Got a minute?
ZeeMuzzy: anything for you, babe. how r u?
JocelynM: "r u"? Hannah must be rubbing off on you.
ZeeMuzzy: u no it! LOL! lk rtng n code.
JocelynM: Ugh! Too much effort to decipher.
ZeeMuzzy: so what's up?
JocelynM: Well, first I wanted to see how the kids were doing. They any better?
ZeeMuzzy: a little. the specialist we're seeing has been really helpful. but it's going to take time. we should have gotten them in sooner, but we just didn't know we needed professional help with it.
JocelynM: No use beating yourself up over it. I'm glad things are getting better.
ZeeMuzzy: me too.
JocelynM: Second, I wanted to talk to you about the retreat workshops.
ZeeMuzzy: hey, that's great! i was wondering how that was going. listen, i've been thinking about the workshop ideas i gave you. i even spent some time last week making a slide presentation on my computer for them.
JocelynM: Wow. And we haven't even scheduled them yet.
ZeeMuzzy: yeah, i know. but i figured might as well,

since i'm best friends with the gal planning the whole shindig. gotta do you proud, right?

JocelynM: That's sweet, Z. But

ZeeMuzzy: i was also thinking of some activities we could do to make it more "hands-on."

JocelynM: Z, wait.

ZeeMuzzy: what?

JocelynM: Well, we had a lot of people give us great workshop ideas.

ZeeMuzzy: oh? so you probably can't let me do more than one, huh? that's cool. i understand. which one do you want?

JocelynM: Actually, not everybody can do a workshop— we just don't have enough time or room.

ZeeMuzzy: that's tough. i guess you're the lucky one that gets to deliver the bad news to them?

JocelynM: Yeah. And you know I don't enjoy disappointing anyone.

ZeeMuzzy: i know. you like to keep everyone happy. you've got a big heart, joc-girl.

JocelynM: Thanks. But that makes it really hard.

ZeeMuzzy: well, you can count on my shoulder to cry on if you need it.

JocelynM: You are sweet, too. Which is why I hate to tell you this…

ZeeMuzzy: tell me what?

JocelynM: We're not going to be able to have you do any workshops. I'm sorry Z.

JocelynM: Z?

JocelynM: Z, are you still online?

ZeeMuzzy: wow. i feel stupid.

JocelynM: No...don't. It's really cool that you were so excited about it.

ZeeMuzzy: was there something wrong with my ideas? or is this because of me and rosalyn?

JocelynM: Neither. We just felt like some of the other workshops would appeal to more people.

ZeeMuzzy: don't sugar-coat this, jocelyn. ros black-balled me, didn't she?

JocelynM: NO! She wouldn't do that. You don't know her, Z. You think you do—just like I did. But she's not like that at all.

ZeeMuzzy: i can't believe this. i worked really hard on those workshops! i was planning to do them other places, like church or mom groups, if they went well.

JocelynM: No reason why you can't still do that.

ZeeMuzzy: a bit hard to get my foot in the door in those places without prior experience. i figured with you doing the schedule, i'd have a better shot this way. "women's retreat speaker" would have given me some street-cred, you know?

JocelynM: I'm sorry. Really. Maybe next year.

ZeeMuzzy: yeah. maybe. you SURE this has nothing to do with ros?

JocelynM: Positive. Are you going to be okay?

ZeeMuzzy: me? you're friends with shrink-girl, and you're asking ME that question?

JocelynM: Look, Z, this rotten attitude toward Rosalyn is getting really old. It's not funny anymore.

ZeeMuzzy: i wasn't aware it was ever funny. what happened was not funny. I didn't realize you were laughing about it like it was some joke.

JocelynM: That's not what I meant. Nobody was laughing about it. But in all our years of snarking about Ros, none of us ever took it seriously. This is different, and I'm concerned about you.

ZeeMuzzy: i'll be fine. you'd better save your worries for your big retreat.

JocelynM: You'll still come, won't you? It wouldn't be the same without you.

ZeeMuzzy: sure. wouldn't miss the Rosalyn 'N Jocelyn show for anything.

From:	Dulcie Huckleberry
	<dulcie@homemakerinteriors.com>
To:	SAHM I Am <sahmiam@loophole.com>
Subject:	[SAHM I AM] Cat problems

Hi girls,

Got a problem—we recently adopted a kitten. MacKenzie, our six-year-old, helped pick him out. His name is Rosie (yeah, it's a girl's name…get over it, it's just a cat). Mac and the twins just adore him. We've tried to keep them from "loving" him too much, but the poor thing can't hardly walk two feet without being scooped up. And half the time, he skulks around, tripping over the shirt or dress the girls have put him in.

Their newest game is to dress him in a nightgown and strap him in the doll stroller. Tom and I are trying to make sure this doesn't happen, but we can't keep an eye on them all the time. And just when we turn our backs, we hear this little mewing sound, and sure enough, the little thing has been roped into playing "house" with our girls.

Problem is, he's started nipping and scratching them. I don't entirely blame him—after all, he's got to defend himself somehow. But it's becoming a bad habit.

He dive-bombs the girls when they walk by and tries to bite their ankles. He's so small, he hasn't been able to do too much damage yet. But he's growing fast!

Any ideas of what I should do?

Dulcie

☺**Instant Message**

ZeeMuzzy: get a pit bull.

Dulcet: What?

ZeeMuzzy: to help with the cat.

Dulcet: And—dare I ask—how in the world is a pit bull going to help with the cat?

ZeeMuzzy: in a cat's mind, i'm sure playing dress up with three little girls has GOT to be a better option than playing chew-toy with a pit bull.

Dulcet: I think the cats of the world should be glad they don't live at your house, dear friend. :)

ZeeMuzzy: oh definitely. some days I would be glad not to live at my house.

Dulcet: I hear you on that! Hey…speaking of the cat, I hear it mewing. Better go check…brb.

ZeeMuzzy: sure.

(Dulcet is idle.)

ZeeMuzzy: dulcie, I have to go. email me later. hope everything is ok.

ZeeMuzzy signed off at 4:28:32 p.m.

From:	Dulcie Huckleberry
	<dulcie@homemakerinteriors.com>
To:	SAHM I Am <sahmiam@loophole.com>
Subject:	[SAHM I AM] Catty-Cake
	(or Ring-Around-The-Rosie)

Okay, Tom is taking the twins to their ballet class, so I'm IMing Zelia, and I hear the distant sounds of a kitty meowing. I walk out of my office and see MacKenzie scuttle through the dining room, looking guilty as sin.

"MacKenzie, what are you doing? Where's Rosie?"

"I don't know." She shrugs, eyes wide.

I am not fooled. But I don't hear any more sounds, so I figure the cat was able to escape and hide. "Leave the poor kitty alone. He won't like you if you keep messing with him."

She scowls. "I don't LIKE Rosie! He bites me!"

"He wouldn't bite you if you weren't so mean to him all the time!"

"I just want to play with him."

"Well, don't blame me if he scratches or bites you. You're asking for it!"

She sticks her nose up in the air. "He's not going to bite me anymore."

She sounds so confident that little prickles of suspicion peck at me. "How do you know?"

Again with the ultrainnocent look. "I just do."

Uh-huh. I'm about to prod further, but my phone rings, so I give her one last glare for good measure, and go back to the office to answer the phone. It is, of course, a client. I end up having to listen to her take the long way around her question.

I hear beeps—like the sound of the buttons on our microwave. MacKenzie! Now what is she doing? I slip on my hands-free headset, and walk to the kitchen, with the client still babbling in my ear.

MacKenzie doesn't see me. She pushes another button. I tiptoe toward her, intending to catch her in the act. She knows better than to play with the microwave.

And then, with something I can only call Mother's Intuition, I know EXACTLY what is in the microwave—

ROSIE!

MacKenzie's finger is poised over the start button, and I'm still several feet away from her. I scream. "NOOOOO!!!!" I dive toward her, my client shrieking in my ear, wanting to know what is happening. Just as her finger touches the button, I shove her to the ground. I've never played football in my life, but I must say this was a beautiful tackle.

I have no idea what my client is saying now. I fling open the microwave, and this orange streak flies at me out of my metal springform cake pan. The streak lands on my HEAD, digging its claws into my scalp with a screech. I think the client hung up on me at that point.

I'm in such pain that I'm yelling—at MacKenzie (whom I've now lost track of), at Rosie, at Tom for being gone, and at microwave manufacturers for making such a dangerous kitchen appliance. The cat will NOT let go of my head, and the more I tug, the more it hurts.

I hear the front door open. A man's voice—that is NOT Tom—is talking to MacKenzie.

"MacKenzie!!! Who is that?"

"It's a policeman, Mommy! I'm showing him the bump you just gave me on my head!"

Oh, lovely. I stumble toward the front door, the cat still clinging to my head.

I point to my cat hat. "Get him off of me!"

The officer's eyes bug out. "Okay, ma'am, just calm down."

"Calm down? After Mac tried to nuke him and my client probably thinks we're all insane and I have a police officer at my door and there's needles in my brain and my daughter has a bruise and you probably think I'm a horrible, abusive, crazy parent, and you want me to CALM DOWN? Get it off! Get it off me!!!"

He approaches me cautiously—out of fear of me or the cat, I can't tell. His hands close in around the trembling kitty. Then I feel something wet and warm dribbling down through my hair and behind my ear. It's not coming from one of the points of pain, so it can't be blood. That leaves…yeah, you guessed it. Rosie got so scared, he peed on my head. In front of the police officer.

Make that ON the police officer.

"Um, ma'am?" He's holding the wet cat by the scruff of its neck.

"Yeah, I know. Sorry about that." I turn to MacKenzie, swallowing the wave of fury that rises just looking at her. "Darling," I grind out, "please get Mommy a towel. Now."

She nearly trips in her haste to obey.

I take Rosie from the officer. "Was there something you needed, Officer?"

"I was driving by and heard screaming. Just came to investigate."

MacKenzie returns with the towel. I offer it to him. "We had a…cat incident."

He nods solemnly, wiping his hands. "I noticed."

"This doesn't normally happen."

"That's…good."

"I think we're okay. Would you like to wash your hands?"

"Thanks. And I think you should get those puncture wounds on your head checked out."

"I will."

"And have a doctor look at your daughter's bruise… which was caused by…?"

"Me tackling her a second before she cooked our cat."

"Ah. Might want to keep a closer eye on stuff like that, huh?"

That earned him a glare of Mommy-Rage. He actually took a step backward.

"And…maybe you should talk to the Humane Society and get some behavior advice."

"For who? The cat or the child?"

Finally, a wisp of a smile. "Both?"

This may be the first time in my life that I've been so angry I didn't dare come within six feet of my daughter. She took one look at me and fled to her room and stayed there until Tom got home. He took us both to the doctor— keeping us on opposite sides of the waiting room and everything. MacKenzie's head is fine. But I got three stitches, and have to take antibiotics in case any germs from the cat pee infected the wounds.

Thank goodness the officer is a dad and understood what was going on, or we could have been in HUGE trouble! I can't even remember which client was on the phone, so I'll have to check caller ID later and try to convince her I'm not insane.

Just looking at the microwave makes me slightly ill.

I still haven't spoken to MacKenzie yet, and it's six hours later. I know the Bible says not to let the sun go down on your anger, but this is just one case where there is no way I was going to cool off in time to make that deadline.

And Rosie? I don't know. I think he's hiding under the couch.

Anybody have recommendations for a cat psychologist in the Springfield area?
Dulcie

From:	Zelia Muzuwa <zeemuzu@vivacious.com>
To:	SAHM I Am <sahmiam@loophole.com>
Subject:	Re: [SAHM I AM] Catty-Cake (or Ring-Around-The-Rosie)

For you, Dulcie-babe—sounds like it describes the scene at your house pretty well:

"…my mother weeping, my father wailing, my sister crying, our maid howling, our cat wringing her hands…" (*The Two Gentlemen Of Verona*, Act II, Scene III)

From:	Dulcie Huckleberry
	<dulcie@homemakerinteriors.com>
To:	SAHM I Am <sahmiam@loophole.com>
Subject:	Re: [SAHM I AM] Catty-Cake
	(or Ring-Around-The-Rosie)

No, it was more like, from Mac's perspective anyway "...my mother screeching, my father yelling at me, my sisters smirking, our cat sinking its claws into my mother's head..."

And our maid? What maid? I'd like to have one of those! Ridiculous that in twenty-first-century America, we don't have what was fairly normal in Elizabethan times. I want a maid, blast it! That way, she can do all that mundane house-keeping stuff like rescuing cats from microwaves. And I could actually get work done without head trauma.
Dulcie

From:	Rosalyn Ebberly <prov31woman@home.com>
To:	SAHM I Am <sahmiam@loophole.com>
Subject:	[SAHM I AM] TOTW December 14:
	Great Expectations

'Tis the season, ladies! 'Tis the season for...
Rehearsals every evening for some Christmas recital or pro-duction of some kind—and of course, you or your child MUST attend or face the wrath of the director...

...Who has called you last minute, begging you to help her out by making fifty shepherd and angel costumes because the person who was going to do it procrastinated and then accidentally blew up her sewing machine...

...So you say yes, because how can you disappoint all those kids? Only to find out that you're also expected to play Dutiful Wife at your husband's office Christmas party to welcome the new boss three nights before the costumes are due...

...And at the party, everyone looks at you weird because you overdressed and HOW were you supposed to know that "semiformal" in their minds meant not having holes in your jeans???...

...Meanwhile, you are chewing your fingernails to the quick for the first time since fifth grade because your child has made it perfectly clear that the ONLY thing she wants for Christmas is her own television set for her room, and that's less likely to happen than you waking up one morning to discover that you now are as beautiful and wealthy as Eva Longoria Parker, so she's bound to be crushed on Christmas morning when all she gets are the practical and acceptable (to you) gifts you've purchased for her....

...Which STILL cost more money than what your husband was hoping for, which means that not only will you have disappointed children, you will have a disgruntled husband...

...Which means that the blessed, warm, golden Christmas that everyone is counting on you to provide, along with happy memories they'll treasure forever IS NOT GOING TO HAPPEN.

So in this scenario, how would you respond? Discuss, please.

Rosalyn Ebberly

SAHM I Am Loop Moderator

"The wise woman builds her house, but the foolish tears it down with her own hands." Proverbs 14:1 (NASB)

From:	The Millards
	<jstcea4jesus@familymail.net>
To:	SAHM I Am <sahmiam@loophole.com>
Subject:	[SAHM I AM] TOTW and Retreat Question

I think I'm not really one who has a right to talk about dealing with the expectations of other people. I'm horrible about that! If anyone comes up with a solution, I'm all ears…er, eyes, as the case may be.

However, I do have a question for everyone about the retreat. Rosalyn and I have been talking about how nice it would be to have a time of worship Sunday morning. I know we all want to keep things simple, but if we did have some sort of service, what would you all like?

Just want to make sure we…um…meet your expectations. (Told you I have a weakness for that!)
Jocelyn

From:	Dulcie Huckleberry
	<dulcie@homemakerinteriors.com>
To:	SAHM I Am <sahmiam@loophole.com>
Subject:	Re: [SAHM I AM] TOTW and
	Retreat Question

Let's do a worship service. Phyllis can preach! Remember, she filled in for her DH at her church when he got strep throat. As for the rest of it—I don't care, as long as we don't have to sing "Father Abraham" or "Zaccheaus Was A Wee Little Man" or "Arkie Arkie"!

Dulcie

From:	Brenna L. <saywhat@writeme.com>
To:	SAHM I Am <sahmiam@loophole.com>
Subject:	Re: [SAHM I AM] TOTW and Retreat Question

Rats! After working in the Sunday School nearly every Sunday since Madeline was six, those are the only songs I know! Actually, I'd like to see us do communion. I usually miss it at our church, and sharing that with all you gals would be really a nice touch.

Brenna

From:	Hannah Farrell <boazsmom@farrellfamilylovesjesus.net>
To:	SAHM I Am <sahmiam@loophole.com>
Subject:	Re: [SAHM I AM] TOTW and Retreat Question

Um, aren't you all forgetting something? We can't have preaching without a PASTOR! And how are you going to have a pastor come when it's all women?

Same thing for communion! It would be like all sacrilegious and everything if we just passed around grape juice and crackers without having a real pastor there to make it official.

I totally think this is a bad idea. Maybe we can just sing a few hymns or something and have someone read a devotional. None of that rock music/love song stuff they call worship that doesn't even like mention God's name or anything! I figure if they could play it on a top-40s radio station, it can't be all THAT spiritual.

Not trying to be a wet blanket or anything, but you guys are awfully irreverent to suggest that we could all just get together and act like we're a church, just cause we're all Christians!

Hannah

From:	Brenna L. <saywhat@writeme.com>
To:	SAHM I Am <sahmiam@loophole.com>
Subject:	Re: [SAHM I AM] TOTW and Retreat Question

< you're awfully irreverent to suggest that we could all just get together and act like we're a church, just cause we're all Christians!>

Um…I thought that WAS what a church is! Just a bunch of Christians getting together.

Brenna

From:	Hannah Farrell
	<boazsmom@farrellfamilylovesjesus.net>
To:	SAHM I Am <sahmiam@loophole.com>
Subject:	Re: [SAHM I AM] TOTW and
	Retreat Question

Obviously, Brenna, you haven't been part of a church for very long. Of course, I guess that's probably obvious since you had a baby outside marriage and all that. Otherwise, you'd know that a REAL church has a pastor and a pastor's wife that runs everything, and he's the only one qualified to do stuff like communion and preaching. And if you don't meet at a church, then it's just a home group or Bible study or something—which doesn't count.

And I don't think this is going to work out anyway because I couldn't possibly go to a worship service run by a bunch of women, and some of the people there won't even be Christians! So I don't see how we can have a proper worship service, and I think it would be disrespectful to God to try it. I think we should all just have a quiet time in our rooms Sunday morning.

I'm not trying to spoil the fun or anything. But we're just all too different and have too many different ideas to actually worship together. And we don't want to do anything wrong. Hannah

⌨Text Message From Jocelyn Millard: For Rosalyn Ebberly

——December 14/5:56 p.m.——
Help! Got so many emails 2day about worship service that my email crashed. Make it stop! Hannah is right—we r 2 different 2 worship 2gether. Some want hymns, some want rock bands, some want candles, some want liturgy, some want preaching!!! WaitN 4 Iona to suggest poetry.

▭Text Message From Jocelyn Millard: For Rosalyn Ebberly
——December 14/5:59 p.m.——
Can't please them all! I never saw such picky bunch of people in my life! Wish I'd never brought it up!

▭Text Message From Rosalyn Ebberly: For Jocelyn Millard
——December 14/6:05 p.m.——
Now you know why I'm in therapy. Moderating all of you would do that to anyone! Okay, I'll try to get them under control. After supper.

From:	VIM <vivalaveronica@marcelloportraits.com>
To:	SAHM I Am <sahmiam@loophole.com>
Subject:	**Re: [SAHM I AM] TOTW and Retreat Question**

And y'all wonder why I don't go to church? Listen to y'all—pecking and squawking like a bunch of chickens. Give me one good reason why I'd want to sit in a worship service like that! At least at the Catholic church Frank's been dragging me to, there's no arguing.

I don't even know what "Arkie Arkie" is, and I gave my kids grape juice and crackers for a snack today—and lightning from heaven did not strike me.

Sunday morning at the retreat, I plan to sleep in, unless y'all come up with some compelling reason why I should join you. I'd get more peace and quiet at home with my kids.

Veronica

From:	Iona James
	<poetsmystique@brokenwrenchandcopperbucket.com>
To:	SAHM I Am <sahmiam@loophole.com>
Subject:	Re: [SAHM I AM] TOTW and Retreat Question

Let's have a poetry reading! Some of the poems we could all sing our own melody to, and that way everyone could have the sort of song they like. And then we could have one really long poem that has Bible verses in it and lots of good insights about God. But it wouldn't technically be a sermon, since we all know that you can't actually learn anything from a poem. So we'd be perfectly safe.

And if we had a poem about Jesus's blood and His body, and we happened to be eating bread and drinking juice at the time, then it would just be a happy coinci-

dence and I'm sure no one could possibly be upset about that, right?
Iona James

From:	Zelia Muzuwa <zeemuzu@vivacious.com>
To:	"Green Eggs and Ham"
Subject:	Re: [SAHM I AM] TOTW and Retreat Question

I like her. Don't you like her?

Iona, babe, how did we survive this long without you? Smoochies!
Z

From:	Thomas Huckleberry <t.huckleberry@showme.com>
To:	Dulcie Huckleberry <dulcie@homemakerinteriors.com>
Subject:	Testing

Hey Dulcie,
I'm just testing out my new computer setup. I think moving my computer to the family room was a great idea. That way you can work in your office without so much interruption.

I had a question, though. Do you think I should take the twins to get new mittens? They've both lost theirs…again.
Love,
Tom

From:	Dulcie Huckleberry
	<dulcie@homemakerinteriors.com>
To:	Thomas Huckleberry
	<t.huckleberry@showme.com>
Subject:	Re: Testing

Looks like the computer is working fine. Sure, take them shopping. Buy two pairs each for them this time. Maybe they'll last for three weeks that way.
Dulcie

From:	Thomas Huckleberry
	<t.huckleberry@showme.com>
To:	Dulcie Huckleberry
	<dulcie@homemakerinteriors.com>
Subject:	Re: Testing

Great! Do you think mittens or gloves would be better?
Tom

From:	Dulcie Huckleberry
	<dulcie@homemakerinteriors.com>
To:	Thomas Huckleberry
	<t.huckleberry@showme.com>
Subject:	Re: Testing

Mittens. We always get them mittens. Keeps hands warmer than gloves. I've got to talk to a client in about five minutes. So taking them sooner rather than later would be a good idea.
Dulcie

From:	Thomas Huckleberry
	<t.huckleberry@showme.com>
To:	Dulcie Huckleberry
	<dulcie@homemakerinteriors.com>
Subject:	Re: Testing

I was thinking of going to the mall. Unless you think we should try to save money and find them at the thrift store instead?

Also, I might go to the grocery store, too. Do you need anything?
Tom

From:	Dulcie Huckleberry
	<dulcie@homemakerinteriors.com>
To:	Thomas Huckleberry
	<t.huckleberry@showme.com>
Subject:	Re: Testing

Go to the mall! I have no idea if we need anything from the store. My client is calling now—gotta go. Have a nice time.
Dulcie

From:	Dulcie Huckleberry
	<dulcie@homemakerinteriors.com>
To:	"Green Eggs and Ham"
Subject:	Shouldn't gripe, but...

Why is it that after OVER TWO YEARS of being a stay-at-home dad, Tom still can't make a decision about buying the kids mittens without pestering me for input? It's NOT THAT HARD! Buy the stinking mittens already and let me work!

Putting the computer in the other room was supposed to mean I'd be interrupted LESS!

Sorry…you probably didn't want to hear that. But I didn't want to say it to him, and it had to be said somewhere. Dulcie

⌨Text Message From Tom Huckleberry: For Dulcie Huckleberry
——December 16/11:32 a.m.——
At grocery store now. Jst wanted u 2 know I love u. U looked cute this morning. Thxs 4 emailing me. Nice to have adult conversation.

From:	VIM <vivalaveronica@marcelloportraits.com>
To:	SAHM I Am <sahmiam@loophole.com>
Subject:	[SAHM I AM] NEED BIRTHDAY PARTY IDEAS!

Seriously, y'all, this is a HUGE emergency! Stanley's birthday is coming up. And even though Courtney's fairy party was—by most measures—a tremendous success, I'm feeling like a gnat in a hailstorm. One of the girls demanded to be taken home when she realized we had no real fairies! She was furious. Said she was gypped and insisted on going home. Courtney was heartbroken, and it made us look stupid in front of the other parents.

So now it's Stanley's turn. So far, since Courtney's party, he's gone to a medieval jousting party where each boy got to try on a real suit of armor, and they hired a swords master to give them fencing lessons. And then there was the "wizarding school" party—complete with a potions class featuring weird, bubbling science experiments. Finally, just last week, there was a NASA-themed rocket party in which the parents rented a zero-gravity machine. Stanley threw up in it, so now that birthday boy is threatening not to come to Stanley's party.

You see why this is an emergency? Our reputation is at stake! What am I going to do to top those parties? I'm starting to feel like I need supernatural powers myself.
Veronica

From:	Iona James
	<poetsmystique@brokenwrenchandcopperbucket.com>
To:	SAHM I Am <sahmiam@loophole.com>
Subject:	Re: [SAHM I AM] NEED BIRTHDAY PARTY IDEAS!

Why didn't you tell me you needed fairies, Veronica? Of course I could have shipped you a whole box. They run quite wild around here—snitching my chocolate chips and hiding one sock out of each pair. Adorable little things, in spite of all that. :)

Of course, with my Irish heritage, I could keep you amply supplied with all sorts of sprites and wee folk. *wink*

Iona James

From:	The Millards
	<jstcea4jesus@familymail.net>
To:	SAHM I Am <sahmiam@loophole.com>
Subject:	Re: [SAHM I AM] NEED BIRTHDAY PARTY IDEAS!

Poor Veronica! You are the victim of your own success, I'm afraid. They've all got sky-high expectations now.

I remember the worst birthday party I ever tried to put on was a pool party for Cassia last summer. It rained and she was mad at me for weeks. As if I can control the weather and made it rain just to ruin her party. We rescheduled, of course, but only about a third of the kids ended up being able to come.

Whatever happened to Pin The Tail On The Donkey?

Jocelyn

From:	VIM <vivalaveronica@marcelloportraits.com>
To:	SAHM I Am <sahmiam@loophole.com>
Subject:	**Re: [SAHM I AM] NEED BIRTHDAY PARTY IDEAS!**

Jocelyn Millard wrote:
   <As if I can control the weather>
   Jocelyn, you are BRILLIANT! Thank you!!!
Veronica

From:	The Millards <jstcea4jesus@familymail.net>
To:	SAHM I Am <sahmiam@loophole.com>
Subject:	**Re: [SAHM I AM] NEED BIRTHDAY PARTY IDEAS!**

Uh…I don't think I'll want credit for whatever you are planning. But thanks anyway.
Jocelyn

⌨Text Message From Katelynn Johnson: For Zelia Muzuwa
——December 18/6:53 p.m.——
Hi ms. m! jst wtd 2 sA av a gud evng. thx 4 letN me babysit. dnt wori bout a ting. w'r gunA av a gr8 tym.

✉Text Message From Zelia Muzuwa: For Katelynn
Johnson
——December 18/6:56 p.m.——
Katelynn ~:o We're glad ur babysitting. bt a lil mor sittN
n a lil less txtN wd B a gud idea, K?

✉Text Message From Katelynn Johnson: For Zelia
Muzuwa
——December 18/6:58 p.m.——
Got it, ms. M!

From:	Zelia Muzuwa <zeemuzu@vivacious.com>
To:	"Green Eggs and Ham"
Subject:	**Guess where we're at RIGHT NOW?**

Brass Elephant—a gorgeous, pricey grown-up restaurant,
complete with chandeliers, marble fireplaces, and Tiffany
skylights. We're here for Tristan's company holiday party. I
am wearing high heels and a cocktail gown so gorgeous,
Tristan is tripping over his own feet because he's staring at
me.

I haven't had a nice evening out like this in MONTHS!
I know we all gripe about how stupid company parties are,
but we're getting adult atmosphere, lobster and a live jazz
ensemble for FREE! Ahhh…I'm just sitting here inhaling
the kid-free air. It's beautiful.

We have a new babysitter staying with the kids. The
daughter of a friend at church. She seems really sweet. And

conscientious, too. Only thirteen but I remember babysitting for large families at that age. She should be fine.

Just wanted to crow a bit to my fab friends. You're here in spirit with me!

Love ya!

Z

This message was sent with BlackBerry.

⌨Text Message From Katelynn: For Zelia Muzuwa
——December 18/8:17 p.m.——
Set off fyr alarm. wz an axidnt. DK h2 turn it off. So loud w'r O/side n firetruck S hre n evry1 askN me ?s +I DK answers, cum hom qik!!!

From:	Zelia Muzuwa <zeemuzu@vivacious.com>
To:	"Green Eggs and Ham"
Subject:	Considering Committing Babysittercide

I'm serious. I don't think I've ever been this angry at a minor in my entire life. I consider myself a fairly open-minded, reasonable person, but THIS???

Right in the middle of this delicious lobster meal, I get a nearly incomprehensible text message from Katelynn about the "fyr alarm" going off. And a second later, my cell phone rings and it is our security company telling us they received an alert from our smoke detectors, and I'm supposed to give them the password if everything is okay so they can call off the fire trucks.

Of course, we had no idea if we even had a home left by this time, so we rushed off. When we got to our house, the fire trucks are there, and my brood is huddled in the cold outside, with a nearly hysterical babysitter whose vocabulary apparently has been reduced to "We didn't set anything on fire! There's no fire! It just went off! There's not a fire!"

And the entire neighborhood, it seems, had no other pressing obligations that evening, because they were all outside watching the trucks and chatting. (WHY does this always happen to us???)

The firefighters finally let us inside. The place REEKED of matches, and the floor was covered with drops of wax. Smoke hung in the air. They'd tried to burn the entire house down!

Tristan didn't even look amazed. He grabbed Seamus's arm and almost shook him. "CANDLES, Seamus? Could we not have even ONE evening without a disaster from you?"

"You don't know it was me!"

"I am not stupid, my son."

Turns out that Seamus (of course) made the brilliant suggestion to Katelynn of "Hey, let's light a bunch of taper candles and run around the house with them!"

Knee-jerk reaction from Katelynn should have been "Over my dead body!" I mean, isn't "Don't play with fire" one of the cardinal babysitting rules that everybody knows?

But NOOOOO. She apparently thought playing tag with lit candles sounded like a perfectly grand way to spend the evening. They created enough smoke that it set off our alarm, which is attached to our security system, so once it went off there was nothing Katelynn could do because she didn't have the pass code to turn it off.

What sort of idiot child would listen to anything my son suggested? Especially when it involved open flame? DUH! Bad idea!!!

And not only did she ruin my Grown-Up Evening Out, but the worst of it is that because of all the commotion, Lishan is terrified to go to sleep now. She's clinging to Tristan and doing everything she can to stay awake.

I really, really could hurt a certain thirteen-year-old baby-sitter! Just wait till I tell her mother! And she's never setting foot in this house again.

It smells like smoke in here. And we were going to come home to a quiet house, take Katelynn home, light some candles of our own, and conclude our Very Grown-Up Evening with some Very Grown-Up Activities. Not going to happen NOW, thanks to Ms. Mensa and her Candle Caper.

Boy I'd like to hit something right now.

Zelia

P.S. And don't EVEN bother sending me a Shakespeare quote at the moment. My sense of humor is allergic to smoke and is now on life support in the E.R.

From:	Chad Ebberly <chad.ebberly@henpec.com>
To:	Rosalyn Ebberly <prov31woman@home.com>
Subject:	Re: What's the REAL reason?

Okay, fine. You want to know why I really decided to quit going to counseling with you? I can't compete! You always have to be the best at everything—even at being completely dysfunctional. I couldn't say two words without you insisting YOUR issues were worse, or weirder or more complicated. It happened to be true—which didn't make it any easier!

Everything is a competition. Even with us. I can't even kiss you without feeling like you're tabulating a score based on frequency and quality and comparing it to your own score.

And heaven help you if you don't come out on top. You obsess and fret about it until everyone wants to run away to the Sahara just for some peace and quiet.

Why can't you just accept yourself for who you are? You don't have to be the best. (Or worst, as the case may be.) I'm tired of it, Ros. Nobody exhausts me like you do—so you can rest assured you're the best in at least THAT.

I quit going to counseling so that you could be the best at being messed up. Although I think you may still have competition with our children. But at least their sessions are separate from yours.

You are already an amazing woman. I love you—for some inexplicable reason. No—it's not inexplicable. But it has nothing to do with whether you're the best or not. You're the best for me, and if you could just get that concept, it would be a huge step forward for both of us.
Chad

From:	Rosalyn Ebberly <prov31woman@home.com>
To:	SAHM I Am <sahmiam@loophole.com>
Subject:	[SAHM I AM] TOTW January 11: Being the Best

Competitive Compatriots,

What's wrong with wanting to excel? With wanting to be the best at whatever we do? Doesn't the Bible commend excellence?

There is too much emphasis in our self-esteem fanatical culture about making sure everybody is equal. That nobody feels inferior or lacking in talent.

When do we get rewarded for being talented? Why is competition suddenly a bad word?

I want to be the best! What's so wrong with that? It's not that I want to make anyone else feel bad. I just want to achieve.

So I say, let's stop shirking from competition! Run away from mediocrity! If you're going to do something, put your whole heart into it!

What do you think? Is it bad to be the best? Is competition wrong?

I wish you the BEST,

Rosalyn Ebberly

SAHM I Am Loop Moderator

"The wise woman builds her house, but the foolish tears it down with her own hands." Proverbs 14:1 (NASB)

From:	VIM <vivalaveronica@marcelloportraits.com>
To:	SAHM I Am <sahmiam@loophole.com>
Subject:	Re: [SAHM I AM] TOTW January 11: Being the Best

I think what my sister-dear is trying to say is that when you've been brought up in a family where even growing was turned into a contest, it's pretty hard to change.

However, sometimes that comes in useful—like when you're trying to throw the absolute most fantastic birthday party in the city! Okay, here's what we came up with for Stanley's party on Friday:

I am going to make it SNOW here in Houston! Yes, really. Jocelyn's e-mail a while back inspired me. These kids—some of whom have never seen snow before, or only a dusting…they're going to get to go sledding, build a snowman, have a snowball fight and all the other stuff I grew up with as a kid in Chicago. Stanley is so excited he can hardly sit down!

Veronica

From:	The Millards <jstcea4jesus@familymail.net>
To:	SAHM I Am <sahmiam@loophole.com>
Subject:	Re: [SAHM I AM] TOTW January 11: Being the Best

Snow? How are you going to do that in Houston, Veronica? Want us to mail you some?

Jocelyn

From:	Rosalyn Ebberly <prov31woman@home.com>
To:	SAHM I Am <sahmiam@loophole.com>
Subject:	Re: [SAHM I AM] TOTW January 11: Being the Best

Oh, my sister has always considered herself practically divine. Mere mortals had best stay out of her way. :)

Rosalyn

"The wise woman builds her house, but the foolish tears it down with her own hands." Proverbs 14:1 (NASB)

From:	VIM <vivalaveronica@marcelloportraits.com>
To:	SAHM I Am <sahmiam@loophole.com>
Subject:	Re: [SAHM I AM] TOTW January 11: Being the Best

Ros The Pot calling Sister Kettle black, hmmm?

Jocelyn is on the right track. Since we can't take the kids to the snow, we're bringing the snow to us! There's a brand-new company in town called It's Sno Surprise and it has Hollywood-style special-effect snow machines. We're going to block off our entire street and it's going to be turned into a winter wonderland! We can even rent sleds from them.

Isn't that amazing? I tell you—this party is going to go down in the history books. We will be LEGEND!

Veronica

From:	Brenna L. <saywhat@writeme.com>
To:	Zelia Muzuwa <zeemuzu@vivacious.com>
Subject:	**Question**

Hi Z,

We got the test results back a couple weeks ago for Little Pat. He has "Global Developmental Delay"—apparently their fancy name for "your kid's definitely behind in everything but we have no idea why."

He's going to have occupational therapy and physical therapy and early intervention through the school system. I'm glad that it's not so bad that they think he's mentally retarded or anything. But Darren is not dealing with it well. He's been avoiding Pat and won't even try to help him with his therapy exercises.

I was just wondering how Tristan feels about Lishan and Duri's problems. Does it bother him? Any ideas how I can help Darren figure out how to accept his son?

I just feel so angry about it! None of us are perfect, especially Darren. What gives him the right to reject his son because of some delays? He acts like he's embarrassed of his own child or something.

Anyway, I just wondered if you had any advice.
Thanks,
Brenna

From:	Zelia Muzuwa <zeemuzu@vivacious.com>
To:	Brenna L. <saywhat@writeme.com>
Subject:	**Re: Question**

Hey, girl. I'm sorry to hear about Little Pat. It's a rotten deal when you find out your kid has problems.

Tristan has been pretty cool with Lishan and Duri. I think our biggest problem was we kept thinking it was OUR fault that they aren't adjusting well. We were blaming ourselves, and the counselor is helping us see that it doesn't have anything to do with our parenting skills. There's nothing we could have done to prevent them from having attachment problems.

Tristan sometimes gets frustrated because he wants to fix everything. He gets impatient at times because he can't make the problems go away. But he's learning—and we're all learning—that this is what it means to love unconditionally. You learn to see the good in your child, even with all the issues and difficulties.

I've learned to appreciate that Duri—for all his food hoarding and insecurities—has a huge compassion for anyone else in distress. As he learns to pay attention to other people and their emotions, it is helping him connect emotionally to them and learn how to bond. And Lishan has poetry living in her soul. The more she expresses that, the more her soul mends and I think she's going to heal eventually. But it's a long process, with as many steps backward as forward, it seems.

For Darren and Little Pat, I don't know, honey. It's one thing for me to say to look for the good in Pat. But you and I can't do that for Darren. He has to figure out how to do that himself. I'll pray that he does. In the meantime, love them both. Love them as hard as you can because they both need you.

Love you, my friend. Let me know how it goes, okay?
Z

From:	Rosalyn Ebberly <prov31woman@home.com>
To:	SAHM I Am <sahmiam@loophole.com>
Subject:	[SAHM I AM] Final Retreat Costs

Tremendous Toddler-Tamers,
The moment you've all been waiting for—attached is a spreadsheet showing the final costs of our little retreat. We tried to work in all your suggestions—so we have an array of excellent workshops. Kathy Keller—our nationally known keynote speaker; three massage therapists (recommended by the hotel), and meals to die for—or at least worth murdering your diet for.

Please note that your retreat fee is separate from your hotel fee. The retreat fee should be paid directly to Jocelyn Millard. The hotel fee is due when you check out.

All the registration info you need is in that document, too, so go ahead and call. We want to see you all there!
Love,
Rosalyn Ebberly

"The wise woman builds her house, but the foolish tears it down with her own hands." Proverbs 14:1 (NASB)

From:	Brenna L. <saywhat@writeme.com>
To:	SAHM I Am <sahmiam@loophole.com>
Subject:	Re: [SAHM I AM] Final Retreat Costs

SIX HUNDRED AND FORTY-FIVE DOLLARS??? Not including the $160/night hotel charge. And not including airfare! Where am I supposed to come up with that kind of money?

This was just supposed to be a little get-together. Share a simple hotel room with a bunch of women I never met before, and hang out at restaurants and the hotel lobby. Do a little shopping. Total of a few hundred dollars—mostly airfare.

Now we have all this other stuff, and it's expensive! I don't know if I can afford to go. I know I put my name down as coming, but I didn't expect it to cost as much as the monthly payment on our farm combine.

I really was looking forward to meeting everyone. Why couldn't you have just kept it simple?
Brenna

☺**Instant Message**

JocelynM: Ros, we're getting flooded with emails! Everyone thinks the retreat is too expensive.

Prov31Mom: Don't worry. Everyone always gripes about the cost of something. But if they want it badly enough, they'll figure out how to pay for it.

JocelynM: And what if they don't?

Prov31Mom: Well, it'll just be less of us.

JocelynM: Do you realize there's an Alaska-sized hole in my bank account labeled "SAHM I Am Retreat" that WON'T get filled if there's "less of us"???

Prov31Mom: Don't get mad at me. You were the one who thought workshops would be a good idea.

JocelynM: And YOU were the one who suggested booking Kathy Keller. This isn't a CONFERENCE. It's just supposed to be a get-together.

Prov31Mom: Everyone was THRILLED about Kathy. And they were THRILLED about the workshops! Look, it's not our fault. They're the ones that wanted all the fun extras. Now they're mad because they have to pay for it.

JocelynM: No. I will have to pay for it.

Prov31Mom: I'll help if it comes to that. Though I really hope it doesn't. I took on some extra financial commitments recently that are making things tighter around here.

JocelynM: Would have been nice if you'd held off on those extra commitments until we fulfilled these financial obligations!

Prov31Mom: Trust me, this couldn't wait.

JocelynM: TRUST YOU? That's all you've said this entire time! I am trying to trust you, but you are making it nearly impossible! Did you know that working with you on this has almost cost me one of my best friends?

Prov31Mom: What kind of friend would ditch you because you're helping plan a great retreat?

JocelynM: Forget it.

Prov31Mom: Look, I know you're nervous. So am I, if you want to know the truth. But this is our very first SAHM I Am retreat. We couldn't just do it halfway. It has to be special.

JocelynM: Why? So everyone would be impressed with us? With you?

Prov31Mom: No. I'm not quite as bad as you all seem to think. I wanted it to be special for THEM. Because they're special. Because they get overlooked and peed on and defied and discouraged and worked to the bone every single day, and I just wanted them to have a couple days off. A couple days in luxury. I wish I could pay for it all myself. I'm sorry it got so pricey. We could maybe cancel some of the extras and just eat the deposit ourselves, if you think that would be better.

JocelynM: You make me so mad.

Prov31Mom: WHAT? What did I do now?

JocelynM: Just when I think I have an airtight reason to dislike you, you go and mess it all up.

Prov31Mom: Is that something close to a compliment?

JocelynM: Don't push it, girlfriend.

From:	P. Lorimer <phyllis.lorimer@geemail.com>
To:	"Green Eggs and Ham"
Subject:	If I hear "Pastor's Wife" again, I will SCREAM!

I stopped at the campus today to drop off my syllabus for this semester's class. I parked along the curb for less than five minutes. I returned to find a hastily scrawled note on my windshield that said, "I would think a *pastor's wife* would have more respect for rules than to park in the faculty parking spot."

I just KNOW it was my advisor. Who else would be that snide? There aren't even any students on campus right now. How dare she?

Then I got an e-mail from one of our church members:

"I heard that you met alone with your male students last semester. I just wanted to caution you that as a pastor's wife, you need to be WAY above even a hint of evil. I'm just concerned. You need to be careful."

I met "alone" with my male students in a cubicle, in the GTA office! Good grief! The thing doesn't even have a door! This is ridiculous.

Then I got a phone call from Julia's teacher:

"I noticed that neither you or your husband were able to come to the parents' meeting yesterday evening."

"No," I said. "I'm sorry. We were both busy."

"Well," she says in an overly perky voice, "we're all busy. But you of all people should know how important it is to be involved with your kids. Save some time next time, okay?"

She might as well have come right out and said it— "Since you're a pastor's wife…"

UGH!!! Apparently I am to be flawless, superhuman and everywhere at once. Just because I'm married to someone who preaches about God does NOT mean I *am* God!

Phyllis

From:	Zelia Muzuwa <zeemuzu@vivacious.com>
To:	"Green Eggs and Ham"
Subject:	I would think that as a PASTOR'S WIFE…

…you'd get sick and tired of being treated like that!

I'm sorry, Phyl-girl. Here, have a Z-Hug: {{{{{{{{{Phyllis}}}}}}}}}

Z

From:	VIM <vivalaveronica@marcelloportraits.com>
To:	SAHM I Am <sahmiam@loophole.com>
Subject:	[SAHM I AM] That's IT, I GIVE UP!

No more birthday parties! EVER EVER EVER!!! Stephenie (who has a Christmas birthday, but we were going to wait until February to have a party) will just have to do without, because I'm not doing this one more stinking time!

The Snow Party was a smashing success. Smashing. Our bank account is smashed. Our window is smashed. Our yard is smashed. And Stanley's foot is smashed—got run over by a rogue sled.

I spent the last three weeks making all the arrangements—filling out an application with the city for permission to close off our block for the party. And then the day of the party, the fire department still showed up because they'd misplaced our application and were going to fine us for code violations. The only way we got out of that is because we had a copy of the application.

It's Sno Surprise filled the entire block with snow. And at first, it was great. The neighbors were taking pictures, and some even got a little teary-eyed because they'd never seen a snow-covered tree before and thought it was beyond beautiful. They were commenting on how the sun made the snow sparkle. I never thought I would ever be homesick for Chicago, but at that moment I was—a little.

That was the last happy thought I had for the rest of the day. It's Sno Surprise covered our neighbor's garden, and they looked as dark as a blue norther. Said we ruined their new rosebushes they'd just planted. Now they're demanding we replace them. They were dormant! How can a dormant plant be ruined by snow? Isn't snow an insulator?

Gotta say, the kids did have a great time. All of them, even the ones I don't know. We had about three times the number of people we actually invited. They made snowmen, and Stanley even helpfully supplemented our supply of thrift-store scarves and hats by "borrowing" MY

100% cashmere scarf and hat. I found them later, muddy and torn, hanging from the branch of a tree in a yard three houses down from us. Three hundred dollars! And they were MY birthday present this year. WAAAHHHHH!!!

They threw snowballs—and it didn't take a couple of them long to figure out how to pack rocks in the middle. We did NOT invite those kids! But that's how my window got broken. And one little girl got a scratch on her arm, and her parents are threatening to sue us.

We tried to keep all the snacks in our yard, but the entire neighborhood now bears the evidence of our snow bash. The neighbors have been calling me all day today to complain about the trash the snow left behind.

It was warm, and the snow began melting, which created a huge amount of mud. Our yard is pitted now where the sleds tore up the grass and people left footprints in the mud. Plus, it froze last night, and this morning the entire street was a sheet of ice. Nobody knows how to drive or walk on it around here. More angry neighbors.

Frank isn't speaking to me, and Stanley is miffed because most of the kids forgot to give him a present—even the ones we'd actually invited! Our neighbors are probably having a meeting right this instant to figure out how to force us out of the area.

So we're legend, all right. We might even be history before this mess is cleaned up. Moral of the story: The creator of Pin the Tail on the Donkey was a genius.

Off to kiss some serious neighbor behind.

Veronica

From:	The Millards
	<jstcea4jesus@familymail.net>
To:	SAHM I Am <sahmiam@loophole.com>
Subject:	**Re: [SAHM I AM] That's IT, I GIVE UP!**

Poor Veronica. Sounds like things kind of snowballed, didn't they? :) But the important thing is this—you won! Nobody can top this. They don't have a snowball's chance in…well, anyway, I'll keep this short, because I'm sure you're snowed under right now with all the cleanup work.

From:	Brenna L. <saywhat@writeme.com>
To:	SAHM I Am <sahmiam@loophole.com>
Subject:	**Re: [SAHM I AM] That's IT, I GIVE UP!**

Yeah, don't worry about your neighbors. I'm sure you'll think of a way to break the ice with them.
Brenna

From:	Zelia Muzuwa <zeemuzu@vivacious.com>
To:	SAHM I Am <sahmiam@loophole.com>
Subject:	**Re: [SAHM I AM] That's IT, I GIVE UP!**

Just for you, babe, with the Bard's regards:
    Merry and tragical! tedious and brief!

That is, hot ice and wondrous strange snow.
How shall we find the concord of this discord?
   (*A Midsummer's Night's Dream,* Act V, Scene 1)

From:	VIM <vivalaveronica@marcelloportraits.com>
To:	SAHM I Am <sahmiam@loophole.com>
Subject:	**Re: [SAHM I AM] That's IT, I GIVE UP!**

I hate you all. MODERATOR! Where are you when
you're needed? Surely this is off-topic!
   :)
Veronica

From:	Rosalyn Ebberly <prov31woman@home.com>
To:	SAHM I Am <sahmiam@loophole.com>
Subject:	**[SAHM I AM] TOTW February 8:**
	A Tribute to Our Sweethearts

Dearest SAHMs,
Since Valentine's Day is in a few short days, I thought it
would be nice to post a tribute to the guys (well, and one
gal) who mean so much to us—our spouses!

When I married Chad, I thought he was going to give
me the entire world. I was expecting a lover, a best friend,
a buddy, a dad, a brother—all in one person. But I found
out that I didn't need him to be all of those things to me.

I just needed him. I haven't always been the easiest to live with…okay, I've NEVER been easy to live with. But he balances me, and somehow I think we're both better people for having had to put up with each other so many years.

It's really nice to finally understand that Chad loves me regardless of what I do. I don't have to do anything at all. I don't know why that was so hard for me to grasp, but in the last few weeks, he's gotten it through my head at last that I don't have to be the best, or the most talented or the most anything to keep his love. And in this disposable world, that's rather amazing.

So what's your tribute to your spouse? It may not be as moving as this one (I DID work on it for three hours this morning while waiting for the sun to rise) but we'd all still love to hear it anyway.

Love,

Rosalyn Ebberly

SAHM I Am Loop Moderator

"The wise woman builds her house, but the foolish tears it down with her own hands." Proverbs 14:1 (NASB)

From:	The Millards
	\<jstcea4jesus@familymail.net\>
To:	SAHM I Am \<sahmiam@loophole.com\>
Subject:	Re: [SAHM I AM] TOTW February 8: A Tribute to Our Sweethearts

I think I can finally say that I'm glad Shane got me a house-cleaning service. It gives me an incentive to make sure I keep things picked up around here! (Yeah, yeah, I know that defeats the purpose of hiring someone to clean for you. Baby steps, okay?)

Shane's always been a decent guy. I like it that he's pretty laid-back and easygoing, because I'm really not. Being around him is relaxing.

Jocelyn

From:	Hannah Farrell
	<boazsmom@farrellfamilylovesjesus.net>
To:	SAHM I Am <sahmiam@loophole.com>
Subject:	Re: [SAHM I AM] TOTW February 8: A Tribute to Our Sweethearts

My Bradley is a FAB guy! We've had our moments, you know, like all couples do. Especially since we got married. But that's just a phase. I'm sure we'll move past it as we get more used to married life.

I'm just really looking forward to our Valentine's date on Friday. We decided we're going to start trying to have another baby! So Friday, we're going out and having a romantic dinner and actually leaving Boaz with a babysitter for the first time. It'll be our first Valentine's Day married that I haven't been pregnant.

So weird—three years ago, I was the babysitter!

Hannah

From:	P. Lorimer <phyllis.lorimer@geemail.com>
To:	Hannah Farrell
	<boazsmom@farrellfamilylovesjesus.net>
Subject:	Babies?

Dear Hannah,

Did I read that correctly? You and Bradley are planning to try to get pregnant again? How will that work with your plan to go to college? Going to school when you have young children is difficult enough. But a baby?

I don't understand. I thought—from our conversations— that you wanted to use your academic talents. I understood that you felt stifled at home and had decided to talk to Bradley about recognizing your independence a bit more. What happened?

Phyllis

From:	Hannah Farrell
	<boazsmom@farrellfamilylovesjesus.net>
To:	P. Lorimer <phyllis.lorimer@geemail.com>
Subject:	Babies?

I TOTALLY do want to go to college, Phyllis. You are like such a huge inspiration to me on that. But I talked to Bradley, and he really feels like God is calling us to build a family right now. In fact, we're going to do the whole "let

God be in charge of your family planning" and starting this Friday, no more birth control for us. So I'll probably have lots of babies!

And you don't have to feel all sorry for me or anything. I've always wanted a big family. I'm not like you. I can be happy without getting more education. The babies will keep me busy. And Bradley would, I think, feel bad if I ended up more educated than him. I can always use my brains to homeschool them.

Besides, I think having more kids will totally bring us closer together. The Bible says that children are a blessing. So if we have more of them, then I'm sure our marriage will be more blessed.

And when it gets tough, you all will be there to cheer me up, right? I'm sure this will work out fine. You can just tell me all about what you're learning in your classes, and I'll enjoy it vicariously.

Hugs,

Hannah

☺**Instant Message**

PhyllisLorimer: Brenna! I'm so glad you're online.

Farmgirl04: What's wrong?

PhyllisLorimer: I can't believe it. I can't believe she's throwing it all away!

Farmgirl04: Who?

PhyllisLorimer: Hannah.

Farmgirl04: Oh. What did she do this time?

PhyllisLorimer: It's that jerk she's married to! He's going to keep her barefoot and pregnant and make her waste all that talent. She's going to end up with 14 kids and never have a moment for herself, and never know what it's like to have her own life.

Farmgirl04: I thought that's what she wanted.

PhyllisLorimer: NO! She was going to talk to him about taking some college classes. Apparently, he doesn't think "the little woman" needs to fill her head with all that "book learnin' stuff."

Farmgirl04: Did she actually say that's what he said?

PhyllisLorimer: Not in so many words. But she implied it.

Farmgirl04: Does she seem unhappy?

PhyllisLorimer: Not at the moment. But she will! I just know it. He doesn't respect her! He treats her like she's a kid. Eventually she's going to resent that, but it will be too late.

Farmgirl04: Well, she DID get married awfully young. And it's already too late to do anything about that. You have to let her live her life. Her way.

PhyllisLorimer: She's making a huge mistake!

Farmgirl04: And even if you could force her to see it your way, how would that make you any different from her husband?

PhyllisLorimer: I know you're right. But it just makes me so angry! I've been trying to help her for weeks! I've been listening to her and giving her advice, and I thought she was going to listen, going to make changes. Assert herself. Not be defined by her role as wife or mother, but actually work at developing everything God created her to be!

Farmgirl04: And she has to go to college to do that?

PhyllisLorimer: It would be a good start!

Farmgirl04: Do you fault me for not being college educated?

PhyllisLorimer: Of course not.

Farmgirl04: Because I'm not as smart?

PhyllisLorimer: Don't be silly. I know that if you wanted to go to college, you'd figure out a way to do it, and Darren would back you up. It's her voluntary repression that's bothering me.

Farmgirl04: Are you sure? Or is it your own?

PhyllisLorimer: What are you talking about?

Farmgirl04: I just think that you might be more frustrated about your own school situation right now, and maybe you were hoping that if Hannah went back to school, too, then you'd have someone to commiserate with.

PhyllisLorimer: I just don't want her to go through what I went through—the feeling of being stifled, of being valued only because you have a womb.

Farmgirl04: That's not how Jonathan treats you.

PhyllisLorimer: True. Maybe it's just the church culture at large. I don't know. I just feel sometimes like if I don't get away from the house I am going to go crazy. Sometimes it feels so meaningless. I can't stand the thought of Hannah sentencing herself to a lifetime of that.

Farmgirl04: Maybe she won't feel that way. Maybe she'll be happy.

PhyllisLorimer: I don't see how she can with a husband that doesn't appreciate her.

Farmgirl04: Then she'll need a friend more than ever. And people do change. Look at Rosalyn.

PhyllisLorimer: Odd seeing you stand up for Hannah. She irritates you incredibly.

Farmgirl04: Yeah. Well, like I said, there's always the hope that people can change. Hannah, me, our spouses, our kids.

PhyllisLorimer: You're pretty wise for being just an uneducated hick. :)

Farmgirl04: And a teen mom, don't forget! :) But thanks.

From:	Iona James
	<poetsmystique@brokenwrenchandcopperbucket.com>
To:	SAHM I Am <sahmiam@loophole.com>
Subject:	[SAHM I AM] A Just Compromise

Dear treasures of God,

Remember a few months ago when I was upset because Jeremy wanted me to get a job? Several of you gave me excellent advice, and I'm pleased to report back that I talked it over with Jeremy and we reached a compromise.

I am going to increase my hours at the coffee shop during the day. And Jeremy is going to work at the music store down the street part-time in the evenings. He will continue with the band, and I will continue writing lyrics for them.

But Tom gave me an inspired idea. I am going to write and sell customized poetry from my home. People will be able to hire me to compose poems for any occasion—engagement, weddings, death, birth of a child—and I will use my art as a monument to mark that special moment in their lives.

Working with any of you would be a special joy, so please talk to me if you'd like me to write a poem for you. A happy occasion would be especially appropriate right now as my heart is full of joy and love.

Soaring,

Iona James

From:	Zelia Muzuwa <zeemuzu@vivacious.com>
To:	Iona James
	<poetsmystique@brokenwrenchandcopperbucket.com>
Subject:	Re: [SAHM I AM] A Just Compromise

Way to go, girl! I knew you could find a solution! Hey, I have a terrific occasion that needs a good poem. Send me your phone number and I'll call you tonight and tell you about it. I'd love to be your first customer!

Z

From:	Rosalyn Ebberly <prov31woman@home.com>
To:	Shelley Dalton
	<shelley@hibiscusmentalhealth.org>
Subject:	Final Session

Dear Shelley,

I just got home from our session today, and I think this is a huge mistake! I'm not ready to end my therapy sessions. I'm really not. I need you. You help me work through so many things that I never even knew I needed help with. And things are going better with my family and with my marriage. And if you dump me, then everything will go back to the way it was! I can't do this on my own.

Please, please, don't dump me. I'll pay a higher fee. We can cut back to just twice a month. I'll do group sessions if you want. Just please don't abandon me.

Rosalyn

"The wise woman builds her house, but the foolish tears it down with her own hands." Proverbs 14:1 (NASB)

From:	Shelley Dalton
	\<shelley@hibiscusmentalhealth.org\>
To:	Rosalyn Ebberly \<prov31woman@home.com\>
Subject:	**Re: Final Session**

Dear Rosalyn,

I think that your e-mail to me proves exactly why this needed to be your final session. You are strong and you are healthy enough now to stand on your own. That progress you've made is going to be reversed eventually if you continue relying so much on me. You don't need me. We've worked enough on the skills you need to continue making positive choices on your own. And you aren't alone. Chad is there to help you, and you are there to help him. And your children are much more stable—they need their mom to be their leader now.

You should feel proud of the progress you've made. It's

always a bittersweet thing for me to say goodbye to a client—I've enjoyed working with you, but at the same time, I'm excited to see you whole and able to function without me. You're at that point now. Be happy about that!

Sincerely,

Shelley Dalton, Ph.D., LPC

Hibiscus Mental Health Clinic

From:	Rosalyn Ebberly <prov31woman@home.com>
To:	Shelley Dalton
	<shelley@hibiscusmentalhealth.org>
Subject:	**Re: Final Session**

Dear Shelley,

I appreciate your confidence in me. I just don't quite feel ready yet. Plus, I really enjoy spending time with you. Could we get together sometime, just as friends?

Rosalyn Ebberly

"The wise woman builds her house, but the foolish tears it down with her own hands." Proverbs 14:1 (NASB)

From:	Shelley Dalton
	<shelley@hibiscusmentalhealth.org>
To:	Rosalyn Ebberly <prov31woman@home.com>
Subject:	**Re: Final Session**

Dear Rosalyn,

I've enjoyed getting to know you, too. However, I don't think socializing outside the clinic setting would be a good idea at this point. I think it would be too easy for you to fall into a therapy mindset since that's been our relationship thus far. You need to prove to yourself that you can stand on your own two feet. It's not healthy to be dependent on me to keep you grounded.

I've really enjoyed working with you and your family. I wish you the best. Keep loving and communicating with each other, and you'll do great.

Sincerely,

Shelley Dalton, Ph.D., LPC

Hibiscus Mental Health Clinic

From:	Rosalyn Ebberly <prov31woman@home.com>
To:	SAHM I Am <sahmiam@loophole.com>
Subject:	**[SAHM I AM] Shelley dumped me!**

My beloved therapist, the rock in my world for two years, told me today that I can't come back. I had my last session. But I'm not ready to go on without her! Can't she see how much I need her? She's helped me so much!

SHE WOULDN'T EVEN GIVE ME THE "LET'S JUST BE FRIENDS" SPEECH!!!

What am I going to do? I don't even want to remember what life was like without her. I feel like she just died. I can't stand it! How could she just do this to me? I thought she cared about me!

I think I'm going to call Chad at work and cancel our plans for Valentine's Day. I don't feel like celebrating.
Rosalyn Ebberly

"The wise woman builds her house, but the foolish tears it down with her own hands." Proverbs 14:1 (NASB)

From:	Hannah Farrell
	<boazsmom@farrellfamilylovesjesus.net>
To:	SAHM I Am <sahmiam@loophole.com>
Subject:	Re: [SAHM I AM] Shelley dumped me!

Gee, that was rotten of her. That's like totally what happened to me my sophomore year. I had this friend, or I thought she was a friend, named Julie and we used to do everything together, and she even said I could date her brother, except that I was strictly a courtship gal so no dating even though he was very hot and a senior, and we had been friends since third grade and she knew all my secrets, but then this new girl came to our school and Julie was all like she's so cool and I was just the brainiac so she told me flat out that she was so over hanging out with me. And I was totally crushed and kept begging her like for three whole weeks to be friends with me again, but she wouldn't. But it turned out okay because I got to know Krissy, and she's a better friend than Julie ever was and would never dump me because somebody cooler comes along, and she's still my friend even though she went off to college and I got married and she's going to travel the world and save dolphins while I have lots and lots of babies. But we're always still connected at the heart, and that's what makes her so great.

I think SAHM I Am is your Krissy, Rosalyn. And who needs a Shelley or a Julie when you have a Krissy?
Hannah

From:	Rosalyn Ebberly <prov31woman@home.com>
To:	SAHM I Am <sahmiam@loophole.com>
Subject:	Re: [SAHM I AM] Shelley dumped me!

Strangely, this was comforting to me. Missing the point, but thank you, Hannah. I didn't expect it to come from you. I was under the impression you thought this loop was a bit crazy.
Rosalyn

"The wise woman builds her house, but the foolish tears it down with her own hands." Proverbs 14:1 (NASB)

From:	Hannah Farrell <boazsmom@farrellfamilylovesjesus.net>
To:	Rosalyn Ebberly <prov31woman@home.com>
Subject:	Re: [SAHM I AM] Shelley dumped me!

Oh, I think you all are total nut bars. But I'm getting used to it. I might even like it in another few months.
Hannah

From:	Rosalyn Ebberly <prov31woman@home.com>
To:	Hannah Farrell
	<boazsmom@farrellfamilylovesjesus.net>
Subject:	Re: [SAHM I AM] Shelley dumped me!

Well, you just be careful—don't get too enthusiastic about it or anything.

"The wise woman builds her house, but the foolish tears it down with her own hands." Proverbs 14:1 (NASB)

From:	The Millards
	<jstcea4jesus@familymail.net>
To:	SAHM I Am <sahmiam@loophole.com>
Subject:	Re: [SAHM I AM] Shelley dumped me!

I think I agree with the basic point Hannah made. Rosalyn, you don't need to have the support of a therapist. She wasn't ever going to be a friend in that way. We all need the support of friends and family. You have us, girl.

Besides, we're a much better bargain—support, empathy, understanding, advice, encouragement…and all for much less than $150/hr.

Jocelyn

From:	Rosalyn Ebberly <prov31woman@home.com>
To:	The Millards
	<jstcea4jesus@familymail.net>
Subject:	Re: [SAHM I AM] Shelley dumped me!

Thanks, Jocelyn. Everyone has been e-mailing me all evening saying basically the same thing. Well, almost everyone…

Anyway, I'm just so afraid of losing the progress I've made. What if I fail?

Rosalyn

"The wise woman builds her house, but the foolish tears it down with her own hands." Proverbs 14:1 (NASB)

From:	The Millards
	<jstcea4jesus@familymail.net>
To:	Rosalyn Ebberly <prov31woman@home.com>
Subject:	Re: [SAHM I AM] Shelley dumped me!

Well, duh, honey. That's where we come in with all that advice and encouragement and stuff I was talking about. We're all cracked pots anyway—we've been waiting years for you to finally give up and admit you're one of us!

Jocelyn

From:	Hannah Farrell
	<boazsmom@farrellfamilylovesjesus.net>
To:	SAHM I Am <sahmiam@loophole.com>
Subject:	[SAHM I AM] MY DAY IS RUINED!

It was supposed to be a perfect Valentine's Day! After we got back from dinner, I was going to light lots of candles in our room, and put rose petals on the bed, and have jazz music playing, and everything!

But Bradley accidentally shut our dog in our bedroom, and the dog peed all over the bed! Our down comforter is ruined, and the mattress smells awful, and there's no time to go buy a new one even if we could afford it!

And I got mad at Bradley and yelled at him for being so stupid, and I never wanted a dog in the first place—it was his idea. And I sat in the bathroom and cried for a whole hour, and now my face looks blotchy and puffy.

Hannah

From:	P. Lorimer <phyllis.lorimer@geemail.com>
To:	SAHM I Am <sahmiam@loophole.com>
Subject:	Re: [SAHM I AM] MY DAY IS RUINED!

Poor dear. Put some cool water on your face, go apologize to Bradley for yelling, and then put your cutest outfit on and enjoy the most romantic evening of your life. Don't let the dog ruin it, for goodness sake! You can always get a new bed later. First nonpregnant Valentine's Day only happens once. Enjoy it.

Phyllis

From:	Zelia Muzuwa <zeemuzu@vivacious.com>
To:	SAHM I Am <sahmiam@loophole.com>
Subject:	Re: [SAHM I AM] MY DAY IS RUINED!

Yeah! And what do you need the bed for, anyway? Come on, a little creativity goes a LONG, LONG way! :)

Z

From:	Hannah Farrell
	<boazsmom@farrellfamilylovesjesus.net>
To:	SAHM I Am <sahmiam@loophole.com>
Subject:	Re: [SAHM I AM] MY DAY IS RUINED!

ZELIA!!!!

Hannah

⌨Text Message From Jeanine Hash: For Dulcie Huckleberry

——February 14/3:23 p.m.——

Hi dulcie this is mom hash i need to talk to you about keeping the kids when you and tom are gone to your conferences in march its not going to work out i dont think because well i just need to talk to you

✉Text Message From Dulcie Huckleberry: For Jeanine Hash
——February 14/4:15 p.m.——
What? Yes, plz call me, or no, I'll cll u. Right away!

From:	Jeanine Hash <ilovebranson@branson.com>
To:	Dulcie Huckleberry <dulcie@homemakerinteriors.com>
Subject:	March

Hi Dulcie!
I tried to call you but you must have a client appointment or something. Anyway, I just wanted to explain why I can't take the girls after all in March. I just found out that one of my friends from high school who I haven't seen in years is going to be in Branson with a bus tour that weekend. I can't miss this chance to spend time with her, and there's no way I can bring three kids with me—that wouldn't work out well, you know.

I'm really, really, REALLY sorry, honey. But I'm sure you can find someone else to watch the kids. Maybe your mom and dad? At least you have a month to figure it out.
Love,
Jeanine

From:	Dulcie Huckleberry
	\<dulcie@homemakerinteriors.com\>
To:	"Green Eggs and Ham"
Subject:	News you won't like

Hey girls,

This has been a horrible day. My mother-in-law dropped a bombshell on us that she won't be able to take the girls when I go to the retreat and Tom goes to his woodworking convention. A friend she hasn't seen since high school is coming to Branson on a bus tour. We, her own family, are getting ditched for someone she hasn't seen in forty-five years!

And MY parents can't take them because they're going to be on a cruise that week. Yeah, they just up and decided last week to go on a cruise. Must be nice.

I called around to some of our friends from church, but everyone is busy that weekend, it seems. Either that, or no one likes my children!

So either Tom or I have to stay home. And, predictably, we got in a big fight about who the lucky person was going to be. I'll spare you the details of that as it really was not pretty.

It comes down to this—Tom feels stifled being a SAHD. I don't blame him—being a SAH-anything isn't exactly the world's most glamorous profession. In fact, a lot of times, it downright stinks. So I get that he wants to have something else to do. He's got a couple other SAHD friends, and some buddies from church, but you know how guys are—

they just don't bond as easily as women do. So he's lonely, unfulfilled and restless.

Okay, fine. My heart goes out to him. For the last couple of years, he's wanted Morris (his stepdad) to teach him woodworking. He's picked up quite a bit, and he's good at it and enjoys it. So when he wanted to go to this wood-working convention and learn more techniques and make some professional connections, I was all for it. But it happens to be at the same time as our retreat.

I felt that since he DOES have Morris to help him get more involved in woodworking on a professional level, it isn't absolutely essential for him to go to this convention. But he said the same thing about my retreat—not absolutely essential for me to go to that, either.

So we were yelling at each other and making absolute brats out of ourselves, and MacKenzie crept into the room in tears.

"I'm sorry!" she wailed.

We asked her what she'd done, figuring she'd created some disaster upstairs while we'd been fighting.

"It's my fault and Aidan and Haley's fault. You're arguing because you have to take care of us. If we weren't here, you could both go on your trips!"

You know how guilt can sock you right in the heart, especially when you know good and well you've behaved like a total skunk? Yeah, that's what happened to me at that moment. And Tom, too, from what I could tell.

MacKenzie went on to say, "I don't think I ever want kids. We're too much trouble."

AAIIIEEEE!!!!

After we both spent the next twenty minutes convincing Mac that it wasn't her fault and that we weren't really mad at anybody (do you think kids know when we're lying?), and that kids really aren't that much trouble (I'm serious—they can't tell when we lie, right?), then we resumed our argument. Only now, it was "I'll stay home" and "No, I should stay home. You go." "No, I insist!" Etc.

So thanks to our own sense of guilt, it was looking for a while like neither of us was going to go anywhere. But I got to thinking…

Tom just doesn't have the support network I do. He doesn't have as many friends, he's on our e-mail loop but only as sort of a curiosity—it's not like it is for me. He doesn't have a dads' group at church like my moms' group. He has one message board for SAHDs, and a couple of SAHD friends, but it's just not the same.

I know that his convention isn't going to solve all that. But it suddenly seemed selfish of me to insist on having my retreat when I have everything else. I have my own business, I have a strong circle of friends, I have a supportive spouse.

I can't really help with the friends part for him, but I can help him with the other two.

So my news is this:

I'm not going to go to the retreat. I'm going to stay home and watch the kids while Tom goes to his convention. I told him tonight it was my Valentine's present to him. He didn't say much, just held me really tight.

I'm sorry. I'm heartbroken that I won't get to meet you all in person. But I think Tom needs this more than I do.
Love,
Dulcie

From:	Rosalyn Ebberly <prov31woman@home.com>
To:	SAHM I Am <sahmiam@loophole.com>
Subject:	[SAHM I AM] TOTW
	February 22: Do-Overs

Lovely friends,

The past couple of weeks, I've been doing a lot of thinking about my life. And I've come to the conclusion that there are a few things I wish I could go back and change.

And I wondered, what are things that you wish you could change? If you could do something over in your life, what would it be?

Rosalyn Ebberly
SAHM I Am Loop Moderator

"The wise woman builds her house, but the foolish tears it down with her own hands." Proverbs 14:1 (NASB)

☺Instant Message

VIM_Vigor: What? No outrageous personal examples? No veiled insults to the rest of the loop? A straightforward, serious TOTW? Are you okay? Are you ALIVE?

Prov31Mom: Sister, dear, am I not allowed to change—hopefully for the better? If you really miss all that stuff, I'll be happy to send you veiled insults. I have plenty of material to work from.

VIM_Vigor: Generous as always, but I think I'll pass. Thanks anyway. So why didn't you post your own response to that question? What do you wish you could go back and change? Or are you waiting until later in the week?

Prov31Mom: I don't think I'd better post my regret.

VIM_Vigor: Zelia?

Prov31Mom: Of course.

VIM_Vigor: Hasn't she unbent yet?

Prov31Mom: Why should she?

VIM_Vigor: You should talk to her.

Prov31Mom: I've tried. Got the cold shoulder. I'm trying to make amends the only way I know how.

VIM_Vigor: And what's that?

Prov31Mom: I'll e-mail you later about it. I have to take the children to school now.

Prov31Mom signed off at 8:26:30 a.m.

From:	P. Lorimer <phyllis.lorimer@geemail.com>
To:	SAHM I Am <sahmiam@loophole.com>
Subject:	[SAHM I AM] Prayers, please

This afternoon, I have to go in front of the advisory board at the university to present my proposal for my dissertation. Hammering this out with my goulish advisor has been torturous. She has delayed me at every turn, refused to answer my phone calls or respond to e-mail, and has canceled our meetings on three different occasions. I had to threaten to go to the dean before she finally decided to cooperate!

We now have a proposal that meets with her approval, as well as mine, and I have to take it to the advisory board— of which she is a member. I'm really nervous. If they don't approve it, I will have to take another semester to work out a new proposal. But they should approve it—after all, as nasty as my advisor is, she wouldn't risk making herself look bad just to make my life more difficult.

I'll let everyone know what happens.

Phyllis

From:	VIM <vivalaveronica@marcelloportraits.com>
To:	SAHM I Am <sahmiam@loophole.com>
Subject:	Re: [SAHM I AM] TOTW
	February 22: Do-Overs

I'll tell you one thing I'd like to "do over"—the birthday party fiasco. I'd do it over by NOT doing it at all! I thought sure-shooting that after the snow debacle, all the parents in our school group would avoid me like an armadillo with cooties.

No such luck! They've been pressuring me to have a belated party for Stephenie, who turned two in December. Said they've never had such great entertainment before. Entertainment! We put several thousand dollars on our home-equity line of credit for their "entertainment." We nearly got sued and fined trying to "entertain" them. And that's all they care about? A few laughs, something to gossip about at play group?

FINE. They want a party? They'll get their party! "Marcello Cinema Proudly Presents…" We're decorating our basement like a 1920s movie theater—well, as close as we can come on a strict fifty-dollar budget. They'll have to use their imaginations—which have shrunk to the size of a frog's nose hair, I fear, by the string of outlandish parties this year.

But we have some GREAT surprises in store for these kids and their pushy parents. I'm really looking forward to it. *evil grin*

Veronica

From:	Dulcie Huckleberry
	<dulcie@homemakerinteriors.com>
To:	SAHM I Am <sahmiam@loophole.com>
Subject:	Re: [SAHM I AM] TOTW
	February 22: Do-Overs

I regret…

Getting this cat!!!

I mean it! He's been nothing but trouble and money from the minute he came through our door. And now he's gone back OUT through that door, thanks to my children's inability to CLOSE the door. I told them and told them, "Shut the door!" Did they listen? NO!

And what happened? Hmm…could it be that the cat ran outside and under the porch? Imagine that. Open door=Escapee Cat.

And who gets to track down the wretched animal so that the three idiot children will stop crying about their beloved Rosie being lost "fow-ever"? Oh yes, that would be me.

It is cold. We had an ice storm yesterday. And I get to

go out and crawl on my belly to try to persuade Dumb Cat that life is better indoors where it is warm and dry.

And of course this had to happen while Tom is spending the day at his mother's house helping Morris strip and refinish an antique sideboard we bought at an antique auction last month.

Off to rescue the thankless animal. Wish me luck.
Dulcie

From:	Marianne Hausten
	<confidentmom@nebweb.net>
To:	"Green Eggs and Ham"
Subject:	Re: [SAHM I AM] TOTW
	February 22: Do-Overs

I can't even look at an e-mail from you, Dulcie, without being sad you won't be at the retreat!
Marianne

From:	Brenna L. <saywhat@writeme.com>
To:	"Green Eggs and Ham"
Subject:	Re: [SAHM I AM] TOTW
	February 22: Do-Overs

I know the feeling, Marianne! I was so excited when Darren and I figured out a way for me to go to the retreat. And all the other Green Eggs will be there, along with Ham, of course, so I thought the whole group would finally get to meet up!

I know we all keep saying "maybe next year" but somehow I don't think that will happen. Betcha something will come up for one of us.

Anyway, not trying to be a downer. I hope you can coax the kitty back inside, Dulcie. Try a kitty fishing pole!
Brenna

☺**Instant Message**
JocelynM: Leave a trail of kitty treats for him. He'll eat them and be lured from under the porch.
Dulcet: Just got back inside from trying that. Brr! It's cold outside! The beast sniffed at the treats but wouldn't come close enough for me to grab him.

☺**Instant Message**
ZeeMuzzy: turn on your hose and spray it under the porch. it'll flush him out, and it won't matter if you make more ice since you already have ice.
Dulcet: Oh yeah, that'll be grand. That way, water can seep into the cracks in our foundation, freeze, and cost us even MORE money in house repairs!
ZeeMuzzy: it was just an idea!
Dulcet: And if I were a cartoon character, I'm sure it would work great.
ZeeMuzzy: okay, okay, i give up. i'm taking lishan to the mall. she needs new shoes and i'm making it a mommy/daughter outing. trying to do the "bonding" thing, you know.

From:	Marianne Hausten
	<confidentmom@nebweb.net>
To:	SAHM I Am <sahmiam@loophole.com>
Subject:	Re: [SAHM I AM] TOTW
	February 22: Do-Overs

I hope it's okay to post about something we got the chance to "do over" and actually got it right this time!

You guys know I've been having a lot of problems recently with my family and playgroup pressuring me about how to raise little Neil. The issue has been that since he's a boy, he should be treated differently than Helene and have different expectations for his behavior. I disagree.

But you know me—always conflict aversive. Well, not this time! I was at playgroup, and Neil was playing with a group of other little boys. They started throwing toy cars at some of the other children. The other moms made wimpy little gestures of stopping it like "All right, we don't throw toys, remember?"

I didn't think that was good enough, so I gave Neil a time-out. The other moms were horrified. "He's a boy! He can't sit still in one place!" They claimed I was scarring him for life.

Normally, I'd just not say anything back and find a reason to leave early. But this time, I decided I was tired of that. I told them, "For thousands of years, little boys were required to sit down and be quiet in school and in church and all the other public places they were taken. For years, males were the artists, the poets, the philosophers, the musicians—and all that required them to sit still and behave in a certain way. I really don't think the male species has changed so much in the last twenty years that they can't stay in time-out for five minutes!"

Nobody said anything. They looked too shocked. Then one of them laughed a little nervously and said, "You only think that because you had a girl first. Boys are different. You'll see." Which made me want to bang my head with a baseball bat or something. But I noticed that some of the other moms were a little more firm with their boys after that. So maybe I made a difference. And even if not—it felt SO good to stand up for myself!

I think I'm too prone to assume that if someone doesn't agree with me, I must be wrong. But I think I was right on this—and it felt good to decide to stand up for myself.
Marianne

✉Text Message From Dulcie Huckleberry: For Tom Huckleberry
——February 22/11:05 a.m.——
Plz come home! Jst long enough to help me get Rosie back inside. Been trying for 1.5 hrs now and am cold and wet and tired.

✉Text Message From Dulcie Huckleberry: For Marianne Hausten
——February 22/11:17 a.m.——
Am on hands N knees, butt in air, in driveway, swearing @ cat. Cat not intimidated. Will kill cat.

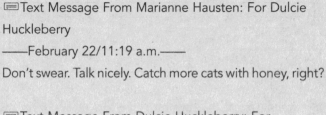Text Message From Marianne Hausten: For Dulcie
Huckleberry
——February 22/11:19 a.m.——
Don't swear. Talk nicely. Catch more cats with honey, right?

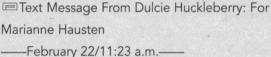Text Message From Dulcie Huckleberry: For
Marianne Hausten
——February 22/11:23 a.m.——
Words nt important. All in tone of voice. High, sweet voice:
Here kitty, kitty, kitty. Come here wretched filthy, horrid
little beast so I can strangle you with my own hands! As
long as said nicely, cat won't know difference.

Text Message From Marianne Hausten: For Dulcie
Huckleberry
——February 22/11:24 a.m.——
Good luck w that. Maybe jst wait till he gets cold and wants
in?

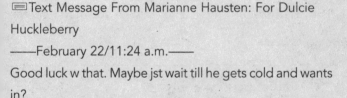Text Message From Dulcie Huckleberry: For
Marianne Hausten
——February 22/11:28 a.m.——
Can't. Girls terrified will run away or freeze to death. Nt
that I would care, mind you, but do have to live with 3 little
girls who care very much. Tom coming home to help.

From:	VIM <vivalaveronica@marcelloportraits.com>
To:	SAHM I Am <sahmiam@loophole.com>
Subject:	**[SAHM I AM] Dulcie's Cat?**

Just wondering if the cat ever came back inside from his outing this morning.
Veronica

☺**Instant Message**
Prov31Mom: Shouldn't you have sent that to Dulcie privately? You know we're trying to cut down on extraneous loop traffic.
VIM_Vigor: Oh please. You wanted to know, too.
Prov31Mom: Well, yeah.
VIM_Vigor: So it's loop business!
Prov31Mom: Remind me never to let you moderate the loop! :)

From:	Dulcie Huckleberry
	<dulcie@homemakerinteriors.com>
To:	SAHM I Am <sahmiam@loophole.com>
Subject:	**Re: [SAHM I AM] Dulcie's Cat?**

I had to call for reinforcements. Tom got home, and we did some strategizing. This was an operation of military proportions. And we were going to use every weapon at our disposal to get the cat back indoors.

First, Tom suggested I try stomping on our porch and yelling to scare the cat out. All I have to show for it is a sore back and hoarse throat.

Then, we waited until Rosie crawled out from under the porch again. We bundled up the girls and eased them outside, warning them to be quiet and not scare the cat. We told Mac and Aidan to block the hole in front of the steps, and we put Haley in front of the other hole on the side.

Should have been simple, right? All they had to do was not move, and Tom and I could chase the cat into the house.

So they were in place. I stepped toward the cat. He skidded across our driveway toward our porch. Tom tried to catch him. Slipped on the ice and thudded to the ground.

MacKenzie slid her way over to him just as the cat shot past her. I screamed at her, "Stay at your post!" She slipped on the ice and fell and started to cry.

The cat ran around to the other side of the porch where Haley was sitting. But she—who can't walk past that cat without picking it up and dragging it around like a doll— saw the cat barreling toward her. She squealed and moved out of the way! The cat dived back under the porch.

Was it asking so much for the girls to just sit there and block the holes? After all, they're the ones that caused this mess! But NO! Now we have Mac and Tom with bumps and bruises, and the twins are chilled.

And that cat is still under the porch!

I'm really rethinking rescuing him from the microwave. Can that be my do-over?

Dulcie

From:	The Millards
	<jstcea4jesus@familymail.net>
To:	SAHM I Am <sahmiam@loophole.com>
Subject:	[SAHM I AM] Veronica's Last Party

I'd really like to hear how the party went. Care to share, Veronica?

From:	VIM <vivalaveronica@marcelloportraits.com>
To:	SAHM I Am <sahmiam@loophole.com>
Subject:	Re: [SAHM I AM] Veronica's Last Party

Absolutely! We planned it for late afternoon, and just finished up. Had a huge turnout. All these parents and children—waiting to be "entertained." HAH! We told the parents that they had to stay, since we'd invited families with two- and three-year-olds.

As each child arrived, we gave them a goodie bag of stuff they could eat while they watched the show. Mostly candy—the higher sugar content, the better. Then we did cake and ice-cream (and presents for Stephenie, of course) right at the start. LOTS of cake. LOTS of frosting. LOTS of ice cream. Yum!!!

We escorted them downstairs and told them they got to watch a really COOL show on our movie theater screen (a large projector screen we borrowed from a friend who borrowed it from work). The parents looked a little confused when they saw that the decorations weren't as elaborate as they'd expected. But they seemed confident that we knew what we were doing.

Which was true. We knew exactly what we were doing. We gave all the kids some extra candy for good measure. Then we turned down the lights. Turned on the movie.

The title came up, "Marcello Cinema Presents…Marcello Family Home Videos."

The parents glanced at each other, looking a bit nervous-like all the sudden. Frank and I snuck back upstairs and out to our hot tub, where we couldn't hear the noise coming from a basement full of bored, sugar-high toddlers and their frustrated parents.

Two hours later, we opened the door, and they straggled out, looking haggard and exhausted. They may hate us now, but you know what?

I DON'T CARE!

As they left, we gave each child party favors—silly string, confetti pops, clapper hands and bubbles. The glares from the parents were sweet indeed.

Well, back to the hot tub! Ashley is babysitting the rest of the kids tonight, and Frank is waiting for me.

Veronica

From:	Dulcie Huckleberry
	<dulcie@homemakerinteriors.com>
To:	SAHM I Am <sahmiam@loophole.com>
Subject:	Re: [SAHM I AM] Dulcie's Cat?

Hi Veronica,

Glad your party went…would "well" be the right word? I'm glad it went the way you wanted it to go. Those poor parents, though!

Just wanted everyone to know the cat is FINALLY back inside! After I stopped yelling at the girls for being so useless, Tom and I went back outside with a big blanket and blocked our porch holes. Then we propped our door open and started chasing the cat. When he saw that all his holes were blocked, the stupid animal ran straight for the open door.

Now he is sulking in the coat closet, but at least he's back inside.

I will not feel sorry for him any longer when the girls treat him like a baby doll. He deserves everything he gets!

Dulcie

From:	The Millards
	\<jstcea4jesus@familymail.net\>
To:	Dulcie Huckleberry
	\<dulcie@homemakerinteriors.com\>
Subject:	**Re: [SAHM I AM] Dulcie's Cat?**

I'm glad it turned out well! I'm surprised you haven't gotten a follow-up from Zelia yet with a Shakespeare quote to commemorate the occasion. Be nice to that kitty, all right?

Jocelyn

From:	P. Lorimer <phyllis.lorimer@geemail.com>
To:	SAHM I Am <sahmiam@loophole.com>
Subject:	[SAHM I AM] She sabotaged me!

I cannot believe this! My advisor hung me out to dry at the advisory meeting this afternoon! One of the other board members voiced a small concern about one aspect of my proposal, something that my advisor should have been able to easily reassure him about. But instead, she said, "This was an area of concern for me, too. I tried to discuss it with Ms. Lorimer, but she insisted on presenting the proposal this way." And then she went on for another FIFTEEN minutes on all the supposed "weaknesses" and "flaws" in my project.

She made it sound as if it was all my fault and that she'd tried to talk me out of it! The result? The board turned down my proposal!

I have NEVER, NEVER been so angry in my life. This is outrageous, and there isn't a single thing I can do about it. She deliberately sabotaged the entire project because…

I don't know. I really don't. I keep trying to think what I might have done to offend her. I've been as nice as I know how to be. I've cooperated. I've done everything she's ever asked me to do. And she just seems to hate me more.

I do not understand! And now I have to explain to Jonathan why this is now going to take an entire extra semester. I'm seriously considering going to the dean and seeing if I can be assigned to a new advisor. I kept thinking if I just kept a good attitude, I could make it work out with her. But I think now that I've been an absolute fool about it.

Where does a pastor's wife go to vent some seriously violent fury?
Phyllis

From:	Brenna L. <saywhat@writeme.com>
To:	SAHM I Am <sahmiam@loophole.com>
Subject:	Re: [SAHM I AM] She sabotaged me!

What's this creep's home address? We'll all go TP her yard for you like we used to do to the teachers in high school who made us mad.

I had LOTS of practice.
Brenna

☺**Instant Message**
HannieBananie: Hi Brenna! About ur post on sahmiam—that's not a very Christian attitude.
Farmgirl04: Beat it, Hannah.
HannieBananie: Why ru so rude to me?
Farmgirl04: Why ru so falsely righteous about everything?
HannieBananie: I'm just trying 2 do what is right! Why does that make u so mad?
Farmgirl04: Dunno. Maybe bc u force it on everyone else. We already have had YEARS of that with Rosalyn. We're all a bit tired of it.
HannieBananie: I'm NOT like Rosalyn!

Farmgirl04: Good grief, she's delusional, too.

HannieBananie: I'm NOT! Rosalyn was trying to be perfect but all the time her life was falling apart!

Farmgirl04: And the difference is???

HannieBananie: My life is GREAT!

Farmgirl04: Yeah, which is why ur giving up your dreams of going to school in order to pop out lots of babies for a man that treats you like an unwanted pet?

HannieBananie: Bradley LOVES me! And I always wanted to stay home and have babies!

Farmgirl04: Then why do you hang on Phyllis's every word about school? And your Krissy friend's school stories? Do you really think that the vicarious experience is going to satisfy you? And Bradley? Honey, what sort of low expectations have you been taught about how a loving husband behaves?

HannieBananie: You don't know a thing about me, Brenna! You don't understand my husband, and you don't know what satisfies me or what I want from my life.

Farmgirl04: That makes two of us, sweetheart.

HannieBananie signed off at 5:53:46 p.m.

From:	VIM <vivalaveronica@marcelloportraits.com>
To:	SAHM I Am <sahmiam@loophole.com>
Subject:	**Re: [SAHM I AM] She sabotaged me!**

What she did to you was rottener than roadkill, Phyllis. I don't blame you one bit for being angry!

You should talk to her. Maybe you've been TOO cooperative. TOO nice. She's being abusive and you're playing the victim. Stand up to her. And I do think trying to get a new advisor would be a good idea. You can't let people treat you like crap. You gotta fight back.

And don't y'all even reply with the "but that's not Christian"—I don't think God made y'all to be doormats. Seems to me if God gave us anger it was so that we could do something constructive with it.

I do like Brenna's TP idea, though. My, that brings back some good memories of high school! :)

Veronica

From:	Dulcie Huckleberry
	<dulcie@homemakerinteriors.com>
To:	SAHM I Am <sahmiam@loophole.com>
Subject:	Re: [SAHM I AM] She sabotaged me!

Phyllis, I'm so sorry, dear friend. That's horrible.

I think Veronica is right—mostly. I think you should at least talk to your advisor about it, and probably your dean, too. This is unethical and wrong.

From:	P. Lorimer <phyllis.lorimer@geemail.com>
To:	SAHM I Am <sahmiam@loophole.com>
Subject:	Re: [SAHM I AM] She sabotaged me!

Thanks, everyone. It means a lot to me—especially Brenna's TP suggestion. Right now, I almost wish you could come do that! (Bad Phyllis!) :)

I've thought about confronting her or complaining to the dean. But what am I supposed to say? I have no documentation to prove that she did, in fact, approve my proposal. It's my word against hers. And as far as the rest of the problems…if I go whining to the dean about it, it will just make me look like all the other religious fanatics on campus complaining about "discrimination." Who is going to take the word of a lowly grad student over a tenured professor? The dean will probably "tsk, tsk" over my inability to resolve this "personality difference" and it will be another black mark on my record.

I don't know what to do. Jonathan was surprisingly supportive and understanding about it. He even offered to go with me and talk to my advisor. Yes, that would really make everything better—hide behind my clergy husband to go talk to a bitter feminist about her mistreatment of his little wife. Sweet and well-intentioned of him, but I don't think so!

I intend to do something stereotypically "female" and gorge myself on ice cream right out of the container. Chocolate ice cream. Goodness knows, I've almost been too nervous to eat the past couple of weeks. I've earned the privilege, I think, after today!
Phyllis

⌨Text Message From Zelia Muzuwa: For Dulcie
Huckleberry
——February 22/6:21 p.m.——
Plz prA. At mall. Lishan missing. Mall lockd dwn. Tell loop.

📧Text Message From Dulcie Huckleberry: For Zelia
Muzuwa
——February 22/6:25 p.m.——
O my goodness! Missing how long? Sent mssg to loop.
Praying.

📧Text Message From Zelia Muzuwa: For Dulcie
Huckleberry
——February 22/6:26 p.m.——
20 min. I thnk. Nt sure exact time. TryN nt 2 panic. Tell Ros
she ws rite. Evry thN she said. Rite.

📧Text Message From Dulcie Huckleberry: For Zelia
Muzuwa
——February 22/6:27 p.m.——
She was NOT right! You'll find her. Will b ok. Everyone is
praying. Even Ros.

From:	Dulcie Huckleberry
	<dulcie@homemakerinteriors.com>
To:	Rosalyn Ebberly <prov31woman@home.com>
Subject:	Zelia

Ros,
It's time to bury the hatchet. Z just texted me and said that
because of this situation with Lishan missing, she thinks you
were right about everything you said. You've GOT to talk
to her and make things right. This has gone on too long.
Dulcie

From:	Rosalyn Ebberly <prov31woman@home.com>
To:	Dulcie Huckleberry
	<dulcie@homemakerinteriors.com>
Subject:	Re: Zelia

Dulcie,
Believe me, I've TRIED! I don't know what else I can do!
You have no idea what I've tried. So far nothing has worked.
Rosalyn

"The wise woman builds her house, but the foolish tears
it down with her own hands." Proverbs 14:1 (NASB)

From:	Dulcie Huckleberry
	<dulcie@homemakerinteriors.com>
To:	Rosalyn Ebberly <prov31woman@home.com>
Subject:	Re: Zelia

Think BIGGER then!
Dulcie

From:	Hannah Farrell
	<boazsmom@farrellfamilylovesjesus.net>
To:	SAHM I Am <sahmiam@loophole.com>
Subject:	Re: [SAHM I AM] Pray for Lishan!

I don't understand! How could a child just go wandering off in the mall like that? How could she be lost for so long?
Hannah

From:	Brenna L. <saywhat@writeme.com>
To:	Hannah Farrell
	<boazsmom@farrellfamilylovesjesus.net>
Subject:	Re: [SAHM I AM] Pray for Lishan!

For crying out loud! If you don't understand that, you had no business babysitting, much less becoming a mother! Grow up already, and realize that a mother isn't all-powerful. We can't control everything. We can't fix everything. We can't make everything work out like it's supposed to. DEAL WITH IT!
Brenna

From:	Rosalyn Ebberly <prov31woman@home.com>
To:	SAHM I Am <sahmiam@loophole.com>
Subject:	Re: [SAHM I AM] Pray for Lishan!

Hannah and everyone,
This nightmare happened because Lishan and Duri have something called "reactive attachment disorder" that makes it hard for them to emotionally bond with their adopted family. I've been doing some research on it, and it doesn't happen to all adopted kids, but the ones that are in orphanages or have difficult early lives are more susceptible to it.

Almost two years ago, I didn't understand this. I just knew that every six months or so, some TV news program had some story about an adopted kid that goes beserk and causes grief for their families. I didn't stop to think about the fact that these stories are sensationalized and hyped, and that for every one of those stories, there are hundreds of stories that go untold—stories about families who face the challenges of adoption with strength and success, and who go on to create beautiful families.

So I posted words about Zelia and her children to the loop that are at the top of my list of things I regret. This is what I would change if I could. What I said then is that Zelia and Tristan had no business adopting their children because "those kids" were "hardwired for disaster." I also claimed that Zelia was too flighty to handle problem children like that.

As many of you will recall, this turned into one of the ugliest, darkest conversations this loop has ever known. And it resulted in my stepping away from the loop for a year to work on my own problems—which were too numerous to list.

I know that it would be tempting for some people to wonder how Zelia could be so careless as to let her child disappear at a mall. Or point fingers to say, "She should have noticed sooner or done something."

I just want to say this is NOT the right attitude. It's not the truth. Zelia and Tristan are amazing parents and what they have accomplished with Lishan and Duri is nearly miraculous. And those two kids are survivors! They have lived through difficulties we can't even imagine, and it is amazing to me that they only have the emotional scars they do have.

I only wish there were more people like Z and Tristan

with the courage to provide homes to children who need them, and the strength to love them no matter what, and the grace and parenting skills to provide a stable home environment for them. It's certainly more than I could do. Much more than I have done with my own family.

So at this time, when we are waiting to hear from Zelia and are praying for a good outcome to what has got to be every parent's worst nightmare, I just want to publicly say I am utterly sorry for the words I wrote then. I've asked Zelia's forgiveness privately, but I want to do so publicly. And I'd like us all to commit to doing whatever we can do to show our support for the Muzuwa family.

Thanks,

Rosalyn Ebberly

SAHM I Am Loop Moderator

"The wise woman builds her house, but the foolish tears it down with her own hands." Proverbs 14:1 (NASB)

⌨Text Message From Zelia Muzuwa: For Dulcie Huckleberry

——February 22/6:55 p.m.——

Found her! Will rite more @ home.

From:	Zelia Muzuwa <zeemuzu@vivacious.com>
To:	SAHM I Am <sahmiam@loophole.com>
Subject:	[SAHM I AM] Lishan is found.

Thank you, all, for praying. I see there are a bunch of loop messages and e-mails to me. It's going to take a while to work through all of them, so please be patient. We are really touched by everyone's concern and prayers. We love you all.

What happened is that Lishan and I were at the mall for a mommy-daughter day out. After we ate supper, I took her into the restroom with me. The stalls were so small there wasn't room for both of us, and the handicapped stall was occupied. So I told Lishan to wait right outside my stall for me. But when I came out, she was gone.

I felt ill. I checked all the other stalls, and raced out into the hallway. I figured she couldn't have gotten too far—I hadn't been in the stall that long. But I couldn't find her. It took me another several minutes to find a security guard, explain the situation and give a description. After a few more minutes of conferring with—I don't know, his supervisor or something?—they locked down the mall.

These past few years since we adopted them, I've struggled SO much with my frustration and even resentment of the amount of time and anguish they've cost us. I've seriously wondered if we made a mistake. And even as they shut the doors of the mall, I feared that not only had I made a mistake, but that the adoption agency, the orphanage and two national governments had made a mistake—a huge mistake of trusting US with these children.

And the fear of never seeing her again—I love her SO much! I couldn't love her more if she'd been conceived in my own womb.

Anyway, that was an awful time. I don't want to relive it, but I do every time I close my eyes.

They found her nearly an hour later, hiding in the women's dressing rooms at one of the department stores. She'd been trailing an African woman who had come into the restroom at the same time we'd been in there. I should have figured it out. Lishan is always looking for her "real" mother. She saw this woman in something similar to Ethiopian clothing, and she followed her. The poor woman didn't even realize she was being trailed! When the security guards tried to question her, she started crying and her English was so broken, we couldn't understand her. But it was clear she had never had any awareness that our daughter was following her, and she was definitely not trying to take her away. I feel sorry for her. She looked so frightened.

I wish I could say that Lishan was overjoyed to be reunited with me. She wasn't upset, just indifferent. I would have given anything for her to have launched herself into my arms and shout "Mommy!" But she has a long way to go before she learns how to share that sort of emotional bond with anyone. And as much as it breaks my heart to acknowledge that, I also have hope that we'll get there—if we can all just keep trying and hang in there.

So that's our little adventure at the mall. Again, thank you everyone for praying. Please keep praying. We need it.
Zelia

From:	VIM <vivalaveronica@marcelloportraits.com>
To:	Zelia Muzuwa <zeemuzu@vivacious.com>
Subject:	**I'm glad you found Lishan**

Hi Zelia,

I just wanted to tell you I'm really glad you found Lishan and that she was okay. I even said a prayer for you. But don't tell my sister—I don't want her to get all hopeful or anything. :)

Speaking of Ros, did you see the e-mail she sent while Lishan was still missing? I just wondered if you'd seen it yet. Ros said she hadn't heard from you.

Veronica

From:	Zelia Muzuwa <zeemuzu@vivacious.com>
To:	VIM <vivalaveronica@marcelloportraits.com>
Subject:	Re: I'm glad you found Lishan

Thanks, Veronica. And yeah, I saw the post from Rosalyn. You're not going to like this, but I really don't know what to say about it. As much as I would like to believe she's had a change of heart, part of me wondered if this was just another way for her to get some more digs in about how messed up my kids are. And even though right now I sort of feel like maybe she was right, it still isn't something I want aired on the loop again.

I just want to handle this privately. The loop doesn't need to know everything.

Zelia

From:	VIM <vivalaveronica@marcelloportraits.com>
To:	Zelia Muzuwa <zeemuzu@vivacious.com>
Subject:	Re: I'm glad you found Lishan

You're right. I don't like that one little bit. How could you read her post as anything but an incredibly sincere effort at reconciliation! Heck, she's never done anything like that for me, and I'm her sister!

She PRAYED for you. And I'm not all that religious, but to me the gesture itself ought to mean something. And I'll tell you something else, too. She did more than just pray. You know that anonymous donor who's been paying for your kids to get therapy all these months?

Yeah. For all her faults, my sister knows how to put her money where her mouth is when it counts. And money isn't something they have in endless supply, either. She would be furious with me for saying anything about it. She only told me earlier this week when I asked.

And I'll tell you what—all her nagging and preaching at me about going to church hasn't done a hill of good. But this…this just might. What she did for you was real. And weird. And wonderful.

If your faith is all it's cracked up to be, I'd think there'd have to be some room for forgiveness somewhere in it. Especially under the circumstances.

Veronica

From:	Dulcie Huckleberry
	<dulcie@homemakerinteriors.com>
To:	SAHM I Am <sahmiam@loophole.com>
Subject:	[SAHM I AM] TOTW
	March 15: Moving Past Our Mistakes

Hi all,

Rosalyn asked me to do the Topic of the Week this week because she's headed to Colorado Springs today to help

Jocelyn get ready for the retreat—and since I'm one of the unfortunate ones who can't go, she figured I'd have time to do the TOTW.

She wanted the topic to be on handling failures. But considering I'm already depressed about not being able to go to the retreat, I decided to make it a little more upbeat a subject.

So everyone who isn't busy getting ready to go to the Springs, why don't we talk about ways that we've found to move beyond our mistakes and failures or turn them into opportunities?

Two weeks ago, I had a chance to do this with my design business. My client, Dorita Jacobs, moved to Branson a year ago and had her house custom-built. Sixty-four and still dyes her hair a bright blond, widowed for eight years. The house is ostentatious—think *Gone With the Wind* meets Las Vegas. I can't believe just one tiny woman lives there.

"Dulcie," she croons to me, "the whole city is buzzing about your decorating skills, honey."

"Thanks, Mrs. Jacobs. I had no idea."

"Oh yes. So I knew you were the absolute perfect choice to help me decorate my living room. I have something very special planned for it, you see."

"What's that?" I'm starting to get nervous at this point.

She takes me by the hand and nearly drags me into her living room. It's just about empty, with soaring cathedral ceilings. There is a large frame draped with a sheet and resting against a chair in the center. The frame is a couple feet taller than me and about six feet wide. I'm guessing it's a portrait. Of her late husband, maybe?

She gently, reverently removes the sheet. I walk around to the front to take a look.

It is a portrait. It is not of her husband.

It is the LARGEST velvet Elvis painting I have ever seen! And it's not even a painting of him when he was young and somewhat attractive. It is from his later days when he was overweight and puffy-looking. And it's not particularly well done at that. He is wearing a Hawaiian shirt and a lei, black leather pants, and is in a pose that reminds me of how my girls look when they have to go potty and are trying to hold it.

Mrs. Jacobs looks like she's in raptures. "Isn't it gorgeous?" she breathes. "I got it on eBay. It's going to be my focal piece for the entire living room. I watch those decorating shows, you know. You're supposed to have a focal piece and decorate the room around that. But you probably already know that." She touches it lovingly. "So…what do you think?"

"It's…" I'm racking my brain for something positive to say. "It's really large."

"I have a large room." She sounds a tiny bit defensive. I'm going to have to do better if I want this job. And while nothing would please me more than to run screaming from the house, my family needs to eat. And if that means staring for the next couple weeks at a middle-aged Elvis who looks like he might have an "overactive bladder"…well, that's life.

"It's just the right size for the room."

She's still waiting for something that sounds like genuine enthusiasm. I swallow hard.

"It's certainly a—" inspiration strikes "—a bold work of art that will be a sure conversation piece." Okay, I was stretching it with the "work of art" bit, but sometimes you just have to flatter the customer some!

Her face lit up. "You see it, too! Oh I'm so glad! I just

knew the minute I found it that it was going to be something special."

"Yeah…" I swallow the lump of revulsion in my throat. "Really special." My voice breaks. My eyes tear up. This might be the project that ends my short career. There is no way I can make this tasteful.

Mrs. Jacobs beams and offers me a flowered hankie. "Oh, I'm going to love working with you! You have such passion and artistic vision!"

Yes, and they're both howling in agony.

Can I just pause the story a minute and tell you that this is what I get to deal with while you all are off on your grand retreat this week? I get to decorate a room around the world's most hideous velvet Elvis painting. ARGHHH!!!

Anyway, how this relates to moving beyond our failures…I won't know until later this week if I was able to turn certain failure into a success or not. So you'll have to wait until then to find out how this ends. But until then, I could sure use your stories of moving beyond mistakes and succeeding despite the odds. I need inspiration!

Dulcie

☺Instant Message

Huck: Are you really that depressed about not going to the retreat?

Dulcet: I'm not suicidal or anything.

Huck: Maybe I should stay home and you can go. You could still get a plane ticket.

Dulcet: No. We already decided. You need to have your time. You deserve it. I'll be fine.

Huck: I feel guilty.

Dulcet: Welcome to the life of a stay-at-home parent. Might as well get used to it. :)

Huck: I'm serious.

Dulcet: Well, tell you what—you use your newfound knowledge gained at this convention to make me a dining table with inlaid mother-of-pearl, and we'll call it even.

Huck: Dining table! Maybe in twenty years if I work really hard. Would you settle for a jewelry box?

Dulcie: Depends on what comes in it.

Huck: You drive a hard bargain, woman. :)

Dulcie: Of course. It's the only way to assuage your guilt. :) Now I have to get back to work—the Elvis Room awaits my final touch of genius.

Huck: The world will never be the same.

Dulcie: Unfortunately.

From:	P. Lorimer <phyllis.lorimer@geemail.com>
To:	SAHM I Am <sahmiam@loophole.com>
Subject:	[SAHM I AM] Talked with my advisor

I did it! I finally did it just this morning. It took me this long just to get a meeting with her—she kept putting me off. But I persisted and she finally ran out of excuses for why she was busy.

I kept Veronica's suggestions in mind and did not come in with a particularly friendly or conciliatory demeanor. I got right to the point—"Why did you kill my proposal in front of the board? If you didn't like it, you should have said so."

"I just thought Dr. Graybill brought up a good point."

"Then you should have said that we'd adjust that part of the proposal to address his concern!"

She wouldn't look at me. "I felt you weren't really as well prepared as I'd expected."

I lost it then. "I was thoroughly prepared, and you know it! I have done everything you asked! I've done almost as much preliminary research for this as I did for my entire master's thesis. What you did to me was unethical, unprofessional and completely uncalled for."

"I'm sorry you feel that way. I disagree."

I almost stormed out at that point, but I couldn't quite admit defeat so easily. I plopped into a chair. "We haven't had the best working relationship, have we?"

She seemed surprised at my sudden change in tone. "I haven't really spent any time thinking about it."

What a rotten liar.

"Well, I have. And I want to know if this is something we can do better on or if I should find a different advisor. What do you think?"

"Aren't you worried about your funding?"

"Funding won't matter if you're going to hold my dissertation hostage to punish me for whatever I've done to offend you!"

She tried to look scornful, but wasn't very successful. "Don't be so dramatic, Ms. Lorimer. It doesn't work for you."

"Just tell me—do you want me to find a different advisor or not?"

She scowled at me a second. "Why did you choose me to begin with?"

"Because I wanted to focus on women's studies in Early Modern Europe, and you are the best choice for that."

"Why women's studies?"

"Because the treatment of women matters greatly to me."

"I find that hard to believe."

"Why?"

"Because I have yet to meet any Christian who really cares about the 'treatment of women.' And I can't respect that. It makes me angry because a lot of us have worked very hard to make the world a better place for women, and you seem to be intent on undoing that work."

There was such intensity and passion in her eyes—I knew she was being uncharacteristically open with me. I sat forward and waited until she was looking at me. "I am not like that. Don't you know that yet?"

"I don't know what to think about you, actually. You're married, you're a pastor's wife, you go to a conservative, traditional church. And yet you speak and act like a feminist. It doesn't add up."

I couldn't help but laugh. "Then I can't win! I'm myself—and I can't help it if that defies your stereotypes."

After that, we actually ended up having a real conversation—probably our first one. We decided that I will remain her advisee, and she is going to push through my proposal after all. I don't know that we have everything worked out yet, but at least we're talking—and that's a step forward by itself.

I'm exhausted now. I'm going to go take a nap!
Phyllis

From:	Zelia Muzuwa <zeemuzu@vivacious.com>
To:	P. Lorimer <phyllis.lorimer@geemail.com>
Subject:	Re: [SAHM I AM] Talked with my advisor

Phyllis, babe,
You are my HERO! You totally rock. I really admire you. It
couldn't have been an easy thing to have that conversation
with her. I know she really hurt you and treated you unfor-
givably. And you still made a final effort to work things out.

That's an inspiration to me—I just wanted you to know.
Z

▭Text Message From Rosalyn Ebberly: For Jocelyn
Millard
——March 15/10:42 a.m.——
Am at Seattle airport. Emergency! Kathy Keller just can-
celled.

▭Text Message From Jocelyn Millard: For Rosalyn
Ebberly
——March 15/10:43 a.m.——
What? We had a contract!

▭Text Message From Rosalyn Ebberly: For Jocelyn
Millard
——March 15/10:44 a.m.——
Son climbed out on roof and fell off. Lucky to have only
two broken ribs and one broken arm. What should we do?

▭Text Message From Jocelyn Millard: For Rosalyn
Ebberly

——March 15/10:44 a.m.——
Invite her to join SAHM I Am? Sounds like she'd fit right in.

▭Text Message From Rosalyn Ebberly: For Jocelyn Millard
——March 15/10:45 a.m.——
Be serious! This is catastrophic! And we're boarding now.

▭Text Message From Jocelyn Millard: For Rosalyn Ebberly
——March 15/10:46 a.m.——
Let me work on it. We'll talk about it more when you get here. As you always tell me—don't worry!

▭Text Message From Rosalyn Ebberly: For Jocelyn Millard
——March 15/10:47 a.m.——
Thank you! I don't handle pressure like this well. I'm glad to be working with someone who can stay coolheaded.

From:	The Millards
	<jstcea4jesus@familymail.net>
To:	P. Lorimer <phyllis.lorimer@geemail.com>
Subject:	**HELP ME!**

Phyllis,
We're having a crisis! Kathy Keller's son fell off a roof, so of course she isn't going to be able to come to the retreat because she'll have to take care of her son and his broken

ribs and arm, but now we don't have a keynote speaker and Ros is freaking out, and I know we sort of snubbed you when we decided to book her instead, but you've always been such a good sport and so now I'm groveling and begging you to forgive us for being so foolish and will you please be the speaker at the retreat?

PLEASE!

Jocelyn

From:	P. Lorimer <phyllis.lorimer@geemail.com>
To:	The Millards
	<jstcea4jesus@familymail.net>
Subject:	Re: HELP ME!

LOL! It's all right, Jocelyn. I was never upset. I've had enough to worry about with school and everything. I'd be glad to come up with something. I'm flattered to be pinch-hitting for the renowned Kathy Keller! Just let me know how long you want me to talk. It will probably not be as entertaining as she would have been—I'm more of a teacher than a motivational speaker. But I'll do my best. Relax. Nobody is going to care.

Phyllis

From:	The Millards
	<jstcea4jesus@familymail.net>
To:	P. Lorimer <phyllis.lorimer@geemail.com>
Subject:	Re: HELP ME!

Care? Of course they're going to care! She was the whole reason some of the moms are coming! Without her, they'll probably cancel, and then we won't have enough to cover my deposit, and our family will be bankrupt and we'll have to fire the housekeeper!

Jocelyn

From:	The Millards
	<jstcea4jesus@familymail.net>
To:	P. Lorimer <phyllis.lorimer@geemail.com>
Subject:	Re: HELP ME!

I did not mean to imply that nobody would come if you are the speaker! You know that, right? Please tell me you knew that!

Jocelyn

From:	P. Lorimer <phyllis.lorimer@geemail.com>
To:	The Millards
	<jstcea4jesus@familymail.net>
Subject:	Re: HELP ME!

Goodness, Jocelyn! You need to go drink a large POT of chamomile tea. I was not offended. Though it does amuse me to hear you fretting about losing your housecleaning help. I thought you hated it. :)

Phyllis

From:	The Millards
	<jstcea4jesus@familymail.net>
To:	P. Lorimer <phyllis.lorimer@geemail.com>
Subject:	Re: HELP ME!

I did, too, until just now when the thought of not having it any more reduced me to tears. I think tea is a very good idea. Only then I'll have to pee, and then I'll have to clean the toilet all by myself!!!

Okay. You're right. I need to stop panicking. How did I let it get to this point? Never mind. Don't answer. I worked with Rosalyn. That's all it takes.

Jocelyn

From:	Brenna L. <saywhat@writeme.com>
To:	SAHM I Am <sahmiam@loophole.com>
Subject:	Re: [SAHM I AM] TOTW
	March 15: Moving Past Our Mistakes

Well, Darren finally had a MPOM (as in the subject line) moment today! I told him since I was going to be gone for the retreat, he had to practice the kids' daily routine today. That meant getting Madeline ready for school and making sure she met the bus on time, and then getting the twins dressed and fed.

He ended up having to spend the entire morning with the twins. And he told me this afternoon, "Little Pat actually knows how to do lots of stuff. He just needs someone to work with him more on it."

"Are you trying to tell me I'm not doing a good enough job with him?" Snippy, I know, but the subject of Little Pat is a sore one these days with us.

"No! You're doing a great job. But I decided to take the twins with me to do chores, and I noticed that he was really interested in the calf. So I helped him give the bottle to the calf and he wasn't scared at all!"

Imagine that. "So have you decided that maybe he's good enough to be your son after all?"

That made his face go all red. "I never said he wasn't good enough!"

"Not in words—but your actions have screamed it for months."

I was thinking great…just great. Here I was due to leave town the next day, and we were going to have a humungous argument. I should have kept my mouth shut, but I am SO sick of his stupid attitude.

But Darren didn't yell back. He put his hand on the back of his neck and looked at the floor. "I know. I'm sorry. I know you don't understand what that was all about, and I'm not sure, either. I just felt like if Pat didn't end up being your 'normal' farm kid, my whole family was going to be really disappointed. They're counting on us, you know, to keep this place running."

"Yeah, I know. So are they disappointed in Pat?"

He snorted. "I don't know. Nobody ever talks about that stuff. But while I was holding Pat, helping him feed the calf, I was thinking about it. And I was being stupid. This is my son. My kid. And that's special, so I'd better not go around whining because he's not up to some ridiculous standard that doesn't even exist."

In most families, we probably would have had a good cry and a hug. But we're just not really like that. All I said was, "Well, all right then."

And he said, "Yeah, okay."

And that was that.

But if you want the poetic finish to this story—everything seems to shine a little brighter now, and I have energy that I haven't had in weeks. And I tell you—Little Pat seems a little stronger, too, even though that can't be possible. Right?

Brenna

From:	Zelia Muzuwa <zeemuzu@vivacious.com>
To:	Brenna L. <saywhat@writeme.com>
Subject:	Good for you guys!

Tell Darren I'm proud of him. And of you. Of course Little Pat is stronger—he's got both of you to love him.

We just gotta keep persevering with these kiddos—somehow we'll all grow up and become better people because we had to struggle together. Right?

Some days, I'm not sure how I'd make it without you, Brenna-girl. You are a real inspiration to me. Thanks, babe.

Z

From:	The Millards
	<jstcea4jesus@familymail.net>
To:	"Green Eggs and Ham"
Subject:	My Last Will and Testament

Hi girls,

This is it. We're done. My life is over. We're going to have to cancel the entire retreat. The hotel we were supposed to meet at had a fire early this morning. It's closed indefinitely. Rosalyn and I checked, and there are no other hotels that can accommodate us on such short notice.

People are going to be furious when we tell them. We don't have any other choice. But they're all going to lose their airfare! And I don't know yet if I'll be able to get the deposit back that I paid.

Rosalyn looks like she's on the permanent edge of puking. And I have the worst headache in my life. Why did we let it get so big? So out of hand? We've been making ourselves miserable all year and for what? To have to cancel two days before the event?

Anyway, I just wanted to let you know first.

Jocelyn

▭Text Message From Zelia Muzuwa: For Phyllis Lorimer
——March 16/9:52 a.m.——
We cn't let them cancel retreat. What r we goN 2 do?

▭Text Message From Phyllis Lorimer: For Zelia Muzuwa
——March 16/9:59 a.m.——
I thought you were upset about retreat. Had a change of heart?

▭Text Message From Zelia Muzuwa: For Phyllis Lorimer
——March 16/10:01 a.m.——

Aw, u kno I cn't stA mad @ Joc! I luv that gRl. Dn't wnt 2 c this ruined 4 her.

☺Instant Message

HannieBananie: Hey Phyllis, I saw you were online. Are you busy?

PhyllisLorimer: No, I'm just doing my best to save the world from imminent destruction once again.

HannieBananie: Really? :-O

PhyllisLorimer: Still a bit concrete-operational, aren't you, kiddo? The retreat is in danger of being canceled. There was a fire at the hotel this morning, and so now we have nowhere to meet.

HannieBananie: Wow! Can't we move it somewhere else?

PhyllisLorimer: Apparently all the hotels are already booked. It's a huge mess. They don't even know if they'll get their deposit back or not.

HannieBananie: I have an idea. Let me do some checking online and make some phone calls. I'll get back to you. Tell them NOT to cancel quite yet!

PhyllisLorimer: ☺ All right. Seems like I just got kicked out of my job of saving the world.

HannieBananie: Forced retirement. I'm younger and cheaper.

PhyllisLorimer: LOL! Touché. All right. Go, Supergirl, go!

📧Text Message From Phyllis Lorimer: For Zelia Muzuwa

——March 16/10:15 a.m.——

Urgent. Tell Jocelyn not to cancel retreat. Hannah is working on an idea.

✉Text Message From Zelia Muzuwa: For Phyllis Lorimer
——March 16/10:16 a.m.——
Hannah?!? Tht child? What cn she do?

✉Text Message From Phyllis Lorimer: For Zelia Muzuwa
——March 16/10:16 a.m.——
Just for that, I am going to make you call her yourself to find out!

☺**Instant Message**
ZeeMuzzy: can i have your jewels?
JocelynM: WHAT?
ZeeMuzzy: your jewels. since you're writing out your will.
JocelynM: Not funny, Z.
ZeeMuzzy: okay. i'll settle for your grandma's china. my grandma didn't leave us anything.
JocelynM: Z! If you just IM'd to gloat, then I have to go. We're busy over here.
ZeeMuzzy: not gloating, friend. i wanted to let you know that i'm on my way to the airport, and i will be in CO Springs this evening. If you or shane could meet me there, i'd appreciate it.
JocelynM: Why are you coming out here? We are CANCELING the retreat!
ZeeMuzzy: no you are not.
JocelynM: Really? And where do you propose we have it at?
ZeeMuzzy: how many women are supposed to come?
JocelynM: About 150.

ZeeMuzzy: did you check the YMCA camp in the Springs?

JocelynM: No...

ZeeMuzzy: hannah did. and we are now booked for our group from thursday through sunday. at a considerably cheaper rate than the hotel, i might add.

JocelynM: HANNAH did that?

ZeeMuzzy: yeppers. looked it up, made a phone call, and had it booked within the hour. should have her organize the retreat next year! :)

JocelynM: Why didn't she just contact me herself?

ZeeMuzzy: uh...i asked her that. she said something about friends being important and that i...well, that i needed an opportunity to mend some fences. *blushing*

JocelynM: She's a good one for surprising us, isn't she?

ZeeMuzzy: uncomfortably good at it.

JocelynM: But won't the gals be upset about going from upscale hotel to a retreat camp?

ZeeMuzzy: better than canceling. sheesh, get a girl a housekeeper and she goes all Beverly Hills on you! :)

JocelynM: Not true! I guess we were just so panicked we didn't even think about that. I'll have to tell everyone to bring camping clothes and their own bedding. Quite a comedown from an indoor pool and massage therapists.

ZeeMuzzy: so? the point is to be TOGETHER. it doesn't have to be a resort. and from what i can tell, the Y camp is really nice.

JocelynM: Okay, I guess we're officially camping. What time does your flight get in?

ZeeMuzzy: i just emailed my itinerary to you.

JocelynM: You'll be staying with me, right?

ZeeMuzzy: i should hope so!

JocelynM: Ros is here, too, since the hotel is closed.

ZeeMuzzy: i assumed she would be. i'll be on my best behavior. i promise.

JocelynM: I really think you should try to

ZeeMuzzy: no lectures, okay? i'm dealing with it in my own way.

From:	Brenna L. <saywhat@writeme.com>
To:	Dulcie Huckleberry <dulcie@homemakerinteriors.com>
Subject:	Here in CO!

Hi Dulcie,

I'm here at the retreat. The camp is beautiful! I'm loving these mountains and this Oklahoma girl can't get enough of all the trees. Good call on Hannah's part, loath as I am to admit that. It's awesome to see all these people in person! We've all got name tags, and we go running around squinting at the tags, and then squealing and hugging when we realize who the person is!

They've got horses here, and Zelia has already managed to get herself thrown from her horse and dumped into a pile of horse manure. And this is just a gentle old trail horse! She's okay, thankfully—the horse, I mean. Zelia has a bruised tailbone and an even more bruised ego, but she'll be fine, too.

Wish you were here. It's supposed to maybe snow a little bit tonight, and we're going to have a campfire and s'mores. I love camping! I'm actually sort of glad the hotel caught fire because I think everyone is a lot happier with this arrangement.

Miss you,

Brenna

—This message has been sent using my cell phone.—

From:	Zelia Muzuwa <zeemuzu@vivacious.com>
To:	Dulcie Huckleberry
	<dulcie@homemakerinteriors.com>
Subject:	Hey girl!

I saw Brenna e-mailing you—don't believe a thing she says about the horse incident! That beast was a monster! I don't know what they were thinking letting such a horrible animal anywhere near retreat guests! I was nearly killed. Really!

Other than that, we're having a terrific time. Jocelyn is starting to be convinced that she can maybe hold off on that will for a while longer. And I am just adoring meeting all these gals that have been my friends for so long. I just wish you were here, girl. But we're all determined to e-mail you a TON so you won't miss out on a thing.

Love you!

Z

This message was sent with BlackBerry.

From:	P. Lorimer <phyllis.lorimer@geemail.com>
To:	Dulcie Huckleberry
	<dulcie@homemakerinteriors.com>
Subject:	How are you?

Dear Dulcie,

We're all here. I am having a very nice time, but so many people—it wears me out! I am writing this from my laptop in my room, and I'll send it when I go to lunch. I know the other girls have already e-mailed you, so I'll try not to repeat any of their news.

I know things now that I didn't know before. The way Z's eyes twinkle when she smiles. The warmth in Jocelyn's voice, even as she's herding us around from one activity to another. Then there's Connie—who is every bit as mother-hennish as she is on the loop, but whose hugs leave you feeling warm the rest of the day. I'm glad her mother is better and that Connie was able to come.

Even Rosalyn—she's every bit as polished as she'd like us all to believe, but there's an earnestness in her eyes, as if she's always watching for an opportunity to please us. I didn't realize that would be there.

And there's Marianne, of course. But you know her secrets already. And Iona—everyone is completely in love with her dreadlocks. She might have started a new SAHM I Am trend! She brought her guitar and read us her poems and sang us songs she wrote for her husband's band last night. We were all teary-eyed by the end because they were so beautiful.

How are YOU doing, though? Are we making things better or worse for you? I keep looking around and it feels like something important is missing, and then I realize—it's you.

Do you want me to call later this evening and we'll chat—just you and me?

Love you,
Phyllis

From:	Dulcie Huckleberry
	<dulcie@homemakerinteriors.com>
To:	P. Lorimer <phyllis.lorimer@geemail.com>
Subject:	**Re: How are you?**

Honestly, I'm miserable. Tom left last night for his convention, so he's in KC now. And it's just me and the girls and all your wonderful, tantalizing e-mails. And I've spent the entire morning trying not to bawl.

But it's so sweet of you all to remember me and try to keep me up-to-date. I hope your talk goes well on Sunday. I think it's good that they canceled all the workshops. Who wants workshops when you can sit around and gab or go ride horses?

On the bright side, my Elvis-themed living room was a raving success! I decided to just go for it and make the room kitschy and retro, in blacks, hot pinks, and splashes of yellow and blue—to give it a Hawaiian flair. I got mod, retro furniture, and a couple of velvet throw blankets and pillows—to echo the velvet in the painting. I even mounted vinyl records on the wall opposite The Painting. It turned out fun and surprisingly cozy. My client was so happy she was in tears. That felt REALLY good.

In fact, the room turned out so well, I'm thinking of entering it in a design contest.

Tell everyone hi for me and that I love them. Even Rosalyn.
Love,
Dulcie (who is currently the most depressing shade of blue in the world)

⌨Text Message From Brenna Lindburg: For Jocelyn Millard
——March 19/1:32 p.m.——
This was a set-up! YOU did this.

⌨Text Message From Jocelyn Millard: For Brenna Lindburg
——March 19/1:33 p.m.——
No idea what ur talking about. Rn't u supposed 2b paying attention to ropes course instructions?

⌨Text Message From Brenna Lindburg: For Jocelyn Millard
——March 19/1:34 p.m.——
Exactly. High ropes buddy course. With HANNAH for a buddy! That's mean. I hate heights.

⌨Text Message From Jocelyn Millard: For Brenna Lindburg
——March 19/1:35 p.m.——
Then b glad ur with Hannah. I hear she's done this lots with her youth group.

📧Text Message From Brenna Lindburg: For Jocelyn Millard
——March 19/1:35 p.m.——
Tht is the point. She should still b IN youth group. N I should B on solid ground. We should all stay where we belong. Nt up 100 ft in air!!!

📧Text Message From Jocelyn Millard: For Brenna Lindburg
——March 19/1:36 p.m.——
Only 50 ft. Which u would kno IF U WERE PAYING ATTENTION!

📧Text Message From Brenna Lindburg: For Jocelyn Millard
——March 19/1:37 p.m.——
Sheesh. Ur such a mom.

From:	Marianne Hausten
	\<confidentmom@nebweb.net\>
To:	Dulcie Huckleberry
	\<dulcie@homemakerinteriors.com\>
Subject:	Live from the ropes course

You won't believe this. Brenna is stuck in the middle of the high ropes course! She didn't look too excited about going up there. I think she especially wasn't happy about being paired up with Hannah. I think Jocelyn did that. But you know Brenna isn't one to back away from a challenge.

She and Hannah had to help each other across a tightrope about fifty feet in the air. Brenna did okay at first, but she got halfway out and looked down, and now she won't move!

Ooohh, I think they're arguing! How awful. Hannah says "Look at my eyes, not the ground." And Brenna says...oh dear, she says, "What would you know about it anyway? You think youth group trust games gives you the experience to talk me out of a panic attack?" That was not very nice, but you know how direct Brenna can be. And she's scared, poor thing. I don't know why she agreed to go up there, except she didn't want to look like a coward.

The ropes director wants to know if Brenna wants to come down. The rest of us rolled our eyes at that. We know her too well. Sure enough, she shook her head. She needs to let Hannah help her, but she's too stubborn.

Hannah and Brenna are talking now. We can't hear them, but I think Hannah is trying to distract Brenna and make her relax. They're each standing on a tightrope, gripping each other's hands. If they let go, they'll fall off the tightrope. Of course, they've got safety harnesses, so they're not in real danger. But I bet it doesn't make Brenna feel any better!

And it looks like it's going to rain! Jocelyn just asked if it starts raining if they'll stop the activity. The director says only if high winds or lightning. I want to know what about hail?

Uh-oh, it's sprinkling. I'd better put away my phone so it doesn't get wet. Sorry to leave you "hanging." ☺ I'm sure one of us will let you know how it turns out.
Marianne

E-mail sent by cell phone

From:	Dulcie Huckleberry
	<dulcie@homemakerinteriors.com>
To:	Marianne Hausten
	<confidentmom@nebweb.net>
Subject:	Re: Live from the ropes course

My darling friend,

You will be DEAD from the ropes course if you don't tell me what happened! This is torture—which, while technically no longer illegal in the U.S., is highly unethical and rather mean. Especially of your best friend!

I don't care if your phone gets a little wet—GIVE ME THE REST OF THE STORY!

Dulcie

From:	Marianne Hausten
	<confidentmom@nebweb.net>
To:	Dulcie Huckleberry
	<dulcie@homemakerinteriors.com>
Subject:	Re: Live from the ropes course

Good grief—violent much, are you? We're all huddled in the supply hut, except for the belayers who have to keep hold of the safety lines. It's pouring out there! And it's cold. I can't believe it isn't snowing. The ropes director told them they have five more minutes and then she's going to lower them by their safety harnesses.

I can hardly see them through the rain, but right before the rest of us dashed for the hut, Hannah had managed to get Brenna to move a few steps. I think they're making progress. If they can get to the end of the line, there's a little tree-house-type enclosure up there that they can wait out the storm in.

It's okay—they're not in any danger. I'm more worried about them all getting too cold and wet. But we'll get them dried off when they come in. It's not supposed to rain too long.

Marianne

E-mail sent by cell phone

📧Text Message From Brenna Lindburg: For Dulcie Huckleberry
——March 19/2:48 p.m.——
Am at top of hi ropes course! Afraid of heights, had panic attack, Hannah for buddy. Pouring rain. But Hannah is my hero—we r in tree house now waiting out storm. Cold, but found blankets. Talking lots about big stuff. Will tell more L8r. Hannah says hi.

📧Text Message From Dulcie Huckleberry: For Brenna Lindburg
——March 19/2:55 p.m.——
Thank God you guys are ok! I was worried. Marianne told me you were stuck. Tell Hannah thank you for rescuing my friend. Love you!

From:	P. Lorimer <phyllis.lorimer@geemail.com>
To:	Dulcie Huckleberry
	<dulcie@homemakerinteriors.com>
Subject:	Did you hear about this afternoon?

I don't know if anyone e-mailed you or not, but there was a huge rainstorm this afternoon while Brenna and Hannah were on the high ropes course. They're okay, but they had to spend an extra hour up in the tree house.

I wasn't there. I was still relaxing in my room. But I talked to Hannah after they returned. Very interesting discussion. It turns out that Brenna and Hannah had a great talk while they were waiting out the storm. Hannah said they talked about being married so young and having children. She told Brenna that being at the retreat made her feel for the first time what it might have been like at college—with so many people around and a group of friends just a door down the hall from her at all times. Brenna said that she'd always wanted to go to college, too, but it's a lot harder with kids. Then she told Hannah that she thinks Hannah should still do it. It won't be like staying in a dorm or sharing a house with a bunch of girls, but that she should use the gifted brain God gave her. That she could do that and still be a good mom and wife. Hannah said it was such an encouragement, she "like totally went all waterworks on Brenna." :)

It sounds as if they are now on an easier footing with each other. Hannah told me that as soon as she got back to her room and dried off, she called Bradley and had a serious discussion with him. She told him that she does not want to always be pregnant and that she would like to come to an agreement on how many children they will have. (Negotiated four, apparently.) She also said she wanted his promise that she could take college classes after those children are school-age. He promised, and we'll just have to see if he keeps his word. I still have mixed feelings about her, but I do admire her for being that frank with him. It's a start.

Brenna denies being responsible for this, but I rather imagine that she had more influence than she's willing to admit. I doubt Hannah will be officially joining the ranks of Green Eggs any time soon, but you know—she really isn't as bad as we all thought. It's been good to meet her. She is so YOUNG! But she's got lots of potential, too.

Miss you, dear one,

Phyllis

From:	Dulcie Huckleberry
	<dulcie@homemakerinteriors.com>
To:	P. Lorimer <phyllis.lorimer@geemail.com>
Subject:	**Waaaahhhh!**

I miss you, too! I can't believe all this excitement happened without me. If you can call me tonight, please do. I am SO lonely now! I just put the girls to bed. The house is quiet except for the miserable echoes of my friends' laughter coming from my e-mail in-box.

Dulcie

⌨Text Message From Tom Huckleberry: For Dulcie
Huckleberry
——March 19/8:15 p.m.——
Get packed. I'll be home in another hour. Your flight for
CO leaves at 11:53 p.m. tonight.

⌨Text Message From Dulcie Huckleberry: For Tom
Huckleberry
——March 19/8:15 p.m.——
WHAT? U R @ convention. & why aren't u answering
phone?

⌨Text Message From Tom Huckleberry: For Dulcie
Huckleberry
——March 19/8:16 p.m.——
Sorry. Was on phone making travel arrangements for you.
Convention is great, but I can't concentrate. Thinking 2
much about u and worrying. So decided pointless to stay
at convention. Was able to get you on a flight tonight but
u and girls have 2 b ready to hop in car when I get there.

⌨Text Message From Dulcie Huckleberry: For Tom
Huckleberry
——March 19/8:17 p.m.——
You don't have 2 do this. I'm fine. Really.

⌨Text Message From Tom Huckleberry: For Dulcie
Huckleberry
——March 19/8:18 p.m.——
Well, one of us is now committed to going to retreat. And
rooming w/ Marianne. Very awkward if person is me. Afraid
u have 2 go. I want u 2 go. K?

▤Text Message From Dulcie Huckleberry: For Tom
Huckleberry
——March 19/8:18 p.m.——
I love you.

▤Text Message From Tom Huckleberry: For Dulcie
Huckleberry
——March 19/8:18 p.m.——
And I adore you.

From:	Dulcie Huckleberry
	<dulcie@homemakerinteriors.com>
To:	Thomas Huckleberry
	<t.huckleberry@showme.com>
Subject:	Thank you!

My darling, wonderful, sweet Tom,
It's Saturday afternoon, and I just wanted to tell you how
the day is going. I'm SO tired—Jocelyn and Marianne
snuck me into the camp about 4:00 this morning. But I got
a few hours of sleep, and then in the morning, I walked over
to the breakfast hall with Marianne—wearing a hastily made
name tag, of course.

It was SO much fun watching people fall over themselves
when they saw who I was! Almost makes up for having to
miss Thursday and Friday. I thought Brenna and Zelia were
going to rip me to pieces trying to hug me. And they nearly
did rip Joc and Marianne to shreds for not letting them in
on the surprise.

It's so wonderful to see them all. We got the Green Eggs and Ham girls all together for the first time after breakfast. We sat around a table and stared at each other. Then Phyllis started to cry, and then we all cried. Even Iona—our newest Egg. And I'm not even sure why.

Then she dived for her notebook and pen because she said crying was cathartic and that she was now inspired at that very moment to finish a commissioned poem she'd been working on. She was muttering something about "saltwater" and "metaphorical tears." Zelia gave her a weird look, and she sort of nodded. But she wouldn't show us the poem. Something about "when all our paths intersect with the perfect point in time" then she'd show us the poem.

She's so weird! We all are, I guess. But these are all the sisters of my heart, and being together…it was like a desert place in my heart I didn't even know was there finally received a soaking, healing rain.

Thank you so much for giving up the rest of your convention for me. You didn't have to. You're going to go to the very next one, even if I have to decorate a hundred Elvis living rooms.

All my love,
Dulcie

▤Text Message From Zelia Muzuwa: For Dulcie
Huckleberry
——March 20/2:20 p.m.——
Hey, surprise-girl! Where ru? Is Phyllis with u?

▤Text Message From Dulcie Huckleberry: For Zelia
Muzuwa

——March 20/2:21 p.m.——
Haven't seen Phyllis. Ask Brenna. Am going to ride horses. Wanna come?

📧Text Message From Zelia Muzuwa: For Dulcie Huckleberry
——March 20/2:21 p.m.——
Wretched, crazed beasts. You be careful!

📧Text Message From Zelia Muzuwa: For Brenna Lindburg
——March 20/2:26 p.m.——
Have u seen Phyllis? Where ru?

📧Text Message From Brenna Lindburg: For Zelia Muzuwa
——March 20/2:27 p.m.——
I think she's in our room. Why? I'm going to play Frisbee golf. Wht ru doing?

📧Text Message From Zelia Muzuwa: For Brenna Lindburg
——March 20/2:27 p.m.——
She suppsd 2 go hiking w/us. Wht she doing in room?

📧Text Message From Brenna Lindburg: For Zelia Muzuwa
——March 20/2:28 p.m.——
Sorry, made me promise not to tell you. But I strongly advise interrupting her.

📧Text Message From Zelia Muzuwa: For Brenna Lindburg

——March 20/2:29 p.m.——
Oh she's NOT. Tell me she isn't!!! Not on a retreat!

📧Text Message From Brenna Lindburg: For Zelia
Muzuwa
——March 20/2:29 p.m.——
Fraid so. Tried to talk her out of it, but she insisted.

📧Text Message From Zelia Muzuwa: For Brenna
Lindburg
——March 20/2:30 p.m.——
Ridiculous! Ok, summon all the Green Eggs. This is an in-
tervention!

📧Text Message From Veronica Marcello: For Rosalyn
Ebberly
——March 20/2:47 p.m.——
Where have you been all afternoon? Better come quick to
the main hall. And bring camera!

📧Text Message From Rosalyn Ebberly: For Veronica
Marcello
——March 20/2:50 p.m.——
Was signing papers to reserve space for next year's retreat.
What's wrong?

📧Text Message From Veronica Marcello: For Rosalyn
Ebberly
——March 20/2:51 p.m.——
The Green Eggs and Ham girls burst into Phyllis and
Brenna's room. Caught Phyllis STUDYING FOR A CLASS!

⌨Text Message From Rosalyn Ebberly: For Veronica
Marcello
——March 20/2:52 p.m.——
Studying! At a retreat! Shocking. Who are the Green Eggs
and Ham girls?

⌨Text Message From Veronica Marcello: For Rosalyn
Ebberly
——March 20/2:52 p.m.——
You really do live under a house-sized rock, don't you. It's
Dulcie, Joc, Z, Bren, and that gang. Thought everyone
knew about that!

⌨Text Message From Rosalyn Ebberly: For Veronica
Marcello
——March 20/2:53 p.m.——
Never knew about it. Why the name?

⌨Text Message From Veronica Marcello: For Rosalyn
Ebberly
——March 20/2:53 p.m.——
Name of private email loop to gripe about YOU. Come
on—you really didn't know? That's a HOOT! Everyone else
knew.

⌨Text Message From Rosalyn Ebberly: For Veronica
Marcello
——March 20/2:54 p.m.——
Just when I thought maybe I really could survive without
therapy…Anyway, so what are they doing to Phyllis?

⌨Text Message From Veronica Marcello: For Rosalyn
Ebberly

——March 20/2:55 p.m.——
They dragged her out of room, to the main hall, and r now making her sing ALL the camp songs we can think of! Singing with her, of course. More gals joining in. Getting wild. Bring camera!

▭Text Message From Rosalyn Ebberly: For Veronica Marcello
——March 20/2:56 p.m.——
Camp songs? Like Magdalena-Hagdalena?

▭Text Message From Veronica Marcello: For Rosalyn Ebberly
——March 20/2:56 p.m.——
Yep. N Smooshing Up My Baby Bumblebee. N Great Green Globs of Greasy Grimy Gopher Guts.

▭Text Message From Rosalyn Ebberly: For Veronica Marcello
——March 20/2:57 p.m.——
I LOVE that one!

▭Text Message From Veronica Marcello: For Rosalyn Ebberly
——March 20/2:57 p.m.——
Hurry up N get over here. We'll sing it again for you. I don't believe it. Phyllis is standing on a table belting out the Chicken Song—complete with the actions. She's gone totally nuts! It's like a sorority party gone wild—only no booze. Weirdest thing I ever saw!

▭Text Message From Rosalyn Ebberly: For Veronica Marcello

——March 20/2:58 p.m.——

Who needs alcohol? And that's what Phyllis gets for studying when she should be having fun. Am on my way over! Do they really have their own private loop to gripe about me?

📧Text Message From Veronica Marcello: For Rosalyn Ebberly
——March 20/2:58 p.m.——

It's a private loop and I'm not on it. I was only teasing. I don't know what they chat about. But who would want a loop just to talk about YOU?

📧Text Message From Rosalyn Ebberly: For Veronica Marcello
——March 20/2:59 p.m.——

Gee thanks. Watch it, sis, or I'll make you sing the Animaniacs states N capitals song with me. Remember we used to be able to do the whole thing?

📧Text Message From Veronica Marcello: For Rosalyn Ebberly
——March 20/2:59 p.m.——

So get over here and let's show them what happens when loop moderators are off duty!

From:	Dulcie Huckleberry
	<dulcie@homemakerinteriors.com>
To:	Thomas Huckleberry
	<t.huckleberry@showme.com>
Subject:	Update #2

Hi again, Tom,

It's evening now, and I just had to tell you what just happened. We were all in the recreation room, enjoying the fireplace and snacks. And then Zelia climbed up on the stone hearth of the fireplace and shouted for everyone to be quiet for a second.

She told us all about the problems they've had with Lishan and Duri, and thanked us again for praying for Lishan when she was lost. It's been so discouraging for her—even more than I realized from her e-mails and messaging. You could see the love and fear for those kids in her eyes, and it broke my heart.

She said, "What Lishan and Duri have taught us is how to love no matter what. And it's that love that makes a family."

And then she said something amazing, Tom. I couldn't believe it. She said, "There's one person here tonight who has especially shown me that kind of love." Her voice got all husky and we had to lean in to hear. "Two years ago, we had a very public falling-out. But tonight, I'd like to publicly honor a woman who has…" And she couldn't say any more. She was crying too hard.

Someone—Veronica I think—shoved Rosalyn to the front. She looked really uncomfortable. I had no idea what was going on. None of us did.

Zelia grabbed Rosalyn and held her, just crying and crying. And then, I saw a tear slide down Rosalyn's cheek. She brushed it away, and then it was like something just broke inside her. She buried her face in Z's shoulder, and all we could hear is "I'm sorry. I'm sorry." And I think that was from both of them.

Nobody knew what to do. Most of us were crying, too. Then I heard Ros say, "Don't tell them, okay? Please. I didn't mean for anyone to know."

Z nodded. And even though we've asked her about it, she won't say a word.

Finally, Z sniffled and said, "Hey do any of you moms have a tissue?" She got nearly fifty offers. The rest of us were using ours.

I don't know exactly what happened, but I think it's safe to say that they've managed to patch things up.

Thank you so much for making a way for me to be here for this. I will never forget this night as long as I live.
Dulcie

From:	Hannah Farrell
	<boazsmom@farrellfamilylovesjesus.net>
To:	Kristina Shaw <krissyshaw@loopy.com>
Subject:	Hi from Hannah

Hi Krissy,

I'm here in CO with all the other moms from my e-mail loop. And they're SO cool! You know, I felt really jealous of you last year when you went to college. Not really because of the classes—I could have done that if I wanted to. But because you were going to go off and live in a dorm and meet all these new friends. I felt left behind.

But now I feel like I have my own group, too. And even though you'll always be my BFF, I don't feel jealous of you anymore. My SAHM friends are really nice. Even Rosalyn's not quite as crazy as I thought she was. And her sister, Veronica, is as heathen as Rosalyn is pious. But I can't help but like her anyway. Even Brenna likes me now, I think. And

Phyllis makes me think hard about things. It feels good to talk to her.

And I hope that these few days Bradley is spending with Boaz will help him appreciate us more. I think it's good to have a break. I don't have to prove I'm a dedicated, skilled mom. I was trying too hard! I didn't realize how tired I was. I think I'll go home and just have more fun.

Oh, Krissy! Even though it's hard, being a mom is really WAY cool, you know?

Gotta go! Love ya the mostest!

Hannah

▭Text Message From Dulcie Huckleberry: For Zelia Muzuwa
——March 20/11:16 p.m.——
Are u still awake?

▭Text Message From Zelia Muzuwa: For Dulcie Huckleberry
——March 20/11:16 p.m.——
Yeah, actually. How did u know?

▭Text Message From Dulcie Huckleberry: For Zelia Muzuwa
——March 20/11:17 p.m.——
Just a feeling. Today was a good day, wasn't it.

▭Text Message From Zelia Muzuwa: For Dulcie Huckleberry
——March 20/11:17 p.m.——
One of the best. I don't want it to end.

▭Text Message From Dulcie Huckleberry: For Zelia Muzuwa

——March 20/11:18 p.m.——
Me neither. Now that we're finally all together, I don't want to let you go. But we have 42 minutes left of this perfect day. Let's do something!

▭Text Message From Zelia Muzuwa: For Dulcie Huckleberry
——March 20/11:19 p.m.——
Like what? By the way, Phyllis is awake, too. I told her she should be sleeping since she has to preach to us in the morning, but she's not sleepy either.

▭Text Message From Dulcie Huckleberry: For Zelia Muzuwa
——March 20/11:19 p.m.——
Let's summon the Eggs. I'll wake up Marianne. Brenna, Jocelyn, and Iona are right next door so I'll get them too. You guys bundle up warm and meet us out at the campfire. It's not that cold, and we can start a fire. Beautiful moon.

▭Text Message From Zelia Muzuwa: For Dulcie Huckleberry
——March 20/11:20 p.m.——
Ur on!

From:	Dulcie Huckleberry
	<dulcie@homemakerinteriors.com>
To:	Thomas Huckleberry
	<t.huckleberry@showme.com>
Subject:	One more update

It's midnight, Sunday morning. I miss having you snuggled beside me. I hope you are dreaming of me.

I'm sitting down by the lake, a clandestine campfire blazing nearby. Brenna, Phyllis, Jocelyn, Marianne, Zelia and Iona are surrounding me. We decided not to waste our precious together time with something as useless as sleeping. So we've been having an impromptu slumber party. Jocelyn raided the supply of snacks she and Rosalyn bought before the retreat, so we're munching on s'mores and drinking hot chocolate.

Giddy and giggly from being so tired, talking faster than our brains can form the words. Huddled together to stay warm, and just to feel each other's physical presence. Trying to store it all up inside to last until the next time we're with each other.

Phyllis may have to read straight from her notes tomorrow, but she said she doesn't care. :)

Online is wonderful, but this moment is perfection. I wish I could hold on to it always.

Love,

Dulcie

P.S. They all told me to say a big hello to the Tiara Man. :)

From:	Rosalyn Ebberly <prov31woman@home.com>
To:	SAHM I Am <sahmiam@loophole.com>
Subject:	**[SAHM I AM]**
	From Iona James, For Everyone

Seashells

By Iona James

Commissioned by Zelia Muzuwa in honor of the first annual SAHM I Am retreat

Rising like Venus from
the sea of things
that are mundane,
they come

not with flawless beauty
of skin or soul
but beauty that shines
for having been tested,

worn smooth by tempest waters
of that which is beyond their control,
they survive.

They are only stones,
Shells,
To many, worth nothing,
But to those that truly see,
They are treasure.
I see! I treasure!
I come
To be one with them.

Shaped by the sea,
we shape the world.

Rosalyn Ebberly
SAHM I Am Loop Moderator

"The wise woman builds her house, but the foolish tears
it down with her own hands." Proverbs 14:1 (NASB)

* * * * *

Dear Reader,

When I started this SAHM I Am journey, my one goal was to tell *our* story—the story of stay-at-home moms—the way most authors could not and would not. I wanted SAHMs everywhere to know that they were understood and appreciated. I wanted to make you laugh on the days that are hard: to feel a little less alone. From the responses I've received from many of you, I dare to hope that I reached my goal.

I never set out to write a series, but thanks to the enthusiasm of my editors and readers, I've had the fun opportunity of continuing the story far beyond what I've ever envisioned. This third (and final) SAHM book was in direct response to those of you who wrote to me asking for another SAHM story. I hope I did not disappoint.

As with the other two books, this book addresses some serious issues, as well as indulges in just plain fun. The most important issue is the reactive attachment disorder that Zelia's adopted children struggle with. This disorder affects not just intentionally adopted children, but domestically adopted and even nonadopted children. It is an incredibly difficult disorder, but there are resources and help available. A good Web site to start with is www.mayoclinic.com/health/reactive-attachment-disorder/DS00988.

We always like to include discussion questions in the books for those of you who choose it for your reading group. If your reading group would like me to make a guest appearance by speakerphone or online chat, please contact me at meredith@meredithefken.com to let me know. I've done this for other groups and it's been a lot of fun. I'm also available to speak to your group or do interviews, etc. Just write me to ask!

Thank you so much for becoming part of the SAHM I Am journey. I hope it's been a blessing to you.

With love,

Meredith Efken

Contact me at meredith@meredithefken.com, or by snail mail at 93 S. Jackson Street #77543, Seattle, WA, 98104–2818. I'd love to hear from you!

QUESTIONS FOR DISCUSSION

On Parenting

1. Marianne is told by her friends and family to have different expectations of behavior from her son and daughter. What do you think? How much of typical girl/boy behavior is biological and how much is conditioned by our culture and our own expectations?

2. Are you, or is anyone you know, struggling with children who have problems like either Zelia's or Rosalyn's or Brenna's? What can we do to provide support and care for these families as they try to meet their children's special needs? If you are one of these families, what would be the most help to you?

3. As parents, we are often pressured—as Hannah suggests—to be everything to our children and be available to them 24/7. Do you agree or disagree, and why?

On Forgiveness

4. Zelia struggles with forgiving Rosalyn, to the point that even her closest friends are growing impatient with her persistent grudge. How would you have counseled Z about this issue? What would you have advised her to do? Have you ever struggled with forgiveness? What did you find helped?

5. Sometimes the hardest person to forgive is ourself. Rosalyn experiences this truth. How does she try to make restitution? Is this a good way? Is there another way she could have made things right? How do you go about forgiving yourself when you know you've been in the wrong?

6. Several characters have to apologize in this story—the Green Eggs and Ham girls, for being unkind to Hannah; Rosalyn, for the long-standing hurt to Zelia; and Darren, for not accepting his son's limitations. Are their ways of apologizing effective? What have you found is the best technique for an apology?

On Competition/Comparisons

7. Veronica's birthday-party competition gets a bit out of hand. What are some other areas in which parents tend to compete against each other? Why do we do that? Is this a good thing or not, and why? What effects does this competition have on ourselves, our children and our relationships with other families?

8. One of Rosalyn's main difficulties is that she compares herself to everyone around her and then feels like she must compete against them to be "the best." Where does this drive to be the best come from, and what can we do about it in our own lives? Is this desire wrong, or can it be healthy if kept in balance? If so, what does that balance look like?

9. Brenna's husband, Darren, struggles to accept his son because he keeps comparing Little Pat to the expectations he had of what a son should be like. In what ways do we do this with our own children? What can we do about this?

On Marriage

10. Several couples in the story (Tom/Dulcie, Iona/Jeremy, Hannah/Bradley) have differences of opinion about who should do what in their marriages and in their families. Iona especially feels as if she is being pressured to give up her art in order to care for the Angel Child, while Jeremy doesn't think he has to make the same sacrifice. What did you think of their expectations of each other? If you're married, how have you handled this issue in your own marriage?

11. Hannah married very young, and it's implied that she may not have been ready for this marriage. Five years down the road, what do you think her marriage is going to look like? What do she and Bradley need to do in order to make their relationship successful? Should she have gotten married or waited until she was older—and why?

12. Bradley wants to have as many children as they can. Hannah has mixed feelings about this. What do you think they should do? How will these solutions affect Hannah's interest in college? What are the pros and

cons of different approaches to family planning? How do you think couples should work together to resolve these differences?

On Culture and Faith

13. Phyllis struggles in the book with the emotional baggage many people have about clergy families. What judgments—both positive and negative—are made about her based on her husband's job? How would you respond in her situation? What would you advise her to do about this problem?

14. Phyllis is also very frustrated by the combative attitude of some of her Christian students at the college where she teaches. What role do you think faith should play in the classroom? What should the attitude of Christian students be in a campus setting?

15. Hannah makes several judgment calls at the beginning of the story about the other women on the loop. She thinks many of them don't seem to be very "Christian," particularly Iona with her incense burning and dreadlocks, and Rosalyn with her emotional issues, etc. If we were to make a list of things we would find hard to accept as Christian, what would that list have on it? Which of those items are only cultural issues? Can a person be a Christian even if they fit something on that list? What should be our response to other Christians who don't look, act or think the way we expect Christians to?

If your group has additional discussion questions that you found generated lively discussion, please feel free to send them to me. I may post them on my site. If you want a link back to your MOPS groups, reading club or other organization, I will consider that, as well. Send your discussion questions and information to meredith@meredithefken.com.